P9-DIB-534

15877

F
Lofts

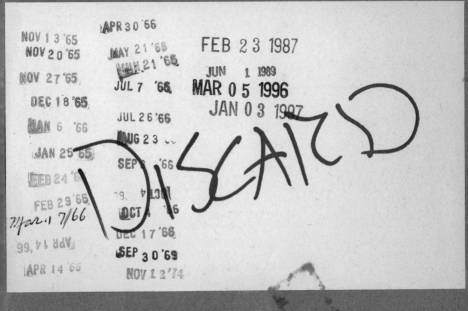

HOW FAR TO BETHLEHEM?

BY NORAH LOFTS

Norah Lofts

HOW FAR TO BETHLEHEM?

A Novel

DOUBLEDAY & COMPANY, INC., GARDEN CITY, NEW YORK

1965

With the exception of actual historical personages, the characters are entirely the product of the author's imagination and have no relation to any person in real life.

*This book is dedicated with admiration and
gratitude to Edward Wagenknecht
who had the idea.*

CHAPTER I

I

i

At some time, too long ago for even the oldest people to remember, the well in the village had failed. The heaviest rains in winter could not replenish it, so it was abandoned, and for at least three generations water had been fetched from a spring which broke out from the rocks on the other side of the hill. This meant that the water-carriers, always women and children, must walk for half a mile, uphill, then down, with empty jars, and half a mile, uphill and down, with full ones.

Women, practical and short of time, had soon found a way to shorten and to ease that journey. Avoiding the road and the hill they cut through the fields that girdled the base of the rising ground, and over the years had trodden a path which halved the length of the journey and was all on the level. In the rainy season the path was muddy and the daily procession of feet churned the mud until it was as sticky as porridge; and for that, too, the women had found a remedy. Certain days in spring and again in autumn were marked as stone-carrying days when everyone using the path in either direction brought a stone, dropped it and trod it in. This custom was older than any memory, but it was still faithfully observed, with the result that between this humble village and its water supply ran a path as hard and firm and flat as the new roads that the Romans were beginning to lay to link city with city.

The solidity of the path had served the women in another way —and not so long ago. Former owners of the land had respected the path as an established right-of-way, one of those ancient things protected by tradition. Seven or eight years ago the field had changed hands and the new owner had questioned the right of people to use part of his land as a public footpath. He intended, he said, to plough up the path and sow corn right up to the base of the hill. The stones, layer upon layer of them, dropped by hands long dead, had defied the ploughshare and the straining oxen. He had then, in a fury, declared that he would fence the path off at both ends. But before he had time to do so his wife had been brought to bed with a child, and several of the village women, pitying her because she was a stranger —and married to such a churl!—had shown her small kindnesses. And apparently even a churl could feel gratitude for nothing more was said about closing the path; indeed the right-of-way was tacitly acknowledged by the placing of large boulders, smeared with ochre, at intervals between the path and the arable land.

Nowadays not only women used the path; horsemen and the drivers of pack animals were glad to take the short cut and avoid the sharp incline; but they could only use it in winter when the field was bare. The packs were often wider than the path and would have brushed against the standing corn, bruising and breaking it; also the animals would snatch a mouthful in passing. So every spring, early or late according to the clemency or otherwise of the season, on a day decided by the rabbi and village elders, posts were planted at each end of the path and bits of red rag tied to them. And there they remained, gradually losing colour in the fierce summer sun until the harvest was in and the field gleaned.

The daily journey for water though time-consuming, and on days when one did not feel vigorous, tiring, had its happy aspect. It was a social occasion, a daily, communal outing. Women mustered all along the village street in little groups, greeting one another, calling exhortations to haste, sorting out their children, sending those who were old enough to do so running ahead so that their behaviour could be overlooked and their ears out of hearing of the gossip. There was little chance that any woman could be sick or in trouble of any kind and stay alone and neglected. If she didn't come out, either to join the group to which she belonged or to give some excuse for not doing so, something was wrong and must be investigated. On the path

and at the spring every bit of gossip was exchanged and repeated; there was a good deal of laughter over homely, very
parochial little jokes, and a good deal of tongue clucking, some
outbursts of sympathetic indignation, sly eloquent glances, some
nudging of elbows. Every one of them at some time or another
had grumbled, to herself, at least, about the daily trudge and
wished that she had a well in her own yard, or access to this mysterious piped water that was said to be available in cities like
Sepphoris; but there was not one who would willingly have
foregone, even in the worst of weather, this daily women's hour.

There was no acknowledged rule about it, but on the whole
women walked in groups according to age and status, it being
unseemly for unmarried girls to listen to talk about marital or
obstetrical problems, and boring for settled married women to
be obliged to listen to the chatter of the young and frivolous.

On this particular March morning everyone was unusually
gay because, at last, after a lingering winter, spring had come.
Overnight the wind had died down, the clouds had vanished
and the sun was shining in a sky the colour of hyacinths. Soon,
of course, they would all be tired of the sun, would shrink from
it and the all-pervading dust, would hide from it in their little
thick-walled, mud-roofed, vine-shaded houses and long for clouds
and cool breezes: but nobody thought of that on this morning.
Spring had come and everybody welcomed it. Especially the
young.

Four young women walked together; two and two because
the path was narrow. They did not quite conform to pattern because one of them was married, the mother of one child and
pregnant again. Rachel walked with her friends for several reasons. One was practical. They would be trusted to carry Joshua,
turn and turn about. He was a fat, handsome, lazy little boy,
nineteen months old and he could walk but preferred to be carried. Married women had no patience with her; they said she
spoiled him: they said, set him down and walk away, he'll follow
quick enough: they issued really horrid warnings about what
would happen to the unborn child if she insisted upon lifting

and carrying that great lump of idleness. Not one of them seemed to realise that if she spoiled Joshua it was because he was the only joy her marriage had brought her. There was her other reason for wishing to walk with the girls. She'd had no wish to be married; she disliked the man her parents had chosen for her. Despite Joshua and the bulge below her girdle, she still felt unmarried, wished that she were, sometimes dreamed that she was, and on the daily exodus to the spring liked to pretend that she was.

On this morning they were talking—as girls tend to do in spring—about clothes. Not new ones, new clothes were rare in their lives, but about the lightweight summer clothes now to be brought out and refurbished; turned perhaps, or dyed, embellished by a few stitches of simple embroidery.

Susannah, shifting Joshua from one hip to the other—really the naughty little boy grew heavier from one day to the next—said:

"You, at least, are sure of a new dress, Mary. What will you choose?"

In Rachel's mind the word "Sackcloth" formed itself; but she did not say it, because the others might see, behind the jest, something of her own private little hell. Nor would it be apt. Mary's parents, unlike her own, had allowed her to have some say in the matter, and the man she should marry in two months' time was good and steady and looked kind. Ephraim, probably sensing Rachel's aversion to him, had not been kind. . . .

Then Rachel, and Susannah and Leah became aware that Mary had made no answer to this, surely most important and easily answered question. They looked at her and Susannah said, "She's off again!"

They had grown up together and the three others knew that Mary had these curious lapses; times when she seemed not to hear or see or be with them in any but the physical sense. They'd learned from experience to leave her alone; for five minutes or so, she'd behave like a sleepwalker, and then blink and smile and take up the chatter where it had broken off. But before they had learned this, when they were still very young, they'd tried to rouse her.

Once, abruptly, she'd been very sick; and once she had cried, so long and so violently that they had been frightened. Mary's mother, Anne, was well known for her sharp tongue and hard hand, and although she herself was never overtly indulgent to her daughter, anybody who made Mary cry was in for trouble.

So they'd learned. Amongst themselves they'd talked about it naturally, and reached their own childish conclusion. Mary's grandmother had been a woman of the desert who had fallen sick and been left for dead by her tribe. Mary's grandfather, a merchant in a small way, had been coming home with his two camels, had found the woman, brought her to his home and in due time married her. Desert people were known to be different; when they were thirsty or hungry or exhausted or tired they could absent themselves from their suffering bodies and so survive, in some mysterious fashion, where other people would have died. There was something about the desert, the three little village girls had agreed, prophets and holy men often came out of the desert. And as they grew older they noticed small differences in their well-loved friend, a peculiarly free-striding manner of walking, a way of holding the head, an outspokenness which was startling in one so modest, and these lapses.

Rachel, looking at Mary and seeing her state, wished with all her heart that she could similarly absent herself from the connubial bed. Leah said:

"Look, the red rags are out. Spring has come!"

"No more donkeys," Susannah said, shifting Joshua again. "What a blessing. I hate walking through dung!"

"We're lucky," Leah said. "We have wood. There are places where women have to gather it and use it for fuel. Imagine having to wait till a donkey passed before you could cook your dinner."

"I don't believe it," Rachel said, and an argument began.

The girl named Mary had sighted the red rags and felt the now familiar feeling of sadness and foreboding and desolation. Spring had come; and with the short smooth path closed to them, the donkeys, with their heavy loads must face the hill. Uphill they slowed down a little, downhill they stumbled, and their riders or their drivers were always too ready to prod or strike. For her the bad season had begun.

She did not hear the question about her wedding dress. She was thinking, with something very near resentment, *why me?* Nobody else cared. A donkey was a donkey, a thing, a beast of burden, provided by God to help man with the business of transporting himself or his goods from place to place. If its pace slowed and a shout proved insufficient incentive to greater effort, a stick or a goad must be used. That was how all reasonable people looked at it; and to think differently was to invite scorn, wonder, amusement. Once, at the sight of a piece of quite gratuitous brutality, she had spoken out, and some of those who heard had laughed, some had been embarrassed for her; the man she had rebuked had been abusive, and worst of all, had hit the poor donkey even harder.

And perhaps ordinary people were sensible; it seemed a pity, almost wrong to allow the sight of a red rag and all that it implied to mar such a lovely morning of sunshine and bird song. Being miserable about donkeys did them *no* service. So stop it; think about something else. Think about spring.

It had always been her favourite season, not merely on account of its beauty but for its promise. Every year, for as long as she could remember, she had felt that before the first flowers faded and the young leaves darkened, something wonderful would happen to her. Many times she had stood by a hawthorn tree, the green and the white just breaking and been certain that some quite unique experience was about to be hers. The silken petals of the first anemones could affect her in the same way—as though they held some secret which if she stayed quite still, and waited, would be revealed to her. Nothing had ever happened, nothing had been revealed. On one spring day, wishing to know whether this feeling were peculiar to herself or part of ordinary human experience, she had so far overcome her natural reserve as to speak of it to Susannah, the most wholly sympathetic of her friends. Susannah said:

"Yes, of course, I feel it too. Everybody does; even birds. It simply means that you're looking forward to getting married."

Mary had almost accepted that. Susannah was a sensible girl, and thoughtful, too, and the explanation was almost feasible, but not quite; the expected thing was less ordinary, less capable of being put into words. In fact it had been silly to try to talk about it at all, because there were no words.

And now it was spring again, and she was not only looking forward to being married, she was properly betrothed; she was in love with Joseph and recognised her good fortune in that respect, was grateful to her parents for allowing her to exercise some choice; she was looking forward, with eager anticipation to her wedding day, to having a husband and a house of her own, and presently, by God's favour, a child. She pictured him, a sturdy little boy, rather like Rachel's Joshua. Yet for all this, the feeling of immanence, of waiting for something wonderful, was with her still, and honesty compelled her to admit that it had nothing to do with Joseph, her feeling for him, or the little house adjoining the workshop.

At this point she returned to herself and her companions and reaching out her arms took Joshua from Susannah, saying:

"My turn now." She settled him on her hip. "By Abraham's beard," she said, "you're heavier today than you were yesterday. If this goes on we shall have to hire you a litter!"

The girls exchanged satisfied glances; that was the way, leave her alone; she always came back, as sweet and good-natured as ever. Susannah repeated her question about the wedding dress.

"It's blue," she said. "And I didn't choose it. It was my mother's mother's. Mother could never wear it, it is too long for her and to cut it would have been a shame: it is such beautiful stuff. My grandfather bought it in Damascus."

"Just blue?" Leah said. "Isn't that Mary all over? I never knew a girl who cared less about clothes. Her wedding dress; and it's blue, and beautiful stuff! What kind of blue and what kind of stuff?"

"It's about the colour of . . . of flax flowers, and I think it is silk."

There were sounds of appreciation, not unmixed with envy. Leah said, sardonically, "She *thinks* it is silk!" She and Susannah then began to speculate as to when it would be their turn, and to describe the dresses in which they would like to be married. Rachel, looking back sourly to her own wedding, thought how much more suitable a mourning robe would have been than all the family finery in which she had been decked; and, unwilling to talk about marriage, fell into conversation with Mary about Joshua.

So, chirping like birds they came to the place just where the field path and the highroad were divided by the outthrust buttress of bare reddish rock from which the water sprang. A very ordinary spring morning in the twenty-fourth year of the reign of Augustus Caesar.

ii

Years and years of wear from the pressure of the mouths of water jars held against the rock to catch the spouting water had altered the formation of the spring which now gushed into a circle of eroded stone which looked as though it had been placed there for the convenience of the women. Each woman rested her jar against the rim, tilted it slightly and waited until it was full. Newcomers to Nazareth, or women who had had occasion to visit other villages, said that this was a quicker and easier way of getting water than hauling a bucket up from a well by a rope.

Few people were in a hurry, most of them indeed were willing to prolong the business, nevertheless there was some rough order of precedence. Married women first, according to age; then girls. And every morning, as the women, like figures on a frieze, moved, stooped, waited, straightened themselves and set their jars on their head, halfway through the married women's line somebody was certain to say:

"Michal's turn." And there would be laughter.

Mary, part of the frieze, standing aside with the other girls would wait for the poor joke and wonder that now, after two years, it should still have power to amuse. Sometimes she felt impatient with them; at other times she would think, It is the measure of the fundamental dullness of their lives. She would wonder, too, if twenty years hence her life would have narrowed down to a point where she must relish an ancient jest and one that had never, at first coining, been very good.

There'd been a time when Michal, a pretty, lively young woman, had taken her rightful place at the spring; then her husband had died, leaving her in a pitiful plight, no relatives at all, nobody to be responsible for her or to fend for her. She'd been reduced to doing the most menial jobs about the village in return for a meal or a bit of cast-off clothing. Then suddenly she had ceased to solicit jobs or charity, had appeared in a brand-new dress one day, the next with scented oil on her hair, soon with bangles on her wrists. There were whispers and raised eyebrows and hard looks and suspicion, soon confirmed. Her tumble-down little house stood on the outskirts of the village, almost next door to the inn on the road to Sepphoris, and men had been seen going in, and coming out.

She must have been very stupid, Mary thought, or very brave, for morning after morning she had joined the exodus to the spring, amazed at first and then tearful to find herself treated as though she were invisible, until she came too near; then she'd be pushed past or jostled. She seemed to think that if she persisted the morning would dawn when she would find herself forgiven and accepted again. She'd had three new water jars broken and two dresses soaked before she realised that the women had outlawed her—forever.

After the last "accident" Mary, then very young, and strictly brought up to respect her elders, had spoken out in a way that Rachel and Susannah and Leah knew.

"It's a shame!" she said, as Michal, finally admitting defeat, fled back along the path, with no water and her pretty dress spoiled. "She did *try*, until she was nothing but skin and bone. We should be sorry for her!"

They'd rounded on her with an astounding ferocity.

"Shame is it? I agree, so it is to hear a girl so young speak in such a way."

"I'm glad your mother didn't hear that," said the woman who intended to inform Mary's mother at the first possible moment.

"I *was* sorry for her. Many's the job I found for her, things I could well have done myself. And when we killed a sheep I remembered her."

"And bread she never lacked; my husband saw to that," said the wife of Hilliel, the rabbi who was also the baker.

Susannah attempted to take Mary's jar.

"I'll fill it for you. You run home," she whispered.

"I'm going to fill my own jar. I haven't done anything. I only said I thought it was a shame. And I still do!"

They were all going to say the same things again, but more vehemently, when an old woman moved and stood near the girls and said to Mary:

"You're young, dearie, and very innocent. You'll learn later that a woman like that is a threat to every married woman. Men are frail creatures. Let it go, now, let it go."

That morning the chatter on the return journey was loud and vociferous. Imagine Anne's daughter, *Anne's daughter* saying a thing like that! And what was the world coming to when any girl, so young should not only rebuke her elders but when in turn rebuked, be defiant? Did you see how her eyes flashed? If my daughter ever dares . . .

Mary knew by the expression on Anne's face that she had been informed. What she did not know and never would was that the informant had obtained little satisfaction from the interview.

"Maybe she spoke out of turn," Anne said, "and she'll hear about that from me. But as for sticking up for a harlot, worse nonsense than that I never heard, even from you, Rebecca! Why the girl's so innocent she wouldn't know what Michal's doing nowadays. That wouldn't occur to you, would it? She thought it was a shame to treat her so because she wouldn't understand *why*. My daughter's been properly brought up, let me tell you."

To Mary she said stern things about respect to elders and being careful about one's reputation. Michal she did not mention either by name or reputation, still being careful of her child's innocence. But of course the girls knew all about it and often discussed it; they thought it was a terrible way to earn a living.

Nowadays Michal drew her water very early in the morning or in the afternoon; and every day, when the procession reached a certain point, the joke about her turn was made, and the women laughed and Mary thought of their dull lives, and of her own, so like theirs, except, of course, for what went on in her head.

On this morning the four girls were last at the spring and then delayed a little because it was Leah's turn to carry Joshua and he had decided not to be carried by her; Rachel must carry him. They argued about this, saying, "You shouldn't; he's too heavy," and each in turn inviting him, cajoling. "Joshua, you ride on me; I'll be your horse," Mary said. But Joshua had his mind made up and knew already that one male mind made up is a match for any number of women.

"I'll take your jar then," Mary said. To carry two jars, one on your hip, one on your head was easy enough, but it took a second or two to lift and arrange both without spilling a drop, and the others had rounded the rocky point and were on the path by the time that she was ready to follow them. She had her back to the highway when she heard the hurried, stumbling hoofs, the laboured breathing of the burdened, the cheerfully callous exhortations of the driver.

Don't look! she told herself. There's really nothing you can do about it, and what you see will haunt you all day and even more at night when you lie down and shut your eyes. Hurry round the rocks without looking, get on to the path, join the others, think of something silly to say.

But you always looked; you were compelled to, if only in the hope that it might not be quite so bad as you feared.

She looked. It was very bad. An aged, decrepit donkey. Three bales, one on either side; a third poised across them. The driver was just a boy, not ill-looking; in his weather-darkened face his eyes were bright and his teeth very white as he gave a rueful grin.

"The short way's closed, I see. That would happen today of all days. Now we've got to get up this hill."

"Oh, please," she said, "don't prod him. He's very old and very small for such a load."

"Just what I said. My very words, this morning. I wanted the black one, half his age and twice his size. With a wreck like this how can I make the journey in one day? I mean to, though!"

He gave evidence of his intention and Mary made a sound of distress.

"You don't want to fret about donkeys—pretty girl like you." His voice was friendly; his glance ran over her with approval, a near-flirtatiousness. Something in her shrank from the glance, but if he considered her pretty, could she use his admiration to help the donkey?

She said, "I *do* fret about them. It may be silly but to see one hurt hurts me. Look, if you'll let him take his time up this hill and not prod him, I'll walk with you, and when we come to my home I'll give you a honey cake and a cup of wine."

"You're a funny one," the boy said. "Where do you live?"

"Just over the hill; in Nazareth."

One part of her mind broke off to consider what her mother would make of this offer of hospitality to a chance-met donkey boy.

"I've got to make a stop there," the boy said; "and any other time I'd be only too pleased to eat and drink as well. It just happens that today I'm in a hurry. My brother's wife has a child— a boy, and tonight he's giving a feast. It would be just my luck to get a long journey, a half-dead donkey *and* an extra load, and the short cut closed."

The boy was wasting no time; as he talked he kept moving and Mary followed him. They were now climbing uphill.

"If you really mind about donkeys," the boy said, giving evidence that he did not, "you could save us a few steps by telling us where the carpenter lives. That bag"—he prodded the uppermost one—"is for him, iron stuff, nails and door hinges and handles. And they're heavy. These"—he prodded the side bales—"don't weigh much really, dyed cotton stuff. Then along comes my master and says, 'You'll be going through Nazareth, drop this on the way.' Just my luck."

She said, "I know where the carpenter lives. I am betrothed to him."

"He's a fortunate fellow," the boy said, concealing under gallantry a certain feeling of surprise. She had an elegance, not of clothing or of manner, or speech, nevertheless an elegance and a delicacy that made it hard to picture her as the wife of a village carpenter. But his interest in her was peripheral. If he hoped to be at the feast tonight he must keep moving. The donkey struggled and made little sobbing sounds. In its browny-grey coat the places where the goad went home ran red.

Suddenly she said, "I can't bear it, I can't bear it. Please, please, let me carry the heavy bag."

He was so astounded that he ceased prodding the donkey.

"Don't be silly. Break your back, that would."

"No," she said, "I'm strong. I'm really very strong. I can carry that bag and you won't even have to turn into the village street. You can go straight along and save time."

The boy realised the truth then. He'd fallen in with a mad woman. Pretty, young, properly dressed, she'd been alone at the watering place; without asking his name she had invited him to eat honey cake and drink wine in her house; she minded about donkeys and said she was betrothed to the village carpenter. Madness was the one and only explanation.

And mad people must be respected; they were possessed by devils. And they were strong. In his own village there was a madman who could straighten a horseshoe between his hands.

He saw himself, at the feast this evening, making a bid for attention: What do you think happened to me this morning, just outside Nazareth? I fell in with a mad woman. And they'd all think of somebody old, with staring eyes and wild grey hair.

He said, "If you want to carry it, lady, you may. But it is heavy. And nails make an uneasy load."

She had already set down the two water jars she carried in the shade of a bush at the edge of the road.

"I can carry it," she said. The donkey, unprodded had slowed, come to a standstill, and stood, drawing breath.

Hardly believing what he was doing and yet thinking what a story this would make, the boy unhitched the bag of ironstuff and laid it upon Mary's back. She put her hands over her shoulders and took the sack by its ears. The donkey, relieved of its heaviest bale, gave itself a little shake.

"Here we go then," the boy cried. "Oy! Oy!"

They moved, considering the incline of the road, at a spanking pace. Mary walked beside the donkey; she could see its eyes, so gentle, so entirely hopeless. The knowledge that she had eased this one load, this one journey, braced and encouraged her. And then suddenly, it seemed, the donkey had tripped ahead and she was alongside the boy.

He tried to think of something that could be said to a mad woman.

He said, "You all right?"

"Quite all right, thank you."

"In some places," he said, "where women carry heavy loads, they wear head-bands. They help, they take some of the weight. But after a time they leave marks, like pack galls."

She seemed to be making rather heavy work of it and an obscure feeling of guilt afflicted him. She asked to do it, he reminded himself. He'd told her it was heavier than it looked.

"I told you it was heavy, didn't I? Had enough? Let me shove it back on him."

"I'm managing," she said, trying not to sound breathless.

She was amazed at the heaviness of the comparatively small sack. Like every other woman of her kind she was accustomed to carrying things, bundles of washing, of firewood, of gleaned corn, baskets of winnowed corn for grinding, baskets of vegetables, water jars, Joshua; but none of them had ever seemed a quarter the weight of this. The position perhaps; she wasn't

used to carrying things on her back; and the boy hadn't exaggerated when he said that it was an uneasy load; points of some
of the nails came through the sack and dug into her.

Think about something else. That was a trick she'd learned
early when set to do tedious jobs like grinding corn or shelling
beans. So she thought about the fine new house which Joseph
was helping to build just outside Cana. The nails would be intended for decoration of the outer doors, nail-studded doors
were evidence of wealth in a country where iron was scarce and
expensive. With rows of nails and iron hinges and handles it
would be a very imposing door indeed. The thought crossed her
mind that Joseph would not be pleased if he knew that she had
carried this load uphill! He was a very kind and considerate man
—it was that which had first attracted her to him.

Then, quite unbidden, another thought slipped into her mind.
A hideous thought. There was another use for nails; the Romans
used them for that slow, terrible punishment known as cruci-
fixion. The Jews stoned their malefactors, and a man could be
knocked senseless in three minutes, and dead in five. On the
crosses men hung and suffered for as much as three days. Oh,
why must she think of that now? Wasn't this load enough, pressing down, hindering the breath, making every step a painful
labour?

The boy could hear her breathing now—worse than the old
donkey at his worst.

"Give over now," he said, almost pleadingly. "It was a daft
idea. You'll do yourself a damage."

She lifted her head and saw that they were almost at the top
of the hill which was marked by a group of trees, old gnarled
hawthorns, bent by years of prevailing westerly winds. And she
saw the little donkey, plodding on with his lightened load. She
shook her head at the boy and the drops of sweat flew off and
spattered the dust. She drew in a breath that hurt her chest like
a knife thrust and said:

"I-shall-get-to-the-top."

The maddest, most stubborn woman he'd ever encountered;
but the guilty feeling moved in him again. He lifted his donkey

goad, intending to dig it into the sack and so lighten it for her. But the stick slipped, or the sack swayed, and the point struck her in the side. A little blood from the goad, and some from the wound crept out and stained her grey gown.

The boy was almost crying. "I didn't mean to do that! It was an accident, an accident!" he cried. "I was trying to help you! Give up, now do! I should never have let you try it."

She seemed not to hear, or not to understand. And he knew that at the feast tonight he would not entertain anyone with his encounter with the mad woman from Nazareth; it wasn't amusing any more. It would be quite a time before he even wanted to think about it.

Mary plodded on, ten steps, counting now; change to seven, seven was a special, mystic number; seven and another seven; must be almost at the top now. And then, swift as flame leaping through dry sticks, pain ran through her, possessing, engulfing; a pain such as she had never known before; a pain that made every other pain a mere discomfort. She cried out in a voice that was to ring through the donkey boy's dreams for years; the sack fell with a rattling thump and she stood swaying, her hands pressed to her body, and then gently collapsed.

The boy stood and swore in three languages. What now? Sling her across the damned donkey and take her into the village. That'd mean carrying the sack himself, and a waste of time finding out where she lived. That wouldn't do. He took her by the shoulders and pulled her to the side of the road, under the shade of the new-leafed trees. She seemed very light and soft between his hands; and she was pretty. It was a shame that a girl like that should be so crazy. He had half a mind to get his water bottle and wet her sleeve and dabble it across her face, try to bring her round; but that meant a further waste of time. And he was a little frightened. After all he had struck her and she was mad; she might come round in quite another frame of mind and accuse him of attacking her. So with another half-guilty, half-apologetic look at the pretty pale unconscious face, he left her; took up the bag and refastened it to the back of the donkey which had snatched this unusual opportunity to take a mouthful of grass. He'd better deliver the bag and get on his way as soon as possible. She'd come round, and she wasn't far from home; or somebody would come along with more time and a less-loaded beast. She'd be all right. But he wished it hadn't happened.

"Oy! Oy!" he cried, and was ready with his goad; but the old donkey had got its second wind and the road was downhill now, there was hardly any need to prod.

iii

It was all exactly right, that was the beauty of it; the thing that she had, through so many springs, expected. Colours sang, music was sweetly scented, scent took on lovely shapes; there was snow, made of white roses, and the stars fell like rain, the moon tasted of honey and all the beanflowers were butterflies, and the hawthorn from which she had always expected a revelation, was an awning, green and white against blue, over this wonderful place where beauty was one and indivisible. This was heaven and to see an angel did not astonish her at all. . . .

iv

Rachel said, "Where have you *been?* We dawdled and waited; and Leah ran back to the spring, but you weren't there. Are you all right? Have you had a fall?"

She could truthfully say, "Yes, I had a fall." Some explanation, however makeshift and temporary, was needed. "After you'd gone, somebody came along, taking the hill road, so I took it too, and I fell. But I've brought you your water."

"I was waiting for it," Rachel said. If she'd had more time, if she hadn't been so scared that Ephraim might come in and scold because his dinner was belated, if Joshua hadn't been pulling at her skirt, Rachel would have questioned her friend more closely. But she could guess. Mary had had another of those spells when her mind was elsewhere, not seen some unevenness in the road, and stumbled; she'd spilled the water and had to go back for more. Following this line of thought she said:

"How lucky the jars weren't broken." And that sounded heartless, so she added quickly, "And that you didn't hurt yourself. But you have been crying."

Suppose she said, Yes, from wonder and joy, and went on to explain; suppose she were Rachel, standing in the low doorway and Rachel were herself, telling such a marvellous tale. Would I, in her place, believe it? Will *anyone* believe me?

She held out her hands, grazed and dirtied.

Rachel said, with solemnity, "Mary, when you're married, you won't cry over a grazed hand. Thank you for bringing the water, I must make Ephraim's dinner now."

Moving on towards her own home she thought, Whom can I tell, with the slightest hope of being believed?

One's mother seemed the obvious person; until one was face-to-face again with that practical, bustling woman, waiting, at the moment for fresh water and slightly irritated.

"What a time you've been! Every day it seems to take longer and longer. In my day we went straight there and back, with a good clout if we loitered. And what have you done to your hands?"

"I fell."

"Carrying that great boy of Rachel's!" Anne said, "So that's the end of that. You can just say that I forbid you to do it again. God gave children legs to walk with. Your dress is filthy too, dust and grass stains." The blood she did not notice for Mary was careful to keep her arm close to her side. At the first opportunity she slipped away and changed her dress.

The day wore on; such a day as no woman had ever lived through. The sun and the warmth had induced a house-cleaning fever in Anne; every mat, every blanket must be taken out into the yard and beaten, every candlestick cleaned, the big chest rubbed with beeswax. And Mary was much less helpful than usual. In the end Anne said, half-serious and half-sarcastic:

"You didn't by any chance hit your *head* when you fell, did you? You're acting as though you were half-witted. What ails you?"

Turn to her and tell her the plain truth and what would happen? She'd drop dead. She was pious in her way, and like all

pious Jews knew the prophecies about the Messiah and his virgin birth; but she would never be able to believe that her own
daughter, whom she was scolding for letting the beans boil dry,
was that chosen one. So belief and disbelief would work in her
as new wine often worked in old, hardened casks; they split; and
Anne's limited, orderly mind, asked to accept and contain this
marvel, would split and she'd drop dead.

She realised, as this momentous day drew to its close that the
only person she could tell was Joseph. He must, in any case, be
told because he was so nearly concerned. Would he believe her?
She cherished one hope here; since he was so nearly concerned,
since so much depended upon him, God would surely have prepared him already. God was omniscient, He would know that
without Joseph's help and support. . . . Don't think of that!
God was just; Joseph, too, on the long walk back from the house
outside Cana, or in his workshop, would have been visited and
enlightened.

To be with someone who knew, who understood and believed,
was such a wonderful prospect that she could hardly wait for the
moment when, supper over, she could slip away and find him.

II

She knew, before a word was spoken, that that hope had been
groundless.

He was in his workshop, making the most of the last of the
daylight, setting his tools in order and brushing some shavings
from the bench to the floor. When her shadow darkened the
doorway he looked up, recognising her with an expression of
pleasure, and then, seeing that she was alone, with surprise.

He lived by himself and properly brought-up girls like Mary,
with mothers like Anne, did not come visiting, almost at dusk,
men who lived alone, even if they were officially betrothed. Once
or twice a week Anne who believed that men, left to themselves,
ate nothing but bread and cheese, would invite him to supper,
and sometimes, afterwards, Joachim, Mary's father, would go

to make his hens secure from the foxes and Anne would absent herself for a little while, and they'd be left alone; but she'd never come to his house unaccompanied and his first thought was that something must be wrong. Carpenters were often called upon when accidents happened for people believed—not without some reason—that a man who could dove-tail two pieces of wood together so smoothly that they seemed to have grown that way, could replace a sprained joint or set a broken bone.

If God had informed him, she thought, he would have come to welcome her, reached out his hands to hers and begun to speak of the wonder. As it was he said:

"Mary! Is anything wrong?"

"No," she said. "Nothing wrong." Disappointment made her voice sound small and woeful. And it was impossible to avoid the thought that had she come to report some physical disaster, the roof of the house fallen in, Anne's ankle sprained, Joachim's leg broken, she could have counted upon him absolutely. Sympathetic, kind and sensible, in any ordinary situation he could be relied upon to do the right thing and do it well. But in this situation . . .

The very sound of her voice dismayed her. She had come to share with him the most marvellous news that anyone, ever, anywhere had had to impart. It should have been announced with joy and pride and the singing of trumpets.

She said, a trifle more firmly, "I came to see you, Joseph, because I have something to tell you, something for you, alone."

His heart gave a great downwards thud. He aligned the handle of a chisel and the handle of a saw with meticulous exactitude. He knew what she had come to say. She didn't, after all, wish to marry him. All along he'd found it difficult to believe in his luck. She was so young, and so pretty, so well-brought-up. He'd been immensely, and pleasantly surprised when her parents had seemed to encourage him; and when, after quite a time of trying to pluck up courage, he had made his formal request to Joachim and he had said, "You'd suit me; but we must find out how Mary feels," he had suspected that Joachim was making an excuse, not liking to say "No" outright.

The trouble was that he was too old for her; age mattered in a society where widows had a very poor time. Any careful father was bound to look ahead and choose for his daughter a man who wasn't likely to die before he had reared a son capable of supporting his mother. Of course, with a rich man it was different; he could provide for a wife. Unless they died early, in childbed, women tended to outlive men and that fact must be taken into consideration when arranging marriages.

However, Mary, so pretty and graceful and gentle, Mary who could have married anybody, had agreed to marry him, a carpenter in his late thirties, not a native of Nazareth, a man who had plied his trade in many far places—he'd even been in Egypt —before settling down. An enormous gratitude had blended with his love for her. Amazement too. And if she had come here, this evening, to say that she had changed her mind, thought better of it, he would not be truly surprised. Sad, disillusioned, but not surprised. He'd bear the blow as a man should, not whimpering; and for her wedding to some younger, luckier fellow, he'd make her a chest, carved all over with lilies, her favourite flowers.

Having, by the arrangement of the tools, gained time to brace himself, he looked up.

He said, "You're shivering. Come into the house and I'll rouse the fire."

She preferred the workshop. The little house that adjoined it, in which once or twice she had, with her father and mother, on formal visits eaten little sweet cakes from Hilliel's shop and drunk wine, had the inexplicable pathos of a place where a man lived alone. It had always been, on those occasions, clean and tidy, but the scent of overcooked food had hung about. And once—whenever she recalled that visit, her heart moved and melted—Joseph had procured from somewhere, a bunch of the white, sweetly scented lilies that she loved; and he'd shoved them into a jar of indescribable ugliness, so narrow necked that the lilies were pressed together, stiffly crowded, and coloured ochre, orange, red, and a peculiarly sharp yellow.

She said, "I'm not cold, and it is lighter here." That was true, the workshop faced West and the last, level rays of the sun—the sun which had risen this morning on a seemingly ordinary day, and was now about to set at the end of a day that had seen the miracle, the germinal birth of a whole new world—shone in at the wide door.

"Sit then, please," Joseph said, and he brought forward the plain stool on which, sometimes when he was tired, he sat at the workbench. As he carried it he brushed his hard work-hardened hand across it to remove any dust or sawdust.

"Now," he said, and moving backwards, perched himself at the end of the workbench which was already in shadow. "Tell me. You look troubled." She would be troubled, if she had come to tell him what he suspected, for she had the tenderest heart in the world.

She said, falteringly, "It's a very hard thing to say. So hard to put into words . . ."

She looked so pale, he thought. Despite the errand he attributed to her in his mind his heart moved towards her; he wanted to make things easier for her.

"If it's anything to do with *me*," he said stoutly, "out with it. I've taken a few knocks in my time. One more won't floor me."

She said, "Joseph, today I saw an angel . . ."

It was still light enough, even where he sat, for her to see his face, shocked, then incredulous and presently frankly appalled. She told him everything, as though by adding detail to detail she could overcome his disbelief. When she mentioned the sack she had carried he turned his head; she looked in the same direction and saw the bag standing there, in the corner. But that proved nothing. She had no proof. She had a fantastic story which must either be taken on trust or rejected, and even as she talked, even as she described the angel, she could see Joseph rejecting it. She could also, in her mind's eye, see herself facing the women at the watering place.

She ended, "I'm not lying, Joseph, I am not mad and I was not dreaming. It happened, everything, just as I have told you. And it *was* prophesied that a virgin should bear a child who would be our Messiah. I don't know why I should have been chosen—I'm as confounded as you are; but the angel said I had been; he called me blessed among women."

She stopped speaking and in the dim, sweet-scented workshop there was silence which stretched on and on until at last Joseph said, as though someone had him by the throat, choking him:

"It is written that the Messiah should be of the house of David. I can trace my lineage back to Solomon. But if you are, as you say, already with child, I am not its father and my lineage has nothing to do with it."

She said, "He will need an earthly father, too."

No truer word was ever spoken, Joseph thought; and wondered that she could speak with such gentle detachment. What about her need for a husband? Why wasn't she weeping and tearing her hair?

He could not rid his mind of the memory of the donkey boy, young, handsome, an obvious young rogue. Horrible, almost impossible to think of, but this was an evening of impossibilities. Suppose that on this spring morning. . . . But then, how could she know, so soon, that she was pregnant? A moon must run its course before any woman could be certain.

But maybe she didn't know that. Maybe she didn't know anything of such matters. Her life had been very sheltered. He had heard of girls so innocent that they thought babies were begotten by kisses. Such girls were rare, but they did exist, and Anne's daughter might well be one of them.

Remembering the boy's shining eyes and white teeth, he thought, magnanimously, that he could forgive a kiss or two. Yet how out of character that seemed! And so did the concoction of such an elaborate and impious story.

"Did he touch you?" he asked abruptly.

"No. He stood under the awning and spoke to me. He said his name was Gabriel." Her voice took on an awed, remembering tone. "He was almost too beautiful to look at, and he had a lily in his hand. He told me another thing too. He said that my

cousin Elisabeth had been pregnant for six months and she is
well over child-bearing age."

This piece of evidence, susceptible to proof, carried less weight
with Joseph than it might have done, since he had never seen
Elisabeth. He said:

"I meant the donkey boy."

"Yes. He hit me. By accident he said, and I believed him. But
not on the head, if that is what you are thinking. Here under
my arm." Then the full implication of the question struck her
and she lifted her head a little and spoke in a different voice.
"The boy," she said, "was a young lout, ill-treating his donkey.
But if I had so far lost all respect for myself and my family and
you, Joseph, do you really think that I am wicked enough to tell
a story involving holy things? Or stupid enough to tell a story so
difficult to believe? Think how much easier it would have been
to have torn my clothes and run screaming that I had been assaulted. Then I should have been sure of sympathy, and everybody would have believed me. I don't think you do." She looked
at his face, wrenched with indecision and misery, and felt sorry
for him. "I cannot blame you," she said, more gently. "You saw
no angel. And I, who did, still find it difficult to believe. I know
that the coming of the Messiah has been foretold, hoped for,
prayed for—and never more than now; but all day I have asked
myself, Why *me?* Yet, when you come to think of it, God has
made strange choices before. Jacob and David, quite ordinary
until they were chosen. Now I am chosen. I vow to you, Joseph,
that everything happened exactly as I have told you."

She longed for him to say, "I believe you." She waited. And
because he loved her, he wanted to say the comforting words
for which he knew she was waiting; but the whole matter was
too great, too solemn to be thus easily accepted. He couldn't say
that he did not believe, he wouldn't say that he disbelieved; so
he sat dumb, looking puzzled and wretched.

She thought, I have failed. And with that thought another
came. Isaiah, in his prophesy of the Messiah, had used the
words, "He is despised and rejected of men." The rejection had
begun here, tonight, in this wood-scented workshop. The first to

reject him was the man who might have been a father to him.
She unclenched her hands and folded her arms across her body,
protectively. Not rejected by me, she thought. It is hard to believe but I know it is true, and if I must I will manage alone,
and still think myself blessed, despite all the ridicule and the
scorn and the pointing fingers.

Again Joseph wondered that she should be so calm. If what
she said about her condition was true—however it had come
about—unless he stood by her she was in a sorry plight indeed.
Anne and Joachim loved her, but their very love would be the
measure of their shock and horror. In them, as in him, doubt
would war with faith, credulity with incredulity. . . .

He said pitifully, "I don't know what to think. I need a little
time to think things over."

She stood up then, and her veil slipped back from her hair
which, freed of the confinement, loosened itself and caught the
last rays of the sun and made a halo about her pale, calm face.

She said, "I came, hoping that God, having chosen me, would
have given you a sign, or that you would have faith enough to
believe without a sign. I was mistaken. But there is no need to
fret or be unhappy. If it is God's will that this child should have
an earthly father, one will be found. It may be that he needs
none. *My* father is another who can trace his lineage from David! Good night, Joseph."

Outside, with the sun suddenly sunk behind the hill's shoulder and the dusk thickening, the night wind chilly after the
warm day, she was afraid. Alone, and cold, and afraid. No
longer the blessed, the chosen, but an unmarried girl with a
child in her womb, and upon her tongue a story that nobody
could believe.

She could see now why the angel had said "Fear not." There
was so much to fear. Her parting words to Joseph had been bold,
almost defiant, but now thinking of her parents, her friends and
her neighbours, she quailed.

For the first time she saw the width of the gulf that divided what people professed to believe from what they were actually capable of believing. At this very moment if someone went to her home and asked her parents, Do you believe that Messiah will come? they would say, Yes, yes, indeed. Put the same question to Hilliel the rabbi and he would answer, Indisputably, it is so written. As late as this morning Joseph, confronted by the question, would have professed his belief. Yet tonight he had been incredulous, despite all her efforts to state her case in a manner likely to lead to belief. She had forced herself to speak calmly, not to weep, or gesticulate or plead. She had known, instinctively, that had she cried and made an appeal to his pity Joseph would have weakened and accepted the situation without accepting the truth. That would have been very wrong. So quietly, rationally, she had offered him the facts, and he had not believed her!

The night grew darker, the wind colder; the feeling of loneliness grew. As she neared her home she knew that she must enter and present her usual untroubled countenance; she could face no more this day. So she leaned for a moment against the thorn fence which her father had planted to keep out the foxes. She felt the prick of the long sharp thorns and thought of the donkey goad. Chosen of God, and then abandoned. She sent a wordless cry, winging through the night—My God, my God, why have you forsaken me?

III

Joseph, left alone, first thought, I should have walked home with her. But she'd gone so suddenly, and there'd been so much to think about.

He got up from the bench, moving slowly and heavily, like an old man and went into his living room. He'd spent this day at home, so he'd eaten at mid-day; bread and cheese would serve for his belated supper. He set them on the table, brought a knife, sat down and felt sick. Up to that point his mind had been engaged in listening to the story, trying to assess its truth and finding possible alternatives. When he had once glanced at the future it had been on Mary's behalf.

What of his own?

His own future, as well as that of Mary and that of an unborn child, lay in his hands; he must make a decision and at the moment he felt incapable of doing so.

His last task before taking on the job at the new house near Cana had been to make a new gateway and a length of fencing for a man who owned a small vineyard, and as part payment he had accepted a large jar of wine which he had set down in the coolest corner of the workshop, intending to save it and contribute it to the wedding feast. He was, by habit, an abstemious man.

Now he rose, took a jug, went to the jar and broke the stamped clay seal, poured a jugful of the wine and hurried back into the house. In the workshop the stool on which Mary had sat was still in position, and something of her presence seemed to linger there, too. He thought uncomfortably that if, at the end of his thinking, he decided that he didn't believe her and did not intend to marry her, he would never enjoy working in that place again. In fact he doubted whether he could go on living in Nazareth, where, even if he could avoid seeing her, he would hear about her.

Get away, he thought. And the question, Where? was easily answered. He could go into the hills and join the guerrillas, the nameless ones, the night-walkers.

He thought about them as he sipped his wine and felt it warm and sustaining after the shock.

It was almost sixty years since the Roman, Pompey, had intervened in the Jews' disastrous civil war, had taken Jerusalem and made Palestine a province of the Empire; the great majority of the Jews had settled down, if somewhat warily and uneasily, under Roman rule. But there were others who refused to accept the fact that the war had ended; there were men who remembered their families massacred, either by the Romans themselves or by his tool, Herod, whom they had made King of Judea. There were ardent patriots, religious fanatics, men with grievances, and they had taken to the hills and seized every opportunity to make a nuisance of themselves. They killed sentries, destroyed stores, stole horses, sabotaged the new road and water works, occasionally even ventured an ambush by daylight. At infrequent intervals individuals, or small groups, were captured and executed. In official quarters there was a tendency to underestimate their numbers and to decry their activities; there were even Jews who deplored their existence, maintaining that they consisted mainly of lawless men, fugitives from justice; but most people admired their courage and their cunning, and the stories of their reckless, spectacular exploits helped to keep alive the spirit of even the tamest town dwellers, backing up the conviction that in the end nobody but Jehovah and his appointed servants could govern the Jews.

Into the ranks of the nameless ones Joseph could disappear tomorrow and be lost. And if what Mary said about her state was true, nobody could blame him; or if they did, he'd never know.

He drank again and was seized by self-pity. Wasn't it hard, he thought, that at his age, having led a wandering life in youth, and now be prepared to settle down, he should have to uproot himself again. He liked his little house; until this evening he had liked his workshop; he liked Nazareth and his neighbours and his customers. Never before had he felt himself to be part of a community; seldom before had he stayed in any place long enough to reap where he had sown in the sense of establishing a reputation for good sound work. Here he was known, Joseph the carpenter, and respected, and trusted. Must he abandon it all?

The alternative was to stay and face a very distasteful situation. An espousal was a serious thing; to cancel it was almost like breaking a marriage. But even if a couple had been married for twenty years and hadn't cohabited for a time, due to separation or ritual abstinence and the woman had said she was pregnant because an angel had spoken to her, the man would be fully justified in putting her away. Wouldn't he? *Wouldn't* he?

He'd have to give his reason, of course. And he could just see

Anne's face, wrenched by shock and horror, Joachim's distorted by anger; and Mary's, full of sorrow and reproach. His fundamentally kind nature shrank from that prospect.

There was another alternative; he could accept her story. He drank again, and then, scowling, went through the whole account again.

He was now down to rock-bottom, weighing and measuring exactly the faith in which he had been born and reared and to which he had paid allegiance, always.

He believed in God; the one and only God who in six days had made the heaven and the earth and all that were therein; the God of Abraham, Isaac, and Jacob, who had enabled Daniel to face a den of hungry lions and Shadrach, Meshach, and Abednego to walk unscathed through a fiery furnace, seven times as hot as an ordinary one. These and a hundred other miraculous stories, he had listened to a dozen times and never doubted; they were now as much a part of him as the calluses on his hands. But they were all long ago, part of the fabulous past, part of "once upon a time." Then, take the prophecies; did he believe them? Naturally; every pious Jew did. Messiah would come, in great power and glory, to deliver His people. But that was all in the future. That was to be one day. . . .

There you have it, he said to himself, lifting the jug again. Belief in the past things and in the future things is easy; but here and now, that's different. Do I believe that Mary, the woman to whom I am espoused, this morning was visited by an angel who told her that she was to bear the Messiah, and that upon that word she became pregnant?

And the answer to that was a downright "No."

There it was, and there was no help for it. No use blaming oneself for one's disbelief, belief was there or it was not there; it would not be commanded. He wished with all his heart that it could be. Because he loved her; he wished he could have given her the answer she wanted. He loved her so much that he wished she had come to tell him that she preferred another man. That, he felt, he could have borne. What he resented—he was facing facts now—was the fact that she had tried to deceive him.

She wasn't stupid; that was one of the things that had attracted him to her. Other women went to the synagogue and, if they were young, clattered their bracelets and looked covertly at young men from the edges of their veils and thought their young, silly thoughts; if they were older they were glad of a chance to be at peace and rest for a moment, or watched how their children behaved. *She* had listened and remembered; and today had tried to use what she had learned.

And yet, and yet, trying to dismiss her as a light, deceptive creature, he could not forget her calm, the dignity and assurance of her last words.

Suddenly he thought, Poor girl, how she will suffer!

The thought of it, and the wine he had drunk made him break out into a sweat. If he repudiated her, what would they do, Anne and Joachim, so respectable, so orthodox? Hide her away, say she was ill, smuggle the baby away the moment it was born and put it out to nurse somewhere far away? Anne was sharp-tongued, Joachim, if displeased—Joseph had once or twice seen him so—sullen and surly. What a terrible life the poor girl would have.

And as he thought of that the last alternative presented itself, and even as he entertained it he knew that it was something that only a pot-valiant fellow would consider.

Why not marry her?

He loved her and she needed him. Why make all this coil about what you believed and what you didn't believe, and God and the prophets. If she had been frail, all the more reason why he should be strong. And he wouldn't, by any means, be the first man to rear another man's child and grow to be fond of it.

She was very sweet and very innocent; somebody had taken advantage of that sweetness and innocence; and she, in turn, had tried to take advantage of him. But that was because he was her only hope. She had agreed to marry him, and he owed her something for that. And he realised that he was, compared to her, old, and a very unromantic kind of fellow. He looked back on his own youth, remembering its fancies and its passions, its moments of ecstasy; it would ill become him to sit in judgement. . . .

Yes, he thought; he'd marry her, because he loved her, because he was sorry for her and because it was the easiest way out for all. And if, by some fantastic chance, her story should be true, and nine months from now she bore a baby with . . . Exactly *how* would the Messiah be born? With wings? With a crown on his head, a sword in his hand? With a countenance of such shining glory that no man could look on it?

How very peculiar that none of the prophets had given the slightest information about that. Dream-ridden, impractical men, they'd spoken of a conception without sin, and of a virgin birth. It had been left to a carpenter in Nazareth, an ordinarily sober fellow who had missed his supper and drunk more in an hour than he ordinarily did in half a year, to ask, How?

He said to himself, Man, you're tipsy! Get to your bed.

But, tipsy or sober, credulous or incredulous, he had decided to marry her; and for that he was always to be thankful. In his ordinary, human, unenlightened state he had, from love and pity, made his decision.

He lay down, and fell asleep. And presently the low dark room was filled with a golden light, and there was the sound of music, and the sweet scent of flowers. There too, exactly as Mary had described, was the angel, a dazzle of whiteness and beauty with great wings, and a lily in his hand. Gabriel!

He would have risen, would have fallen to his knees, but he was paralysed.

"Joseph, thou son of David," Gabriel said, "fear not to take unto thee Mary, thy wife; for that which is conceived in her is of the Holy Ghost." If he could have spoken then, Joseph would have said that he had already decided; but awe held him speechless. "She shall bring forth a son, and thou shalt call his name Jesus; for he shall save his people from their sins."

Then it was dark again, and silent. The night wore away and in the dawn Joseph woke.

Very often, he knew, dreams were conjured up out of what

had happened during one's waking hours; twisted, sometimes almost unrecognisable, but you could, if you gave your mind to it, find the link. It did not seem to him unduly marvellous that he should have seen, in a dream, an angel exactly as Mary had described it, even to the lily. But there was one thing about this dream that could not have been the product of anything he had been told or imagined. That final phrase—"from their sins." That was, and the sensible, practical carpenter recognised the fact, something new, something he could never have imagined or dreamed. Messiah, when he came, was, by common belief, to save his people from their conquerors; he was to re-establish the throne of David, justify and re-instate a proud people. But Gabriel had said, "for he shall save his people from their sins," and that was such an original, revolutionary idea that it could only have come direct from God.

And although the idea that God, the one and only God had through a dream, communicated directly with him, the village carpenter, just as He had communicated with specially chosen people in the past, in the once-upon-a-time, Joseph felt curiously calm. He now understood Mary's attitude on the previous evening. "Rest in the Lord and wait patiently for Him." "The Lord is my shepherd, I shall not want." The certainty was like a rock. Yet, as over even the most solid rock, a climbing plant may throw its comparatively unimportant growth, over the certainty there were the purely human considerations; he must get to Mary and assure her; he must make arrangements for hastening on the wedding.

The village was hardly stirring when he walked to her house. The door was still closed and he knocked on it. Mary opened it and her face, already pale, whitened when she saw him. He took a step backward and signed to her to follow him.

"Have you told them?" he asked in a low voice.

She shook her head. She had come home, feeling forsaken of God, and thinking that she must tell them, the sooner the better, and found them both busy, preparing the eggs that her father would, in the morning, take into the market at Sepphoris. Anne, with a damp cloth, was wiping each egg clean from the clawmarks, the dung, the bits of nesting chaff, and Joachim, taking them one by one, was holding each egg against the candle-light. To sell an egg with an embryo chick in it, or with a blood spot or a meat spot would be to lose customers. In Sepphoris ordinary housewives, or the slaves who bought for bigger house-holds, must always be able to say, "The eggs we buy from Joachim are always fresh."

She'd stood there for a moment, visualising what would hap-pen if she suddenly gave them the news. She'd tried Joseph the one to whom, mentally and emotionally, she was closest and he had not believed her. So from her parents she had turned away and gone to bed.

"I'm glad of that," Joseph said, in answer to her shaking of the head. "I've come to ask you a great favour." He was aware that in the shadowy room behind the open door somebody was moving, listening, alert. He raised his voice a little. "I know weddings, and the preparations for them mean a great deal to brides and their mothers. But Cana is seven miles away, I have to leave early and I get back late. I'm tired of coming home to a dead hearth, tired of making my own breakfast. . . ." Whoever moved in the shadow had come nearer, was listening intently. "The day after tomorrow," he said, "is the day for weddings. I've come to ask you, Mary, to marry me then, instead of two months hence."

Even had he not had his dream her face would have been sufficient justification. Joy, gratitude, wonder, completely trans-figured it. He had thought it over, he believed it.

She said, "Oh, Joseph!" and looked on him with love.

"What is this? What is this?" demanded Anne, able no longer to remain a silent listener and coming to the door.

"I want to put the wedding forward," Joseph said.

"I heard you. There's selfishness for you! Marry the day after tomorrow—with the guests bidden for eight weeks ahead. So you're tired of fending for yourself and to spare yourself just that short time more, you'd do Mary out of her wedding day. In the whole of my life I never heard anything so preposterous!"

As in the early days, faced by Mary's mother he felt all hands

and feet and angular elbows. He said, as awkwardly as though
his request had been made from purely selfish motives:

"I thought if Mary didn't mind . . ."

Mary said, "I don't, I'd be glad."

"You be quiet," Anne said. "You're so soft, you'd stand by the
door and give away your nose for a whistle if anybody asked
you!" The tone in which she said that was almost rough, yet she
was expressing, for the first time, fully and freely, her inmost
opinion of her own daughter. She was so tender-hearted, so
easily troubled, so altogether, in Anne's opinion, unfitted for the
hard battle that was ordinary life, that somebody must stand up
for her, protect her, save her from herself as it were. And Anne
had hoped that Joseph would be that somebody. That had been
her only reason for showing him any favour; he was getting on
in years, he wasn't and never would be rich; but she had thought
him kind and reliable. Now he was the very one to come along
with this most selfish suggestion.

"We," Anne said, giving the contemptible fellow a fierce look,
"have relatives, on both sides of the family, scattered all over
Galilee and Judah. I have a brother in Capernaum and another
in Bethsaida; Joachim has two sisters in Shechem. And there's
Zacharias," she said, naming, with some pride, the husband of
Mary's cousin who was a priest in the Temple. "How do you
think they're going to feel when they hear she's been married
without their presence? It's all very well for you to come stroll-
ing along and suggest getting married the day after tomorrow,
just because you've spoiled your breakfast. Things aren't done
like that in decent families."

Mary said, "At least my dress is ready."

"So it may be. But nothing else is."

Joseph felt rather than saw that Mary was looking at him
with appeal. What could he say?

Speaking almost as the words came into his mind he said:

"What I said to Mary wasn't the whole of it. When we set
the day I didn't know this job was coming up, did I? Now I can
see I'm going to be so busy that it'd be very inconvenient to take
three days off then. This week I could do it." From first to last

a properly celebrated wedding in humble families went on for three days, with richer people it could extend to six.

"Too busy to attend your own wedding!" Anne exclaimed. "That's the first time I ever heard that."

From behind her Joachim said, as he fastened his girdle: "What is going on here?"

Anne turned and in short sharp words informed him. Joachim looked at Joseph who appeared to be embarrassed and awkward, at Mary, who seemed to be on the brink of tears, and at his own belligerent wife. And he thought, Why of course, they're in love and it's spring, poor fellow he doesn't want to wait any longer. On top of this understanding thought he felt the instinctive impulse to side with one of his own sex.

"Well," he said, when Anne had finished, "I can't see so much amiss with that. Unless Mary minds. It's her wedding; it's for her to say."

"I'd like to be married the day after tomorrow," Mary said.

"That's settled then," Joachim said before Anne could speak. "Now perhaps one of you would come in and give me my breakfast."

Speechless, Anne flounced into the house.

Mary said, "Oh thank you, Joseph! I can never thank you enough. You do believe me?"

"I believe you," he said.

Her joy at being believed was so transcendent that he decided not to mention the dream yet. He'd save that for an unjoyful day. Looking ahead he could see plenty of that sort to come.

CHAPTER II

At the foot of the stone stairs that led up to his tower, Melchior turned and looked at old Senya; she'd never been, in his opinion, particularly bright, and now, with age, her wits as well as her hearing and eyesight were failing. He had to say things over and over again, and even then could never be sure that she had heard and understood. Her own few remarks she repeated so often that had he taken any notice of what she said, he would have found the reiteration quite tiresome.

Wrapped up against the cold, muffled and shrouded in the remnants of several garments, once of varying colour but now from age and dirt a uniform dun, she crouched by the pitiable fire.

"Senya," he said. She was his slave, but as always he addressed her with gentle courtesy. "Senya, you did understand me?" Her head like a tortoise's emerged from the carapace of wrappings and turned towards him. "I am going up now and I shall not be down until tomorrow morning. Don't call me and don't cook any supper for me."

He had told her that twice before and she had merely nodded and grunted. This time she said:

"Master, there is nothing to cook. Nothing. Nothing at all. When what we have is eaten, we shall starve."

"I'll think about that tomorrow."

She had been muttering about the nearness of starvation for quite a long time now; sometimes he took no notice, when he did he always soothed her by saying he would think about it presently.

"The pig is hungry, too," she said in her flat old voice. He was the cleverest man in Korea, maybe the cleverest man in all the world, but in many ways he could act like an idiot, and he was acting that way about the pig. It was good housekeeping to have a pig in a pen to eat the household scraps and panful of meal now and again, and this year, as in former years, she had bought a little pig, the runt of a litter; very cheap it had been because the man who had sold it thought it would be dead before she got it home. What she had been trying, without success, to make Melchior see for the last fortnight, was that when there was so little for people to eat there were no scraps for pigs, and when there was no money, there could be no meal. The pig was losing flesh, and its hungry squealing, shrill enough to pierce the constant buzzing in her ears, made Senya perpetually aware of its plight. However, Melchior was her master, the pig was his, bought with his money—she looked at the little jar which stood in a niche in the wall, an empty jar now—and she would never dream of doing anything about the pig until Melchior told her to.

"I'll think about the pig, too; but presently."

In the bitter depths of her heart she said to herself, Always presently, always tomorrow, shuffling things off; so he has brought ruin to himself and hunger to us both.

But when he had disappeared around the first turn of the spiral staircase and was reasonably certain not to turn back and tell her again what she had fully understood in the first place, she roused herself, took a knife and with a savage, a self-mutilating cut, halved the bit of stale bread, the bit of hard cheese that lay on the bench. Then, opening the door, she stole out into the bitter wind and went to where, at the base of the tower, there was a basket, attached to a long rope. She slipped her offering into it, covered it again and went back to the fire.

Only a few minutes earlier, showing him the poor portions of bread and cheese, she had said, "Master, this is all we have!" And he had, for a moment, brought his mind back from the wide fields of the sky where it ranged, and he had looked closely at the food.

"Enough for today," he had said, quite contentedly. "Halve it between us." It had never occurred to him to say, Halve it fairly, because for years it had been understood that whatever there was was to be thus divided. And under his eye, attentive for once, she had made a fair division. Now she had given him half her portion; because he was her master, and because she had loved him slavishly for more than fifty years. He wouldn't notice; he never noticed anything; at least not anything on that level; that was why they were in this sad state.

The pig, having seen Senya come out and go in again without throwing him so much as an outside cabbage leaf, squealed angrily. Senya, going into another of the little rooms at the base of the tower to smooth Melchior's sleeping mat and his blanket, thought, He did say tomorrow! and thought how good a bit of roast pork would taste.

Melchior, climbing steadily, indeed briskly, the spiralling stairway that clung to the tower's outer wall, deliberately put the old woman's words out of his mind. Poor, poor, yes, he knew they were poor; but one good thing about eating scantily was that you stayed spry and lively. How many men of his age, seventy-five, could go up and down these stairs as he did, he asked himself. Very few. Leading the life he did—he had not set foot outside the tower since he'd sold his last bit of land, and that must be at least five years ago—if he had eaten full, he would be heavy and scant of breath, an occupant of a carrying chair. As it was, only lately had he rigged the rope and the basket as a means of getting things to the top; previously he had carried them.

Undoubtedly the worst thing about being poor was the cold. It was spring now, the snows had melted, the frost-hardened earth was softening, but this process added a dampness to the chill of the wind which blew from far inland where it was much colder than in sea-girt Korea. He could see the damp on the stone wall, feel it in his bones. Years ago, when the tower was newly built there had been braziers here and there on the stairs, and no fewer than three in the room at the top. When he'd moved here he had brought three slaves, Senya and two young males who had scampered up and down the stairs carrying food and water and fuel for the braziers. In those days he'd had a bed in the room at the top, and a big bell in an aperture; he had only to ring it. . . . He did not grieve over the vanished service, the lost comforts, but he did feel the cold. He was glad to wrap rags, like bandages, over his cloth shoes and well up his legs. And all through the winter he wore his one wadded robe, a good garment in its day, now stained and faded. But spring was on its way; the winter solstice was three months past. In a rush the warm weather would come, and he could wear his other, unwadded robe, and Senya, as in other years, would take this one and wash it, beat the lumped wadding into fluff; and the sun, shining into the room at the top of the tower would cherish and revive him.

Poverty, self-imposed, was tolerable. He had, he knew, only himself to blame for his state. He'd been a most fortunate young man. His grandfather had come out of China in the train of that great, that almost legendary warrior, Wiman, and in the carve-up of the conquered territory he had received enormous tracts of land which had passed eventually, undiminished, to Melchior. If, when he had come into his heritage the tower had been built, he could have stood at the top of it and looked in every direction and known that all he could see he owned.

His father he could not remember; both his parents had died young and he had been reared by his grandfather who, because he was a Chinese and had no learning, had a great respect for it. One day the boy Melchior had made some remark or observation —he could not remember the exact circumstance—and his grandfather had said, "I think you may be a clever boy. You shall go to the university in Pyongyang." Pyongyang at that time prided itself upon being one of the most cultured cities in the world. Korea had, long ago, been colonised by Chinese who had brought their own culture, their own learning with them. General Wiman's invasion had been a reconquest, almost an invasion of barbarians; and there had been times, when in the muted, learned atmosphere of Pyongyang's schools Melchior, because of his ancestry, had been made to feel that he was almost a barbarian. That had made him pursue his studies more diligently. He'd learned eagerly, everything, even some rudimentary

Greek. Less than a hundred and fifty years before the great Wi-man conquered Korea, a Greek named Alexander had marched into Asia, intending to conquer India. He'd failed—Melchior now knew exactly why—but his tongue had spread along the routes, had established itself in many places, become a means by which men of widely diverse cultures could communicate. In Pyongyang, where no born Greek had ever been, a place that no Greek had ever heard of, the young Melchior had learned Greek of a peculiar kind, together with history, mathematics, and astronomy.

Astronomy had been from the moment he was introduced to it, emotionally his darling and financially his downfall. The moment he had come into his inheritance he had built this tower, at vast expense. Glass; that was the trouble. He must have glass, and only one country in the world knew the secret of its making. Egypt, a place immeasurably far away. But intrepid traders, voracious traders had held open the tenuous lines between East and West. Ask in Pyongyang—as Melchior had asked—for glass, and it was like dropping a stone into a pond; the ripples spread. Months, even years, later you had glass, fragile stuff, carefully packed, gently handled, carried on the backs of camels, donkeys, horses and mules and men, moved by stages, paid for by stages, but arriving at last and costly beyond all reckoning. He'd grudged nothing; he had planned a great tower with a glass dome, and he was not surprised or dismayed by the fact that when at last it stood on the hilltop, just as he had visualised it, nine-tenths of his heritage was expended.

And in a way he had been right not to care; he had what he wanted; and he had a tenth of his patrimony left, and that would have sufficed to keep any ordinary careful man for as long as he lived. He simply hadn't been careful. Could he be expected to come down, in the middle of some calculation, or the careful drawing of a chart, to deal with a dishonest steward, a defaulting tenant? The idea was absurd. He'd said, "I'm busy." He'd said, "I'll deal with that tomorrow." Now and then, faced with the problem in some way that forebade escape or deferment, he'd said, "I'll sell something."

With what remained of his estate he could not be bothered. Nor could he be bothered with friendships or any social contacts that made demands upon his time. When the tower was new there were men who had known his grandfather, men who had studied with him in Pyongyang, men with marriagable daughters. All splendid people he was sure, but to him as troublesome as flies in summer. Hundreds of times he had said, "Yes, thank you, I will come," in answer to their invitations. Then he had forgotten all about them.

So his fortune had wasted away and his life had narrowed. Now on this very cold morning, with spring imminent, he owned his tower, a small vegetable garden in which, presently, Senya would plant vegetables, Senya herself and a hungry pig. Nothing else in the world.

And there was not a happier man in the world. . . .

Downstairs, Senya, having straightened Melchior's sleeping apartment, moved back to the fire and looked at it with a gloomy eye. It was almost dead and she must go out in search of fuel. She looked at the miserable scrap of bread and cheese that remained and realised that she must do something about food, too.

In the past she had been in the habit of going down into the valley and hiring herself for some hours during the busy season, doing field work for which casual labour was welcome. Bent double, she'd planted rice in wet paddy fields, and then cut and carried it. She'd planted vegetables too, and gathered them. She'd picked and packed fruit. She'd cleared fields of stones and with the same stones built fences. She'd spent hours and hours in the stinking place where hides were scraped and the hair, mixed with glue, was beaten into felt from which hats and shoes were made.

Of these activities Melchior knew nothing. She'd timed her goings out and her returns very carefully. She never left the tower until he was safely at the top, and she was always back by sunset which was the usual time for the evening meal. He had not, of course, noticed her small but invaluable contributions to the household expenses. It must be at least five years since

Melchior had sold that last strip of land and had come in, trusting her absolutely, and put the money in the jar that stood in the niche. Even his bemused mind must have recognised something of the situation, for he had said, "That's the last, Senya. Make it go as far as you can."

Having said that and set the jar back in its niche he had gone straight up the stairs to what he called his work and she, in her mind, called his toys. And she had gone across to the jar and counted the coins. How wicked, she thought, the way good men are cheated; had that field been mine I should have haggled and sold it for at least twice as much as this. And then she had realised, for the first time, fully, that Melchior not only trusted her —she had known that—but that he was depending upon her.

So, shameful as it was for a slave born in the family house, and reared therein to do such a thing, she had gone and sought casual labour. Always far down in the valley where she was not known. And always, if questioned, she had said that she came from Pyongyang. Sometimes she had added the information that she was a widow.

It had worked until last year. Then something had gone wrong inside her head; far worse than the buzzing in her ears. When she stooped—and all field work involved stooping—she'd turned dizzy. Naturally she had ignored this, just as she had ignored her aching back, her stiff knees and elbows. But, working on through the dizziness, she had fallen and lain unconscious. She always came round, as good as new, and no harm done; but she'd had such spells so often, in so many different fields and orchards, that now no one would employ her. There was a superstitious belief that to have a worker die, at work, brought bad luck.

There were still things she could have done, inside houses; she could have cooked, preserved fish and meat, mended, done anything that did not entail much stooping; but the trouble was that in the valley there were only rich families who had slaves and servants of their own to do such work, or poor ones who would never hire domestic labour. The same problem had bedevilled her one or two begging expeditions; the poor had nothing to spare and in the big houses the servants had chased her off, calling her a dirty old woman.

Today the situation was desperate, she must go out to find fuel, and if it were humanly possible, something to eat tomorrow.

When she opened the door the pig squealed in anguished anticipation; she gave it a calculating look as she passed. Nothing but skin and bone now, and it would be worse tomorrow. Tomorrow she must by some means gain Melchior's attention and make him understand about the pig. It seemed strange that such a clever man should be so stupid about simple things.

Still, she was his slave and she must do her best for him. In addition, she loved him very much. She had lost her heart to him more than half a century ago, when she was fifteen and he a handsome young man of twenty. Oh, how handsome he had been, tall and slim and elegant, with such bright eyes and glossy black hair, and such beautiful manners. The old master had been alive then, the tower did not exist and they were all living in the magnificent house that stood halfway down the slope, overlooking the valley. She was the youngest of the female slaves, and the prettiest, and it was quite usual for masters, young or old, to take a comely slave girl to bed. She remembered the dusks of summers long ago, when the young master was home from his studies, and the night wind blew softly and she'd haunted the courtyard outside his bedroom and yearned for him. She'd done her best to attract his notice, putting oil on her hair and scent on the palms of her hands. If someone then, with the gift for seeing, had told her, You'll live alone with him for thirty years, sharing a fire and a dish, how wrongly she would have interpreted it, how overcome with joy she would have been.

Bodies grew old, she thought, shuffling down the hill; handsome young men turned into thin, frail ones—but she still thought Melchior good-looking, for his age; and in comely girls the sap dried up, till they were like old twisted trees and nobody would believe that once they had worn flowers behind their ears and been desirable, and almost died of their own desiring.

In the end even desire failed.

But duty remained; and a kind of fondness, and that was why

she was out here in the biting wind with the mud seeping through the rags that wrapped her feet instead of remaining indoors and thinking that it was a master's duty to provide his slave with at least one meal a day.

After a time she drew level with the big house under whose warm-coloured, curving tiled roof both she and Melchior had been born. She had never visited it to ask for employment or charity; it was too near the tower; she might be recognised and so bring shame upon Melchior; and Melchior, looking out from his tower, might even have seen her. Also she had felt a curious reluctance to go back there where life had run so comfortably in the old days.

This morning she thought about the past. The old master had possessed a sternness unknown to his grandson, but he had been just, and there had never been a mistress to make things hard. The old mistress had died in childbed, and Melchior's mother had died, with his father, in the time of the great sickness, two years before Senya herself was born. In the comfortable house life had been pleasant; plenty of fuel, plenty of food, plenty of tea. Of all the things she had lacked in recent years Senya missed tea most. It came from China and was very expensive, so it had been one of the first things to be cut out. Melchior seemed not to notice; he drank hot water without comment or complaint, but Senya still yearned to see the green leaves uncurling and yielding their flavour and fragrance, and the water changing colour. Between a bowl of hot water and a bowl of tea there was all the difference in the world.

She came back to the present. Either the wind was stronger than usual or meagre feeding was telling at last in increased feebleness; she was making very slow progress. Ordinarily she would have been in the valley by this time and here she was, still skirting the wall that surrounded the big house. It offered some shelter from the wind and she paused to gather strength. Through an archway she could see into the main courtyard. It wore its winter look. The big tubs of lilies had been taken indoors and every rose tree had been loosened from its stake, bent over and swathed in sacking. Very soon now it would look very different. Spring, when it came, came at a bound. She remembered how, for several years, she had watched the rose trees being unshrouded and straightened, and the lily tubs brought out, with excited anticipation. Maybe on some warm, scented evening *this* year Melchior would notice her and she would be able to give her maidenhead where she had already given her heart. That was all she asked.

It had never happened; and all that wasted hope and emotion might have been a sadness and a hurt to remember, but for one thing. If she had failed to make her humble way into his bed, so had women not so humble. Many men, with silk-clad, tiny-footed, jewel-shining daughters, had desired that rich, handsome young man as a son-in-law, and Senya had watched fearfully, feeling that she could hardly bear it if he took a wife without first taking her, yet knowing that she must bear it and give no sign for fear of ridicule. That misery, at least, she had escaped. Melchior had taken the sky as his bride, and such a rival any woman could accept, not gladly, but with fortitude.

She stood in the shelter of the wall and realised with dismay that this morning, even if she forced herself on, down into the valley, she would never climb back again. Old, yes, she was old, her ears buzzed as though bees were swarming there, and when she stooped she grew dizzy; but she'd never felt feeble before. Now she did, her legs trembled under her and she felt dizzy without stooping. It occurred to her—and it was a shocking thought—that if she was to have anything to offer her master when tomorrow morning he came down from the tower, she must ask for, and obtain it from *this* house.

She turned and looked back at the tower, a long grey finger pointing to the sky with a glass dome at its tip. It seemed far from where she stood, skulking in the shelter of the wall, to where her master was, high in the glass dome. But he had that wonderful glass, the thing he claimed to have invented.

Some years ago, but she could remember the day with clarity because it was the one and only time that he had ever shared his real life with her, he had come down with a tube, like a section of bamboo in his hand and he had said, "Look through that,

Senya, and tell me what you see. No, put it to one eye and close
the other, now, what do you see?" It had been summertime and
the door in the base of the tower had been open and he had
handed her the thing with its end pointing outwards. So she
had obediently closed one eye and applied the other to the end
of the tube and seen nothing, a blur, and she'd been confused,
torn between her wish to please him, since the toy was evidently
of importance to him, and her inability to guess even what it was
that she was expected to see. And then, suddenly, she had seen.
A tethered goat, eating grass.

She'd said, "I can see a goat."

And that had been exactly the answer he wanted. He said:
"Now, take the glass away and look in the same direction,
Senya. Can you now see the goat?"

She could not.

"Try the glass again."

She did so, and there was the goat, so close that she felt that
by reaching out her hand she could have touched it.

"I see it now," she said. Then he'd snatched the thing from
her and said:

"It brings distant things close, doesn't it? It will be of inestimable value to me in my work."

After that she had felt less happy about her own work, fearing
that even when she was far away in the valley he might turn
the glass in that direction and see her as plainly as she had seen
the goat and the grass. But in time she had realised that he only
turned the glass upon the stars or the moon, and the fear had
left her. This morning, however, because she was about to do
something that outraged her own standards, her fear of being
observed sprang up again, lively enough to make her turn and
look before rounding the corner of the wall and making, in a
furtive way, for the entrance to the kitchen courtyard.

Although she had never yet been back to what in her mind
she always called *the* house, she knew who lived there. A big fat
man who had made a fortune from running houses of prostitu-
tion in Pyongyang. A very disreputable way of making money,
as the man had realised. So, with one child born and another

about to be, he had sold his houses, moved into the country and bought Melchior's family house and several little farms. He was said to be an oppressive, unmerciful landlord. It was also said that his temper had been embittered by the fact that people in other big houses would not befriend him, called him Bawd-master and did not seek to ally their families to his by marriage. All this Senya had heard from the tongues of gossips. She had heard it said, also, that her master was at fault for so demeaning himself as to sell the house of his fathers to such a man.

And now, after all these years, she was about to demean her master even further, and demean herself too, by begging at the kitchen door.

It was terrible, and she knew it; and it was all her master's fault; he'd wasted his substance, just as he was at this very moment wasting the pig which, killed a week ago, would have provided several succulent joints, and killed tomorrow would hardly have enough fat in it for basting.

The kitchen door was firmly closed against the cold; but even her buzz-ridden old ears could hear the sound of voices, of laughter. When she knocked there was a momentary silence, then a voice said, "See who that is." Another voice said, "Ordering me about! Go yourself, lazy-bones." The first voice said, "Lazy-bones, am I?" And there was the sound of a scuffle and more, louder laughter.

Senya knew, intuitively, that there was no master, no mistress within this house. She remembered hearing somewhere that the Bawd-master, old now and his bones creaking, often took himself and his family South to winter in a less rigorous climate.

Slaves left in charge, she thought, growing arrogant and fat in idleness, the worst possible people to beg from. This opinion —based on experience—was confirmed when the door was opened by a young woman who said, after one glance:

"Whatever you're selling, we don't want any."

With the suddenness of a lightning flash from a summer sky, the idea came to Senya. She said in a wheedling, cajoling voice, not her own:

"You'll want what I have to sell, dearie. So will those within.

I can read fortunes. True ones. By the lines in your palm, or by the tea leaves in a bowl, I can tell what Fate has in store for you."

And wasn't it marvellous! She could have said, I'm starving, my belly is empty, my legs shake and my head spins from hunger, and they'd have turned her away. A few words of rubbish and there was the girl at the door all attention, and a voice from within saying, "A fortune-teller is it?" And in less than a minute she was inside the warm, the food-scented, the oh-so-familiar kitchen.

Melchior climbed the stairs and reached the one at the top, much wider than the rest, with, straight ahead of it a solid door, and to the right an aperture with a slatted shutter. This he opened and hauled up the basket, which, as was his custom, he had packed himself. For some reason quite outside his comprehension old Senya appeared to resent this sensible labour-saving device; she had offered to toil up the stairs with whatever was needed, and when he had pointed out to her that they were both now too old for such needless exertions, she'd turned sulky. Whenever she packed the basket something went wrong with the contraption because she seemed unable to understand the necessity for packing the basket in a balanced way. So now he did it himself. He knew—or thought he knew—exactly what was in the basket today. At the bottom a few handfuls of charcoal for his brazier; the last of the supply; a full jar of water, and as a counterbalance on the other side a larger wine jar containing a very small amount of rice wine, also the last of the supply. Between the two his half of the bread and cheese. Ample for all his needs for the next twenty-four hours. He carried the basket into the glass-roofed, circular room and set it on the floor. Then he looked about him with that sense of satisfaction, of homecoming which the room never failed to evoke.

All around the room, broken only by the entrance door and another leading to a little side chamber, ran a wide flat bench, set at just the right height for a man standing or sitting on a high stool to work at. On this bench, this morning, several charts, drawn on paper or parchment, and smaller pages covered with closely written figures or words, lay exposed. Others, neatly rolled, lay on shelves beneath the bench. In the centre of an empty space stood a box without a lid; in it lay his tools, his astrolabe, his compasses, his loadstone, and the glass which Senya remembered. There were pens, too, and sticks of coloured chalk, ground to a fine point; there was a knife and an ink jar.

The centre of the room was clear except for the three-legged brazier and a tall ladder with a stout strut at the back of it and at its top a platform upon which a man could sit or lie. The whole place was noticeably neat, even clean. Dust was never allowed to gather upon the oldest, the least used chart or map.

It was noticeably cold, too, perched on the hilltop, and above bench level all of glass: he looked wistfully at the brazier, already laid with a few dry twigs and lumps of charcoal. But he must not be extravagant. Soon, when the sun reached its midday height, the tower would become warm; then when it went down and night fell it would be colder than it was now; he must reserve his fire for the night. So he tucked his hands into his sleeves and went and stood by one of the charts, studying it.

He wondered if there were, somewhere in the wide, outer world, anyone who, looking at this chart, would understand it. There were astronomers in Pyongyang—it was there that he had gained a rudimentary knowledge of the subject—but, and this thought roused no pride in him, they were not of his calibre. How could they be? He had given his whole life to the study; they were men of divided interests; they gave lectures, reared families, took regular meals and spent a great deal of time in useless talk.

There were astronomers in the West, too; he even knew the names of two cities famous for their experts, Babylon and Alexandria. But a thin smile moved his lips as he thought, They hadn't done very well by Alexander. If he had been on that great general's staff he could have warned him that his attempt to conquer India was doomed to failure, a waste of time and money. Mars in decline, Saturn in the ascendant. Hopeless! He could have foretold, too, the break-up of the Empire Alexander did succeed in establishing; in the third house there was every augury of disintegration and division.

To be honest, though, there had in the last month or two been moments when he would have been glad to talk to a really skilled, truly learned fellow scholar; not in order to indulge in the futile, wrangling arguments such as he had witnessed and sometimes taken part in during his student days. He would have liked to hold out this chart and say, "What do you make of it?" Not because he was unsure of himself; a pregnant sky was as unmistakable as a pregnant woman; some new thing was augured; probably a comet; he would have welcomed another opinion about that.

He was now well away, and no longer aware of the cold; and Senya need not have feared his observation. If he had by any chance have looked out and downhill and seen her about to enter his old home he would merely have thought that she had shuffled out to have a gossip with some of her own kind. There had been a time when she would go out with some regularity and stay away for hours; women had an infinite capacity for gossip.

When Melchior had decided that he could no longer afford the house and the tower, and had also argued that to live on the spot would be more convenient, he had taken Senya, the two young male slaves, and enough furniture and gear for their needs. The rooms at the base of the tower were small, however, and much had been left behind and sold with the house. So the kitchen looked very much as it had done when Senya left it. The great chopping block still stood in one corner; several enormous cooking pots hung on the wall, and on a shelf were the blue-and-white lidded jars, left behind with some regret. Not that she'd have had any use for them lately, being unable to afford the spices and exotic herbs they were designed to hold. Onions and salt had been the only flavourings she had used for years, and the onions had been home-grown.

There were three people in the kitchen. The young woman who had let her in, an older woman with a full-fleshed face and

hard-looking eyes, and a boy on the verge of manhood. Their
easy, holiday-making air confirmed her guess that they had been
left in charge of the house; she knew the situation; little to do,
nobody to oversee them. Here they were, at mid-day, drinking
tea and eating . . . what were they eating? She used her nose as
well as her eyes. Delicious! Small savoury dumplings, packed
with chopped pork and herbs. She'd made many in her time.
And if her master would agree to the killing of the pig before
it starved to death, she would again—if by some means she got
some flour, some herbs.

The woman said, in a rousing, challenging way:

"Well, what about these fortunes?"

Senya, disturbed from her meditations, started and blinked.
What fortunes? Then she remembered, and said:

"Oh yes, the fortunes. By palm or by tea leaves? And I have
to be paid, you know."

"We could have guessed that! How? In cash or in kind?"

On any previous day, asked that question, she would have
said "Cash." She was a shrewd, shrill bargainer and down in the
village invariably managed to get more than her money's worth.
But now—she thought swiftly—she simply didn't feel able to
walk the rest of the downhill way, face the bustle and shoving
in the market, haggle, and then, carrying bundles, climb all the
way back. And she thought of the storeroom that adjoined the
kitchen; in the old master's day it had been a treasure house of
good things. Hams and strings of sausages and bunches of salt
fish had hung from hooks, there'd been barrels and sacks of flour
and honey, soya meal, dried peas and beans, rice, jars of oil and
vinegar and wine. She turned dizzy again at the thought of the
abundance. And doubtless it was the same now. The Bawd-
master had a bad reputation as a landlord, but nobody had ever
suggested that he was a stinting, niggardly master. So she said:

"Pay me in food." And as she said the words she could see
herself carrying away food for two, perhaps even three days.
And she could see Melchior, tomorrow coming down from the
tower top and being so surprised and pleased to find that she,
whom he had left with a bit of bread and cheese, had somehow,

miraculously, produced a real, belly-filling meal. He wouldn't ask how; he'd just enjoy it and say, as always, "Thank you, Senya, a very good meal."

"Food it shall be, then," the woman said. She was plainly the one in command, probably the cook. "I'll have mine in the tea leaves."

The girl said, "Me too." The boy said, "I think I'll have mine by hand."

Senya watched, enviously, mouth-wateringly as the two women drained their tea-bowls. And then she did her very best. She knew absolutely nothing about telling fortunes, but she did know what everybody wished to hear—impossibly favourable things. She was handicapped by her lack of knowledge about this household; in kitchens you found born slaves, like herself, bonded people, who must serve a certain term, and free people working for hire. And since status governed the future with an iron hand, a would-be fortune-teller must needs be very careful. She was careful; and she managed to offend every one of them. Staring into the meaningless pattern made by the tea leaves and thinking of what she would have wished to hear when she was this woman's age she told the cook that she would have children, beautiful children, and the cook, now the secret mistress of the old Bawd-master, chanced to desire nothing less. She told the young woman what surely any girl would wish to hear; many lovers, she said; and the young woman, who had one lover to whom she was utterly devoted, heard in that her doom. For the boy, regarding the delicate, uninformative palm that he offered, she foretold a future that was possible to any young man, slave, bonded, or free; because of all things the army was the most powerful; masters of every kind were always being asked to contribute to the army—that was a polite way of putting it. So she told him that he would be a soldier and a very successful one. The boy, a homosexual, who was waiting for one of his master's friends, a rich man of the same mind, to buy him and dress him in silk, was not pleased by this prospect.

It struck Senya, as the boy withdrew his hand, and she abandoned the trance-like attitude that all the fortune-tellers she had ever encountered had adopted, that they were an ungrateful lot. What had they expected? How had she failed?

The cook said, "Well that is that. Now we will pay you." She poured hot water into a cup and sprinkled tea leaves on it; she took a long-handled spoon and caught one of the savoury dumplings, and put it into another bowl.

"There you are," she said coldly. "Eat and drink." The three of them withdrew a little, whispering amongst themselves, saying, each one speaking from his own inner dissatisfaction that this was no true teller of fortunes, just a dirty old woman who shrank from downright begging. Take no notice, they said.

To Senya the bowl of tea was very welcome. In good conscience she could drink it and enjoy it; but the lovely little dumpling presented a problem. If only she could get it home, unbroken, what a meal it would make for her master when he came down from his tower tomorrow morning. Five minutes in a pan of boiling salt water and it would be as though it had been freshly made. Draining her bowl of tea, looking at the dumpling and repressing a fierce desire to eat, to taste it, she said:

"I would like, if you please, to take it home with me, to eat just before I sleep. One sleeps ill on an empty belly."

She could see, by their faces, that they were now hostile. And the hostility took the form of opposition, even to that simple request.

The cook, thinking what pregnancy would mean to her, said:

"Eat it. You asked for food, and that is food. Eat it!"

"I can't," Senya said, thinking how awful, how unnatural it would be for her to eat a delicious savoury dumpling while her master ate stale bread and sour cheese.

They whispered together. The cook said:

"Eat it. You shall have something to take home with you."

"Eat it," the girl urged, wondering how long it would be before the one, the chosen, deserted her and she must console herself with the many.

"Eat it," the boy said, contrasting what she had foretold with what he had hoped for.

So she ate it and it was so delicious that she abandoned the restrained manner of eating which she had adopted when, years ago, Melchior had said, Come, sit and eat, Senya, while the dish is hot. She allowed her teeth to clash, her lips to slap audibly, and somehow that added to her enjoyment of the dumpling.

Then, all suddenly, the boy said:

"I've seen you before. It's bothered me, all the time. You serve that crazy old man who lives in the tower."

Shame and disgrace; Melchior's slave, going about trying to tell fortunes, begging for food.

She said, "What tower? What crazy man? I come from Pyongyang."

"Then you must," he said, "be sister to the old woman who waits upon the madman in the tower at the top of the hill."

She could not disgrace her master, so she denied him.

"I may have a sister of whom I know nothing. And I know nothing of madmen in towers. I am from Pyongyang. A poor widow."

The cook said, "And you want something to eat this evening. I will fetch it."

Well, that was what she had come out for; something for her master to eat tomorrow; and she had achieved it. Scooping up the last bit of dumpling, Senya said, "Thank you. Thank you kindly."

The cook came back and handed to Senya one of those woven reed baskets in which fish and fruit were often carried. Such baskets were made by blind children in Pyongyang; some charitable ladies saw to it that there was always a supply of reeds, and they bullied shopkeepers into buying the baskets. A large household could collect four or five in a single day, and it was regarded as an unworthy act ever to hand back the baskets; if you had a use for them, well and good, if not they should be burned or dug into the garden to rot and enrich the soil; only thus could the orphans continue to eat, the ladies to be charitable. The basket she now had in her hand was closed by a sharp wooden skewer which pinned its edges together. And it weighed beautifully heavy. She was so glad that she had chosen to be paid in food, for no sum she would have dared to ask could have bought so much solid heavy provender.

She pushed her hands into her ragged multiplicity of sleeves and bowed, expressing her gratitude again and again. The hostility she thought she had sensed had vanished by this time, and they all smiled at her. The boy said, "Enjoy your supper!"

"Oh, I shall. I shall indeed. There is enough here for many meals. On the morrow's morrow I shall still be blessing you."

They smiled.

After the warmth of the kitchen the outer air struck even colder than before; and because she had lied she was compelled to walk away, downhill, as though making for the valley and the city beyond it. That was not all wasted effort, though, for she found, half-buried in the thawing mud a sizeable log, and later, when she had turned and was climbing back by a path which did not lead past the big house, she found several small bushes which the winter had killed; she grubbed them up, roots and all. She was fully loaded as she made her way up the steep incline below the tower, breathless and rather dizzy, but too happy to mind. Food and fuel for two days.

The pig squealed when it saw her and then again, even more loudly when she passed it by without a glance.

She relighted the fire first, feeding the feeble flame twig by twig and then putting one of the roots in place. The log was damp, and she laid it in the hearth where it could dry out a little. Then, as excited as a pampered wife who on New Year's Day had received a prettily wrapped parcel the contents of which she could not guess, she opened the basket and gave a yelp of dismay. There was nothing edible in it at all.

What had weighed so heavy were some shards, the broken remains of a heavy jar, and a piece of dried plaster from a crumbling wall, and a great bone, bare and bleached.

She remembered the way the three had whispered together, planning this; the way the inexplicable hostility had given way to smiles; the latent cruelty in the way they had forced her to eat what she had wished to bring away. Who could have believed that there were people in the world so lacking in all feeling, so downright wicked as to have played this heartless trick on her? I did them no harm, she thought. And all at once she was crying.

Her life, pleasant compared with that of most slaves, and quiet, had for years been a hard one; she had suffered her share of aches and pains, but she came of a hardy stock, possessed of an animal-like patience and fortitude and she hadn't wept since she was a girl, taking the wilted flower from behind her ear, smelling the wasted scent on her palms, knowing that it was all useless. She had wept then, slow sensual tears. Now she wept tears of rage and disappointment, and guilt because she had eaten the dumpling, because she had let herself be deceived. Oh, how she longed to punish them all; not realising that she had done so; that the cook would lie down tonight counting days on her fingers, and the young girl wonder how she could bear many lovers when she loved but one, and the boy dream of the harsh fabrics, the discomforts, the rigours and dangers that made up a soldier's life.

She cried for some minutes, with harsh, angry-sounding snorts. Then she realised that the light was changing. Soon it would be dark.

The day was ending. What a wasted day. The night would come, and the morning; her master would come down from his tower and she would have nothing to offer him except the half portion of a half portion of bread and cheese—and they both seemed to have grown smaller while she was away. The thought brought her back to her ordinary dumb, doggedly enduring self. She mopped her eyes and blew her nose on one of her sleeves and asked herself, What can I do?

Outside, the pig also saw daylight declining and cried aloud his hunger and despair.

I shall kill the pig, Senya said to herself.

Never before, in all her years of servitude, had she acted in defiance of an order, even an unspoken one. Every time that she had mentioned the pig, during these hungry days, she had been inviting Melchior's order. It had not been given. That might be simply his usual dilatoriness about everyday things, or it might imply that for some obscure reason of his own he did not wish the pig to be slaughtered. But she intended to kill it. For many reasons.

One she recognised; plain sense; an unfed pig lost flesh.

Another she recognised; there was nothing else to eat; and it took some time to dress a pig carcase and make it fit for food.

Another she recognised; she now had fuel.

One reason, good and valid, she never even thought of. The feeling of fury, the desire for vengeance, had been building up in her ever since she opened that basket. Rage must be vented on something or somebody. The pig was the only available victim.

Savagely she sharpened the knife on the hearthstone.

A pig-killing is never a pleasant affair; and when the butcher is an old woman, enfeebled by long malnutrition and already exhausted by effort and emotion, and the pig is young and lively and madly hungry, several macabre touches are added to what is at best a bloody business. But her mind was set, and she had him cornered at last and she cut his throat, slash, slash slash, one for each of the people who had made a fool of her that day. Once it was done she was calm. Outside, in the pen where the pig had spent his short, hungry little life, she disembowelled him, carefully saving such of the offal as was edible. Then, as dusk fell she dragged the body indoors and with one last expenditure of energy, managed to get it suspended from a hook. She added another root to the fire and set a pan of water to boil. Soon, slowly, because she was tired, but doggedly, she began to dress the carcase.

For Melchior, high in his tower, the time had passed unmarked. The sunset, pink and purple, golden and a clear cold green, spreading all over the sky to the West, brought him to his senses. This day was almost spent. And inside the tower the cold had clamped down again. The sky was still clear however.

He lit his brazier, not without difficulty. In his vague way, on the outer rim of his mind he had never ceased to wonder at the fact that Senya, in many ways so witless, could set flint to tinder and in almost no time have a fire going. Whereas he, who could, had he been asked, have explained exactly why flint struck on iron made a spark which lit the tinder, must strike twenty times. But in the end he had his fire, the twigs caught and he blew upon them, gently, and presently the charcoal caught and began to glow and give off a faint warmth.

He then took the water jar from the basket, and opened the door to the little side chamber which was a stool room, with a chute which ran all the way down the side of the tower into a cess-pit at the bottom. He made use of it; then he poured water into a bowl which stood on a tripod, a bowl which even then would have commanded a good price and which presently was to be priceless, to him just a pretty, useful bowl, and carefully washed his hands. The used water he poured down the chute. Amongst all the other things which he must deal with tomorrow was the bringing up of at least two full jars of water so that the chute might be thoroughly flushed. Senya's awkwardness about the rope had somewhat defeated him there. Clever as she was at making fires and in other ways, she had never quite managed the business of sending up that extra jar of water that was needed. But no matter. If he had been right in his calculations, tomorrow he would be a free man, able to give his mind to things like flushing the chute and providing food for himself, Senya, and the pig. He was not so stupid as not to have realised that Senya thought him foolish over the pig. He knew very well that a young pig must be fed, must be fattened all through the months until autumn when it would be fit to kill. But until this moment he had foreseen a situation in which he might need another sheet of paper, and the pig was his one saleable asset. So he had been able to ignore Senya's hints, and the pig's squeals; for work came first, and he was prepared to say, "Take the pig and sell it and bring me back a piece of paper or parchment, whichever is handier."

He went back into the tower room and sat down by the brazier. He reached for the basket and found the bread and the cheese. More than he had expected to find. Enough for twenty-four hours, he had told himself, and here was enough for two days.

The old woman's whining voice, talking about imminent starvation, came back into his mind. Women *worried* so, he thought. Food and fuel, the contents of the cooking pot—that was about as far as their minds could reach, poor creatures! And he felt a little guilty pang; he might have seemed oblivious to the plight in which he and Senya and the poor little pig were involved; but actually he was not. He'd seen this crisis coming quite a long time ago, and he knew how he must deal with it. Tomorrow or the next day he must go down to Pyongyang and offer to teach. To a man of his kind, after so many years of quiet, dedicated study, of separation from the world, the idea was appalling, but he had faced it, and faced it now, without flinching.

He'd been, he realised, careless and remiss, especially lately, but he'd been absorbed. Tonight—unless his reckonings were very much amiss, and after a day's final, critical scrutiny he couldn't see how they could be—a comet would start on its elliptic course. Melchior's Comet. He had foretold it, on his charts; he had marked its probable course. And having seen it, having proved his worth as an astronomer, he would go down and hire himself out for regular salary; and old Senya could have her tea, her honey and flour and soya meal and everything else which he knew she had missed and craved.

Eating his meagre meal, slowly, fastidiously, he refused to think of himself, back in his old age in the crowded corridors, the packed halls of the university, facing all those lumpish young men, sent—as he himself had been sent—to get a smattering of learning. There might be one, just one, similar to himself, just one who cared for learning for its own sake, not as a means by which to gain respect from the vulgar, or to obtain a job. That one might be worth teaching.

Mumbling the stale bread, the hard cheese, he thought of that potential one and refused to think of the hundreds who had no wish to learn.

Then he took one mouthful, no more, of the rice wine, to clear the crumbs from his mouth. And he was ready. The sunset had died into a faint yellow line between the earth and the sky. Now, now, he thought, I am about to know whether I was right or wrong. He took his glass from the box and carefully climbed the steps of the ladder. For some reason always on the ladder, never on the stairs, he remembered that old men were prone to fall and their bones were brittle. One day he was going to think about this oddity, it had something to do with the solidity of what you climbed upon; on the stairs you didn't see how far away the earth was; climbing the ladder you were conscious of the floor. Also, of course, he must carry the precious glass as though it were his child, his son, his firstborn. He mounted carefully, full of expectation.

When he descended he came down the ladder like a cat dislodged from a wall. It was black night except for the stars and a small pink glow from the brazier. He found a stump of candle, made a light, pulled his stool up to the bench, reached for the chart and his tools and set to work. He breathed in quick, shallow gasps and his heart thudded so heavily that the vibration shook his hands. He had been right; the sky had been pregnant, and it had brought forth, not the comet that he had expected, nor an ordinary star to add to the existing myriads. He had half-foreseen, and then witnessed the birth of the star of stars. Now he must make certain adjustments to his chart and work out the full meaning of what even his cautious mind recognised as a phenomenon.

When he had finished, in the bitter cold hour before dawn, he said to himself, Greater than Alexander! And he thought, It may be that I am the only man alive who knows this, and if that is so . . . He straightened his bowed shoulders to take the weight of the enormous responsibility. The expression of awe upon his face gave way to one of determination.

He reached for a map and spread it. It was unsatisfactory; all maps were; too many blank spaces. It was curious that men had never yet succeeded in making maps of the solid earth—which could be walked upon and surveyed—anything like as complete and accurate as the charts which he and others had made of the unreachable sky. But no matter. There would be other maps, in other places. The one he held had been made on the assumption that Pyongyang was the centre of the world; map-makers in places blank on this map would have worked on some similar assumption; he would have to find his way as he moved.

Now he must think practically. Amusement brushed the surface of his mind as he remembered that on this day, just dawning, he had intended to be practical; had meant to go into Pyongyang and stick his head into the scholastic yoke and work for his keep, like an ox. There was a joke, one which it was unlikely that he would ever be able to share with anyone. For a moment the completeness of his loneliness appalled him. And so did his penury. He had no money, no friend from whom he could borrow.

But he had one asset, his tower. And for that there was only one potential buyer—the University at Pyongyang. He felt a momentary regret that he had not bothered to keep on good terms with the governing body of the university; he had refused, or neglected, invitations to lecture to the students or to dine with the faculty. Still, what he was offering to sell was unique, they must realise that. If they failed to, if they hesitated or haggled he must sell it to a speculator, not for what it was, the best observatory in the world, but as a collection of stone from which many houses could be built, and a collection of glass, enough to glaze many window openings . . . but he hoped that it would not come to that.

Pushing away the distasteful thought he busied himself; he took his chart and the map, rolled them tightly and slipped them into a hollow bamboo case. He pushed those of his tools that he thought he might need into the loose front of his robe. Then, holding the tiny wafer of candle in his hand he looked about the room in which he had spent his life, his youth, his energy. He never expected to see it again. He was, after all, seventy-five years old and he was setting out on a journey such as few men had ever faced. Destination unknown. There would be deserts and mountains and rivers; there might be wild animals, robbers, places where war was being waged. He thought of all the hazards and did not quail. Only one thing mattered, and that was that he should get there in time and tell what he knew, what the stars had told him.

From habit he closed the door carefully behind him and then hurried down the stairs.

The room at the bottom smelt of smouldering wood, and of an old woman who had not washed or changed her clothes since last summer, and of something else which he could not identify. Senya lay asleep by the fire; in better days, with fuel more plentiful, she had often scorched her outer clothing, but there was little danger of that now. Against the wall there was something pale, something that had not been there in the morning. He raised the dying candle and peered. Ah, the pig! Killed and dressed.

Even in his haste and excitement he had time to think how strange it was, that she had known! When people lived, in close company as he and Senya had for so many years, it seemed that they developed a link—Greek expressed it best, telepathy. He had sometimes thought that this was a subject worth investigating. Once, up in the tower, he had been stricken with such pain in his back that he had only just managed to crawl downstairs, and when he reached the kitchen Senya had been brewing the stinking liniment that he needed. And another time, in Pyongyang, buying paper and ink he had suddenly thought, Salt! and had bought a block and carried it home and Senya had said, "I needed salt, master."

Now she had known, by that same peculiar means, that he was about to make a journey and would need food to take with him.

He roused her gently. Credulous people believed in a dichotomy, soul and body; they believed that when a person slept the soul left the body and that if the body were too abruptly wakened the soul might not find its way back. Melchior held no beliefs of that kind, but he was not a man to scorn the beliefs of others, so he called her name, softly, then more loudly and only when she stirred and groaned did he put his hand on her shoulder and give her a little shake. She opened her eyes and said, in alarm:

"Is it morning?"

"Very early morning. I see you have killed the pig."

She gave him the lie which had come to her overnight, comforting, sleep-inducing.

"Master, the pig died. The pig died of hunger."

"You had the good sense to dress it at once. It will be edible," he said. And she saw that he was pleased that the pig was dead and ready to eat; she wished she had not lied about the manner of its death.

"I scalded and scraped it, master," she said with eager servility. "If you wish you can have liver for breakfast."

He said, "I have no time for breakfast. I must go into Pyongyang. But I should be very glad if you could cook some of the meat, cook it well, with salt, so that it keeps. I could take some on my journey."

"Your journey? Master, what journey? To me you said nothing of a journey."

"I knew nothing, until a little time ago. I must go now. I must be in Pyongyang early; to sell this tower and buy a camel."

"A camel?" She had an irritating habit of picking a word from what he had said and repeating it. "Master, where would you be going on a camel?"

"That I do not know. To the South West. I shall learn as I go. Senya, I shall need my hat."

It was so long since he had been out of doors and needed his hat that for a moment she stood, perplexed, saying the word "hat" over and over. Then she remembered that she had put it carefully away, and went and fetched it, and offered it, respectfully. He set it on his head and it was incongruous wear with his soiled, faded robe, for it was a hat of quality, made of good felt, black, and lacquered all over to make it rainproof. She wished she had had more warning; he could have stayed in bed one day and she could have washed his robe.

"Now," he said. "I don't know how long this business will take. I shall be back as soon as possible. Meanwhile, cook some of the meat, cook it hard, with plenty of salt, so that it travels well."

He stepped into the morning air, which though cold seemed a trifle less so than yesterday's.

"And if you need fuel," he said, astounding her, "there is a fence around the pigpen, and as there is now no pig, it may be burned."

She realised that she herself would have gone past the pen a hundred times and never thought of that.

Then, picking over all that he had said in so short a time, she recalled that he had said he intended to sell the tower. *And what is to happen to me?* I'm old and feeble, nobody would give a handful of meal for me. I'm old, I'm useless, my ears buzz and if I stoop I fall down; I am of less worth than a worn-out donkey. The tower is my home. When it is sold I shall be homeless, after all these years. The thought was all the more shocking because she had never, in all her life, given her personal future so much as a glance; well-born families such as Melchior's never discarded their slaves however old and tiresome they might become; broken in body and sometimes of mind the old creatures squatted about, certain of their rice bowl and a spare-rib to gnaw on.

I shall starve to death, out in the open, like a dog with no owner, she thought; and again she wept.

Weeping she tugged up the stakes of the fence and made the best fire the little kitchen had seen for years; weeping she hacked away at the pig's carcase, choosing all the best pieces for him to take with him. The salt of her tears fell into the brine as she cooked. Yet she cooked carefully. He might be planning to abandon her, but he was her master still, and her beloved. He'd ignored what she had offered, so shyly, so passionately all those years ago; though courteous always he had ignored her warnings; and now he was about to ignore her plight; but that made no difference.

It was after mid-day when he came back, riding on a camel. Not a good one. A single glance from her smoke-reddened, tear-blurred eyes told her that. It was an old camel, with a hard life behind it. He would have done better to let her do the buying;

but then how could she? Yesterday she had been unable to even reach the village; she could not today have walked to Pyongyang.

He was pleased with his camel, and with all his other arrangements. And he had not forgotten her.

"I realised," he said gravely, "that this had been your home for many years, Senya; so I included you in the contract. You are to be the caretaker. Students will come and go, because this is now the chief observatory in Pyongyang, and so long as you feel able to stay here and keep the place tidy, you are the caretaker. But you are also a free woman; and when you no longer wish to work you will receive a pension—enough to live upon. You do understand me, Senya?"

She began to weep again and to thank him; but he cut her short.

"Is the meat ready?"

"It is cooked, but still hot. Master, you are not leaving *now!* The light is fading; soon it will be night."

"I intend," he said, "to travel much by night. And I must leave at once."

"But why? Why is there such haste?"

"Because of what I know. I fear that only I know this thing. There is a warning to be given. And not a moment to waste."

She packed as much of the still-warm, greasy meat as she could cram into two of the reed baskets, and then went out and helped Melchior to attach them and the bamboo chart case to the camel. Then she stood back.

Now all was done; the last service rendered. The heart which she had thought broken on summer evenings long ago, broke anew.

Something of her dumb misery made itself known to Melchior.

He said, "You have served me so well, Senya, that I never missed the others. I think I shall call this camel by your name."

The misery was not eased; he tried again.

"You will be safe and comfortable. I put it all in writing. You are a free woman and will be paid for what you do here; and when you can no longer do it, you will still be paid. You understand?"

She took his hand and bowed over it.

"May all the gods and the spirits of your ancestors and of mine, have you in safe-keeping, wherever you go, my master."

He looked at her, seeing her properly for the first time now that he was unlikely ever to see her again. Poor old woman; poor faithful old woman, grown grey and bent in his service. He stooped and for a second laid his cheek against hers. A gesture of love.

At last! she thought, and felt repaid for everything.

CHAPTER III

The relatives to whom Anne had referred with pride, Mary's cousin Elisabeth and her husband, a Temple priest, lived in a hill village within walking distance of Jerusalem; and there Elisabeth had made a garden which was justly famous. Elisabeth herself, by nature a woman somewhat silent and reserved, warmed when speaking of her flowers and herbs, her fruit and vegetables. She would say that the garden was her own creation; and that was true. Just over forty years earlier, when she had come, a bride of seventeen, to this house the ground around it had been an unsightly waste, its thin soil trodden hard over the stones that lay near the surface, and nothing grew except a few tough weeds. Former occupants of the house had used the space as a drying ground for linen, and a place to throw rubbish.

She had begun to work on the garden immediately after her arrival, for then she found time heavy on her hands. She had been the eldest daughter of a large family, always busy. Now, with Zacharias so often absent on his Temple duties, she was much alone with little to do. She was not the kind of woman to make friends quickly.

Zacharias, in his spare time, had helped to clear away the rubbish and to remove the largest of the stones and to dig a little. He was a leisurely mover and teased her about the haste with which she worked herself. Gardens, he said, weren't made in a year. She was too reserved and shy to tell him that she wanted all the heavy work done in a month or two because she hoped soon to be in a condition which would render digging and stone-hauling unwise. As she worked she often thought to herself, Next year! She saw a plump healthy baby lying on a mat in the shade, then taking a few tottering steps.

But at the year's end she was still able to work; to gather

basketfuls of stones and take them out and throw them amongst others on the hillside and then refill the baskets with the fine silty soil which the rain washed down from the hills. She had planted trees, a fig tree near the house door, almond, apricot and plum and apple trees along her boundary; young trees that would grow as the child grew. For she was certain of a child next year.

So year had succeeded year and hope had died a long-drawn-out death. By this time she knew her neighbours and had more than once heard women with several children mourn a new pregnancy. "Another mouth to feed," they said. Once, when her herb garden was well established and known, a woman had come to her and after some half sentences and evasions had voiced an enquiry and a request. "There are seven already and my man is poor; how shall we manage?" Elisabeth, explaining with some embarrassment, that she had nothing of that kind in her garden, had thought how inexplicable, how seemingly unjust God was. An eighth child to a woman already overburdened, and her own arms still empty.

The woman had found what she sought and almost died of the bitter brew and that child was never born.

Nobody, not even Zacharias, had ever heard Elisabeth repine. Only her garden knew how often, coming back from the well or from the market, she would walk with rapid, agitated steps and wring her hands and cry, "God, my God, why? What have I done? What has he, your servant, done that we should be cursed?" The flowers had held their innocent faces towards her, offered their perfume for comfort. Very slowly, grudgingly she had abandoned hope, and without realising it, had allowed the garden to fill the empty place in her life. In some ways it was like a child; it needed constant attention; it progressed in little steps; it was something that she had made. In hot, dry summers she would go twice, three times to the well; on the much-travelled road into Jerusalem she would gather dung. The garden flourished and was beautiful; even the fence that divided it from the road was a thing of beauty, thickly covered with morning glories, so gloriously blue, and thicket roses, coloured like a summer sunset. And all within the fence, the flower-beds, the herb patches, the vegetable strips were neat and tended and precise, the living embroidery which she had worked upon the stony hillside.

And it had been, appropriately, in the garden, that the miracle had happened. It had been an autumn evening, mild and mellow, and she had been gathering fallen leaves and heaping them in a corner where, through the winter they would rot into the cool, dark substance which in the early summer of next year, spread around the roots of trees and flowers, would help to prevent the soil from drying out.

Zacharias had come to her there, looking as he always did after his spells of duty in the Temple, pale and tired. She had risen, rubbing her hands together and said:

"Supper is ready."

And he'd mouthed at her, his lips moving but making no sound. He used his hands, touching his lips, beckoning her into the house.

She thought, He's had a seizure! And a great weight of guilt fell upon her. She hadn't valued Zacharias as he should have been valued. She'd thought always about the child, and then she had transferred her attention to the garden, not realising that despite all she had been singularly blessed, having a good husband.

"You're sick," she said. But he shook his head and would not take the arm she offered to help him into the house. And she, watching him, saw that he walked as usual, if anything more vigorously.

"What is it?" she asked, and he shook his head and smiled.

Inside the house he had gone straight to his own special table, taken up a waxed tablet and his stylus and written something and held it out to her. She could read a little. Early in their marriage, sensing her unspoken discontent, he had taught her to read, even to write a few words. But her heart had never been with her studies, and his vague hope of turning her into another Anne, a woman he knew, childless, a widow, but happy because she was studious, had been defeated. Still, Elisabeth could read, and having read what he had written, and reread it, in case she had made a mistake, she had looked at him and said:

"Can you hear? Nod, if you can."

He had nodded.

She said, "It is impossible. I am too old."

He snatched back the tablet and wrote, "Remember Sarah."

She said, "Yes, I remember Sarah, but that was all long ago, in the days of the Patriarchs. Nothing like that could happen *now.*"

She was expressing the feeling of many Jews of her time; the age of miracles was past.

Zacharias wrote again, "Great things impend. This child will be the forerunner."

She read the words and looked at him a little fearfully. Except for her barrenness they had been a happy couple, but there were great tracts of his mind, even of his life which she could never hope to understand. He was a priest; he was allowed by right to enter the inner court of the Temple where no lay person could go; he was deeply religious, almost a mystic.

She asked, "How do you know?"

Bit by bit, writing brief, succinct sentences, he told her how, in the middle of his duties at the altar he had seen an angel, Gabriel, who had said that their prayers were to be answered and that she would bear a son, to be called John; a very special child who was to prepare the way for the Messiah.

"And I was struck dumb," the last sentence read.

Her fear and her uneasiness grew. One did not contradict one's husband; one did not argue with a priest of God. But she was unable to rid herself of the thought that he had been taken ill—visions often accompanied illnesses.

"Otherwise are you well?" she asked.

He nodded and wrote, "I am happy. You?"

"Yes," she said untruthfully, "I am happy." In truth she was puzzled, incredulous, miserable about her incredulity and worried about him. All that evening she fussed over him, treating him as she would treat a man who had had some severe physical shock. When, just before bedtime, she presented him with a steaming bowl of her famous herb brew which her neighbours had come to regard as a panacea for anything short of a broken limb, he had broken into silent laughter, and reaching for his writing tablet, wrote:

"I am not sick. I am to be dumb until the child is born. Punishment for disbelief. Be warned!"

It was the first time in over thirty years of married life that he had ever shown any sign of levity, and that, somehow, increased her uneasiness.

Long after he was asleep she lay by his side and thought it all over and asked herself, How shall I know? In her childbearing days a woman's life was ruled by the moon. A disturbance, an interruption could be noticed, interpreted with joy or with dismay. She knew; there was no woman in the world, she thought, who had more closely checked her reckonings. A day's delay and she had hoped . . . But it was a full ten years since the moon's courses and hers had ceased to be connected. Ten years ago since she had, at last, abandoned all hope. And Zacharias' admonition to remember Sarah had a peculiar sting. For quite a few months she *had* remembered Sarah with whom it had ceased to be after the manner of women, and she envied that long dead woman very greatly. But ten years . . .

Zacharias remained dumb and Elisabeth remained dubious. But changes came, things the most realistic and incredulous of women could hardly overlook. Her skin regained its lost bloom, her hair its lustre; the early morning nausea made itself felt. And her body, like a ripening fruit, began to swell.

One day she could say to Zacharias, without any reserve at all, "It is true!" And on his tablet he wrote, "I told you!"

She was unthinkably happy, but embarrassed, too—and there again, ashamed of her embarrassment as she had been of her disbelief. Women always pretended that they could not reckon, but they were sharp enough where another woman's age was concerned. There wasn't a woman at the well or in the market who wouldn't know that Elisabeth, the wife of Zacharias, was fifty-seven years old, and even if she could bring herself to tell them the truth, was there one who would believe it? Not one.

They'd look on her as a poor self-deluded creature, afflicted with one of those slowly killing growths in the womb, pretending to believe that she was with child. The herbs she grew and the draughts she made from them had brought her into contact with many people, sick of mind or body, and she knew about the fantasies such people wove. She hated the thought of such a fantasy being attributed to her.

So she had refused to leave her house. Zacharias had written his protests and she had said, "When the child is born, I will go out with it in my arms, or ask them in to see."

Everyone in the village knew that Zacharias had lost his power of speech and imagined that this fact had so upset Elisabeth that she was unable to go to the well or to market. A girl, extravagantly rewarded for such service, delivered water daily and Zacharias bought everything that was needed in the markets of Jerusalem. That Elisabeth's distaste for going out and exposing her state was no mere whim had been proved to him by her attitude to her cousin Mary's wedding. It was due to take place when Elisabeth was in her eighth month; a good time, really, all the early inconveniences and dangers over and done with, and a pregnant woman, moving slowly, commanding deference, could take, amongst friends and relatives, her rightful, proud place.

But Elisabeth had said, "I cannot go. I love my cousin Mary, and if I could see her alone I would gladly go. But there's Anne —imagine how she would look at me—and there'll be women of my age trying to arrange marriages for their granddaughters. Zacharias, I could not face it. Please, write and say that your duties at the Temple will prevent us from attending."

He had intended to write, but he had never been obliged to do so, for in Elisabeth's sixth month, Mary's wedding date still two months away, they had had word that Mary was already married. Rabbi had communicated with rabbi, link by link, a chain that reached over the eighty intervening miles, and Zacharias and Elisabeth were in due time informed that to suit Joseph's convenience, the marriage had been put forward by two months. It had therefore been a small wedding, and had lasted only one day.

Elisabeth was relieved, and yet concerned. It sounded as though Mary, that sweet, gentle creature, might have chosen a selfish man. After all, a girl's wedding day was her one great day; and she shouldn't be cheated of it to suit the bridegroom's convenience. If a man had never given the woman he chose any consideration and meant never to give her any, he usually allowed her that one great day, thinking nothing of his own convenience.

"I hope she will be happy," Elisabeth said, looking back over her own marriage which, apart from that one lack, had been so very happy. "We must send her our gift."

They'd spent time and thought on it; nothing of wood, Mary was marrying, they knew, a carpenter, so she would be well supplied with anything in that line; and Elisabeth, though she had not seen her Aunt Anne for some years, knew that anything practical, linen, blankets, bowls, could be counted upon to come from her.

"She's very fond of lilies," Elisabeth said. "And I will send her a dozen good bulbs; but from us there should be something more." She knew that with Zacharias in regular employment and—as in Nazareth they would still think—childless, something generous would be expected of them. And one day, without warning, Zacharias, setting down the stores he had carried, and smiling, showed her the exact thing. It was a coin, known as a rose jekkal, the rarest and most valuable coin in the world. Not only for its worth, for its beauty. On one side, not imprinted but embossed, there was a full-blown rose, exact, even to a thorn; on the other there were symbols, words perhaps, in a language nobody could read. For the rose jekkals came from far, far away and if four of them reached Jerusalem in a single year, that was the most. They were eagerly sought after and the woman who could hang a rose jekkal amongst the coins of her headdress was a proud woman indeed.

Zacharias held the lovely coin on his palm and invited her approval; dumbly, like a trained hound.

Elisabeth said, "For Mary?" and he nodded.

She said, "It is beautiful; and with the lily bulbs, a fine gift. How clever of you. Where did you find it?"

He wrote on the tablet which he now always carried.

"At the money-changer's stall."

It was just right; a thing of beauty, a thing of value, a suitable accompaniment to the lily bulbs. And yet, Elisabeth thought, turning to the hearth, not right, in some mysterious way. Mary, as she remembered her, had such a lovely brow, so calm and smooth, with the hair growing back from it in such a pretty way. For some reason it was difficult to imagine Mary, the young Mary, with the usual coin collection dangling between the curve of her eyebrows and the curve of her hair. It would seem a deformity.

Nonsense, nonsense, Elisabeth told herself, Mary, like every other married woman, would now begin to make the collection of coins for the headdress which constituted, in fact, every respectable family's nest egg. And Mary, who loved even the wild cornflower, would love the rose.

Lifting the pot from the hearth, she said:

"We must find a trustworthy messenger to carry it." And she said again that it had been clever of him to obtain it. She said, "If I thought I could get in and out of Nazareth without seeing Anne, who, though she is my aunt, is younger than I, I would take it myself. I think that Mary is the one woman in the world whom I could tell, and be at ease with."

Zacharias wrote on his tablet, "Go." He was sure that she had only to cross the threshold and she would be released. It was said—though he'd never tested the theory—that one could confine a hen by drawing a chalk circle; and there were times when Elisabeth, in her present state, seemed to him to be similarly confined by a barrier of which only she was aware.

While the subject was still under discussion they received a letter, written in a large, squarish hand and in the black graphite with which carpenters marked measurements on rough boards. The journey had smudged it but it was legible. It said, simply, "My name is Joseph, Mary my wife who is your cousin would like to visit you. Friends leave for Jerusalem on the twelfth day of the month and she could come with them." The bearer of the letter, a pedlar, in Jerusalem to stock up with what he called "pretty things" said that he was intending to return to Galilee and would carry their reply. Zacharias wrote that Mary would be most welcome.

Elisabeth, though delighted at the prospect of seeing Mary and having her under her roof, was perturbed again. In the first months of one's marriage, if it were a happy one, one did not give much thought to cousins, or propose an eighty-mile journey in order to visit them. She remembered how, last time they met, at the wedding of another cousin, her Uncle Joachim had said that when Mary was old enough to marry he hoped it would be to someone she *liked*. Elisabeth, a conventional woman, could see an element of danger there; girls so often liked men for all the wrong reasons. How, at the age of sixteen or seventeen, if properly reared, could they know anything about men, know what to look for and what to avoid? Such things were better left to parents who had some standard of judgement, some experience, and cool heads. Mary might have made a mistake, been misled by good looks or a persuasive tongue.

And yet the letter had something frank and straightforward about it; and would a selfish man—and such the wedding arrangements had indicated Joseph to be—have written at all, been willing so soon to spare his bride from his bed and his hearth?

She turned the letter about as though it might have some hidden information to offer; and in a way it had, for it was written upon the back of a draft obviously from the skilled hand of an architect; the plan of a large house, almost a mansion, and in the lower left-hand corner were the words *House of Nathaniel in Cana*. A possible explanation occurred to her; Cana was seven miles from Nazareth, and if Joseph were working under pressure he would not get home until well after dark, on some nights perhaps not at all. He might have qualms about leaving Mary alone. Mary might not wish to be left alone. Against that explanation must be set the fact that Mary's parents were in the village. . . .

Well, she must wait; when Mary came she would tell her everything, no doubt, for despite the disparity in their ages on the few occasions when they had met they had always been congenial.

The family with whom Mary was travelling as far as Jerusalem was on its way to attend a *bar mitzvah* of a young relative there, and they were very merry. The weather was fine and warm, not yet the blistering heat of high summer; in the fields the crops were ripening, poppies and cornflowers abounded, vetches and honeysuckles threw their tendrils over every fence and post. The father of the family had made this journey several times before and knew many short cuts, through fields and by-ways, and Mary was always glad to leave the highroad where sights, distressing to her, were to be seen.

After Gibeon, however, they kept to the road and joined up with other foot-travellers, for the hills were full of robbers, apt to attack any small party.

There was so much chatter and laughter that there was little chance to think much. A mile short of the city their ways parted. The head of the family issued a hearty invitation to her to enter the city with them and partake of the hospitality in his relative's house—everybody was welcome on such occasions; and it was a shame, he said, to be so near and miss a chance of seeing Jerusalem. But she was anxious to see Elisabeth, and anxious to be alone. So, thanking him, she said that she could see the city under Zacharias' guidance almost any day. And when they had made certain that she had only a short distance to go, and that over a safe road, they left her.

It was now seven weeks since the angel had visited her and they had been seven weeks of unreality and confusion. The wedding, so hastily arranged, yet, in Anne's capable hands, so correct; a girl's great day; to her part of a waking dream. Clad in her grandmother's beautiful gown, receiving compliments and good wishes and gifts, she had felt utterly detached from it all. She thought of women she knew—some of them women to whom marriage had brought little happiness—who cherished some trinket or piece of clothing, whose worn faces would brighten, whose harsh voices would soften as they said, "I wore it at my wedding." Yet here she was, with as much reason to be glad and grateful that she was being married as any woman ever had, looking at the smiling, friendly faces and thinking, If only you knew!

She'd looked at Joseph, too—the one person who did know—and saw with consternation how he had changed in a handful of hours. He'd always worn his years lightly, taking few things seriously except his work, and her; he'd always worn a cheerful, carefree look, in accord with his roving, foot-free life; it had been so easy to visualise him shouldering his tools and going off to see what the next place had to offer. That was all gone now; and his new air of responsibility which would have been right and only slightly touching in a young man just embarking upon the serious step of marriage, in him was very touching, giving him an elderly, almost a troubled look. She made up her mind to be the best possible wife, always cheerful, patient, and kind; she would love him forever and try to make up . . . Her thought jolted to a standstill. Make up for what? Being chosen by God?

And so it had gone on.

Rachel, with the lazy Joshua astride her hip, had offered her a present, a handsome oil jar. "I hope you'll be very happy, Mary," she said, and all her willing could not prevent her voice from revealing her doubt that any woman could be really happy in marriage. Then, in a different tone, she had added, "And I hope you'll have a boy, like this, but less lazy." And Mary had thought, dizzily, Suppose I said that I knew I should have a son, and that he will be the Messiah. Rachel would recoil, and probably be so shocked she'd drop Joshua.

The grooms lifted and carried her to her new home; and she thought, You little know whom you are carrying besides me! And there the ritual vase, the symbol of virginity, was broken, and the feast began. Joseph had cleared the workshop for the purpose, and Anne, loudly complaining that she had had time to do nothing, had done marvels. There was wine which Joachim had been saving for the wedding, and Joseph also had a jar; he gave it a peculiar look as he produced it, saying that it was not quite full . . . as though that mattered!

The feast had been very merry; most of the guests lived lives on or only just above subsistence level and were as much exhilarated by the food as by the wine, though there was plenty of that, the company being so much smaller than it would have been if held on the appointed day. (Years later, she was to remember this, to think, There was plenty of wine at my wedding; and out of kindly pity for the embarrassment of a family less well-provided, make a suggestion that was to result in what was to be known as the first miracle.)

Then it was dusk; there were children to put to bed, animals to feed, hens to shut up against the prowling foxes. The company began to disperse. Anne threw her arms about her daughter in one last, protective gesture; from this hour on the kindness and the chiding and the sheltering care must come from another, from this fellow who, in Anne's view, suddenly seemed quite incapable of taking her place as Mary's guardian. She said:

"My dear, I wish you every joy," and then, hearing and despising the tremor in her voice, said sturdily and rather crossly, "It has been a pleasant day. But there should have been three!"

The age-old feud between the loving mother and the husband had claimed another victim.

Joachim, very slightly inebriated—and why not?, it was, after all, his daughter's wedding—sobered up suddenly and took Joseph by the shoulder and said in a voice not completely void of menace:

"Use her gently. You understand me?"

"I do indeed," Joseph said. And he thought, That is the final irony; if only he knew!

Quiet had fallen upon the little house, and on the workshop, littered with the remains of the wedding feast.

Watching her own hands as though they were those of another woman, Mary had lighted, in her own house, her own lamp.

Joseph said, "What a day this must have been for you!"

"And for you," she said.

And he had thought, God is not blind. Far better me than some untried, amorous boy.

He said, "I shall sleep in the shop. I've slept in many worse places. You take the bed and I hope you sleep well."

She'd reached out and taken one of his big work-hardened hands in hers.

"Joseph, this was not of my choice. It happened. It happened to us both."

"Yes," he said. "It happened." Something almost like resentment tinged his voice as he thought of what the present moment might have been, but for what had happened. Hard on them both.

"It happened," he repeated, "and we have to take it as it is. You don't look to me as though you've slept much these last two nights. Try to sleep now. This is God's doing and we must leave the outcome in His hands."

She said impulsively, "I know why you were chosen, Joseph! You're the best man in the world."

He said, "No. I reckon I just happened to be handy." He shouldn't have said that, he knew as soon as he had said it, and made a clumsy attempt at a joke. "Praising myself! It's the best thing you can say of a carpenter—he's a handy man."

In the morning the struggle between the real and the unreal tilted a little. She was in her own house, using her own bowls and knife and spoons, taking bread from her own crock and making Joseph his piece to take with him to eat at mid-day. He went off to work and presently Rachel called for her to go to the spring. She was grateful to Rachel for having broken through the rule about married women walking with married women; she dreaded their eyes, their sly questions. They knew, or pretended to know, many signs which told whether a marriage had been successfully consummated or not. Rachel said, "Are you happy?" and she said wholeheartedly:

"Very happy. I have a good man." And there was that thought again, If only you knew how good.

Leah and Susannah joined them and chatted girlishly about the wedding; and suddenly, there with her friends on the familiar path, she was overwhelmed by loneliness. She thought with longing of Elisabeth and wished with all her heart that she lived nearer.

Towards evening, making a meal with which to greet Joseph on his return, things seemed ordinary again and continued so until, in the middle of eating, Joseph said:

"Mary, I've been thinking, on and off all day. What are we going to tell people? And when?"

"I don't know. I wanted you to believe me, and you did. Beyond that I haven't thought. But I suppose we must . . ." She shrank from the thought of the disbelief, the jeers, even from the commotion that would be aroused by those who did believe. Almost sternly she said, "It is the truth. And it is something that concerns every Jew."

"Every Jew," Joseph agreed quickly, *"and a lot of others as well."*

"What others?"

"Herod for one." As he spoke the name of the King, far away in Jerusalem, she realised how narrow her own imaginative view had been; limited to Nazareth, to—to be honest—the women by the spring.

"I thought of him on my way to work this morning. He's got less right to the throne he sits on than I have; and he knows that. I can't imagine he'd dance for joy to hear that the promised heir to David's throne will be born in nine months' time."

"That is true—but I should never have thought of it."

You could see why a child—even such a child as this—needed a father and a mother; this was the kind of thing that men thought of, and women did not.

"There's another thing, too, the Romans. I know our beliefs mean nothing to them, but they'd see danger. The Jews aren't all that settled yet. Start a story of Messiah about to be born and the national feeling would stir. The Romans know that, and they'd stop at nothing to forestall it. This is something we should take into account, Mary. They, or Herod, might easily do you an injury. Herod is a master-hand at arranging accidents for people he wants out of the way. And there is yet another thing . . ." There was the faint hesitation, the near-embarrassment with which she was to become so familiar. "Nothing you were told sounded as though we were to go shouting from the housetops."

"No," she said slowly, thinking back. "That is true."

"Then why not wait," he said, rather as though they had been arguing. "Once he's born, he'll be the Son of God. How he'll be born or what we should expect is a mystery to me, but once he's born, God will take care of him, or perhaps he'll be born able to take care of himself. It's you I'm concerned with now, and I can see danger for you. Silence may be part of the plan. After all, you didn't go running to tell your mother, did you? You came to me. And now I have this feeling . . ."

She said, "I should be glad to tell nobody. It's such a very difficult thing to put into words."

He nodded. "I know. With most situations, there's some guide, other people have been the same way and left their tracks. We're in a situation nobody has ever been in before. We have no guide. I think it would be wise to say nothing until we have some sign."

"Unless," she said, "I should see Elisabeth. I might not even have to tell her; she might know. Gabriel told me about her, he may have told her about me."

He was amazed, as he was to be again and again by the simple, matter-of-fact way in which she spoke of the archangel—as though he were a neighbour, not the awesome, shining presence from the thought of which his own mind shied away.

He said, "Yes, it is a pity she doesn't live nearer." And there the conversation ended for the moment. Into his mind, though, had flashed the thought of how lonely she must be with a secret of such magnitude that he had urged her not to share with anyone. It was different for him. He had his work, his workmates. Now that the anxiety that had been with him all day was allayed he knew that there would be hours on end when he would not give the matter a thought.

But the thought of her loneliness, brief though it was, had dropped a seed, which rooted and grew, and one day, again as he ate his supper, he said:

"How would you like to go and visit Elisabeth?"

She said, "I would like it very much. But how can I? Who would look after you?"

"That same stout fellow who's looked after me since I was so high," he said, measuring a height from the floor. "Joseph, the carpenter."

She laughed. "You couldn't be in better hands. But think of my mother; all her plans for the wedding spoiled because you didn't like coming home to a dead hearth; and then, in a few weeks, I go gadding off to make a visit."

"My fault," he said. "I underestimated—a thing that has brought many good carpenters to ruin. You could tell your mother, and anyone else who was interested, that we're now working such long hours that it would be better for me to sleep on the site. The masons have reared a good lodge and they'd admit me, I'm a craftsman. I've only made that trudge in order that you shouldn't be in the house alone. . . ."

"Is that true?"

"In part; for your mother, wholly."

"Then she'll suggest that I go back home."

"Not if I have made other arrangements. And I have. I've been keeping my ears open. Joel and all his family are off to Jerusalem very soon. You could travel with them. Suppose I wrote to—what is his name?"

"Zacharias."

"To Zacharias, and made all the arrangements? Then you could go to your mother and say Joseph has done this and that and she will not question it. Would you like that?"

"More than anything in the world. . . ." And then she realised, What a cruel, what a dreadful thing to have said. There were forms of brutality that had nothing to do with sticks or goads.

"I didn't mean that the way it sounded," she said. "I love you, as no woman has ever loved a man before—not having the reason for love that I have. But as we are . . . and if you are sure that in the masons' lodge you will eat well . . ."

"Masons," he said, "eat like kings, every day. So much build-

ing is going forward that when they contract they can stipulate
two meat meals every day. Shall I write the letter?"

"If you would. If you are sure . . . You see, you know, you
believe, and you understand; but there are times when a woman
needs another woman; and Elisabeth is the only one, the only
one to whom I could talk."

"I'll write it now," he said.

So now, here she was, within sight of Elisabeth's garden
which she had never seen, but recognised from descriptions
given by various members of the family and, more modestly, by
Elisabeth on the rare occasions when they had met and sat and
talked together, quietly in the midst of hubbub. That a miracle
should have happened to Elisabeth was not in the least surprising to Mary; Elisabeth was a rare person; she had borne that
curse of a Jewish woman, childlessness, with great gallantry,
without a complaint, without jealousy of luckier women. She'd
endured loneliness—his Temple duties often kept Zacharias
away from home for two or three days together; and out of her
frustration and solitude she had made beauty on a bare hillside.

As Mary walked, swiftly now, eager for their meeting, towards
the place of colour and perfume that was Elisabeth's garden, she
saw her cousin emerge from the house door, empty a bowl at the
root of a tree and then stoop and straighten up with a bunch of
yellow flowers, marigolds, in her hand. And it was true, Elisabeth, in the fifty-seventh year of her age, was heavily pregnant.

She had never doubted it; Gabriel had told her and she had
believed, just as she had believed what he had said about her own
state; but there was a difference, a very great difference, between
believing in your mind and seeing with your eyes.

She hurried forward, calling her cousin by name, and Elisabeth, on her way back into the house, halted and turned and
came to open the gate in the flowery fence.

"Mary!" she said; and Mary said, "Oh, how I have longed to
see you!" They were about to embrace and then Elisabeth took
a step backward and turned pale and sweat sprang out, like
beads on her brow and upper lip.

"*You!*" she said. "You, Mary! *You* are to be the mother of the

Lord to whom my son is to be the forerunner. You, blessed above all women."

Mary said, "You did not know?"

"Until this moment, no. But the child did. It leapt as I spoke your name. So late and never a movement, I was worried. But he leapt, recognising you and the child you are to bear."

"Gabriel did not tell you?"

"I never saw him. He appeared to Zacharias, in the Temple. He was dumb-struck, and dumb he has been ever since. Did you . . . did you see him, Mary?"

"Yes. He told me about you."

"The chosen, the blessed one," Elisabeth said. And because ordinary words were too ordinary, too worn to be used at this moment, there in the flowery garden they broke into one of those antiphonal chants of the kind which from time immemorial their race had used as a vehicle for praising God. Chanting and extempore song making came easily to Jews in emotional moments. Deborah, in song, had celebrated the defeat of Sisera; David, in song, had lamented the death of Jonathan.

"Blessed is she that believed," chanted Elisabeth; and Mary sang, "My soul doth magnify the Lord . . ."

The meeting set the tone for the whole visit. For two happy months Mary lived in an atmosphere of understanding and acceptance so complete that on one occasion she brought herself to mention to Zacharias some of those prophecies that caused her such foreboding. Zacharias reached for his tablet and wrote, "He shall see of the travail of his soul and be satisfied, it is written. You too." Elisabeth read the words aloud, and added, "John may have a hard life, also. The path of the forerunner is never easy."

They agreed that all that they could do was to ensure the children a happy childhood, to rear them to be strong. They were oddly in accord in never doubting that to begin with, at least, these would be ordinary human babies. Without realising it they were thus rejecting the pagan ideas that had come to Israel with the Seleucid invaders, stories of gods and goddesses born in some supernatural way, springing to birth full-grown, armed, with winged feet and similar fantasies.

In Mary's company Elisabeth's reserve and fear of ridicule or pity disappeared completely; she moved about the village again and allowed Zacharias to write letters announcing her news. Two female relatives offered to come and tend her in childbed.

"They are experienced; and it would be more seemly," she said to Mary, almost apologetically, for it meant that Mary's room would be needed.

"I must go home," Mary said. "Joseph will need me. The house at Cana should be near completion, now."

Zacharias, inquiring round through another priest, found a group of pilgrims to Jerusalem, about to return to Galilee; and with them Mary walked home, knowing that the first thing she must do would be to tell her mother that she would have a child in mid-winter.

Anne's feelings—greatly to her own surprise—were divided. She was delighted with the news, delighted at the prospect of becoming a grandmother; to her delight she gave loud and repeated expression; but she also thought, Poor Mary, so soon! She'll hardly be accustomed to being a wife before she'll be a mother, hardly be used to managing a house before being called upon to manage a child as well. And all the natural fears that women have when told such news by their daughters rushed uppermost, exaggerated in her case by her protectiveness towards this child of hers who was so unlike her; not very robust, too sensitive. These feelings took expression in a great outpouring of advice, some sensible, some sheer superstition. She also said, again and again, how fortunate it was that they lived so close to one another; "I'll look after you," she said.

The visit to Elisabeth had bridged for Mary the gulf between the real and what seemed unreal. She knew now; and to her mother and her friends she no longer felt the impulse to say, If only you knew! She could think of the day when they *would* know; when what had been revealed to her would be revealed to them. And she turned upon them the smile that was to embrace the world.

CHAPTER IV

Every time that Gaspar rode into his city with its towers and its arches and its tinkling fountains something happened between his shoulder blades, a prickling uneasiness, as though he were a dog whose hackles were rising. Always, somewhere between the Gate of the Rose and the Fountain of the Maidens, he would turn to Kalim, or whoever rode on his right, and make some remark. "Jexal looks well today," or "How it stinks, this place," or "Still standing, I see." Such words would bring him reassurance; it *was* his city, the heartbeat centre of the region he had won by his sword.

He never thought of it as his home; if he lived here and ruled for sixty years, and went out and came in again every day of those sixty years it would never be, he knew, with any sense of homecoming. In the desert three black huts, a few hobbled camels, a dung fire smoking into the evening air never failed to move him with the sense that he was rejoining his own; to a lesser degree he could feel it in the grasslands, where a huddle of clay huts stood by a patch of beans and rye, and there was the smell of sheep and a dog barking. In the city he would always be a stranger. Its people had accepted him with despicable alacrity, had settled down, were smiling and placating; the city itself stayed inimical.

On this morning, at the usual place, he turned to Kalim and said:

"Our city has put out the banners!" It was true; in the ten days of their absence the place had burst into bloom; trusses of flowers, pink and purple, blue and white and yellow, hung over every balcony, sprawled over every wall. In the open spaces around the fountains the trees had shaken out their green.

He had heard people say that it was the most beautiful city

in the world. It was immensely old, and for the last thousand
years had been very rich. The soft-living, careless people had
planted trees and flowers, had reared beautiful buildings, made
fountains, when, in Gaspar's opinion, they would have been
better employed in looking to their defences and bringing up
their boys to be hardy and brave. He'd watched the city for a long
while before he finally moved against it; more than once he had
entered it on foot and mingled with its people in the streets and
markets. They were arrogant in their assurance; buying and
selling, eating and drinking and making merry was all that mattered to them.

When, at dawn on a summer morning, now almost four years
ago he and his Five Hundred had swept in, the city had been
taken as easily as a peach from a tree.

Kalim, in answer to his remark, smiled, showing his splendid
teeth, and said:

"Very gay banners."

Gaspar returned the smile with a ferocious scowl.

"You're riding behind me again! How many times must I tell
you that I want none of that nonsense?"

Any hint of the formality that hedged kings about roused the
same uneasiness in him that the city inspired. He was the leader
of the Five Hundred; that he could accept, it was a right he had
won, being able to outride, outfight, outwit and, if necessary,
outfast them all. He expected loyalty and demanded obedience,
but lately they had tried to give him more. There'd even been a
suggestion that he should wear the crown and call himself King—
and that suggestion had not come from the city people, but
from the members of the Five Hundred. The idea filled him
with horror which was almost superstitious. The city rot setting
in, he thought.

To Kalim he now said:

"Nine times out of ten the man who rides second is plotting
against the one ahead!"

"That I should live to hear you say that to me!" Kalim exclaimed. Then he mastered his rage and said, "I'll tell you something, Gaspar; you're becoming a fearful man." It was, and he

knew it, about as insulting a thing as one member of the Five Hundred could say to another. He hastened to explain. "Fearful not of hurt or of death, but like a child in the dark, fearful of what is not there!"

"What I fear is there, Kalim; I know its face, I know its name. Anything, anything that could tend to make us like them!"

He jerked his thumb towards a group of Jexalians, out for the first time in their summer clothes, standing idly admiring the prismatic colours made by the sunshine in the spray of the fountain.

"You're still upset about Lakma," Kalim said shrewdly.

Gaspar turned in his saddle and looked towards the last riders in the group.

"Upset? Not any longer. I've settled him. I hope"—he gave a rueful grin—"that I've settled that for good and all. I have only ten fingers; Lakma broke one for me."

"You broke his head," Kalim said dryly.

Gaspar allowed himself a more wholehearted grin as he remembered how, three months earlier, Lakma, one of the Five Hundred and a man of mature age, not a silly boy to be easily persuaded, easily forgiven, had wanted to marry, to take as his legal wife, a girl of the city, a daughter of the defeated ruling family, a princess. "You want to *marry* such rubbish!" Gaspar had said, in horrified astonishment. "Take her, use her, such women were made for use; but to stand up in the Sun's eye and mingle your blood with her dregs! Man, have you thought? If you do that and she bears a boy, he will be entitled to your place in the Five Hundred, to your horse and your sword. A half-breed, with soft straight legs and black eyes!" Nothing more scornful could be said of any man's potential offspring; the race of which the Five Hundred was at once the remnant and the flower had eyes as blue as a summer sky, and believed that boy babies were born with bowed legs, ready shaped to a horse's barrel.

"That I will not take, even from you," Lakma said.

"It is a truth that I will not withdraw."

"Then we fight," Lakma said, leaning upon his immemorial rights.

"The weapons to be of your choosing," Gaspar agreed.

They could fight it out on horseback, using staves or swords, or on foot, barehanded. Lakma had chosen a mounted contest with staves, and he approached the conflict with a divided mind. If he won, he must be prepared to accept the duties and responsibilities of leadership, a daunting thought; on the other hand the girl, very young, very appealing in her dark, exotic way, had fired his blood. As soon as the fight had begun he had no time for thought at all, for Gaspar had fought like a madman; his place as leader was at stake, and so was something, to him equally important—the absolute necessity of preserving, pure and untainted, the blood of his people.

In the end Lakma had taken the crack on the head which had dismounted him, and it was some days before he was in a fit state to speak the ritual words, "You are right. I apologise." Gaspar had relented then, and the errand from which they were now returning had been taken for Lakma's benefit. A small party of them, led by Gaspar, who always took advantage of any excuse to get out of Jexal, had ridden into the desert and hunted until they found four black tents by a spring of water that sprang from an outcrop of rock and then ran away and was lost; and in the tents there were three females, not yet mated. "Take your pick," Gaspar had said. Lakma had chosen the youngest, the most comely, and together they had stood in the Sun's eye at mid-day, he had slashed his wrist, the girl's father had slashed hers, their blood had been mingled and the marriage was made. A sheep had been killed and roasted, and at the feast Lakma had professed himself well pleased with his bride. They were bringing her back now and within a year, with any luck, she'd bear him a son, with blue eyes and red hair, and before he could walk he would be riding on a sheep's back, getting ready to be a horseman, in time to be one of the Five Hundred.

Now they were clattering across the bridge, so rightly called the Golden Bridge, for, though nobody thought of it nowadays, it was to this bridge across the tumbling river that the city owed its origin and its prosperity. The bridge made possible the continuation of the trade route towards the East, to the fabled lands of India and Cathay. Once a simple, serviceable structure of stone it had been many times enlarged and beautified. This morning the water swollen by the melting of the snow in the mountains was emerald green, marbled with white foam.

"Lakma," Kalim said with a pretence of resuming a conversation, "left marriage too late. Whims multiply with the years."

Gaspar's scowl returned. He knew what *that* meant. And in his heart he admitted the rightness of it; it was ridiculous that he should go about, arranging marriages for other men and remaining celibate himself. But marriage demanded intimacy, and he had never attained that, even with his men, even with his grandfather who had reared him. For as long as he could remember he had been self-contained, self-possessed. The idea of going, unclothed, unarmed, and submitting himself, even for the briefest space, to the embrace of another human being was repulsive to him. Yet, paradoxically, he regretted not having a son. If now he ever saw a woman whom he *could* marry—and he simply could not imagine what kind of creature she would be—and she bore him a son, the boy would be handicapped by his youth in comparison with the sons of other members of the Five Hundred; be he ever so hardy and bold and worthy of leadership, it would take him years to attain it.

He said, "Kalim, when you find me entertaining a whim, tell me; in blunt terms. Then *you* can break my finger and I'll break your head, if I can."

Kalim gave a little snort of laughter. *That* was what gave Gaspar such an ascendancy, not only over the bodies of the Five Hundred, but over their minds as well. He always saw through what was said to what was meant; he always went straight to the point and he never lacked an answer. Even when he was old and feeble—and let that day be long deferred—he would be a man to be reckoned with.

They were now approaching the Palace, an ornate building to which successive Kings of Jexal had made additions and alterations. Three hundred years earlier, Alexander had marched through Jexal on his way to India and the Jexalians, following their established policy, had welcomed him. The then reigning King had arranged for one of his sons to go to Greece, "to learn the ways of the West," and that young man, when he returned, had set his mark on the Palace, and to less degree on the city.

Gaspar hated the Palace more than he hated the city; it provoked in him, in exaggerated form, the same uneasiness. For more than a year after his conquest he had slept in one of his people's felt huts, reared in the Palace gardens, and he would have been sleeping there still but for a rumour that had reached him. The people of Jexal were saying that he dared not sleep in the Palace because he was afraid of the spirits of the old Kings. On the night of the day when that rumour reached him he had moved into the Palace and slept in the vast bed, all golden posts and silken hangings in which the last King of Jexal had slept on the night that had ended with a bloody dawn. He'd slept there alone, lying down as he always did in his tent, wearing his leather breeches and with his sword to hand. With the doors wide open and the window unshuttered it had not been too unbearable, had not inflicted too great an outrage upon his distaste for houses, his dread of being shut in.

In former days one wing of the Palace had housed Palace officials; there were hardly any left now and the apartments were occupied by members of the Five Hundred who were unmarried, or whose wives were amenable to communal life. Some women had preferred houses of their own and they had had wide choice of the splendid establishments formerly occupied by Jexalian grandees.

Another wing had been given over to administrative offices. Gaspar had reduced officials to the minimum; he had seen no reason why a man who checked the market dues shouldn't pour himself a glass of wine when he wanted one, or why customs officers needed uniformed public servants to help them on with their shoes. The administrative service was now much depleted and about three times as efficient as it had been.

One official Gaspar had retained. He had been known as the Grand Vizier, and he was still the Vizier, but no longer Grand.

He was fat and flabby, as all officials—indeed most Jexalians past first youth—tended to be, but he had his wits about him. He'd been cunning enough to hide himself well away when the city was sacked, and sensible enough to appear before Gaspar wearing a plain brown woollen robe, and lucky enough to speak the tongue of the ordinary people who had dealings with the country dwellers. True, he spoke it with a lisping refinement, but it was understandable; and what he said made sense. He had said, "Lord, you have taken this city. Fifty miles down the river stand the ruins of a city similarly taken when my grandfather's grandfather was a young man. Trade died there and the people perished or fled. A few goats now graze there amongst the fallen stones."

"I know it. I have camped there."

"A city lives by its trade," the Vizier said. "And trade needs men who can read and write and keep accounts and make visitors feel welcome and safe. Fighting men are not shaped for such work."

That was true, Gaspar reflected. And although he hated the city and all its ways, he had taken it, he knew, because he wanted it, as it was, rich and prosperous. Who wanted to be master of a mass of deserted ruins? What he wanted, he realised, was an ideal city, rich and prosperous, lively and flourishing, but not soft and decadent. So there and then he and the Vizier had made their bargain, and it had all worked out very well; the Vizier had traded in his former grandeur and its accompanying insecurity for a less obvious but far more real power and Gaspar had, here and there, abrogated part of his authority, saying, "Maybe you know best about that." Jexal had continued to flourish.

In former days whenever the King of Jexal had moved in or out of the Palace there had been a great commotion; trumpeters had blown upon their silver trumpets, attendants had stood, evenly matched on each side of the twelve shallow steps. Gaspar had done away with all that. The small cavalcade clattered into the space between the fountains and the serried cypresses flank-

ing the Palace steps and Gaspar swung himself from the saddle
and left his horse to the boy who had come running. The others,
reining in, prepared to disperse. Gaspar waited until Lakma, with
the girl, uncomfortably perched on the saddle before him, drew
level, and then put his hand on the man's knee. "I wish you joy,"
he said, and turned, and began to mount the Palace steps which
were so shallow that any active man must take them three at a
time.

His Vizier was waiting for him, ready to report upon what had
happened in the departments for which he was responsible during the last ten days. None of it was important. He had never
been able to rid his manner of servility, but at least he had learned
to stand upright and speak like a man, and not to keep saying
"Lord." He ended his account by saying:

"Benjamin, the carpet merchant, arrived yesterday. Is it your
wish to ask him to supper?"

Gaspar brightened. He liked the old Jew who visited Jexal
every second year with a long train of handsome mules and went
away laden with the choicest products of Jexal's looms. On Benjamin's former visit he had been scornful of the Vizier's suggestion
that he should receive the old man. "A carpet pedlar!" he had
exclaimed.

"He buys our best," the Vizier had explained. "He is a man of
substance, noted for his honesty. He is also a speaker of tongues
and a great carrier of news. As you say, a carpet pedlar, but an
aristocrat of pedlars."

"That would be something to see!" Gaspar had said. "Ask him
to supper." They'd had much interesting conversation then, and
he now looked forward to another. But two years! How fast time
flew in a place where it was reckoned; in the desert, with little
to mark one day from another, it had moved slowly.

"And Lord, there is one other thing," the Vizier said.

"Yes?" He spoke sharply, knowing that nowadays the Vizier
only used the honorific term when broaching matters of importance—in his own eyes at least.

"The boy, Malchus, very humbly asks if you could spare him
a moment of your precious time."

"Malchus?" For a second Gaspar was at a loss; then he remembered. The old King had had several wives and the youngest of them, when the city was raided, had hidden herself and her two children; they had remained in hiding for a week, and when they were discovered the blood lust had been appeased. The girl, Ilya, had been twelve or thirteen then, the boy some two years younger, and Gaspar had said, more in contempt than charity, "I don't make war on children!" And *that*, he now reflected sourly, had cost him the use of a finger, for it was the girl, Ilya, whom that fool Lakma had wanted to marry.

"What does he want with me? If my memory serves I told his mother to apprentice him to a useful trade."

"She did so," the Vizier said in a voice carefully void of all expression. He could remember the two beautiful, pampered children, their old father's darlings, petted by competitive courtiers and officials, Prince Malchus and Princess Ilya. . . . Four years ago, and in another world. "He works as a smith. He chose that, being fond of horses."

"Very sensible. And what does he want from me? Permission to set up his own business?"

How he bristles, the Vizier thought, at any mention or reminder of the old days in Jexal.

"He did not state his business. Today is the spring Festival of the Horse, and although it is no longer a public holiday—by your command—the smithies are idle. So he came and I allowed him to wait and said that I would tell you he was here."

"I'll see him," Gaspar said. "In the Balcony Room."

It was the only place in the whole huge Palace in which he felt moderately at ease, and that was because, strictly speaking, it was not a room at all; it was a bulge in the corridor which led to the private royal apartments. Once, more than five hundred years earlier, a Queen of Jexal had paused there, looked through the lacy marble of the wall and seen beyond the cypresses and the flowers of the garden the green river tumbling down. It was, she had declared, the best view obtainable from the whole Palace. Her doting husband had had the wall removed, the floor extended, so that she might the better enjoy her view. The doted-upon Queen and the King who had doted upon her were long since dead and forgotten; for many of their successors the balcony had been only a draughty place, to be hurried through, between the public audience chambers and the private rooms; but Gaspar had seized upon it as a place where he could feel moderately at ease and not suffer the shut in, stifled feeling that the rest of the Palace inflicted.

The boy, Malchus, came in and Gaspar looked at him with interest and curiosity and distaste and grudging admiration, all mixed. Fourteen? Fifteen at most, but with none of the awkwardness of the boy-meets-man stage. He was roughly, even poorly clad in a tunic of undyed homespun, now a trifle tight; his shoes were such as only the poorest wore in Jexal, that prosperous city, wooden slabs shaped to the foot and held in place by a thong which passed the great toe and its neighbour and tied about the ankle. And at the end of his thin boy's arms his hands hung, disproportionately large, coarse, scarred, ingrained with black that no amount of washing would remove. Yet he seemed quite at ease . . . at home. At home! Gaspar thrust that thought away, but with a commentary; he always felt at home in a felt tent, he'd been born in one; this boy had been born here, so naturally . . .

"Well," he asked harshly, "what do you want with me?"

Malchus said, "I was advised not to say 'Lord' to you or to use any other term of respect. So please, do not attribute the omission to incivility."

"What do you want?"

"I wish to call your attention to the plight of my sister, Ilya."

"I know all about her. She's given me quite a lot of trouble. Lakma, one of my men, wanted to marry her. I made him think better of it."

"Yes," the boy said. "That is why I am here. Ilya is now almost seventeen years old; she is very beautiful. It is time she was married."

"Marry her off then."

"That is easily *said*. My ambitions for her are, I assure you, moderate. Our nobles fell in the battle. Lesser men, but rich enough to keep her in comfort, may look upon her lustfully, but they avoid us, partly through fear of how you might regard their linking themselves to the royal house. I had one hope, which your man Lakma seemed about to fulfil."

"And I prevented him."

"You did. Could you tell me why?"

"I don't hold with mixed marriages."

"Have you ever thought about them, coolly, without prejudice?" the boy asked. "Believe me, I have not come here to anger you. You rule, we obey; but this is one city, it cannot forever be occupied by two peoples. Marriages would weld them into one." Then, while Gaspar was thinking of some retort that would suitably express his anger at this audacity, Malchus said quickly, "Not that I ever thought Lakma a fit match for my sister. It would be much more suitable if you yourself married her. As Queen my sister would command the loyalty of all our people."

Gaspar glared at him. The audacious young cub! He wanted to stamp, to shout, to laugh and jeer; but there was something about the boy's manner, so matter-of-fact, so fundamentally dignified, that he checked himself, gripping his hands, hurting the stiff, ill-set finger.

"The loyalty of your people!" he said sneeringly. "And what's that worth? Didn't I win it, between dawn and mid-day?"

"The loyalty of fear," Malchus said. "There is another. The loyalty of the heart."

"And *that* made a brave show, didn't it, when we rode in?"

"More than three thousand died."

"So they did. Like sheep, running this way and that."

"Taken unawares," the boy said hardily. "For a thousand years my people had been here, living in peace in this valley, cultivating the arts and the skills that can only flourish in peace. That is true, you know. *Your* women can do no more than to tread wool into felt; they never have time enough, or peace enough, to set up a loom."

That was truth and Gaspar faced it with distaste; but, skirting round the situation in his mind as once he had skirted around Jexal on his horse, he hit upon the boy's vulnerable spot.

"We're barbarians," he admitted. "And now I'll ask you something. Where's this loyalty of the heart you talk about? You would wish to marry your sister, first to Lakma, then to me. By the Sun, if I had a sister I'd slit her throat sooner than see her give a cup of water to those who had killed one of her kin!"

"That," Malchus said, "I do not doubt; but then, Lord, you said it yourself. You are a barbarian."

"And I rule here," Gaspar said. "Do you realise that for that saucy remark I could have your head?"

"My head," the boy said, "you are welcome to. For a long time it has been nothing but a nuisance to me! If you want to see me quake, threaten my hands!" He held them out as he spoke, unsightly with their calluses, a half-healed blister, but steady. Gaspar had a fleeting doubt whether he, unarmed and helpless in the presence of an all-powerful enemy, would have been so steady. To make up for that doubt he spoke with increased gruffness:

"I want neither your head, your hands, nor your sister, boy."

"Have you ever seen her?" Malchus asked. Before Gaspar could snap out his answer, no, and he had no wish to do so, the boy turned, gracefully, without haste and called, "Ilya." Evidently a prearranged signal, for immediately from between the pillars that separated the Balcony Room from the inner corridor, the girl came forward.

Gaspar's idea about what made a woman desirable were based upon strictly practical considerations. A marriageable girl should be young, upright and strong, equally ready for childbirth or hard work; she should bear the signs of health on her skin and hair, she must be one of his own race. That her demeanour should be modest and her attitude meek was taken for granted; all decent parents saw to that.

In no way did this girl, born a Princess, conform to these standards. She was pale, with the pallor of an indoor life, of careful protection from wind and weather; this and her huge, artificially darkened eyes, gave her a look of ill-health; she was very slim, almost frail, with delicate wrists and ankles, narrow hands and feet. Her black hair, exactly like her brother's, clung in little lustrous curls to her head. Gaspar's sharp eye noticed

even that her ears had been pierced for the wearing of ornaments, but she wore none; and her dress, something the colour
of the water of the river just below the balcony, though of silk,
was worn, in places mended. A fine wife she'd make, he thought
contemptuously, visualising her carrying and hauling, drawing
water, collecting dung for the fire, grinding corn and cooking,
all without interrupting the process of breeding and bearing.
What in the world had got into Lakma, he wondered. Then the
girl looked him straight in the eyes and he wondered no
more. . . .

His first reaction was one of genuine shock and horror. If
his sword had broken in his hand at a critical moment, or his
horse had failed to obey the pressure of his knees, or as he set
down a cup he had drained to the dregs he realised that he had
been poisoned, he could not have felt more sharply the sense of
having been betrayed. He'd just looked at her, asking himself
what such a woman would be good for, and she had looked at
him and given the answer. Made for delight! The very marrow of his bones moved and melted as he thought of the form
that delight would take.

"Go now," Malchus said, as though aware that his object in
producing her had been achieved.

"You go, too! Get out of my sight," Gaspar said, trusting that
the shortness of his breath would be attributed to wrath. The
boy stood his ground.

"You see, she is beautiful; and she is ripe for marriage. She
has been well reared; but now the jewels that she and my mother
had on them at the time of our ruin have all been sold. I earn
little. *What will her future be?*"

"That," Gaspar said, "is hardly my concern." He was so angry, with himself, with the boy, with the girl, with the Vizier
who must have connived, that he could hardly think of anything sufficiently spiteful to say. But he did his best. "Lakma is
safely married, now," he said. "Maybe in six months' time he
could take her as his concubine."

"Sooner than that I would kill her." He gave Gaspar a steady
look, and now the man could see the likeness between brother

and sister; in the hair, the shape of the skull, the way they held their heads. A look of race, unmistakable in man or beast.

"Have I your leave to go?" Malchus asked.

"Just a minute. You . . . you work as a smith, don't you? What about *your* future? Have you ever considered joining the army?"

He had reorganised the remnant of the Jexalian army, taken away most of its privileges and trappings and officered it with his own young men who were waiting their time to be admitted into the ranks of the Five Hundred. It was now fairly efficient and growing more so every day; and he was always careful to have some part of it well to the fore when he entertained travellers or emissaries from other places. Let nobody go away with false ideas; he had taken Jexal because he was the leader of the finest fighting force in the world, and because Jexal had been ready for the taking. Nobody was going to take it from him.

"It is my intention to become a soldier as soon as I am old enough. Sons of your men are admitted when they are fourteen; the rule is that a Jexalian born must be sixteen."

"And how old are you?"

"Fifteen."

"Well," Gaspar said, with sudden geniality, "we'll make an exception in your case. I'll give the word and if you present yourself tomorrow you will be accepted. Soldiers earn more than smiths, so you'll be able to look after your sister."

Why had he added that?

"I am indeed most grateful," the boy said, without looking grateful at all; and Gaspar knew that nothing he did, nothing would inspire true gratitude in this cub; if he fetched out the crown and set it on his head, and bowed his own head and kissed his hand, he'd take it as no more than his just due. Such a boy could be dangerous; he must be watched!

"We don't play at soldiers, now," he said. "You must work hard. I shall keep my eye on you. You may go."

"I thank you. I shall work hard," the boy said. He turned and walked away, unhurriedly and with a lithe grace. Somewhere in the corridor he called, "Ilya, where are you?" and it struck Gaspar that the words were an echo of words spoken only four years ago, but in fact unimaginably far away, the words of two children, silk-clad and carefree, playing in the long corridor of the Palace that was their home. Getting fanciful, he told himself scornfully.

It was a relief, at the end of the day to sit down to supper with Benjamin, the old Jew who bought and sold carpets.

In the old days, if the Vizier was to be believed, supper in the Palace had occupied the whole evening and lasted far into the night. It had been a social occasion, a nightly feast, with many guests and three or four times as much food cooked as could possibly be eaten. Gaspar and his Five Hundred had come straight from a life where they thought themselves lucky if in the morning they could place slices of tough raw meat under their saddles and at the day's end remove it, flattened and softened in fibre, and find fuel enough to char it black on the outside. Often enough they had eaten it raw, tasting of leather and horses' sweat. Bread had been a luxury, so had any vegetable or fruit.

From such a life they had plunged, in a single day, to life in this city, which straddling the trade routes from East to West, offered every delicacy known to man. A wide belt about the city itself was devoted to market gardens, to farms where pigs grew fat and calves were bred to be eaten young. There were imports, too; fruits from plants too delicate to flourish even in this sheltered valley and fish, not the well-nigh indestructible salted and smoked fish which was a rare luxury in the desert, but fresh fish, reared in great pools on the fish farms, and other fish, cunningly preserved in oil and spices, brought from far places. There was even one delicacy, fish eggs in oil, sealed into jars, that came, by painful stages, from some unknown place in the North East.

For a time they had all eaten gluttonously: and if they had simply been sacking the city and intending to move on, gluttony would have been in order, even a duty, since a man should build up reserves when he could, against the hungry days, as a camel did, or a fat-tailed sheep. But they were not passing through; they were here to establish themselves, and very soon

Gaspar, in whom the desert-bred respect for food was lively, had issued orders. Nowadays, even in the Palace, one main dish was served, fish or flesh or fowl, with all the bread, cheese, or fruit that a man needed to attain the full-fed feeling. The horde of master cooks in the kitchens, mourning the waste of their acquired skills in rearing airy towers of spun sugar, the moulding of marzipan into flowers and animals, the making of small many-coloured cakes that melted on the tongue, had been set to useful tasks, often menial. And in the Great Hall where parasitic officials had feasted Gaspar sat down to eat with those of the Five Hundred who had no homes of their own, or preferred the company of their fellows, and any chance-comer upon whose right to be there Gaspar and the Vizier were agreed.

There had been a time when visitors showed obvious signs of nervousness. Jexal had been taken by barbarians and in many people's minds barbarianism and cannibalism and reasonless killing were closely associated. But gradually the word had spread, the new régime was different, definitely uncouth, but it was disciplined; and Gaspar was not a bad fellow; difficult to talk to, being ignorant of Greek which Alexander's short-lived Empire had made almost a universal language.

On this evening, because, despite his embargo on the many public holidays, people were still celebrating, in a muted way, the Festival of the Horse, none of the Five Hundred was present and Gaspar and his guest sat down alone; not in the Balcony Room which would ordinarily have been Gaspar's choice were the company to number less than ten, but in a small room, on the ground floor, handy for the kitchens. The Balcony Room, his chosen refuge in this place, had been spoiled for him by the morning's experience.

The old Jew, who had washed his hands and his feet in an anteroom, gave his ritual greeting, "Peace be on this house."

"Peace be upon you and yours," Gaspar responded. It was curious, he thought, how, from the very first, he had felt an affinity with this old man who came from the West, who was a trader. It had been partly explained when, during their first meeting, the old man had said that his people had once, long ago, been a desert people; and they had taken a city called Jericho in very much the same way as Gaspar had taken Jexal. Another partial explanation lay in the fact that Benjamin reminded Gaspar of his grandfather, though there was no physical resemblance between that fierce old warrior, lean and leathery, all scarred from his many battles, and the plump, peaceable Jew. Yet there was a likeness; perhaps it lay in the fact that both men have the impression that they had lived long, seen many things and been little impressed. And there was the similarity of greeting and leave-taking. True, Benjamin said, "Peace be upon this house," and Gaspar's grandfather said "upon this tent," never having seen a house; but the intent was the same. And the ritual reply was identical.

"And now," Gaspar said when the mutton and rice had been served, "what is the news in the world?"

Benjamin had learned, on his previous visit, how limited Gaspar's knowledge was. Tell him now, for instance, about the increasing size and importance of the port of Caesarea—a thing of great importance to one who regularly shipped cargoes of carpets and rugs to Rome and a dozen other places, and what would it mean to Gaspar who had never seen the sea or a ship? He considered and discarded several things and then said:

"The news that most closely concerns me is a plague that has broken out amongst the slaves in Tyre. They are the ones who fish out the murex, from which the purple dye is made; and they have died more quickly than they can be replaced. So for a year or two there will be a great shortage of the true purple colour."

"Our carpets then, already dyed, should increase in value," Gaspar said, and was instantly ashamed. City talk. Tradesmen's talk!

"That is so," the Jew agreed placidly, "and today, in my buying, I took that into account. I paid more for any carpet with purple in it; and I warned your people of the shortage."

Gaspar narrowed his eyes. "Now why should you do that? They couldn't know. They'd have sold at the old price."

"God would know," the old man said simply. "And the man

who profits by another's ignorance can not lie down at peace with his God."

Possibly in its far distant and now-no-more-than-legendary homeland Gaspar's people had had gods, religious beliefs, and ceremonies, but if so they had been left there, with everything else that could not be carried on horseback or travel on its own legs. All that remained to them as drought after drought had forced them to move farther and farther to the South West, was a primitive kind of sun worship, strictly practical in its purposes. It was convenient to have some form of ritual to mark a permanent marriage from a passing association; it was convenient to know that when a man said, "I swear by the Sun . . ." what he said thereafter was likely to be the truth. There was no mysticism about it; nobody imagined that the sun had any interest in him or demanded anything from him. They kept one festival, on the day when the sun stood highest in the sky and meat was plentiful, since that was the time when young bull calves and rams were ready to be eaten, must indeed be weeded out to prevent overgrazing. Gaspar was about as far from understanding what Benjamin meant when he said "God" as any man could be. He remembered that on his former visit, telling stirring tales about famous men of his race, the old Jew had several times mentioned God and some completely unbelievable things that he was supposed to have done.

They talked of other things and then Benjamin, looking grave and leaning a little forward, asked:

"Are Pella's activities known to you, or am I the first to bring the news?"

"Pella," Gaspar repeated, knotting his brows. "Who is he?"

"From what I hear, he claims to be a son of the old King of Jexal. There was a son, I remember, who got on very badly with his father and went to live in Armenia. That would be almost twelve years ago now. I have no liking for carrying bad news, but I thought a word of warning wouldn't come amiss."

"A son of the King lives here, in Jexal. He was in this place this morning. He's no threat to me, so why should I be warned against one in Armenia?"

"Ah, but he is no longer there, or so they say. He is in Rome, trying to interest Caesar Augustus in his cause."

"His cause?"

"His claim to the throne, *here.*"

Gaspar knew Caesar Augustus by name; he ruled in some place half a world away, separated from Jexal by deserts, by mountains and seas and dozens of other kingdoms; and he had won his right to rule by his sword, just as Gaspar had won his. So much he knew from talking to travellers, and that was the sum of his knowledge. He was not perturbed, but he was puzzled.

"What does it matter to the King of Rome who rules in Jexal?"

"Nothing. But that is the way the Romans work. They seize upon someone else's quarrel and march in to restore order as they call it. They did it in my country. Order they restored, but not the ruling house. They set up a puppet king, Herod of Idumea, who is not even a Jew. Worse, he is not even a good man."

"And you really think it likely that they would come *here?*"

"Who am I to say? Their decisions are unpredictable, their methods are not. They reach out and establish themselves and then they build a road to link the new possession with the old. And this I have noticed: Augustus sees himself as a second and greater Alexander; Alexander moved to the East; it seems to me not unlikely that Augustus should turn his eyes this way."

Gaspar made a grunting sound. "This needs thinking about."

"It does. In your place I should think of it often and heavily," the old Jew said gravely; he liked this strange young man, this barbarian with whom from the first he had felt at ease. The next remark must be worded carefully, he thought. "In Roman eyes Pella's claim is legitimate enough to justify action on their part —if they wish to take action. Of course there is another possibility . . ."

"And that is?"

"Something else I have seen done. An emissary may come to you, secretly, and suggest that you pay tribute; a ten per cent levy on all the goods that pass your custom houses. Then, if you agree to pay, you are Rome's friend, and Pella will one day be fished out of the Tiber. Body of a man unknown."

"And we," Gaspar exploded, "who fight hand to hand and would never betray those who had eaten our salt, are called barbarians!"

"My people," Benjamin said, "were once equally scrupulous. There was a woman called Jael who killed, with her own hands, the leader of an invading force. It was a laudable action, but she is not reckoned amongst our noble women; it is held against her that she had first fed him."

"In many ways your people and mine sound somewhat akin," Gaspar said. "Tell me, how do your people accept the rule of Rome?"

Like all really pious Jews Benjamin tended to overlook the vast numbers of his countrymen who had settled down under Roman rule and concentrated rather upon the few who were rebellious, the guerrillas in the hills who still actively carried on the war, the civilians who thought up cunning ways to avoid taxes. Unwittingly he painted for Gaspar an entirely false picture, leaving him with the impression that Rome's hold on Palestine was infirm and feeble compared with his hold upon Jexal. By the end of the evening the conscientious old Jew realised this and tried to give his host some idea of the strength and magnitude of Rome, but it was like warning a child who had never seen water except in a jar or a goatskin against the danger of drowning. Gaspar simply did not understand. And somehow Benjamin let slip the fact that in Jerusalem six hundred legionaries were stationed. Gaspar said:

"There are Five Hundred of us. The Jexalians had an army of seven thousand." And it was all very well to say that Rome was different. How different? And why? This man was a simple soldier from the desert, with no more imagination than the table on which he leaned his elbow, no more comprehension of politics than he had of mathematics—and five hundred seemed to be the limit of his reckoning.

The time for parting came. Benjamin said, "I thank you for your hospitality. Peace be on this house."

Gaspar said, "Go in safety, and return soon. In my tent you are always welcome."

He realised that his tongue had slipped and smiled, waving his hand. "My tent!" he said.

Soon after he went to his bed and slept and dreamed that a thing, brute faced and very hairy, but recognisable to him in some mysterious fashion as Pella, was about to rape the girl called Ilya and that he was going to her aid, with his knife in his hand, but someone from behind hit him, a sharp chopping blow on the wrist and his knife had fallen to the floor and the noise of its falling had wakened him, short of breath and sweating at every pore.

After that she had haunted his dreams. Most often she was in some distressful situation from which, always impotently, he tried to save her; sometimes the situation was reversed; at such times most commonly he was dying of thirst and she, ploughing her way through the sand, was bringing him water. She'd stumble and spill it, or she'd reach him and the cup, the jar, the gourd she carried would be empty, or full of something undrinkable, horse's urine, mud, chaff, a crumpled silk scarf which he desperately pulled out, yards and yards and yards of it.

He never mentioned his dreams to anyone—to whom could he mention them? Outwardly life went on. He issued an order that he had been meditating for a long time. All the beggars in the city were to be rounded up, confined in one place and given one good meal a day. He'd hated the sight of them himself and had seen them through the eyes of visitors, a blot, a scar. The Vizier said, "But if it is known that we *feed* beggars they will flock in, from Babylon, from Samarkand." "Not on *my* terms," Gaspar said, "when I say beggars I mean those incapable of making a living; the blind, crippled, and witless. Any able-bodied fellow who wishes to eat the bread of idleness can be *made* blind, crippled, or witless." So beggars had ceased to infest the streets and there were less than twenty in the asylum he had provided.

He had issued another order, too. Anybody coming into Jexal

from the West was to be brought to the Palace and interrogated. He always asked about the Romans, and so far he had learned nothing more than Benjamin had told him; Pella's name had never been mentioned.

To the Vizier Gaspar had mentioned Pella, introducing the subject by demanding why he had never been informed of the man's existence.

"Because, to us, he is no longer alive. Ten, twelve years ago, he took his portion and went away, forever. Not only is his name never to be mentioned; in the book of records it was blotted out; it is as though he had never been born."

"Why?"

"He was . . ." The Vizier hesitated, choosing his words carefully. "I will not say a bad *man,* but a bad Jexalian, and a bad son and a bad prince. Always he was in opposition to his father and his family, so much so that if his father said, 'It is a fine day,' he would say, 'Not so!' He gathered about him a few of the same mind, young men who could not agree with their elders. Then there came the time when it is necessary that he should marry and beget an heir. Since he was so high"—the Vizier measured the height from the floor—"he has been promised as husband to a princess whose people have been our friends always. Peace and much trade had resulted from that promise. But will he marry her? No, he will not. He has fallen in love"— the Vizier's voice was edged with scorn—"with a woman in the market, a woman who sold doves for the Temples; she was a widow. On his knees his father beseeches him, saying marry the one you are promised to and beget a son, that is all I ask; the market woman can be your concubine. But that does not suit Prince Pella . . ." The Vizier's face turned pale and sweat shone on his brow. "If my old master could hear me, he would have my head for that! No, that does not suit him. It is his wish, his intent, to bring the market widow, the dove-seller, into the Palace and make her Queen, crowned with his mother's crown. The result of this you can imagine. Every well-born lady in Jexal insulted; the King, whose daughter has been passed over, ready to make war; the market people insufferable from pride. Not to be contemplated. So he is given his portion, he announces publicly that he is no longer prince, or heir, or any connection with the ruling house and he goes. To Armenia, it is said."

Gaspar listened to this sorry little story with a sneaking feeling of admiration for Pella, a man of some spirit, he thought, not a Jexalian at all.

"Suppose," he said, "just *suppose,* that he came back, with an army behind him, to claim what he claimed to be his right."

"He renounced all rights. Between the dove-seller and Jexal he chose once and for ever."

"So you said. But if it came to choosing between him and me; what then?"

"You," the Vizier said, "valued Jexal enough to fight for it; he flung it away like a worn-out shoe. Also, there is this to be said . . . You said I was always to speak the truth to you, and the truth now I dare to speak. We are subject to you and to your Five Hundred, but with you we feel safe. When the battle was over it was over, some lost their positions, some their mansions, but our lives are safe. With Pella nobody would be safe. He gave up Jexal once for a market woman; he would give it again to the foreign army that re-established him. He was a man of no judgement. May I ask . . . Is it likely that we must make this choice? Has he, in the face of all that he vowed, some plan to return?"

"Not that I know of. I was talking idly. And still talking idly, I ask this: If Pella should ever come, the boy Malchus, the girl Ilya, where would they stand?"

"Against him, whatever that involved," the Vizier said promptly. "He and his mother, and the two princes who were killed did everything in their power to make life miserable for the young wife and her children. Malchus, I assure you, has no ambitions; except to be a soldier. With three elder brothers he never expected to inherit the crown and now that you have allowed him to be a soldier he is content—and your devoted subject."

That Gaspar doubted, but he let it pass, hoping that the

Vizier would now speak Ilya's name, since he couldn't without betraying his interest, speak it again himself.

"For the girl I am sad," the Vizier said, "as I am sad for any girl for whom no husband can be found. My old master so doted upon her, his only girl child, that no offer made for her pleased him. This one was too old, this too young, this had bad teeth and the other was of known bad temper. Thirteen years old and not promised, when he died; for a Princess, and so pretty, a thing unknown. And now too late. Unless—and this I also dare to say because you said that from me you would take nothing but the truth—if you would marry her. What a wonderful thing that would be, and how pleasing to all the people."

"When I marry," Gaspar said, "it will be to please myself, not the people."

"But naturally," the Vizier said.

Time passed; no emissary came from Rome offering a ruinous friendship; there was no news of Pella. The year passed its peak and began to decline; travellers from the West grew fewer; soon would come the season when snow would lie on the mountains. Gaspar busied himself with his army and his defences, never naming Rome as the enemy even in his mind, but being ready because, as he had reason to know, all men are enemies to those who possess something covetable.

Then, on a crisp bright morning, the Customs Officer in the post on the Northeasterly road out of Jexal reported the arrival there of an old man, almost half dead from hunger, riding a lame camel: his name, he said, was Melchior and he came from far away, from a place called Pyongyang. He seemed to be a scholar, he had spoken in two or three strange tongues before trying the one which, with difficulty, the Customs Officer had understood.

"And which tongue was that?" Gaspar asked the Vizier who had brought this report to him.

"Something between the market speech which I use to you and the speech of the Five Hundred which you use to me."

Coming from that direction the old man could have no news

of Rome or of Pella; he was not, like Benjamin the Jew, a rich and valued customer; there was no real reason why Gaspar should receive him. But lately he had welcomed any diversion which would prevent him, in the evening hours, from brooding upon his own foolishness with regard to a pale, frail girl with great dark eyes.

So he said, "Kinship of tongue should indicate kinship of blood. Ask this Melchior to eat supper with me."

"If the report is to be believed," the Vizier said, "he and his camel may be dead by suppertime."

"Where are they now?"

"A swift runner brought the message and I came straight to deliver it. They may by this time have reached the bridge."

"Order a meal; bring the old man to me, and look after the camel."

Had the King of Jexal given such an order in the old days it would have been relayed and subdivided and its execution delayed; but things were different now and in a short time Melchior and Gaspar made their fateful meeting. Gaspar, well-used to assessing a man's physical state, saw at a glance that the old man was in the last stages of exhaustion, and near starvation point as well. But he was courteous. He put his left hand in his right sleeve, his right in his left, and bowed so that for a second his queer round hat looked like a shield. Then he raised his wasted face to Gaspar and said:

"It is charitable of you to invite me to eat with you; but you are only prolonging a useless life."

The words, spoken in a weak voice, and, to Gaspar's ear, strangely accented, were only just recognisable. Their meaning seemed obscure.

"Sit down," he said. "Food is ready."

A servant brought in a dish, hastily prepared and the old man eyed it so avidly that Gaspar said:

"Take a mouthful or two of wine first, to make way. Then eat slowly. With fasting the belly shrinks."

"You have known hunger?"

"Many a time."

The wine ran down hearteningly and presently Melchior began to pick at the food.

"You have travelled far," Gaspar said. "Where is Pyongyang?"

"To the East. By the shore of the Yellow Sea."

Gaspar had never heard of the Yellow Sea but he was skilled now in concealing ignorance, so he nodded and asked:

"And where are you going?"

"That I cannot tell you, because I am uncertain myself. This may sound strange to you, but it is fact. In Samarkand I consulted a map, said to be new and accurate, and I think I was bound for Jerusalem or some place a little to the South of it. Not that it matters. I know now that I shall never get there. I have failed."

"In what way?"

Along the road, making an ineffectual attempt to bargain, or —since his money gave out—to beg, Melchior had tried to explain something of his errand and its urgency; he had always been laughed at. So now he was cautious.

"I had a message to deliver," he said. "A message of the utmost importance, something that only I knew about. I realise now that I am an impractical man. . . ." He brooded for a moment, ignoring his food, then said in a more vigorous voice, "On the other hand, had I foreseen the difficulties and the expense or realised how money becomes of less and less value as one moves Westwards, there was nothing I could have done. I sold all I had. My own wants are meagre, but to keep a camel in condition is very expensive. And the ferries . . ."

He looked at Gaspar with his old unworldly wise eyes and said with a thin smile that looked as though it hurt:

"Have you ever been obliged to pay for a passage, with a camel, across a wide river, by ferry?"

"No."

"You have then been spared the worst evidences of human rapacity. I have made five such crossings and they have ruined me. It is not, one admits, easy work, and there are certain risks, especially with a camel aboard; but I can see no excuse for saying that the ferry fee is so much and then stopping in mid-stream and demanding as much again. Or, as once happened, allowing me to land on the farther bank and then pushing away, threatening to carry my camel back to the other side unless I paid more. I hesitate to say that such practices are unknown in my own country, I have led a retired life. And it is possible, of course, that strangers are exploited everywhere. Oh, not here," he added hastily, "here I have been most kindly received, and I am grateful indeed. And I ask you to forgive, if you can, my showing a miserable face at your hospitable table. The thought of my failure distresses me."

"I am interested," Gaspar said, "in your having a message to deliver to some unknown destination. How can that be?"

"Ah yes. I am an astronomer. I read the stars in their courses; and I read this message plain and clear. It is just possible that others have read it and are now on their way, I can only hope that that is so. But I was better equipped, I think, than most of my kind, so it seemed to me essential that I should take action. Perhaps you are one of those to whom astronomy is foolishness. In that case I will not bother you with details."

"In the desert," Gaspar said, and he felt a pang of the old homesick feeling, "the stars are a reliable guide. That is all I know of them."

"In the desert, as on the sea, for navigational purposes, certainly, they have their uses. And the star I follow has never failed me. But the stars have other purposes. There are combinations, movements . . . things which, if you will excuse me, can only be properly discussed by those who understand. What I *cannot* understand"—some petulance crept into his voice—"is my position. To this study I gave my life and a considerable fortune and I read the message. But it looks as though it would have been better had I spent my time studying what it costs to feed a camel or how to charter a ferry boat, and why it is that in one place a coin will buy a whole sheep and in the next, only a few miles away, a mere bowl of weak mutton broth. It is ignorance of such things that has defeated me, *not* lack of will or weariness, frustrating as the latter can be at times." He gave a great sigh.

"You said that your destination might be Jerusalem," Gaspar

said. He recognised it as the home of Benjamin the Jew; the place which the Romans had taken as he had taken Jexal, but the Jews had not settled down tamely as the Jexalians had done; they were, by all accounts, still rebellious, and he thought of them as a potential weak spot in the defences of a potential enemy.

"Do you know it?"

"Only by word of mouth."

"Who rules there?"

"A King named Herod; but I understand that he is a hollow man. A tool of the Emperor of Rome."

"Emperor," Melchior repeated thoughtfully. "It is possible, then, that my errand concerned him and his family. Does he live in Jerusalem?"

"He does not. He lives in Rome, and from what I hear he is a rogue."

"Indeed?" Melchior sighed again. "Oh well, no matter. Whoever was concerned, in whatever place, will have no warning from me. I have done what I could, I have spent all I had, I have begged, I have starved, all to no avail." But even as he said it the small quantity of wine he had drunk, the food he had eaten had revived him and he was willing to snatch at the frailest hope. He looked at Gaspar with a calculating eye, and then took note of his surroundings, hitherto ignored.

"You are a man of wealth and power; if you could bring yourself to believe in the importance of my errand and help me on . . . The child's family would surely repay you, since part of my errand is to warn them against his death by treachery before he is weaned. If I could be there in time, I would tell them to whom they owed the child's life and I would ask them to reward you. . . ." He broke off, deterred by the inscrutability of the hard young face of the man with whom he was pleading. "I am unaccustomed to begging," he said, with great dignity, "and believe me, for myself I would never do it. But for the sake of a child with such a destiny, and in such danger, I humble myself and ask you, sir, to lend me a camel and enough money to take me to Jerusalem."

That word again!

"Eat, while I think," Gaspar said and leaned his chin on his hand.

His thinking was simple and direct; he had little imagination and was incapable of visualising anything not related in some way to his own experiences. When he thought of the Roman army, said to be a great one, he saw, in his mind's eye, the old Jexalian army, a great mass of strutting men with plumes and banners and silver trumpets, and remembered how easily it had gone down before the charge of his Five Hundred. And when he thought of the guerrillas in the hills of Judea of whom old Benjamin had spoken, he saw them as men like those of his own Five Hundred in the days before the great battle, skulking, watchful, hard men awaiting the chance to strike.

One of the first rules of fighting that he had ever learned was that one should attack before one could be attacked, and that the battle should take place in the enemy's terrain, so that his tents, his flocks, his womenfolk and children suffered. Another thing he knew was that of all weapons surprise is the most deadly.

He sat there and remembered how, in the months before he swooped down, he had come, on this pretence or that, into Jexal, mingling with its people, marking the strengths and the weaknesses. What he had done once he could do again: And what better disguise could he adopt than that of travelling companion to this star-bemused old man?

And deep under all these thoughts, so deep that he need not trouble to face it, was another—that by absenting himself, by moving about and making plans, he would escape from the spell which the girl Ilya had cast upon him.

Finally he lifted his chin from his hand and said:

"I am minded to come with you."

"You do not trust me?" Melchior asked haughtily.

"What? With one camel and twenty gold pieces in a bag? Do you think that of me . . . ?" He had been about to tell Melchior who he was and what he owned. "No," he said, "I have a fancy to see this city, Jerusalem. And I think that you would travel faster and more safely in the company of a practical man like me."

"That is indisputable," Melchior admitted. Hope was now lively in him; the food and the wine had had their full restorative effect, his plea for aid had not been rejected; he was himself again. "When can you be ready to go?"

"Tomorrow morning," Gaspar said, thinking of what he must first do. Melchior shook his head.

"Oh no! Haste is of the utmost importance. I have lost time already, with Senya so lame."

"This," Gaspar said, "is a thing I do not understand. You say that according to the stars this child has a destiny, and yet according to the same stars, he may die before he is weaned. One or the other may be true, but not both."

"Ah, that is what is so difficult to explain to one like you. The stars indicate: they do not rule. They say what may happen, not what will. There are indications, and counterindications, always, and in this case both are very clear. It is—how shall I put it simply? A woman goes to market and buys a length of woollen cloth. Let that cloth represent what the stars *indicate*. Now of that cloth the woman may make a gown for herself, breeches for her husband, a blanket for the bed. She cannot, of woollen cloth, make a silk robe or a muslin veil, but within limits the choice is hers, and her choice can represent the counterindications. Have I made that plain?"

"As plain as it ever will be, to me," Gaspar said, giving up. "So, haste is of importance; but we shall make good speed. We shall travel on swift . . ." He had almost said "horses," but hastily substituted "camels, *riding* camels." It would never do to ride one of his horses, if he wished to pass unnoticed; everyone who ever came to Jexal noticed and commented upon the beauty, the strength, the spirit and docility of the horses. His tribe had brought with them from their remote Mongolian homeland all the rules governing the treatment of horses, and had preserved them strictly. It was an offence to strike one except on the rump, and then only with a rod as thick as a woman's smallest finger.

And if water were scarce and of horse or man only one could drink, the horse drank, which was sense, since the horse could carry the man; and a man could suck a pebble and reflect that privation toughened him.

It was an irony, Gaspar reflected, that because his horses were so good he must ride a camel.

"Even so," Melchior said doggedly, "I should prefer to move on today. I am already late." If they were to travel together, on camels, and with money provided by this man it was important that from the first he should understand the urgency of the errand. It was not a question of whose will should be paramount —or at least that was not how it appeared to Melchior's dedicated mind; but it was *his* errand, *his* responsibility, therefore *his* must be the authority. He was grateful, in a fashion, but gratitude was irrelevant.

"Give me an hour," Gaspar said. "Lie down." He pointed to one of the couches, hardly ever used nowadays. "Rest yourself while you may. I will go about my preparations."

He went out and sent for Kalim, Lakma, and a third man, Tembur, his three most trusted comrades. He told them that there was something to the West that he wanted to look into, that he was leaving in an hour and could not foretell the time of his return. He left Jexal to them, he said, and would not insult them by giving orders; they knew the rules as well as he did; trivial matters they three could deal with; things of importance must be discussed by the Five Hundred in solemn session, each man speaking in turn.

Their absolute trust in him was evidenced by the lack of protest, of questions. He had always led them successfully and this proposed absence fell neatly into pattern with his behaviour in the past. To the West they knew lay many petty kingdoms, similar to that of Jexal: another raid in the spring, perhaps; or maybe at last he had taken one of their many hints, and was going to look for a wife.

"Go in peace and come back with joy," they said.

When he came back he would find everything as he had left

it; they were his brothers, bound to him by that which the boy
Malchus had, in his flowery, Jexalian way put into words, "the
loyalty of the heart."

When all was ready, the camels already kneeling in the courtyard, Gaspar went to rouse Melchior; he did it by taking the
old man by the shoulder and was almost shocked to feel the
bones so prominent under the faded blue robe, and the bones
themselves so frail and light. Melchior, accustomed to sleeping
lightly and brokenly, was awake at once, on his feet and ready to
go.

"There is one thing," Gaspar said. "Of Kings and courts I am
ignorant, but I think that if we visit this Herod he might expect
gifts. What shall I bring?"

"My gift I carry in my head," Melchior said. "And I also am
ignorant of Kings. But all men like gold."

Gaspar had a pouchful of it, but that he might need for the
journey. However, he knew the very thing—the crown that had
rolled from the dead head of the old King; the crown which,
before they understood his mind, some of his followers had
wished to see on Gaspar's head. "It would impress people," they
had said, and he had retorted that he could impress people in
his own hat, or know why not.

"Wait here. Eat again," he said, remembering the bones; and
he strode along to the bedchamber where, unwillingly, he had
slept to defy the rumour that he was afraid. The King of Jexal
had died there, by his own hand—which showed, Gaspar had
always thought, what manner of man he was. Seeing the battle
go against him he had run to his room and stabbed himself, and
the crown had fallen from his head and rolled into a corner. It
and all the other pretty, womanish things he had worn, rings
and necklets, armlets, jewelled pins, had been put into a chest
into which Gaspar now thrust a hasty hand and brought out a
crown. It consisted of three golden circlets, the largest just the
size of a man's skull, the others smaller, linked by curved struts;
circlets and struts were set with jewels, rubies, sapphires, emeralds. The triple crown of Jexal. A pretty thing, but no wear for

a man. Now the other . . . Gaspar wasted a moment looking at the Queen's crown, a filigree coronet, all set with pearls, was the right wear for a woman; at least for some women; it was difficult to imagine it upon the head of any woman he had ever seen in the market. It was difficult, in fact, to imagine it upon any but one woman! Upon that thought he let the lid of the chest fall with a crash. The triple crown he slipped into a soft leather bag and tightened the thong. He was ready.

It was, by this time, not much more than an hour before sunset, and as they rode towards the Western gate, called the Water Gate, Gaspar looked towards the mountains, measuring what remained of daylight, and because he had as yet no experience of Melchior's method of travelling, thought that really they might as well have waited until morning. But he did not resent the early start, for already he felt an uprush of relief at leaving the Palace and the city and all that they meant, behind him.

The wide street that led towards the Water Gate was not a busy thoroughfare at this season and the people who were in it were all women, walking purposefully. Gaspar scowled at them; he knew where they were going—to the Temple which stood just within the city wall. In Jexal there were nine Temples, dedicated to various gods and goddesses, and Gaspar regarded them all with distrust and suspicion; but he had never issued an order that they should be closed. What he had done was to inculcate and foster the idea that no man worth the name would go running, trying to placate an irate, or cajole a friendly, god, and his policy had worked so well that nowadays only women and a few old men frequented the Temples. This had made priesthood an unremunerative occupation, not attractive to recruits. The time would come, Gaspar told himself, when this superstitious thing, conducive to fear and the shuffling off of responsibility, would die out of its own accord. Already in Jexal it was fashionable to swear by the Sun, and to be married by the mingling of blood.

He was thinking this, not without complacency, when he recognised, in one of the women, the girl Ilya. Her walk was unmistakable. He intended to ride past without turning his head and he almost managed it, but in the last second the temptation to look, to see whether she was as lovely as his memory of her, was too much. So he turned and once again they looked into one another's eyes.

She made a little sound of astonishment, recognising him in his stiff felt hat, leather jerkin and baggy trousers, the horseman, mounted on a camel; then she began to move more swiftly, almost running beside him, and lifting her face. She said the word he had forbidden:

"Lord," she said, "Lord!" And because he wished to conceal his real identity from Melchior, who up to this moment had regarded him, he was sure, simply as a wealthy and charitable man, he checked his camel's pace; and because being obliged to do so angered him he said gruffly:

"What do you want with me?"

"To thank you," she said. "To thank you from my heart for what you have done for Malchus. He is so happy now."

She spoke the true Jexalian tongue, removed from his own by the softening, refining influence of a thousand years; Malchus, who had worked with common men in the smithy, had seemed to lisp, and there were times when Gaspar was obliged to ask the Vizier to repeat himself; upon Gaspar's ear what she said fell with all the appeal of a woman speaking with a lilt, an intonation, just understandable and no more.

"I am glad to hear it," he said. "Happy soldiers are good soldiers, as a rule." Then he added the little extra, "Temur speaks well of him."

Something flashed in her eyes. It said—if he read it rightly and he thought that he did— Because I thanked you for breaking a rule on my brother's behalf, don't imagine that I value Temur's good word!

Then she said, "You go a journey?" and she looked at the camel, comparing it, he knew, with the horse he ordinarily rode.

"I go a journey," he said.

"Then take this," she said, "to preserve your most precious health in evil-smelling places." She reached up and thrust into his hand a little package, wrapped in linen. "Ishtar will not

grudge it," she said. She stood back and raised her hand, in perfect imitation of a member of the Five Hundred taking leave.

"Go in peace and return in joy," she said.

He was having his first experience with camels; they were
more gregarious, less near-to-human than horses. The one he
rode and the one Melchior rode had always been a pair, measuring their paces. His, held back, fretted and fidgeted, and Melchior's ridden forward, was fretting and fidgeting too. In one
wild moment of confusion, the package in his hand, the camel
restive, the mockery of her leave-taking and his need to take one
last look at her, all mingling, he could do no more than call back
the traditional, tribal response to the leave-taking:

"Stay in peace; I shall return."

Then his camel, straining forward, drew level with Melchior's,
straining backward, and the two fell into even pace. And as they
did so he realised the nature of Ilya's gift. The scent assaulted
him, the dominating scent of what he called the city stink. It
was frankincense. In a curious way it represented all the alien
way of life, the ritual, the king reverence, the god worship, the
decadence of the city he had made his own and yet distrusted.
And having it thrust into his hand by that woman, of all women,
roused such a violent distaste in him that for a moment, wishing
to throw it from him, he was unable to do so; he was paralysed
by disgust.

"The brazen slut!" he said to Melchior as the two camels,
order restored, moved forward happily. "Accosting me with her
stinking rubbish."

Melchior sniffed. "Rubbish? It smells like frankincense; believe me, in many places it is worth more than its weight in gold.
This King—did you say his name was Herod?—would find that
an acceptable gift, I think."

"You give it to him, then," Gaspar said; and to his relief found
himself able to move, to hand the package over. "But so long as
you carry it, try not to ride between me and the wind. I hate the
stuff."

"On which side of you I ride," Melchior said mildly, "is of no
matter to me. So long as we move forward. Perhaps I should

have told you. I am old, I need little sleep. I travel by night. Then, when the camel must rest, I take my reckonings by the star and mark my charts. You are young; you may find my way somewhat tiring."

Never, since he was ten years old and about to be taken, as a great favour, on his first desert raid in the company of men, had anyone spoken in that mildly admonitory, challenging voice to Gaspar. And then the voice had been his grandfather's, the voice of a man tried and proven, tough as leather, tempered as steel. To hear the echo now, from this old man, so frail, so just-brought-back from death by starvation, so sharply snatched back from despair, wiped out of Gaspar's mind every thought, every emotion except that of the primitive feeling of competition. Rome, Herod, Jexal, Ilya were all forgotten as he said:

"Ride ahead, my friend. And when you are tired, let me know."

CHAPTER V

Upstairs, in a cool airy room overlooking the terrace, the Lady had settled down to gambling, and downstairs her slaves were hoping, even praying, that her luck might be good. Her temper, at all times disagreeable, became savage under provocation, and nothing provoked her more than to lose at games—unless it was the failure of a tenant to pay his rent.

Balthazar stood a little apart from the rest with his arms folded so that the stiffened fingers of his right hand were held between his other arm and his body in a cradling, cosseting gesture. He was a scribe, an accountant, and his right hand was most precious; its gradual, increasing disablement gave him great anxiety.

He was not praying for the simple reason that he did not know to whom, or to what to pray any more. Years back, in Tyre, he tried all the gods, and one after another they had failed him. He watched, with gloomy detachment as one slave killed a dove and offered it to Aphrodite and another took four bleached bones from a bag and arranged them in a pattern and made a ritual gabble. Poor things! Upstairs the dice would fall as they would, indifferent to anything that was done down here; and if they fell unfavourably for the Lady, tomorrow everyone would suffer, more or less. He would suffer more than anyone except the Lady's body slaves, for he must every day, sometimes many times a day, go and stand in the dread presence. He cradled his right hand a little more closely remembering what she had done to it on one occasion, and might very well do again.

A great wave of hopelessness washed over him. Lately he had been prone to moods of miserable despair. Being a thoughtful man he attributed this, in part to his age; he was forty years old and the last of youth's hopefulness had drained away; he was no longer capable of feeling that around the next corner something better might be in store. I have, he admitted to himself, been disappointed too often.

The first of his disappointments had happened when he was twelve, a happy though sometimes hungry boy living in some nameless part of Africa, so far inland that on maps he had studied later it was just blank space. It was near a great river, not the Nile, and his tribe had its home where the river spread out over the flat land, making innumerable wide muddy shallows where the crocodiles had lurked, one eye watchful above the water's surface, ready to snatch at women who came to fill their gourds, and at men who came to fish.

The tribe had a god, the Great Crocodile, N'Zana. They believed that the ordinary crocodiles were his minions and that if they did certain things and observed certain rites N'Zana would favour them and keep them safe from his servants. Once a year at a time calculated by the old wise men of the tribe, three girls, virgins, without any physical blemish, were chosen and taken to a special hut where, no matter how low the food supply might be, they were fed and kept idle in semidarkness, so that at another date they might be brought out, sleek and fat; then they were oiled and garlanded with flowers, and to the beating of drums and the yelling of their fellow tribesmen, they were cast into the river and immediately torn to pieces.

Once a favourite sister of the boy who now bore the name of Balthazar had been one of the chosen virgins and he had not accepted it in at all the right spirit. His father had rebuked him, telling him that it was an honour to give a virgin to N'Zana, but he could not resign himself. All through the fattening season he moped and pined and when the day of sacrifice came he had hidden himself away and wept. Not long after, a woman going to the river for water had been snatched and drawn under and devoured and the boy, fearful of his father's wrath, but curious and rebellious had asked how could this be. The price of protection had been paid and where was the protection?

"You are my son," his father said; "but you do not always obey me. That crocodile was a disobedient son of N'Zana. He will be punished."

The forty-year-old Balthazar could tell himself that had he had any sense he would have learned his lesson then and there and spared himself much disillusionment. But at the time he had accepted it, and when, being twelve, he had been most painfully initiated into manhood, he had received his pierced crocodile tooth—the badge of a full man in his tribe—with pride, and had worn it for some months; until the slavers came, in fact.

The slavers came in the night, and N'Zana made no move to save or protect the tribe who once a year had given him their choicest virgins, and at all times the choicest joint of any beast they killed, the tribe whose chief, on ceremonial occasions, had worn the symbolic crocodile skull. N'Zana, said to be many times larger than the largest crocodile ever seen in the river, and to have four times as many teeth, had not come up from his hidden place and lashed about with his great tail, or snapped with his great teeth. He had done nothing. So the huts were all burned, the very young and the very old were left to starve to death with no one to care for them; the others were marched off, their necks thrust into forked sticks.

They had marched for many days, a long chain of misery; some had died. Those who lived were taken to the banks of another great river, the one which Balthazar now knew as the Nile; and there they were packed into ships, as closely as fresh-taken fish were packed into baskets, and taken to a place called Egypt where everything was strange and terrifying and the houses were as many as, and as tall as, forest trees.

There someone had rubbed powdered chalk upon his feet and he had stood on a block and several men had fingered his arms and legs, forced his mouth open and studied his teeth. Later that day, with other boys of about his own age, he had been taken into one of the tall houses and suffered something worse even than the initiation rites. The pain had been terrible and very hard to bear, with none of the hope, the pride which had enabled him to bear the elders' slashing and slitting; that had been destined to make him a man; this was destined to make him something less than a man. All that the initiation rites had conferred this more agonising process took away.

When he recovered—which every boy so operated upon did not do—he was tested as a singer. One of the results of the operation was to preserve whatever voice a boy possessed, and a slave who could sing and play some instrument was of enhanced value. Balthazar proved to have no ear, nor any potential skill as a potter or a painter which, after singing, were regarded as the employments most suitable for the truly black, woolly haired slaves brought from far inland.

"You have no skills," the owner of the slave-school told him, not angrily, but as a plain statement of fact. "I see nothing for you but to be a guard and escort for women."

By this time Balthazar had acquired a smattering of several languages and had talked to many people and learned a good deal; he knew that the life of a harem attendant was not an enviable one. It was tantamount to being a human watchdog, and who cares for a watchdog? Women, he had been told, were profoundly cunning and deceitful, and when a deception was discovered, who was beaten? The watchdog who had failed to be watchful enough. Also women quarrelled amongst themselves, and who must step between them lest they come to blows and damage one another's looks? Again the watchdog. Women, again, seemed from the tales he had heard, to bear a curious, deep-rooted enmity against his kind. Some of the tales he had heard were quite horrifying; and although amongst his tribe he had been regarded as a courageous boy, courage seemed to have left him with his manhood. He was very sensitive now, both to pain and to mockery.

All the things he had heard were not horrible, however; there were many tales about slaves who had been clever, risen to positions of trust, managed to save money somehow and had purchased their freedom, or so endeared themselves to their owners that they had been set free. There was one whole layer of society which consisted of freed men. Some of these even owned slaves themselves. It was, however, generally agreed that once the harem curtains had closed upon a half-man, he would stay there, like the other inmates, for life.

So, timid as he had become, Balthazar thought he must risk making one suggestion. Bowing his head, he said:

"Master, I am worthless. But I think I could learn the abacus."

The slave-trainer looked at him with astonishment. The arts of reckoning and of penmanship were regarded as too intellectual for slaves from far inland who could sing, make pleasing patterns with colours, mould pottery, mime amusingly and play the clown—all physical things, extensions or refinements of what came naturally to them, of what they would have been doing if left in freedom in their own homeland. The use of the mind was a different thing altogether; some people doubted whether they even had minds. Dubiously the old slave-trainer cast an experienced eye over the boy; a good lively eye, he reflected, and a promising forehead.

"We can but try," he said. "Fetch an abacus."

Eighteen months later he was able to put upon the market a property practically unique; a young, neutered slave who could read and write and reckon accurately; who was docile and teachable and reliable; and black, with the black's well-known powers of endurance and ability to eat almost anything. Most slaves who could read and write were Greeks or Semitics or half-breeds who resented their condition and were shifty or sickly; often they were men who had fallen into slavery on account of debt and tended to be followed about by hungry families, which made them attempt to be dishonest.

To the Greek merchant from Tyre, in Alexandria on business, and astonished by the price asked for Balthazar, the trainer said:

"Within three months you will think it too little."

And within three months the Greek was almost of that opinion; for in addition to all his other qualities the boy proved to be completely honest. The Greek, himself, a profoundly dishonest man, subjected Balthazar to the most subtle and cunning temptations his wily mind could devise and Balthazar never cheated him of a penny. And when a trader—bribed by the Greek to do so—offered him a bribe, Balthazar refused it, with the extraordinary excuse that there was no column for such things in his accounts book.

At the end of a year—it took so long to convince the merchant completely—he was able to say to his wife:

"Now, when I go on business there is no need for you to go downstairs and dull your pretty eyes checking the accounts. Balthazar is quite honest, or he has such a mania for accuracy that it amounts to the same thing."

In his work Balthazar was happy; but within himself he was always aware of a yawning emptiness. The sense of loss which he had felt after his mutilation had increased rather than diminished through the years. His sleep was haunted by dreams, pleasant in themselves but dreadful to recall when he woke because he would dream that he was a whole man again, back in his home by the great river, hunting and fishing with the men by day, and at night snug and happy in his hut with a woman who was always—this was the shocking part—the sister whom N'Zana had taken.

He was now enlightened enough to see the Great God of the Crocodiles for what he was, something that men in their fear of the ordinary crocodiles, and their impotence, had invented for their own comfort. He had lost his faith in N'Zana at the same time that he had lost his freedom, but deep inside himself he had a hankering for the comfort which only faith in something outside himself could supply. As he grew older and his need for an emotional outlet grew, he began to think about other gods, the gods worshipped by all these clever, busy people who had no fear of crocodiles.

In Tyre there was no lack of them; the flourishing polyglot port had much to offer to anyone seeking a god or a goddess. There was the Phoenician Baal in his many forms; Baal Tamar of the Palm Trees, Baal Perazim of the Wells, even Baal Zebubm, Lord of the Flies. His groves were everywhere. For the convenience of visiting Egyptians there were Temples to Isis and Osiris; for Greeks Temples dedicated to Zeus, Aphrodite, Diana, and a dozen more; the Romans had reared Temples to

Jupiter and Venus; the Babylonian goddess Istar had her sacred place, and so had the god recently brought from Persia, Mithras.

They all had one thing in common with one another, and with N'Zana, Balthazar discovered; they all liked presents; and presents he was prepared to give and able to give. On certain days of the year it was customary for masters to give trivial sums of money to their slaves; females spent these sums on finery for themselves and whole men spent them on finery for their women. Then, occasionally, after some particularly profitable transaction, the Greek would toss a coin or two to Balthazar; openhanded merchants would do the same. And he earned money too, by writing letters or making a reckoning for some unlearned fellow. Many slaves, commanding such resources, would have bought delicacies to eat, but Balthazar, often hungry in childhood, was quite content with the food in the Greek's kitchen, simple, monotonous, but sufficient. Nor had he any need to spend his little income on clothes, the Greek took pride in his slaves' appearance, and Balthazar, in the counting house, in the public eye, was better clad than most. And women, those ever avid, never satisfied creatures who made such demands upon a man's pocket, meant nothing to him.

So, bearing gifts, he made a slow round of the groves and Temples and underground shrines; looking at first for a place to rest his heart, for something to fill the great emptiness caused by the loss of freedom, of manhood and belief in N'Zana. It was much to ask, and he never found it. After his twenty-fifth year he asked something else, something simpler, of the gods. In his twenty-fifth year his right hand had begun to trouble him.

Laying down his pen one afternoon, he had stretched his fingers, as usual, and they had resisted the stretching movement and remained cramped, as though still clutching the pen he had laid aside. It had been a long day and he had written small, paper being expensive, and the cramp did not cause him much concern. In an hour it was gone and his fingers were as flexible as ever. But day by day the condition grew worse until there came a time when he went to bed with his fingers still bent about an invisible pen. In the morning, for a long time, his hand was better; and then one morning he woke to find his fingers still contracted, and in the centre of his palm a curious bony bump. After that, offering his flowers, his doves, his expensive spices he had asked of the gods not a resting place for his heart but a cure for his fingers, and the answer to the one request matched exactly the answer to the other. Nothing.

He could still write, which was something to be thankful for —but thankful to whom? His fingers, cramped into a writing attitude and clenched about a pen, could still do their work. But they were growing worse and abandoning the gods, once and for all, he took other measures. He gave his money to a man who took his afflicted hand and thrust it into a pan of almost boiling hot mud; to a woman who filled his palm with oil and gently rubbed and pressed and prodded until the oil had been absorbed; to a man who had attempted to press the fingers and the bony protuberance of the palm, flat between two boards, excrutiatingly painful and quite ineffective.

He had tried to learn to write with his left hand, practising surreptitiously; and his left hand could write, but in a fashion quite unsuitable to the narrow columns of an account book. It wrote a large, sprawling hand, square and ugly, and no amount of determination, no amount of practise, could make it write otherwise. And looking ahead into the future Balthazar saw himself like a chariot horse, injured at the races and sold, doomed to drag out a limping, ill-fed life, dragging a heavy cart until it died. He was a writing slave, and of what use was a writing slave with a crippled hand?

He was in this particularly vulnerable state when one of the house slaves died, died mounting the stairs to the living quarters and dropping, as he fell, a tray laden with porcelain dishes from Cathay in the far East, which the Greek in one of his travels and transactions had managed to acquire. Over the dead man nobody had mourned, but the Greek's wife's lamentations over the broken dishes had been loud and long.

The slave bought to replace the dead man was a Jew, named Eliezer, and he was, by his own account, a slave by choice. His aged father had fallen deeply into debt; "He was seventy, I was his youngest son. Unknown to me he had sold all that we had, and borrowed money from a Samaritan who demanded heavy interest. He was about to be shamed and disgraced. The Samaritan agreed to take me, and to cancel the debt. So I am a slave. But my father's debt was paid and I have obeyed the law Thou shalt honour thy father and thy mother. I was misled. By our law no slave can be held for more than seven years. Whatever his value, in the seventh year he must be set free. But other people have other laws and I have now been in bondage for twice seven years and my father, if he is still alive, is doubtless in debt again, being a fool in business. Still, I did what I could."

Balthazar was much impressed to learn that a man could voluntarily sell himself into slavery, that hated state, and even more impressed by Eliezer's indomitable cheerfulness which was not the cheerfulness of the light-headed and thoughtless kind which seemed to be the only kind available to slaves, and which Balthazar himself had never attained. This cheerfulness, he discovered gradually, was based upon hope and faith, both rooted in a religion, which as it was revealed, bit by bit, was astonishingly different from any of those he had sampled. Eliezer's god was a spirit who had on earth no physical representation at all and who demanded not the occasional present or the bowing down in this place or that, but control of a man's whole life, from the moment he waked in the morning until he fell asleep at night. "It is the Law," was Eliezer's explanation of everything, down to his refusal to eat certain kinds of meat and his frenzied attempts to do as much of the seventh day's work on the sixth as was possible. The reward for keeping this law might come in this life, "Jehovah never deserts a just man," Eliezer said, and it was plain to Balthazar that Eliezer still, after fourteen years of slavery, was hopeful for liberating action from his god; but this life was not all, a just man could count upon life after death when he would be gathered to his fathers and enjoy everlasting felicity.

It took some time for Balthazar to learn all this, since his work lay in the counting house and on the docks, and Eliezer's kept him to the domestic side of the house, but whenever they could they drifted together and the talk took a religious turn. One evening Balthazar stretched out his right hand which he usually concealed as much as possible and laid it on Eliezer's knee as they squatted together in the dusty courtyard.

"Look," he said.

"A handicap to anyone," Eliezer said gravely, having looked. "And doubly so in a scribe."

"If it were yours and you prayed for a cure, would *your* God answer you?"

Eliezer hesitated and then said:

"No. In the old days there were prophets who could work wonders; Elijah restored a dead child to life; Moses made a dry path through the sea. But there have been no prophets for the last five hundred years. Besides"—he hesitated again—"if Jehovah answered that kind of prayer nobody would ever be sick or blind or crippled . . . or a slave."

"Have you ever prayed, outright, for your freedom?"

"As I would ask for a melon from a stall? No. I have asked my God not to forget His servant in his bondage and exile. And that prayer He has answered."

"How do you know?"

"In my heart," Eliezer said simply. "In his heart a man knows whether he is forgotten by God or not."

"How?"

"He becomes melancholy. Perhaps I can best explain to you by way of a story . . ." He told Balthazar the story that all Jewish children knew, the story of their first King, Saul, who was forgotten by God and went melancholy-mad. And then by contrast he told another story, that of Job. He ended with a quotation, "Though He slay me, yet will I trust in Him."

Balthazar dimly realised that though this god of the Jews offered no remedy for the contracting fingers, he might offer some remedy for the apprehension with which he himself regarded the future, and also, almost equally important, something to fill the emptiness within him. When Eliezer said, "In my heart,"

Balthazar had understood, because his need was the need of all men, all the Temple-frequenters, the sacrifice-offerers, the need to feel that somebody, somewhere, saw you as an individual and *cared*.

After that talk he became assiduous in his questions. Did Jehovah have a Temple?

Yes, indeed, Eliezer said; it was in Jerusalem, the most beautiful and holy building in the world. It was the ambition of every pious Jew to visit it, at the Feast of the Passover, at least once in his life. Eliezer told Balthazar in great detail about the building of the Temple—which he had never seen; its destruction by Nebuchadnezzar, its rebuilding by the liberated Jews, under Ezra, by people who worked with a trowel or a shovel in one hand and a sword, a club or a dagger in the other—that made a stirring tale; and finally its enlargement and beautification by Herod.

"And here, in Tyre?" Balthazar asked. "Your god has no Temple here?"

Eliezer suddenly looked uncomfortable.

"One God, one Temple," he said. "In other places we have a meeting house, a synagogue, where the Law is read and expounded and the songs of praise chanted."

"There is one in Tyre?"

"There is one in any place where any number of Jews are gathered together."

"And you go to it?"

"When I can—which is not very often. A house slave has little leisure," Eliezer said. "Listen!" He jumped up with what Balthazar could only puzzledly regard as relief at the sound of the bell which summoned him.

There was then a time when Balthazar, hot foot after this, the last of his gods, found Eliezer very odd and evasive, which was strange, because to say the least a scribe-accountant by even talking to a mere house slave, honoured him. But the day came when Balthazar could say to Eliezer:

"I am interested in all that you tell me of your god. When next you go to your synagogue, tell me. I will ask leave to go with you."

Eliezer's face took on the peculiar colour which all pale-faced men showed under any strain.

"That is not possible," he said, avoiding Balthazar's eye.

"Because I was not born a Jew?"

He could see Eliezer wavering between tact and honesty. Honesty won and Eliezer said:

"It is not that. It would be better if you asked no more and accepted my answer—it is not possible."

"Because I am black?" He'd never been particularly conscious of his colour; it was true that most of his kind were slaves but that was because of their misfortune, not because of their colour, and there were plenty of men, quite as black as he was, who came to Tyre to visit or to trade and were regarded as the full equal of anybody except a born Roman citizen.

"No," Eliezer said; and he lifted his eyes and looked Balthazar straight in the face. "It is written, it is the Law as given by God to Moses. No man, maimed as you are, can enter the congregation."*

The forked yoke of the slave trader had fallen upon his neck, the gelder's knife had agonised him; but neither had hurt him as these words did. This was the final blow, because he had been all ready to give his heart, his whole being to this god of Eliezer's, who was a spirit and who answered prayers by gifts to the spirit and not to the body. He had been ready to say, with Eliezer, "Though He slay me, yet will I trust in Him," and "Yea, though I walk through the valley of the shadow of death, I will fear no evil." That was how he had always wanted to feel, how he was prepared to feel. And now . . .

"Your god is a very unjust god, Eliezer. And inconsistent, too. If, as you claim, he is a spirit, concerned with men's hearts and minds, that is a senseless rule. This thing," he said, in an angry voice that was in sharp contrast to his ordinary mild utterance, "was done *to* me without my wish or consent. No reasonable

* Deuteronomy. Chapter 23 Verse 1.

man would hold that against me, far less a god who, as you claim, sees and understands all."

"I am sorry," Eliezer said, "but I cannot help it. It is the Law."

After that Balthazar had finished with gods.

About a year later the Greek came home from the docks where he had been supervising the unloading of one of his ships, on a hot day and complained, in the counting house, of a headache and feeling of stiffness in the neck. His wife had sent for a physician who prescribed some remedies and rest in a darkened room. But next day he was worse, with high fever and pains in all his limbs.

Downstairs in the slave quarters somebody said:

"Cleo, bring your ball and look into it and tell us, will he live or die?"

Cleo was a young Nubian girl, recently brought into the household; she was a skilled hairdresser and spent most of her time in the bedchamber of the Greek's wife. She owned a ball, about the size of an egg, but rounded, of black obsidian, and she claimed that by looking into it she could see events that were yet to happen.

Balthazar, from the first, had regarded her as a fraud, and her fortune-telling as a means of gaining attention. But twice—this was undeniable—she had been right; once when one of the master's ships was overdue she had cradled the ball in her hands and looked into it and said, "It is wrecked. It has gone down in the sea." And once she had foretold the sex of an unborn child. Everyone else was much impressed but Balthazar considered these prognostications to be lucky guesses.

On this evening she brought her black globe, warmed it between the palms of her hands, stared fixedly at it and at last announced in a flat, dull voice:

"He will die."

There was a general groan, for the Greek merchant was, as masters went, lenient and conscientious.

"All men die," Balthazar said, a little sharply, the verdict being unwelcome to him, too.

"He will die on the second day," the young Nubian insisted. Then she pushed the globe into Balthazar's hand and said, "See for yourself."

He stared and was overcome by amazement; there, pictured in the polished black surface was the bedchamber of the Greek, his dead body on the bed and the embalmers busy with it.

After a long silence, during which he stared and stared, Balthazar protested:

"Yes. I see him dead. But there is nothing to show whether he will die on the day after tomorrow or in twenty years hence."

"Look closer. How many white rings enclose the picture?"

"Two," he said in exactly the voice he would have used if asked a question in the counting house.

"So!" the girl said. "He will die on the second day."

As she spoke the picture faded from the globe, and standing there with it, blank, in his left hand, Balthazar realised that he had just experienced something new and strange; he had seen something that had not yet happened as though it were already past. The obsidian was cold and heavy in his hand; he gave a little shudder.

"Put it away," he said.

Two days later the Greek died and the house was filled with the mourning wails of the slaves, to which were added, for a short time, those of the widow. But she recovered rapidly and began, in a level-headed way, to turn all the assets she had inherited into cash so that she could return, wealthy and independent, to her native Corinth. She had always, she said, felt an exile in Tyre.

The slaves began to plague Cleo to look into the ball again and see, if she could, what would happen to them who were to be marketed in just the same way and the ships, the storehouses, and the pack animals. Several times she made unsuccessful attempts: "I see nothing." But one evening, having warmed the ball carefully, she looked into it, gave a moaning cry and fell senseless. The ball rolled from her limp hand and somebody picked it up and gave it to Balthazar.

"You saw our master dead. See what is in store for us."

"It is better not to know," he said, remembering how Cleo had cried out. But they insisted and he was curious, in a way, himself. So, almost flinchingly, he looked and he saw himself, rather finely dressed, riding a camel in company with two other men who wore peculiar hats; one round, the crown running steeply into the brim, very much, in shape, like the roofs of the huts of his own tribe, the other a kind of cap with a white crown and a black brim. On his own head he wore a turban, made from a silk scarf, and his robe was richly red.

"You see something," the slaves cried. "Tell us. Tell us what you see."

"A happy future for all," he said, wondering about the meaning of what he had seen concerning himself. They crowded round, demanding details, individual forecasts. In his hand the ball had gone blank again and cold and heavy.

"I had no time to see small things," he said, handing the thing to one of the women who stood by Cleo. "I can only tell you that you were all happy."

But Cleo hanged herself from a beam sometime during the night and what became of the black ball nobody ever knew.

The widow retained Balthazar to the very last; there was a great deal of reckoning to be done; he knew about the business, and her husband had considered him to be honest. Several times in the ensuing months he was able to save her from those who would have taken advantage of her sex and her ignorance. Every time this happened and every time he made a shrewd or useful suggestion, she said, "You shall be rewarded," and he would think about the money piling up, how enormously rich she was, and dream that in the end she would write him his paper of manumission and set him free. In the globe he had worn the clothes, ridden the camel, of a prosperous freedman and he knew that could he once attain his freedom he could become prosperous. He could set up as an accountant and scribe, and charge for his services. Perhaps the two men with whom, in the vision he had been riding, were clients of his, merchants from far away, glad to make use of his knowledge of languages and of currencies.

All this pleasant speculation ceased when the widow, wearing the aspect of one who has performed a good action at some cost to herself, told him that she had sold him to a Roman.

"I could have obtained a better price for you," she said, in warm, complacent tones, "but I bore in mind how well you have served me lately, and the state of your hand. With your new master you will not be required to write so much, or so small. Theodor Metellus is growing old and losing his sight. You will have an easy life with him, just reading to him and writing a few letters. I hope you are pleased," she added, changing her tone as she saw the sagging disappointment in his face.

He was bitterly disappointed, and also dismayed. The Romans, as slave-masters, had an unsavoury reputation. Hardly two generations had passed since the Roman world had been rocked by a great uprising of slaves, led by Spartacus. It had been put down with the utmost severity, but it had not been forgotten; Romans still regarded their slaves as potentially dangerous and behaved to them accordingly.

Contributing to his dismay was the knowledge that he had been sold cheaply because, in slave-market parlance, he was "unsound." And, as with pack animals, the way in which a slave was treated was in direct relationship with value. There was also the question of Latin; his, picked up by use in the streets and the counting house was not of the kind that a Roman gentleman would require or expect.

He wondered once more, as he had wondered many times before, what Cleo had seen in the obsidian to make death preferable. And how reliable was information from such a dubious source? The black ball, like the gods, like the widow, had let him down.

There was nothing to be done, however, and on the appointed day he took his little bundle of possessions and moved across the city to the residential quarter where fine villas stood, remote from the noise and bustle of the quays and the business quarters. It was with a certain amount of relief that he noticed that the slave who admitted him looked well-fed, well-clad, and cheerful.

Metellus was a lawyer who had enjoyed a considerable reputation, both as a scholar and an orator; he was old now, and on account of his eyesight, virtually retired, though still active in a consultant capacity. His great dread was that he should become dependent upon his slave secretary—he had seen that happen with other ageing men—and for a long time he resisted Balthazar's well-meant attempts to make himself indispensable. "I am still capable of doing that," he would say; or "Don't take too much upon yourself, Balthazar." And long after he had ceased to see at all he would reach out blindly for a paper and say, "Let me look." In the end, however, he succumbed to his new slave's genuine ability, desire to please, and gentle manner. As much friendship as could exist between master and slave existed between them; Balthazar was made free of Metellus' considerable library and they spent hours together in talk.

Metellus was a Stoic, and without in any way aiming to convert Balthazar—for how can a man be persuaded into an intellectual state—he introduced him to that stark, impersonal creed, the reverence of natural principles, the respect for reason, the uncomplaining acceptance of one's fate. They talked of Zeno, of Cleanthes and Chrysippus, and of Posidonius, whom Metellus tended to decry as being "too mystical." It was a far cry indeed from the doves of Venus, the groves of Baal, but after all, Balthazar would reflect, they had failed him, Stoicism could not do that. It had one fault, however; it underestimated the importance of a man's emotional life; it was a creed, Balthazar realised, for whole men, for aristocrats, for men whose emotional needs had been satisfied elsewhere. Nevertheless, adherence to it gave a man dignity; see how uncomplainingly Metellus accepted his blindness! In such company Balthazar found it easier to disregard his contracting hand. Also, the widow, greedy, false, and selfish as she had been, had also been right in one thing. With less writing to cram into constricted spaces his hand suffered less from cramp.

This leisurely, comfortable, peaceful life lasted for five years; towards the end of that time Metellus had become entirely dependent upon Balthazar whom he called "my amanuensis." Fewer visitors came to the secluded house; every year there were new young lawyers appointed, men to whom Metellus was merely a name, a man whose books could be consulted in any library.

One young man, however, was a regular caller. He was a lawyer named Marcus, born of a Roman father and a Syrian mother. Partly because of his mixed blood—for though in a multi-racial Empire racial equality was paid some lip service, truly Roman Romans regarded themselves as superior to all others—and partly because he had indulged in practises not considered strictly ethical in legal circles, he enjoyed small esteem amongst his fellows and it pleased him to be received in the house of a man, who, though old and blind, was of unblemished reputation. He was fond of saying, "I must ask Metellus' opinion on that." Then his hearer would say, "Metellus? Is he still alive?" And Marcus would say, "Very much so; I dined with him yesterday."

To Balthazar, Marcus always behaved with arrogance. "I have something to ask you, but that can wait until we are alone," he said more than once. Most often Metellus would say, "If you ask me something and I need to refer to a book, Balthazar can find it quickly." Or, "You can speak freely before my amanuensis, I like to have him near in case I need something." Balthazar regarded the young lawyer with a dislike somewhat out of place in a true Stoic and occasionally showed it, murmuring a correction of a date or a name, sometimes even going so far as to say, when asked to fetch a book, "There is no need, sir. I have that passage by heart." Metellus would smile and say, "You see, Marcus; he is my eyes and my memory, and, I suspect, a better lawyer than either of us."

But the evening came when, on Marcus' arrival, Metellus himself sent Balthazar out of the room on a reasonable excuse: and as soon as he had gone, he said:

"I want you to do something for me. Write that man a paper of manumission and I can sign it now. Then you can hold it until I die."

"I trust, sir, that that day will be far distant," Marcus said politely, and truly, since his friendship with Metellus lent him status.

"I think not," Metellus said calmly. "I am older now than most men live to be; and I have had warnings." A Stoic did not waste time describing symptoms, except to a doctor from whom he hoped for relief; nor did he invite sympathy. "You know what to write," he said; then, as he felt for the edge of the paper, fumbled it into position and signed it, he added, "I am reasonably sure that if Balthazar knew of this it would not affect his behaviour one iota except to make him grateful and more doggedly devoted. And that would irk me. So you keep it and regard it as part of my will. The contents of a will should never be divulged."

"I will hold it safe, and trust that it may prove an ineffective instrument, sir."

"And what may that mean?"

"Only that you may outlive him."

"Then you wish me ill. To replace him I should need a nurse and a scribe, and still be at a loss for a companion."

A bare three months later Metellus died, in his sleep. The young man, Marcus, remembered his mother's sister, a woman of wealth who lived in Edessa and from whom he had great expectations. She was always in trouble with her stewards; free men, freedmen, slaves, she'd tried all and never been satisfied. So he destroyed the paper of manumission, and at the sale of Metellus' effects bought Balthazar very cheaply, having ostentatiously drawn attention to his afflicted hand. Then he personally conducted Balthazar to Edessa so that his aunt might thank him, face to face, for his thoughtfulness and consideration.

Knowing nothing of how nearly he had missed being set free, Balthazar could hardly be said to be disappointed. Now and again he thought that if Metellus had not died so suddenly, had he had time to realise that he might die, things might have been different. On the other hand his Stoic creed might very well have influenced him to think that Balthazar was a slave as naturally as he himself was blind; unpleasant states both, and to be borne without complaint.

He was glad to learn that although Marcus had bought him, he was not taking him into his service. Stoutly he braced himself to learn new ways, to fit into a new household, to be obliged, probably, to learn another dialect, to please, if possible, his new mistress. He was thirty-four now, the extreme adaptability, the resilience of youth had gone.

Within a week he realised that he had fallen into the clutches of a woman not entirely sane. The Lady, as everyone called her, had been so corrupted by great wealth and almost absolute power that she did not know her own mind from one hour to another and her rages were frightful to see. In a rage she had no respect for anything, not even for herself. Balthazar had seen her, in a stamping temper, pull out her own hair and throw it away from her as though it were obscene. And Marcus must have been disappointed by the reception of his present.

"I don't like eunuchs!" the Lady had said. "They're always eating." She rapped out, in gross terms, the reason for their thinking food so important. Then she said:

"What's wrong with his hand? What use to me is a steward who can't write?"

In happier circumstances Balthazar would have gloated over Marcus' discomfiture, and tasted to the full the irony of hearing Marcus, who had always seemed to despise him, lauding his abilities and virtues.

"I'll believe all that when I have reason to," the Lady said. And to Balthazar, "Straighten your fingers, man!"

"Madam, it is impossible. They have grown this way. For many years now."

"Let me look," she said, less sharply; almost kindly; and innocently he had extended his hand.

She took it in hers which were satin-soft, plump, decorated with many rings, pretty, feminine, harmless-looking hands, but they were strong as steel as, with a quick movement she clutched his wrist in one hand and with the other attempted to bend back the crooked fingers. It hurt much more than the pressure between the two boards, for then the contracture had not been so complete. Balthazar's black face turned grey, sweat sprang out on his forehead, he was obliged to lock his teeth to prevent the escape of a cry of agony. Worst of all, as she flung him back his hand, was the sight of her face with its look of pleasure, of satisfaction. A person who enjoys the pain of others, he thought, with a feeling of complete despair; and I belong to her!

To Marcus, immune from physical ill-treatment, she said:

"And why should you bring me a black? You know I loathe them. They stink!"

"This one is clean," Marcus said placatingly. He might have been speaking of a pet dog, house-trained.

Balthazar realised that never until now had he plumbed the depths of humiliation which being a slave involved. How fortunate he had been hitherto. First the old slave-trainer in Alexandria, anxious only to produce the most marketable product; then the Greek, busy with his money-making and valuing anything which contributed to it; then the Roman, reasonable and just, and in the end dependent. He had been a slave for a long time, but this was his first taste of slavery.

Now, at the end of six miserable years, he stood apart while his fellow slaves called on their gods, and worked their magic and upstairs the Lady shook the dice box. And he was empty, of hope, of vigour, of everything except what he knew now to be a nebulous dream. Suddenly he could not bear any longer the company of his fellow slaves, so he went to the open door and sidled out into the courtyard.

This was a very different place from the dusty, dung-scented yard of the Greek's house in Tyre. Every corner of the Lady's

house was swept and scrubbed, polished, fussed-over. This courtyard was enclosed on three sides by the walls, with their arched
openings, of the house itself; the fourth was the terrace with its
marble balustrade, upon which, at intervals, were set marble
vases filled with flowers. Immediately below the terrace the land
fell away, first to the Lady's pleasure ground, and then, lower,
the vegetable garden, and below that again, the orchard. Still
farther down the slope were the towers and the roofs of the city.
On suitable days, midway between the winter's chill and the
summer's heat people would sit on this terrace with the Lady
and congratulate her upon her view and she always accepted
the compliments as though she had made the slight slope with
her own hands.

Tonight, in the darkening, slightly purplish twilight, the rail,
the struts, the vases of the terrace's edge looked black against
the sky. From overhead came the sharp rattle of the shaken dice
box and the shrill voices of excited women. Balthazar moved to
the edge of the terrace and stood there thinking of tomorrow,
and of all the tomorrows that would follow after. To a certain
extent, during the last six years, he and the Lady had come to
terms, terms of her choosing. He was of value to her, he knew,
and to a certain extent she trusted him; in the service of any sane
woman his position would have been assured and he would have
been immune from ill-usage; but in this woman there was something dark and dreadful, unreasonable and perverse; the thing
which had once, when he had done her a service that nobody
without a knowledge of accountancy and law could have done,
had made her, thanking him, suddenly take off her shoe and hit
him in the face with it, and split his lip and make the blood run.

He stood on the dark terrace, thinking his dark thoughts and,
without realising it, staring at one of the black curving urns,
freshly planted that day with sweet-scented flowers.

And there he was, dressed as before, with those two men, instantly recognisable; and this time they were riding into the
gateway of what could only be a great city; he could see the high
walls to the left and right, made of enormous blocks of stone and
within the walls tall towers and the upper stories of buildings

that must be either temples or palaces. The gateway and as much
of the street as he could see was as crowded as the busiest parts
of Tyre.

He stared and stared in amazement—not that he should be
seeing a vision, for while it was happening it seemed to be real,
the only thing happening in the world—but that the men with
him should have been so instantly recognisable, their faces as
familiar as though he had known them always. The old man,
very thin, with high cheekbones and mild, study-wrinkled eyes,
the young man with a face like a hawk's: queer company for
one another, and queer company for him.

From the upper room came the sound of a slight crash, followed by a cry. Balthazar gave a little start and instantly the
picture was gone; there was the black, smooth-sided urn, no
different from its fellows.

He at least had something to think about during the next day,
when the Lady, who had lost heavily, was so intent on making
everyone wretched that her ill-will extended even to peasant
farmers she had never seen, men who wrested a meagre living
from an outlying estate of hers, two days' journey away to the
East. They were all, she shouted at Balthazar, to pay increased
rents, either in cash or kind, and he could tell them so when he
went, at the end of next week, to do the rent collecting. It was
not a prospect that he relished. They lived such miserable lives,
already, that sometimes when he left them he would compare
their lot with his; a slave was reasonably certain of his next meal,
at least; then as he walked and the distance between him and the
Lady decreased, his pity for them would change into envy.

Her losses on that evening had convinced the Lady that she
was on the verge of penury; everybody's ration was reduced, and
when Balthazar asked could he have a new pair of shoes before
he set out on his long walk to the estate she said, "No. Wear
what you have," and hit him on the head with a heavy silver
comfit box which happened to be handy. "And don't pretend
that hurt," she said as a slow trickle of blood ran out of his hair
down his forehead. "A skull of wood, and woollier than a sheep!"

That evening he went, as he had gone every evening since that of the disastrous gambling party, and stared fixedly at the urn in which he had seen the picture. He knew that by doing so he was merely inviting yet one more disappointment, but he felt drawn to the place, to the urn. He remembered Cleo and how she had often said, "It has nothing to tell me." What governed such things, he wondered. Were those two men—and himself—there, in the urn and he unable to see them? Had he merely imagined the experience which had now visited him three times? Or was it, each time, a dream? In which case, over the death of his master, he and Cleo had dreamed the same dream almost simultaneously.

While he was thinking in this way, something moved in the dark depths of the urn. It was a star, much larger, much brighter than any of those that scattered the heavens and it moved, perceptibly, down, down until it was very low; then it seemed to swell and splinter into something that he could never describe, a great burst of glory and beauty and wonder, very real and yet unreal, as though colour had sound, and sound had taste, and taste had shape. An entirely new world, he thought, obliged to close his eyes against the dazzle of the revelation.

When, timid and dizzy, he opened his eyes again the urn was as it had been at other times, and loneliness weighed on him like a sickness. To whom could he say, I saw a star burst and the world was made new, with no more slavery, men of all colours made equal, the rich giving their goods to feed the poor? And if there had been one to whom he could say it, how feeble and ineffective the words would have been, how incomplete the other's understanding. And how, even to himself, could he explain that this vision was inextricably connected with the two men in peculiar hats. But it was. . . . And he must, somehow, find those two men.

He went to his bed and lay and gave serious thought to a subject he had not really considered since he was a boy in the old slave-trainer's establishment in Alexandria—how to run away and not be caught. In a civilisation based upon slavery this was an extremely difficult thing to do, and doubly difficult if you hap-

pened to be black. And the punishments devised for runaway
slaves were deliberately designed to deter all but those already
made crazy by ill-treatment. In addition to being black he was a
eunuch—and no free man, save an ecstasy-drunk priest of Baal
who had mutilated himself, was that.

Still, he thought, sturdily, even a black man, even a eunuch
might have bought himself free, or been manumitted.

Now, he thought, pursuing that thought, if my master the
Greek, or my master Metellus, or my mistress the Lady had
manumitted me, I should carry a paper, signed or sealed.

The Lady had never troubled to learn how to write her name,
but she had a seal, a great square topaz set in silver, which, when
she pressed it into the hot wax which Balthazar had prepared,
left in the wax a sheep's head in the centre and in each corner
the initials of her personal and family names. (Her father's
wealth had been made from sheep; once there had been a great
sickness and thousands of sheep had died; his had stayed healthy
and he had been able to sell a ewe in lamb for the price usually
charged for a tiger, an elephant, or a fully trained performing
bear.)

She never, even in a temper, let the seal out of her keeping,
and demented as many of her actions were Balthazar knew that
there was no hope of presenting her with a forged manumission
paper, amongst several others and getting her to seal it. Where
anything concerned with business or money was concerned she
was very shrewd. But he had, in his possession, many of the little clay tokens which it was his duty to give to tenants in ex-
change for their money, their corn, their jars of oil, or wine
which constituted their rent. Every quarter, as he went round,
he issued new clay tablets, a different colour for each new quarter, and collected the old ones.

It was just possible that he could smear the face of one of these
stamped tokens with oil and press it against some fresh-dribbled
wax. He would then have a replica of the Lady's seal. . . .

Next day he wrote himself a document of manumission,
phrased, although he did not know it, almost in the very words
which Marcus, that clever lawyer, at Metellus' bidding, had

used. Then he forged the seal. Transferred from topaz to clay and from clay to wax and then to wax again it lacked the sharp, immediate impact of the original; but looking at it critically he thought it would fool most people.

There were other, cunning little moves to make. In the ordinary way he spent two days on his journey, two days rent collecting, two days on his way home. But this time, before he left, with the forged document tucked into his breast, he said:

"My Lady, the increase in rents that you have ordered, will bother these people and may cause some delay. The usual rent they have, hidden in the wall or under the floor, if it is in cash; put aside in barn or storehouse, if in kind. Faced with the increase most of the tenants will be obliged to run to the money-lender, or fill other sacks and jars. I say this because this may take me more than six days."

She said, "Did I not make myself clear? I want this increase; I *need* it. And you are to stay there until the last penny, the last grain of corn, the last drop of oil or wine has been yielded up."

"That might mean, my Lady, that I should be absent for two weeks."

"What of it?" she said. "Do you think that I shall pine for the sight of your ugly face? I know what you are thinking of. In this house you eat full and sleep soft. For two weeks you'll miss your comforts. Three even, if some of them have to sell their children to meet my demands."

Yes, it might even be three weeks before she missed him and said, "Where is Balthazar?" And after that, at least two days' grace, waiting, wondering, expectant. And then the hue and cry; runaway, a neutered slave, black, the fingers of his right hand bent, aged forty, hair turning grey, when last seen wearing . . .

He knew it all, he thought, as he passed from the Lady's presence for what he hoped with all his heart would be for the last time. Once she knew, and the news was out, everybody would be on the alert, avid for the reward.

But he had, at least two, at best three weeks; he had, if challenged, his forged document; and he had on the one hand his hope, on the other his despair. If he failed, if his dream like everything else in his life simply led to disappointment and he was brought back, he would take his fifty lashes and his branding, and he would die. . . .

On the night before he left he gave sensible consideration as to the best direction to choose. The really practical thing, he knew, was to go to the estate at Babila, spend a day collecting the rents that were immediately available and then disappear from there; he would thus acquire money for his journey, he could buy the camel and the clothes which, in his vision, had seemed to be his. But this procedure was distasteful to him, not only because he had never stolen a penny in his life, but because it seemed wrong to start out in pursuit of something unspeakably wonderful by committing a theft. Also—and it was amazing how even a slave could find reasons for not doing what he didn't want to do—to act in this way would be to act exactly as the Lady, when he failed to turn up, would guess that he had acted. She would send first to Babila, two days' journey to the East; by moving Westwards at once he would add four days to the time he had in hand. So he would go West; taking with him the few coins he was allowed to purchase food. Apart from that he had nothing, for in Edessa—or at least in the Lady's household —the charitable custom of making small money presents to slaves on certain days, was not honoured; nor had she allowed him to write a letter or make a reckoning for anyone other than herself. He had attempted it in his early days in Edessa, where there were plenty of ignorant persons willing to pay for such a service. The Lady had said, simply and spitefully, "If you can't find enough work to keep you busy on my business, just tell me, and I will help you." He had known what that meant!

So, meanly clad, his shoes already broken, and with just money enough to purchase one evening meal, he set out, very early in the morning, and since he would be looked for first in the East, turned West as soon as he reached the city's boundary. Then, for two days, he dared not use the highway for fear of being seen by someone who knew the Lady and might recognise him and report. Walking across country in this way was a slow process, for he was traversing a belt of highly cultivated land upon which Edessa depended for its market produce and the plots were divided by walls of stone loosely piled one upon another, by fences, by irrigation ditches. Also there were no shops where food could be purchased. On the first day, except for the "dawn-bit" which he had eaten before setting out, he ate nothing at all; on the second, seeing a woman outside a lonely little house, milking a tethered goat, he had approached her and asked could she sell him something to eat. She rose to her feet, looked at him, with fear and then, searchingly, all round; looking for his accomplices.

"I am alone," he told her. "And I am not a beggar; I can pay."

Her expression did not change, but she nodded, and taking up the bowl of milk, went into the house, walking in the stiff-legged way of one who wishes to hurry but deliberately refrains from doing so. He heard the bolt on the inside of the door jolt into place.

He stood there, feeling disheartened; without eating he could not travel; and he realised again that a slave's life, though full of humiliation, and, in the power of anyone like the Lady, pain, was a sheltered one; he had been used to eating regularly. Even in Edessa when the Lady was angry or needlessly economical and the quality and quantity of the food had been reduced, there had always been something, served up at regular times.

Resolutely he cast his mind back to the days of his youth, particularly to the brief period between his initiation and his capture, when he had been allowed to go with the men on their hunting expeditions. They never went out until the food supply of the village was almost exhausted, and what little there was left in store stayed there for the support of the women and children. In the morning they would say, "Tonight we eat full." But often enough there were days when they had no success and lay down with empty bellies. They'd thought nothing of it; nor had he, then. The forty-year-old Balthazar thought, I am not the man my father was. Then he thought, Naturally not; I am not a man at all. And he wondered whether the Lady had been right when she said that eunuchs thought of nothing but eating.

Next day, still moving West and travelling across country, he was fortunate and fell in with a woman more brave, or more charitable, than the first. She sold him some wheat porridge, cold, and set almost as firm as bread, two small onions, and a cup of goats' milk. He carried the onions with him, and ate them just before he lay down under a wall and went to sleep.

On the third day, after a long laborious climb up a ridge of rising ground, planted on its lower slope with olive trees, above that bare and rocky and very damaging to his poor shoes, he found himself looking down upon a road, carrying considerable traffic and running—he took his bearing by the sun, slightly South West—North East. He scrambled down the ridge and joined the traffic that was going, so far as he could judge, away from the direction of Edessa. There were trains of pack ponies and donkeys, trotting along in a haze of dust; camels swayed under their loads. There were mounted men and ladies being carried in litters, and so many people on foot that Balthazar felt himself to be reasonably inconspicuous.

Hunger bothered him again and presently he had proved that he had no skill as a beggar; nothing came his way that day, and the situation was made worse by the fact that all along the road people were eating, and there were places where food could be bought. Bread freshly baked in a village shop smelt delicious and brought the water into his mouth; so did the sight of a pedlar, resting against his pack and eating the leg of a chicken.

Towards evening he came to an inn. Poor travellers who were prudent and determined to get good places for themselves on the covered platform that ran around the yard, and good places for their beasts in the enclosure, were already settled and eating the food they had brought with them; from doors and windows in the inn itself came the odours of the meal being cooked for wealthier people who could afford to eat indoors, in comfort. Balthazar paused. There must be a great deal of work to be done in an inn at such a moment; animals to be fed and watered, dung to be swept up, dishes and pots to be washed. He turned in and at the door asked, most meekly, whether there was anything he could do in return for a meal.

"I don't encourage beggars," the innkeeper said. "Puts people off if they think they're going to be accosted and bothered."

"I wouldn't accost or bother anyone. I'd just do anything you'd have me do, whatever it was, in return for something to eat."

To that the innkeeper did not even bother to reply; he pursed his lips and whistled, and from somewhere a dog appeared, and without a bark or a snarl or any evidence of hostility, sank his teeth into Balthazar's wrist, and held him.

"That'll do," the innkeeper said; the dog loosed its hold and backed away.

"Now you be off," the innkeeper said, "unless you want another dose."

Outside the place he was obliged to stop and tear a piece from his tunic to make a bandage for his wrist which was bleeding profusely. It dawned upon him—and this hurt more than the dog bite, or the blisters, just beginning to break on his feet, or the hunger-gnaw in his belly—that he had come out on a ridiculous errand, hunting for two men he did not know, who might even now be travelling in exactly the opposite direction. Even at this low moment he did not doubt their existence; they were as real to him as the surly innkeeper, but he was beginning to fear that he might die of hunger, and never find them.

Miserably he wandered on, and in a short time heard, from the side of the road where there was a clump of myrtle trees, the sound of several men's voices, laughing and cursing; the scent of charred flesh reached him. He ventured cautiously around the trees and saw that he had stumbled upon a group of soldiers, Roman soldiers, who had bought, or commandeered, a suckling pig, and made a fire and were now endeavouring, clumsily, to cook it by using their swords as toasting forks. Even as he watched, it slipped and fell into the fire which spat and sizzled.

"Jupiter give you a pig for a first-born," one of the soldiers said. "We want it for eating, not for a burnt offering." He reached out and, taking the pig by its hindleg, retrieved it.

Balthazar moved forward, a shadow emerging from the shadows and said in the faultless Latin he had learned from Metellus:

"I could cook it, if you would permit me."

At least they were not frightened and did not turn upon him eyes of fear or any of the emotions that fear engendered.

"See," one of them said, "didn't I tell you that this was enchanted country. We need a cook, and one walks in."

"In disguise!" another said. "As unlike a cook as any I ever saw—and I've seen a few. Can you cook, fellow?"

Balthazar had never cooked anything in his life; but he had seen cooking done.

"I can cook that pig," he said.

"Then cook it," said the man who held it by the leg, "and shout when it is ready for eating." He gave the greasy, half-charred little body to Balthazar and turned away. The others turned away too, towards a dim lantern that stood on the ground. They were Romans, the dominant race and to them it did not seem strange that out of the dusk service should come and offer itself. One of them, just beginning to throw the dice, was annoyed when Balthazar came behind him and asked could he borrow his knife. No slave of the Lady's was allowed to carry a knife or anything capable, in the most farfetched circumstances, of being used as a weapon of offence or defence.

Handed the knife, Balthazar cut two forked branches and planted them firmly in the ground, one at each side of the fire. Then he cut a long, stout stick and forced it through the body of the suckling pig; the protruding ends he lodged in the forks of the branches and the pig hung there, near enough the heat to cook, far enough from it not to char. He sat down by it, now and then replenishing the fire, now and then giving the long stick a turn so that another portion of the pig was brought in contact with the heat. A mouth-watering smell overpowered the scent of charring and spread about the little camp. One of the men turned and called:

"How long will it be?"

"Not long now, sir," Balthazar called back. He thought how tender the white flesh would be, the crackling how crisp, the fat how sweet, and was obliged to wipe his mouth on his sleeve.

For the first time in many years he remembered Eliezer, who would have starved before he would eat pig meat, or hare, or venison. At the time he had respected Eliezer's respect for his Law and admired him for it; now it seemed ridiculous. Though no more ridiculous, he thought, than casting yourself into a hostile world on account of a dream, a waking dream. Then, because every man must attempt to justify his own form of madness, he thought that after all his action might not have been so ridiculous, even if he never found the men he was looking for. If he could keep alive and stayed on this road while the Lady hunted for him around Babila, he might come to a city large enough to hide in and set himself up as a street-corner scribe. In that there'd be none of the wonder and glory he'd come out to find but one thing he'd dreamed would have come true. No more slavery. He'd thought that that had applied to the whole world, but maybe he had been mistaken; maybe it applied only to him.

Presently he tested the meat with the knife; the point ran in easily, even in the thickest part of the leg. He threw earth on the fire to deaden the heat and then carefully lifted the forked sticks and planted them again a little way away.

"The meat is ready for eating, sirs," he said, and walked a little distance away.

"I want my knife," said the soldier who had lent it.

Balthazar, apologising, brought it back; by this time the others had fallen upon the meat as though they were starving, and Balthazar licked his lips.

"You hungry too?" asked the knife-lender in an offhand, but good-humoured way. "Move over, Varro. There you are." He turned back to Balthazar and offered him a chunk of meat from the point of the knife. Nothing had ever tasted so good.

He slept that night under the myrtle trees, and was wakened by the clatter the soldiers made as they moved off. He ran to the place where the pig had been hacked to pieces and breakfasted on the scraps of meat which still adhered to the scattered bones. The meal and a night's rest had restored his spirits and his hope of meeting the two men was lively again. He resumed his walk, studying carefully anyone who rode a camel.

On that day he made less progress for the blisters on his feet had begun to fester. By mid-day the dog bite on his wrist was troubling him, too; when he let his arm hang it throbbed like the worst kind of toothache. But he refused to be discouraged by his sores, or by his marked ill luck in begging. He was now on one of the great highways of the world and anyone who lived beside it and had a charitable heart could have stood and given away all that he possessed in forty-eight hours; and those who carried their food with them were concerned lest their supplies should not last to the end of their journey. In three days after leaving the soldiers he ate twice, once on a half-rotten apple which a fruit-seller threw out because it might contaminate the sound ones, once on a piece of barley bread given to him by an old woman who was eating as she trudged along with a bundle of laundry on her head.

He arrived at the caravanserai at the crossroads in the dead hour of the afternoon on the seventh day. It was an imposing place, occupying the whole corner between two of the four roads that met. Just inside the yard which gave upon the wide open space where animals were stabled was a stone drinking trough, and a little girl, with one shoulder higher than the other—and, he presently saw, one leg shorter than the other—was emptying a wooden bucket of water into it.

He said, "May I drink?" Finding anything to drink had also been something of a problem on the highway; people were actually *selling* water!

"It's for beasts, really," the girl said. "I'm just going to draw another bucketful. I'll bring you a cup, if you like."

"This will do," Balthazar said, cupping his hands and drinking eagerly. She limped away. He splashed the lovely, the beautiful, the free, cleansing water over his face and head. He ripped off his makeshift bandage and plunged his wrist, with its aching, festering wound deep down into the trough. He was about to kick off his shoes, climb to the edge of the trough and ease the sores on his feet in the same way, when the girl came limping back. His thirst slaked, he looked at her more closely; she wasn't dressed like a slave.

"Are you," he asked, "the daughter of the house?"

Her thin little fingers touched first the folds of her dress, worn and dirty, but in its day a dress of quality, and then the silver ornaments in her ears.

"These are for show," she said. "I am a slave."

"Oh," he said; and he was a little disappointed. She was kind, she'd offered to fetch him a cup, and a child learned its attitude from its parents; he had hoped that the father might be kindly too, and let him do a job and give him a meal.

"Could I speak to your master?"

"Not now. Not for an hour. He is asleep; or in bed with *her*."

"I wanted to ask: Is there any job I could do to earn myself a meal?"

"A lot of people ask that. He always says 'No'—except to fortune-tellers. After they've eaten, most people like to have their fortunes told. If you can tell them"—she looked at him dubiously—"you would be welcome; but not otherwise."

"I'm so hungry," Balthazar said, "that to get a meal I'd become a fortune-teller."

"I can give you something to eat. Every day we cook more than enough." She spoke eagerly. "Wait there," she said, and pointed to a nook made by the house wall not running quite in line with the lower wall that enclosed the place where travellers' beasts were herded. "That," she said, "is a good place. I go there when I cry."

He went and sat down, eased off his shoes, unwound the dripping wet bandage and looked at his wound. It was worse; that dog must have had poison in his teeth! His whole wrist was puffy and hot, and from the two punctured holes yellow pus was oozing, giving off an offensive smell.

The girl, and although she limped, she moved quickly, came and presented him with a wooden platter, heaped, piled with what was plainly the remainder of several main dishes.

"It doesn't look very appetising, but it is all good," she assured him. "I've lived on it for three years."

"It looks good to me," Balthazar said, digging his fingers into the rice, the bits of gooseflesh and mutton, the leaves of artichokes, the cabbage. Looking at the girl he judged her to be about thirteen, so if she had been here, living on left-overs for three years she must have fallen into slavery at an earlier age than he had . . . or perhaps she had been born one. . . .

"Three years," he said, "you have lived here for three years?"

"Three, thirty, three hundred. I lose count of time. She"— she raised her eyes to the blank, recently whitewashed wall that jutted out above this secluded little corner—"she marks every hour and one new wrinkle under her eye rocks the house. I," she said, tapping her flat little chest, "am a slave, but, sometimes I think, less a slave than my master. She is very pretty and has a heart of stone."

"Is it because of her that you come here to cry?"

"Sometimes. Sometimes it is for my family in Antioch. Sometimes"—she looked away from him—"it is because of the things I have to do. I have to . . . sleep with men," she said.

Balthazar, chewing on a gristly bit of mutton, looked at her and wondered what sort of man it could be who would wish to go to bed with her, so immature, so crooked? She sensed, and indirectly answered his question.

"In the dark," she said, "when they are eager and inflamed by *his* promises, they use me. Afterwards they are . . . ashamed, and angry with themselves, and with me. Afterwards, when a pretty girl would get smiles and presents, I get curses, and blows. You see," she said simply, "*she* won't have a pretty girl in the house. She uses her bed as a stick to hold over my master; it would never do for him to have another bed to go to." She looked at him, saw comprehension and sympathy in his eyes, and went on. "She wouldn't have another woman of any kind in the house except that she, the wife of an innkeeper, the daughter of a pig-butcher, thinks herself a lady and must be attended in her bedchamber. And it is impossible," she said, "quite impossible for anyone to work as I do, in the yard and the kitchen, and still have hands smooth enough to handle hair as it should be handled."

Something in the way in which she had said "pig-butcher" prodded Balthazar's memory.

"You are a Jew?" he asked.

"Yes. My father is a shoemaker in Antioch; three years ago he fell ill; more than three years ago, I have been here for three years. Jews are well liked if they are thriving; when they fail to thrive they have no friends except other Jews, as poor as themselves. He owed money, not much, but some, for leather, for thread and wax, also rent for the house, and those to whom he owed came in a body and said he must sell something and pay his debt. He offered to sell his tools but they were worth little. My brother was four years old, my sister still at the breast. If my father had sold himself they would starve. So, weeping, and in great sorrow, he sold me." She raised her chin a little. "Sometimes a pedlar, a friend of my father, passes this way and we send messages. Always my father says that he is saving to buy me free, to be patient and keep the Law and work well and freedom will come; always I send back a message to say that I am happy and have a good master and mistress. I think sometimes that this is contrary to the Law, 'Thou shalt not bear false witness,' but it harms no one and comforts my father and my mother."

"And observes the Law about honouring them."

"You know about that," she said eagerly. "You know, when you came to drink at the trough, something in my mind said, this is not a beggar, this is a prophet! And it is strange that I should think that, since you are not a Jew. But you know our Law."

Balthazar nodded. "A little." He racked his memory for some words, used by Eliezer, and applicable to this child's case. He found it. "Sorrow may endure for the night, but joy cometh in the morning!"

"Oh," she said, her ugly little face transfigured, "you do know! That is a saying from . . ." She broke off as a loud, ringing female voice called, "Susie!"

"I must go. I've wasted time . . ." she said, and limped hastily away.

Balthazar stayed where he was in the sheltered angle between the walls, the hidden place where Susie came to cry. The meal he had just eaten weighed upon him with a comforting, enervating weight. His wrist, freed of the rough, bloodstained bandage and recently cooled in the trough hurt less than it had done.

He dozed. The somnolent, dead afternoon hour ended with an inrush of travellers, anxious not to be on the road after dark, anxious to secure room for themselves under the tiled awning which sheltered the platform that ran about the enclosure for animals, or, if they were rich a private sleeping chamber and a place at the table where the meal was served for such as could afford it. Balthazar roused himself, not without self-reproach. Indirectly he had justified the Lady's jokes about eunuchs; out in search of the indescribable, the wonder for which there were no words, he was still a slave to his need to eat and sleep.

He rose and stretched himself and took a step or two out of the secluded corner into the main entry of the yard. He was thirsty again and intended to take another drink from the trough.

He never took that drink; for as he emerged from behind the corner of the house, two men, on camels, sagging, exhausted camels quite unlike those he had seen in his vision, rode into the yard. And their faces, their hats, everything about them, except that they, like the camels, looked utterly exhausted, was exactly as he had seen them in his waking dream. Even the hats, about which there could be no mistake.

He ran forward with all the joy, the incredible excitement of one who finds a dream translated into fact.

"You are those I have been seeking," he cried, in his weightless tenor voice. "You follow the star. I beg you, take me with you!"

They looked at him with blank, uncomprehending faces. And of all the bad moments in his life, that was quite the worst.

CHAPTER VI

Melchior and Gaspar had not been travelling a week before the younger man had learned one very useful lesson—toughness had little to do with appearance. The old man, so frail and so thin, was never the one to suggest that they had travelled far enough for one day; and to Gaspar, not yet accustomed to the motion of his camel, the days, extending far into the night, seemed very long. In the end he was compelled to protest, not on his own account—that he would have been ashamed to do— but on account of the camels.

"By the Sun," he said, "no wonder you lamed your other camel! These will drop dead under us if you go on this way."

It chanced that he first said this in a desolate place; had it been in a town or a village, Melchior would probably have answered that they could buy fresh camels; but even he could see that *here,* should the camels fail, there would be nothing for it but to go ahead on foot. So he said:

"You were right when you said that I needed a practical man as a companion. I never thought of the camels!"

"But you must yourself be tired," Gaspar said.

"My bones are tired," Melchior said; "but they have been tired for so long that I no longer notice them."

And when they halted, wherever that might be, by the roadside, to eat food that they carried, or in the crowded caravanserais, the day was still not ended for Melchior; he must take out a chart and make his complicated reckonings, the results of which were never to his liking. "We must move faster," was always his verdict. The need for haste obsessed him, and soon another problem arose. "Night by night," he said, "I grow more doubtful about our destination; it lies South of Jerusalem. Of that I am almost sure."

Gaspar, who had come out with the intention of seeing Jerusalem, and Herod too, if that could be managed, always tried to console him.

"You told me, on the first day we met, that this child was to be born of a royal house; and Herod is King in Jerusalem. It may be that he has a Palace for winter and a Palace for summer, or one in the city and one in some quiet place, suitable for a breeding woman." The Kings of Jexal had owned a Summer Palace, on high ground above the river, and Gaspar spoke with some assurance. "We must make first for Jerusalem, and there ask."

When he said this for about the twentieth time Melchior, who had never denied that this might be the most sensible thing to do, suddenly said:

"And in what tongue?"

The matter of language was becoming a problem in itself. As they moved Westwards the dozens of dialects and mutations of the tongue which was common to them and which had been carried by the successive waves of emigrants from their original homeland, had become less and less of service to them, and Melchior had been obliged to fall back upon his book-learned Greek, a language he had never heard used and every word of which he must pronounce in all possible ways before he made himself understood. So long as they were moving, all unknowingly, along the road which Alexander and his men had twice travelled, where wounded men, exhausted men and various camp-followers had stayed and sometimes remained, Melchior had managed, not without difficulty, to make himself intelligible enough to buy what was needed, to ask a few questions and obtain answers. As they moved Southwestwards they had found that nobody at all understood any variation of their common tongue, and fewer and fewer people could understand Melchior's version of Greek. When Melchior asked, with a slight bitterness, "And in what tongue?" they had been moving, for several days, through a region where educated people spoke Latin and the common people some form of Aramaic—as varied and as seemingly universal as their own tongue was in the areas

reached by successive impacts of the great Mongolian invasions.
Gaspar answered the question in his usual blunt way.

"That," he said, "I must leave to you, Melchior. You are the
scholar. I am merely the provider." And that, Melchior realised,
was not said as a reproach, it was, like most of Gaspar's statements, plain fact. Food, for man and beast, accommodation,
tolls at bridges and ferries, everything had been paid for from
Gaspar's pouch. And the man himself was a good fellow-travel-
ler; tireless, uncomplaining. And considerate. Many times he
had insisted that in a caravanserai Melchior should occupy a
private room. Private rooms were few and costly. Ordinary travellers slept on a kind of platform, sheltered by an awning which
ran around the open space where animals jostled and brayed
and scratched and moaned. Gaspar always, when they slept in
a caravanserai, chose to sleep there, not in a private room. "I
like to sleep in the open; but for you I will buy a room," he
would say. "You have your work to do, and coming back would
disturb us all; also, since you sleep so little, you must sleep
soundly, undisturbed by a child crying or an ass braying." In
many ways Gaspar behaved to Melchior like a son—the son he
had never had. They depended upon one another, and it worried Melchior a little that though Gaspar's contribution to their
journey, the gold he carried, was acceptable everywhere, his
contribution, his book-learned Greek, was becoming less and less
of value. Also it was evident to him that Gaspar's goal was Jerusalem.

There was something else, also, that troubled Melchior. Gaspar's curiosity and interest in people that he himself would have
passed without a second glance. "Are they soldiers? Roman soldiers?" Gaspar had asked once, with some excitement. "Ask.
Find out." And he had checked his camel, and Melchior's had
immediately slowed down too. The men had been Roman soldiers, and Melchior admitted that it was clever of Gaspar to
have guessed so shrewdly; but what of it? What did Roman
soldiers matter? You could waste time, most valuable time on
things like that. And some of the soldiers, not understanding
what Melchior said, made gestures that even he understood, rude.

. . . On the whole the standard of manners and of hospitality declined as they moved Westwards, and, unless they were being grossly cheated, prices were still rising steeply. Melchior had realised before reaching Jexal that he had no skill as a bargainer; Gaspar had never bargained in his life and was, in addition, unused to handling money, and seemed not to notice prices at all.

The strain, the haste and fatigue, differences in character and in objective, even the sense of being so dependent upon one another, would have resulted in bickering had Melchior not been so naturally courteous and Gaspar the heir of a long tradition of respect towards elders: but on the day when their path converged towards that of Balthazar they had almost quarrelled.

Gaspar, who had always believed that he could outride and outfast any of the Five Hundred, which meant any man alive, was galled to find that this old man, skeleton-thin, was not only prepared to stay on the jolting camel for at least an hour after he himself was reeling with fatigue, but that he was also more indifferent towards food. On the morning of that day, having slept in the open, they had eaten the last scrap of food that they carried, Melchior insisting that Gaspar should take the larger share. "You are young," he said, "and accustomed to feeding well." But he had waited, with obvious impatience, as Gaspar gulped down the stale bread, the bit of stinking cheese. His overnight calculations had been very unsatisfactory. "We shall be late," he said, with dismal certainty. "This child will be born, at latest, four days after the winter solstice, and after that there are a few days' grace. Then, if I am not there, all my efforts will be wasted. We must press on today."

They had pressed on and just as the sun was setting had reached a point where the road sloped steeply down towards a huddle of roofs that indicated a sizeable town. Gaspar pointed to it and said:

"We stay there for the night."

"Oh no. We shall be there before it is full dark. We must travel until moonset, at least."

"Our food is exhausted, our water-bags are empty, our camels are spent. To go farther would be folly. Tonight we seek an inn and have a meal of cooked meat. We buy stores for tomorrow. The camels restore their strength. Tomorrow we shall travel faster."

"I have no time to waste upon meat or stores or camels," Melchior said stubbornly. "I told you from the first that my errand was urgent. Nothing else matters. I must press on."

"Then you go alone," Gaspar said, and as soon as he had said it, realised his folly. It was now a long time since anything he said had been understood by any save Melchior; difficult as it was to find in these parts people who comprehended the old man's other language, such people were to be found, and they constituted the sole hope of making contact. Melchior, equally dismayed, remembered that Gaspar had the money in his pouch.

He said, "This country is more thickly inhabited; if we ride on until moonset we shall reach another town."

"That I wouldn't count on. Unless you show some sense, Melchior, you will arrive at the place after this"—he jerked his head towards the little town—"in worse case than you arrived at Jexal."

"There was nothing wrong with me when I arrived there," Melchior said petulantly. "My camel was lame, that was all."

"You have a short memory! You were so nearly starving that I was obliged to warn you to eat little and slowly."

"Very well, I was starving and I am prepared to starve again. A man with his mind set can endure a little starvation and take no harm!"

That was the kind of thing which Gaspar was accustomed to saying, not to hearing said, and it irked him.

"Camels can't live on their thoughts," he said. "Go ahead, if you wish to be stubborn, and see how far you get!"

Melchior thought that over. Something of the despair he had felt as he limped into Jexal, returned and made itself felt again. From that despair Gaspar had saved him.

"You have been very good, very generous," he admitted. "You are hungry and you are weary, and part of my mind tells me that you are sensible. Particularly as regarding the camel. It occurs to me that Senya may have gone lame because of an empty belly. An empty belly shows no symptoms, gains no sympathy; lameness does both. If we halt here"—the first houses of the town were now alongside—"will you agree to start out *very* early in the morning?"

"Very early," Gaspar said.

So, when they reached the inn, they had turned into the yard, and had been immediately accosted by a beggar of exactly the kind that Gaspar most deplored, the kind he had banished from the streets of Jexal.

Ignoring him, he nudged his camel forward, Melchior, more courteous, even to a dirty stinking beggar, said in his rusty Greek, "I am sorry, I have nothing." And to that Balthazar replied in the Greek of the counting house of Tyre:

"I ask nothing, except that you should take me with you as you follow the star."

"Star! Did you say star? What do you know of the star?"

He gave his camel the signal to kneel and dismounted with stiff haste. He was ready to think that this was a fellow astronomer from some far, far place, who having done work similar to his own had reached the same conclusion, and the thought set his heart pounding from excitement.

Two lengths ahead, farther into the yard, Gaspar's camel in some extraordinary way had sensed that its companion had knelt and been dismounted, and since what was right for one was right for both it knelt without waiting for the signal. The innkeeper, watching from his doorway, saw two men, not impressively clad, and a third whose appearance was a disgrace, and two wilting camels, obviously in the last stage of exhaustion; so before Balthazar could answer Melchior the man rushed out, crying in Aramaic:

"Not there! You block the entrance!"

Neither Melchior nor Gaspar understood a word he said, but they realised that they were being shouted at; Melchior turned upon the man a look of dignified inquiry, Gaspar one of a ferocious hauteur. The combination silenced him.

Balthazar said to Melchior:

"He says we block the entrance to the yard."

"Only for a moment," Melchior said. "Would you tell him that we wish these beasts taken to the enclosure, watered and fed, as much as they can eat? For ourselves a supper, with meat, and a room inside the house."

While Balthazar was obligingly translating these orders Melchior watched him, taking more fully into account his poor condition: he'd share his supper with him, he thought, though it was unlikely that he would be welcome inside the house, either by the innkeeper or by Gaspar, with his so-sensitive nose. But all that could wait. They must first discuss the star.

His first reaction to Balthazar's blurted tale was one of deep disappointment.

"Ah," he said, "a clairvoyant! Not that I decry clairvoyance, but unlike astronomy it is an inexact science, if indeed it can be called a science at all. Still you are here, and you recognised us; and you are the only person I have met in many months who seemed to have an awareness of this star at all." He pondered the significance of this.

"You will take me with you? I beg of you. I will serve you, wait upon you, be your slave," Balthazar said, willingly putting his head back into the yoke from which he had so recently freed it.

Melchior thought of Gaspar and his money pouch; he looked back to the time when he had been rich and independent, and to the time when he had been poor, but independent, and he gave a sigh that came from his heart.

"That is not easy. And it is not for me to say. I have nothing of my own. All I ever had was spent in the pursuit of knowledge. To accompany us you would need a camel, a good camel . . . But wait here. I will speak to my companion."

He went into the house where in a public room Gaspar and a few other travellers who could afford the luxury were consuming the mutton and the onions and small crusty loaves of fresh-baked bread. He intended, as he took his place, to appeal to Gaspar in much the same way as he had done in the Palace at Jexal, but looking sideways at the hard young face, he had a better idea.

"There is a man who could be of inestimable use to us," he remarked in an almost offhand way.

"That black beggar!"

"He is not a beggar by trade. He is a man of education. He speaks the tongue that has served me fairly well, so far, but has become less and less useful lately; and he also speaks the language of the country. It has worried me, to think that we might reach our destination and not be able to make ourselves understood."

"That is a thing to consider," Gaspar admitted. It was not a situation which his own mind would ever have presented to him, but now that it was put to him by someone else he was able to visualise it quite clearly.

"Are you suggesting that we take him with us?"

"It would be a convenient arrangement."

"But he stinks! Washed and reclad he might be tolerable. And he would need a camel."

"He would need a camel," Melchior agreed, picking at his food and looking at Gaspar from the corner of his eye.

"Could he fit himself to travel with us, *very* early in the morning?" Gaspar emphasised the *very* just as Melchior had done earlier.

Remembering the almost wild urgency in Balthazar's voice and eyes, Melchior said with assurance:

"Oh yes; he would be ready."

"Then he'll need some money," Gaspar said, feeling for his pouch. How many? Unconcerned as he had seemed about the cost of things he had realised that his money had lost value as he moved Westwards. But even here, surely, ten would be enough. He passed the coins, unostentatiously, into Melchior's hand. "And tell him, from me, to do something about that running sore on his arm," he said.

Melchior took the money with a feeling of relief and of triumph, and of gratitude.

"I hope," he said, "that you will have reason to regard this as money well-spent." He picked up his plate and went back to the yard where Balthazar waited, patiently, sitting against a wall.

"It is arranged," Melchior said. "You are to come with us, if you can obtain a camel, and fresh clothes and be ready to set out before sunrise. Also you must wash and find some remedy for the sores on your arm and your feet. Here is money."

He held it out and Balthazar's eyes bulged. He'd seen such coins—but only on three widely separated occasions—in the counting house. The most valuable coin in the world, not only because it was so heavy, of such pure gold, but because of its beauty. It was greatly in demand, not as currency, but as a decoration. Men who could afford it hung their women with gold coins both as a means of advertising their wealth and as a form of investment; and a rose jekkal was of all coins the rarest and most sought after. Any woman lucky enough to own one wore it in the very centre of her forehead, exposing the side which showed the full-blown rose which gave the coin half its name.

"Ten! I don't need ten," Balthazar said when he had caught his breath again. "Two will buy all I need and leave a great deal over."

"It must be a *good* camel," Melchior reminded him. "We must travel fast. And in this country everything is very expensive. When last we filled our camels' food bags the man who supplied us took one of these."

"Then he was a thief and you were cheated. Grossly cheated. There, also, I can be of service to you. I am an accountant, of great experience. I recognise even a rose jekkal, and know its worth."

"Take two then," Melchior said. "And look, I have brought you some food." He held out his hardly touched supper.

"That was a kindly thought; but thank you, I have eaten. Not long ago. And even had I not, I could not waste time on food just now. I have a lot to do."

"You," Melchior said, "are a man after my own heart."

"And you are one of those of whom I dreamed. I knew that once I could find you, all would be well."

Melchior carried his plate back into the house. The fat had

congealed as the food cooled and it was no longer the appetising dish that it had been; he ate it without noticing, absent-mindedly and in haste. He still had his charts to consult, his reckonings to do.

"You still here?" asked the innkeeper who had been called out of the house to settle a dispute between the two men who each claimed that the other's donkey had eaten his donkey's food. "I don't like beggars hanging about my yard. But you did a good service, speaking for those strangers, so take this. And be off." He pushed a penny towards Balthazar who pushed it away and said:

"I wish to buy a camel, a *good* camel. Perhaps you can tell me where to go."

Innkeepers always knew what was for sale and where; they advised travellers, and if a sale resulted they were given their percentage.

"I myself have a camel to sell. A prime camel, young and swift. A merchant came here and fell sick; we nursed him tenderly, my wife and I, but he died." Balthazar gave a little inward shudder at the thought of what that tender nursing had been. "He owed us a great deal," the innkeeper went on, "and we shall never be fully paid. There is the camel and some clothes of the kind that there is no demand for in this place!"

"Show me the camel, and also the clothes."

"Show me your money."

Balthazar held out the two rose jekkals, gleaming against his pinkish palm.

Two of them, the innkeeper thought; one for his pretty wife to flaunt, one to sell!

"Come with me," he said.

Balthazar knew, even before he saw it, that the camel would be a good one; and he knew, with absolute certainty, that among the dead man's clothes would be a dark red robe, and a head-scarf of the same colour, striped with blue and woven with a silver thread. And they were there, together with everything else, down to the very shoes which he had seen himself wearing in his dream. Exultant, bemused, one half of him gloated and rejoiced, the other half, the accountant half, stayed unmoved and bargained shrewdly. The innkeeper craved the two rose jekkals and they were too high a price to pay for an untried camel, however good-looking, and a dead man's clothes. A full bath of hot water must be included. "Oh yes, yes," the innkeeper said, "the maid shall prepare it."

"Also," Balthazar said, "I need ointment for my blisters and the place where the dog bit me on the arm."

"We have, in this town, a woman most skilled in the making of ointments and potions. She keeps her own bees, and grows the pink Cistus that yields myrrh," the innkeeper said, thinking of his percentage. "She lives a little way along this street, in a house with a broken fence. It is late," he said, "and when you are bathed and reclothed, it will be later still. But if you tell her that I sent you, she will open her door."

"Very good," Balthazar said, spreading his open palm to which the two rose jekkals were now stuck. "The camel, these clothes, enough change to buy the ointment. *And*," he added in a fierce tone, alien to his own, "the freedom of the little lame girl."

"But consider," the innkeeper protested. "Even for two rose jekkals, that is much to ask. Also the crooked one does not belong to me. She is my wife's slave."

"Then you must ask your wife; does she wish for two rose jekkals to hang on her forehead or not."

For the first, for the only time in his life Balthazar felt omnipotent; on this side the fulfilment of his dream, on this the possession of two rose jekkals. . . . And yet, thinking of the little lame girl, he was sad. Tomorrow the pretty, hard-hearted wife of the innkeeper would buy just such another and treat her just as badly. And then he remembered what he had seen when the star splintered and revealed the new world that was about to come. Save the little girl now, he thought, because it was obvious that unless something was done she would not live to see that new world; the next poor creature to fall into the hands of the innkeeper's wife might be stronger, more resistant. We must play for time, Balthazar thought. He said:

"Well?" in the stern tone he had cultivated for use with the Lady's tenants.

The girl is clumsy and is always crying, the innkeeper reflected, and Ophelia does nothing but grumble about her. The next one may not be so very unattractive and maybe when Ophelia is angry with me and bars me from her bed, I could . . .

"It is a bargain," he said, and stretched out his hand, itching for the touch of the two rose jekkals.

"You must write the girl her paper of manumission," Balthazar said.

"But there is the difficulty. I shall need the services of a scribe. I myself cannot write."

"I can," Balthazar said. "You, I presume, can make your mark."

"I make a good mark; it is recognised and given credit as far away as Antioch," the innkeeper said, with some pride.

"That is well. Now, we will have the camel tethered alongside those of the lords with whom I leave in the morning; my bath will be prepared, and these clothes brought to its side. When I am reclad I will write the paper and you shall make your mark thereon."

"It shall be done. You wish to take the girl with you?" The innkeeper was prepared to believe almost anything by this time; for to a man who had seen two, *two* rose jekkals in the palm of a filthy, sore-ridden beggar, nothing could come as a surprise.

"No. Once free, she will make her own way to where she wants to go," Balthazar said. "Now, what about my bath?"

When he was dressed he wished that he had a silver mirror, as large as the one on the Lady's dressing-table, in which to behold himself, but there was none; however the way in which the woman herbalist received him assured him that he looked respectable and well-to-do. He smiled a little sardonically as he reflected that had he arrived at her door little more than an hour ago, begging a crust, she would have bolted it against him in terror.

She made ointments of all kinds she said; he asked for the best, and she said the best ointment deserved the best jar. She had a number of little pots on a shelf, most of them made of the coarsest thickest clay, one or two of fine, almost translucent alabaster. As she turned to take one of these down he stopped her, indicating the ordinary jars.

"What a pity," the old woman said fretfully. "The clay pots break easily; these"—she laid her gnarled finger almost caressingly upon an alabaster one—"last forever, for all they look so fragile."

"But once my sores are healed and the ointment used I shall have no use for so small a pot."

"This is my best ointment—smell for yourself; full of myrrh, my own. A smear tonight and another in the morning and you'll never know you had a sore. And it keeps, in fact it improves with keeping. Are you sure you won't change your mind?"

"I am sure."

She was grieved, and spooned the ointment into the little clay pot almost reluctantly.

He went back to the inn and anointed the broken blisters on his heels and the inflamed bite on his arm and then wrote out a paper of manumission worded exactly like his own. The innkeeper made his mark gladly; his Ophelia was delighted at the prospect of wearing a rose jekkal in the middle of her forehead and had said that for such a coin she would give six slaves, had she six to give. He was anxious to get to bed with her while she was in such a good mood.

"There you are. Now you are free, child," Balthazar said. "You can go and find your family in Antioch. Never lose this; never part with it. It is your freedom."

"Even if it meant nothing," the little girl said, clutching it to her flat chest, "I would keep it to remember you by. It smells of you."

He had written it after using the ointment, without washing his hands.

In the morning another and less favourable comment was made upon the ointment odour.

"Yesterday," Gaspar said, "he stank of dirt and rotting flesh; today he stinks like a harlot." As he said that he became aware that for several days he had not been conscious of the scent of the frankincense which Melchior carried at the bottom of his camel-fodder bag. When he had caught occasional whiffs of the fragrance he had blamed them for the way in which his mind reverted to Ilya. Yet now, with the scent forgotten, he still thought of her. This realisation made him annoyed, so he regarded Balthazar with disfavour.

"Come along, come along," he said irritably. "I thought we were in a hurry!"

"It was you," Melchior reminded him mildly, "who warned me against pushing a camel too hard early in the day."

Yet although he regarded Balthazar as his protégé, to be protected from criticism and, in an oblique way, spoken up for, he watched the black man's fumbling mounting and inept management of the camel with some dismay. With money, with language he would be a valuable companion; but if he slowed down progress he must be jettisoned at once. Nothing, nothing in the world must be allowed to delay them now.

Balthazar was aware that he was on approbation. Melchior, so considerate overnight, seemed different this morning, preoccupied and remote; in Gaspar he sensed a latent hostility—perhaps he felt that his money had been wasted upon fine clothing. If he could have spoken to Gaspar direct he would have explained that the clothes were not new, that he had driven the shrewdest possible bargain. But he did not dare disturb Melchior's thoughtful intensity by asking him to translate; and he could see that he must give all his mind to the problem of managing this animal—he had never ridden a camel before. He must also, for as long as they were together, endeavour to be of service, to make himself indispensable.

Gaspar wished that he were on horseback. A good horse could outrun a man's thoughts. On the other hand, any man worthy of the name should be able to govern his thoughts and prevent them from dwelling on the charms of a pale, frail, entirely unsuitable girl.

"Ask him," he said, jerking his head towards Balthazar, "whether he knows anything about the Romans."

"Yes, indeed," Balthazar said, when this question had been translated. "For many years I lived in the household of a Roman lawyer—as an accountant. I speak Latin. My Latin is very good; superior to my Greek or my Aramaic."

Melchior gave this information to Gaspar, hoping that it would cheer him. He attributed the younger man's mood to his having been compelled to rise so early. He was a rich young man, and rich young men were not accustomed to rising at dawn. He told Gaspar what Balthazar had said, and added:

"Is it not fortunate that we should fall in with one who knows so much about the people in whom you are so interested?"

Thinking of Ilya again, Gaspar said shortly:

"Very fortunate."

CHAPTER VII

I

The announcement about the new taxes came as a shock to everybody. It was made in typical, sly, Roman fashion. Probably notices were put up in public places, probably the tax-farmers, already informed, had begun to spread the news; but in Nazareth, and hundreds of other small country places, it was left to the local rabbi to make sure that everyone understood.

Harvest was over, the heat of the summer was past when Hilliel the baker, wearing his prayer shawl, stood up to break the news. The Torah had been taken out, read and solemnly replaced; the whole congregation had joined in the last chanted praise and people were preparing to disperse when Hilliel, at the raised reading desk spoke, not in his formal, synagogue voice, but as though making a remark across his bakehouse floor.

"I have been asked," he said, "to tell you something. It is not a thing I wish to speak of in this dedicated place, so would you, please, go out and wait under the sycamore tree. It is," he added, "something of importance. Please wait."

In the synagogue women and men sat separately; at the doorway Joseph, joining Mary, slipped his hand under her elbow and said:

"Would you rather go home? Your father or your mother can tell us whatever it is this evening."

Anne came every evening, whether or not she had seen Mary during the day. She had been delighted, transported to learn that her daughter was to have a baby. "So soon!" she had said to Joachim. "To tell you the truth I always thought Joseph was just a mite *old!* But no youngster could have done better." Then, immediately, she had fallen into the ambivalent state of mind of women in her position; there was nothing to having a baby, nothing at all, no need to fuss. If you were sick, you were sick

and you ran off to be sick in some private place; and if your
back ached, it ached and you bore it without complaint. Bearing
children was what women were put into the world for, a pregnant woman was a fulfilled woman and she should be joyful.
But, there was another, a darker side to this whole business.
There were women—Anne could have named three or four—
who had been careless, who had pushed or pulled or heaved
things and lost the baby in a welter of blood and pain; and there
were women who had craved things out of season and either
not mentioned their craving or been denied what they craved,
and their babies had been born too early, too late, ailing, de-
formed, even blind. "If you hanker for anything," Anne had
said, on the first day when she knew that with any luck she
was to become a grandmother, "you just tell *me*. Joseph is a good
man, but no man can understand these things. Tell me, and I'll
sell a calf—after all I rear them, all by hand; and I'll send to
Sepphoris for whatever it is, *whatever* it is." With her managing
nature she had been slightly disappointed that Mary had never
expressed any desire for something which, unobtainable in a
village like Nazareth, would be for sale in a great new city like
Sepphoris, only a good hour's walk away, and the most completely Romanised city in Galilee. On the other hand, she had
been pleased, and proud that her daughter wasn't being fanciful
and whimsical. Pleased and proud. Puzzled, too, by Mary's dis-
inclination to discuss her condition or the actual date when it
might be expected to end.

"But you must *know*," Anne had insisted, and she had gone,
in great detail, into the intricacies of that calendar which, never
written, never acknowledged, yet governed women's lives. So
many days and a doubt, so many more days and a certainty, so
many more and a delivery. Every woman, however simple, could
do that reckoning.

Mary had never contributed anything to Anne's reckonings,
she had never contradicted and Anne had thought, How fortunate that she will have me, and not be dependent upon the midwife! And every evening, every single evening, she had walked
down the village street, always with some excuse, in order to

make sure that Mary—we mustn't fuss or treat this as anything but an ordinary happening, part of ordinary life—was well, needed nothing and was taking care of herself.

She had joined them now and was subjecting her daughter to keen but tactful scrutiny, speaking as she did so about the latest acquired of her many remarkable bargains, a length of the very finest linen, straight from the loom and only needing to be bleached before being fit for a baby's use. "You'll be surprised when you see it," she said, "it's not the kind of stuff you see every day; it's more like silk. Fit for a prince!"

What was wrong with that, she wondered, seeing what she called "that funny look" on Mary's face. In the next second she had explained it to herself; Mary was frightened that the implied assumption of the child's sex might be unlucky. "Or a princess, come to that," she added.

At that moment Hilliel, divested of his prayer shawl, emerged from the synagogue and moved towards the little mound out of which the sycamore tree grew. Joseph, in a lower voice, repeated his question and Mary said:

"No, let us wait. It won't be long."

Hilliel cleared his throat and said:

"I've been asked to tell you, first, that we're all to be taxed anew." There was an outbreak of groaning and Hilliel, when it had died down a little, said, "Yes, it is unlikely that there'll be reductions—I've never known them go down. The second thing is this—there's to be a new register, and to help with its making every man is to go back and register at the place where he was born."

This was greeted by a brief astonished silence broken by one voice saying in dismay, "But I was born in Beersheba!"

Mary and Joseph looked at one another and each saw that the other's face had whitened. They'd never spoken about the matter—though they had both heard the prophecies read and quoted often enough to know that Bethlehem, David's city, was the destined place for the birth of the Messiah. The truth was that almost immediately after Mary's return from her visit to Elisabeth, they had ceased to talk about the baby in any but the most ordinary human terms. This reticence had not come about by arrangement, or by the imposition of the will of one upon the other; it had simply happened: as though the truth would have been too much to live with day after day and they must take refuge in the pretence that everything was ordinary and normal.

The people were now battering Hilliel with questions.

"When is this register to be made?"

"By the last day of the month they call December. For us mid Tebeth."

Satisfaction stirred in Anne's heart. As well as she had been able to reckon—with so little help from Mary—that would mean that Joseph, who would have to walk from Nazareth to Bethlehem and back again, might be away at the time of the birth. Men were nothing but a nuisance at such times, so she'd be glad to have him out of the way; and his absence would give her the perfect excuse for having Mary home; with a little persuasion she would stay there until her purification rite. It couldn't have been better arranged.

The crowd did not share this feeling.

"What's the idea behind all this?" a man asked.

"I know no more than you. But I can guess. I think the Romans are using the tax as a cover for a census taking."

"By *our* Law forbidden. On them the guilt! But that could have been done without uprooting so many."

"It's a scheme to ruin us all," said the disgruntled man from Beersheba who had just counted how long he would be away from his smithy.

"It can hardly be that," Hilliel said. "Ruined people can't pay their taxes. It may have something to do with our names. I believe the Romans find them difficult. Maybe they thought that if all the David-son-of-Davids were together on a given day it would ease matters. But I don't know. All that I was asked to tell you I have told you."

He stepped down.

Anne, losing no time, said, "Mary, don't give a thought to being alone. You must come and stay at home, with me, until it's all over."

Mary said, "Thank you. It was kind of you to think of that so quickly; but I shall go with Joseph."

Surprise, and the deepest possible consternation held Anne silent for some seconds; then she said, in a voice that made the dispersing congregation halt and turn and stare:

"Go with . . . Are you out of your mind? Ninety miles, on foot. In your last month! Child, it's impossible. Never, in all my days have I heard such a witless notion. Mid-winter, too!"

Even as she spoke she realised that she was making no impression. To a woman of her competent, managing nature, not to be able to manage this—after her own marriage and child-bearing, the most important event in a woman's life—seemed unbearably frustrating. The hurried, ill-attended wedding had been bad enough, but at least that had been a challenge, and to arrange things in a short time as well as most women could have done in a long one had given her a secret satisfaction. This was quite different. The possibility that her grandchild should be delivered and swaddled by other hands than hers made her feel positively ill. Angry, more vehement sentences began to form in her mind, but a glance at Mary's face informed her that railing would do no good. So she tried cajolery.

"You didn't mean that. You spoke without thinking. Suppose, just suppose that your time should come when you were far away from me. What would you do? How would you manage? You hadn't thought of that, had you? You come back home, my dear; back to your own room, so snug and cosy, and let me look after you." Then, without allowing Mary time to speak, she added a cunning touch. "If for no other reason, you must think of Joseph. He could be there and back in the time it would take you to get to Bethlehem. You wouldn't want to waste his time, would you now?"

Mary knew her mother. When chiding, and coaxing and craftiness failed, she could always fall back upon that reliable weapon, a fit of weeping. It would be horrible to see Anne crying because of her. Had they been wrong not to take her into their confidence? She said gently:

"Mother, I have thought of all these things, and I still want to go with Joseph."

This would happen! Anne thought furiously. So good the girl had been all through the early, the usually most trying days, never a complaint, never a whim: and then, this! The most ridiculous, the most senseless, the most dangerous fancy surely that any woman in that state had ever entertained.

Well, there was nothing for it. Humiliating as it was, she must appeal to her son-in-law.

She looked at him sternly, daring him to go against her, and said in a deceptively reasonable way:

"This isn't for us to decide, Mary. Let's hear what Joseph has to say."

He'd annoyed her about the hurrying forward of the wedding day, and without knowing it she was jealous of him because he was now closer to Mary and more in control of her than she herself was, but she had faith in his good sense. He'd heard everything that she had said to her daughter, standing by, saying nothing and looking a bit sheepish; he *must,* not being a fool, give the answer she wanted. But he did not: he said:

"I'd like Mary to come with me."

"You great goat!" Anne said. "Can't you see what a risk you'd be taking? I thought you, at least, would show some sense. Can you give me one reason, one sound *good* reason for dragging a woman, in her last month, all that way, far from her home and her kindred?"

"She wants to come, isn't that reason enough?" he said mildly. "I shall be there, I shall take care of her. And if the child *should* be born in Bethlehem that wouldn't be so much amiss. I was born there, and my father before me."

"Spoken like a prince!" Anne exclaimed, losing her temper completely. "The ancestral roof! And you told me yourself you had no kin there or anywhere else. Very well, have it your own way; and blame yourself if this baby is born in a ditch. All that walking!"

"Mary will have no need to walk," Joseph said. "I intend to buy her a donkey."

"You do that," Anne said furiously, "then she'll have a pair!"

She turned away abruptly, knowing that she was about to cry, and even now not wishing to upset Mary. Her way led up the street, theirs led down and when they had walked for a minute Joseph said:

"In her place I should feel just the same."

"So should I. Poor Mother! Just for a moment I wondered, should we have told her? Ought we to tell her now?"

"She has no discretion. The kindest of hearts, the best of good sense, that I grant. But if she disbelieved she would shout her derision, and if she believed she would whisper to this one, or that. It is better that she should think you wilful and me stupid."

For a long time, almost ever since her return from her visit to Elisabeth, they had kept up a curious pretence that everything was ordinary. It had been their defence against a truth too strange to take its place in everyday life, a light too bright to be looked at without blinking. Hilliel's announcement this morning had brought them face to face with the truth again.

Mary said, "It is all coming true, is it not? Word for word. All the Jews in Galilee and Judah wondering why that order should be given, and only we know the answer. I have so often wondered lately how I could mention Bethlehem to you. And I need not have worried."

"I had thought of it," Joseph admitted, "the truth is, and it shames me to say it, I *forget*. Not wholly, but as one half-forgets a dream. Day after day, my work; I come home and there you are, with my supper ready; sleep and then work again. Sometimes I wake in the night and the full realisation smites me, I wonder, I look ahead and I sweat. Then in the morning, off to work, everything so down to earth; and the truth, God forgive me, seems like something I dreamed."

She attempted to put into words the result of hours of thought.

"Don't you think, perhaps, that that is how God wanted it to be? We're the human part; the ordinariness is our contribution; all we have to contribute, really. I fix my mind on that, Joseph. He's to be born an ordinary human child, and how could that be if all the time his parents were walking about thinking that their child was the Son of God?"

"Sooner or later, though, that thought must be faced."

"I know. But it's like Bethlehem; there were we wondering how to mention it even, and it's all arranged for us. God will look after all that part of it." She took his hand. "Oh Joseph, while we can, let us cling to the ordinary. There's so much to come that won't be. . . ."

So much, she thought. All those *dreadful* prophecies about being wounded, bruised, and then slaughtered. It *said*, "He is brought as a lamb to the slaughter." Surely, never before, in the whole history of mankind had any woman conceived and carried a child whose fate she knew, from the first. She'd known, of course, all along, but in the early days, especially after her visit to Elisabeth, she had been filled with ecstasy and mysticism. But day by day, as the child grew and weighed heavier, became more and more part of her, her sorrow for him, her protective feeling, grew. He would be great and glorious, he would be the Son of God; but human, too, vulnerable to pain, and she, his human mother, must grieve and suffer, for him.

But these were thoughts she could share with no one. Alone in the kitchen of the little house, laying out the Sabbath food, cooked on the previous day, she did pause for a moment, gripped her hands together and said, "God, I must leave it to You. All I ask is strength to bear what comes." Then, carrying the dish, she went in to Joseph and said gaily:

"Mother was annoyed, wasn't she? Calling you a donkey! If she only knew, to my mind that was a compliment."

Smoothly, beautifully, she had made everything sound safe and ordinary again.

II

Despite all the mutterings and the prognostications of ruin, the carrying out of the latest order from Rome caused less upheaval than had been anticipated. The order was regarded as harsh and

tyrannical and, as always under any kind of threat, the Jews
united. Farmers who, because they were born in or near Nazareth, need make no journey, or only a short one, undertook to
keep things going on the farms of those who must face longer
journeys. An old smith who lived in comfort with his well-mar-
ried daughter in Sepphoris walked all the way from that city to
tell the man who must go to Beersheba that he would take charge
of his forge while he was away; he made no favour of it, it
would be as good as a holiday, he said, to get his hands on tools
again.

Joseph was less fortunate in finding a substitute and was faced
with the closing of his carpenter's shop when he heard through
Hilliel, who had heard from the rabbi at Japha, half an hour's
walk away to the south, that a carpenter named Aaron there
would be willing to undertake any urgent job, if Joseph would
leave a chalked notice on his door directing any possible customers to *his* shop.

In later days, amongst his many other worries, Joseph sometimes wondered about Aaron and how long he had done two
men's work before wiping that notice off the door at Nazareth.
But when he came back there were the chalked words, renewed
again and again, and one of his first visitors was Aaron, carrying
in his hand a small bag of money and in his head an exact account of every piece of work he had done on Joseph's behalf.

Only men, the taxpayers, the putative recruits should there
ever be a general call up, were compelled to register, but Mary
was far from being the only woman to accompany her man;
there were women who disliked the idea of being left alone,
women whose men did not wish them to be alone, and a multitude of women to whom the prospect of a family reunion was
irresistible. Relatives unseen for years could be visited, children
shown off, marriages arranged. The women, less politically
minded and in many cases less informed about the Law, would,
with the slightest encouragement, have made the whole thing
into an outing—or in the case of those who remained in their
own homes, an opportunity to show hospitality. The men took

a more dour view, looking upon the new taxation with dread and upon the census with distrust.

In Joseph's household the preparations were complicated by two incidental things. The first was Anne's inability to accept the idea that Mary's child might be born far away, under some other woman's eye. She wept, she cajoled, she threatened to accompany them, and then withdrew the threat when she realised that two of her own brothers must return to Nazareth for the census and would have to be looked after.

"Muddling about and walking just at that time," she said, weeping again, "the baby'll most likely be born by the roadside."

"That won't happen," Joseph said firmly. "We intend to start early. And she won't be walking, she'll be riding."

"And being jolted, which is just as bad!"

Mention of the riding reminded Joseph of the other complication. Over the matter of the donkey he had yielded to Mary and in his heart felt that in doing so he had made a mistake. There was a donkey, very old, more than a little lame, that belonged to a man named Micah who had a little brick-kiln, and on this sorry animal Mary had set her heart.

"But it's lame," Joseph said.

"It wouldn't be if it had some rest. If we could buy it now and feed it up a little . . ."

Joseph's mind underwent the by-now-familiar dichotomy; this woman, my wife; this woman, chosen of God to be the mother of His Son.

"If only I could afford it," he said, "you should have a white pony with red harness."

"I'd much rather have Micah's donkey, who is already my friend. I give him crusts and cabbage leaves, and though he is so roughly treated, he's very gentle. Please, if you really think I need a donkey, let it be that one."

Joseph had given in hastily because he was afraid that she was about to cry—and in all the time he had known her he had never once known her to use tears as a weapon as so many women did. Actually she had been on the brink of tears, thinking of the hopelessness of it all. Micah would buy another donkey, younger, stronger, which soon, from ill-usage, would be as lame and dejected looking as this one. You couldn't save them all.

And then, for the first time, her mind touched upon the other side of those direful prophecies. *He* can, she thought. He will be God, all-powerful, and at the same time He'll be human. He'll know about pain and being hurt, about bruises and stripes. And when all the prophecies have been fulfilled and He emerges in glory, He'll do something for humble, helpless things. If necessary, she thought, I shall ask Him: I shall say, Please do this for me, your mother. . . .

It didn't do to pursue such thoughts, they made her feel frightened and dizzy.

"I shall take some tools," Joseph was saying. "You never know. Most people have a job for a carpenter and never get around to sending for him. I could shore up a beam or respoke a wheel in return for a night's lodging, maybe." For with them, as with hundreds of other Jews, ready money was short. In the country a good deal of trade was still being done by a system of barter and many families had difficulty in gathering enough coined money to meet the demands of the tax-gatherers.

As well as the tools they would carry food of the kind that would not spoil by keeping. The task of providing this was taken out of Mary's hands by Anne who, in the last few days before the departure, never visited without bringing some offering. A smoked mutton ham, a great jar of pickled eggs, a cheese the size of a millstone; dried figs, raisins and dates, a string of salted fish; a huge honey cake. . . .

"At least you shan't starve, you wilful girl!" she said, beginning to cry again. Then, mopping her eyes with the edge of her veil, she said, "And what, pray tell me, is this that I hear about that ass of Micah's? Is it true? On that very first day Joseph said you should have a donkey to ride. Does he call that bit of carrion a donkey?"

"I chose it," Mary said. "And it is now not a bit lame; there's gloss on its coat too. It will get me to Bethlehem."

"I no longer understand you," Anne said. "I reared you well

and you were always meek and amenable. Now you are very headstrong. Rushing off to Bethlehem, without the ́slightest need. At such a moment, too! And on a broken-down donkey. . . ." She began to cry again.

This was all such a far cry from the annunciation on the hilltop, from the moment of ecstasy in Elisabeth's garden, that one human mind could hardly be expected to contain, to deal with it all. Should I, Mary wondered, have taken my mother into full confidence from the first? But I knew then that she would think I was mad, and if I told her now she would think the same. This predicament and the discomfort it causes me is part of the price I must pay.

She said, "I want to see Bethlehem because it was Joseph's birthplace and a place of importance in our history. You yourself told me that first children are often as much as two weeks late. The donkey is sound now. Can you not take comfort in the thought that I may go, and be back?"

"It is possible, I suppose. But I wanted you to be with me, in your own room, being looked after."

"Then my uncles, Dan and Asher, would have had to look for lodging elsewhere. Are you sure"—Anne, the provider, could surely be diverted by any question concerning food—"that in giving us so much to take with us, you have not depleted your stores?"

"I never, as you should know," Anne said, instantly diverted, "take one mutton leg from the chimney without putting another one in. And the same with the cheese, before the ripe one is eaten another is ready. For the lesser things I still have time in plenty. Your uncles haven't so far to come."

"Still, they'll be hungry and happy to taste your cooking again," Mary said swiftly, for at the word "far" Anne's eyes had filled anew. But her distress did not prevent her from being practical.

"You *may* be right about getting back to have the baby here; but don't, for pity's sake, forget to take the baby's things. And don't be brave. Oh, I know I've brought you up not to make a fuss of an ache or a pain, but there are times when a woman can be *too* brave. At the first sign of a pain, make for a respectable house with a decent woman in it. I shall hope and pray that you're not taken on the road, but if you are . . ." She fumbled in her dress and pulled out a little bag. "Twenty sestertii," she said, producing her hoard with justifiable pride. "Enough to pay for your lodging and the services of a good midwife."

Overcome, Mary said, "You are the best mother in the world!" and as though the praise had in some manner restored her to herself, Anne said, almost in her old sharp way:

"I only hope that your child will never bring you as much grief as you have me, just lately."

They set out at first light on the appointed morning. Mary rode on the donkey which also carried two bags, one of food—the jar of eggs had been left in the house—one of clothing, everything the baby would need, and one change of linen for each of them. Joseph shouldered his bag of tools. To him Micah's old donkey resembled a careful housewife's bowl, once broken and mended with strips of linen soaked in flour-and-water paste. It might look all right, but the flaws were there, and under stress it was likely to collapse.

It worried him, and he was worried that he should be worried. It showed such a lamentable lack of faith. There was no *need* for anxiety, he told himself, again and again. It has been foretold that the Messiah should be born in Bethlehem, and there he would be born, even if the old donkey fell dead.

When he thought such a thought he would enjoy a feeling of relief, but the carefree moments never lasted. God will provide, he'd think, and I do believe that; but *through* me. I'm responsible; I was chosen. After all, he'd think, every pious Jew believes that Jehovah sent the ravens to feed Elijah, and could do the same any day, yet we work for our daily bread. And I believe that Jehovah will bring us to Bethlehem, but I must act and think as any ordinary, prudent man in my circumstances would do. And then, there he'd be, worrying away again.

After a while, when the donkey flagged, Joseph added the bag of food and then the bag of clothing to his own load; and that moment, which might have been one of recrimination was sweetened by a laughing reference to Anne's sharp remark about Mary's two donkeys. Then, on a long, uphill stretch Mary said she would walk for a bit and when Joseph protested she said, "Walking is good for women in my state. Remember that one of my grandmothers was a desert woman, and when the desert people are on the move between two wells they dare not stop and risk disaster to all because a woman is about to have a baby. She walks to the last moment, bears her child, swaddles it and walks on."

"And sometimes dies," Joseph said sombrely.

That was another thing that worried him. The sacred writings told of an immaculate conception, a virgin birth, but they said no word about what happened to the mother. There were times, horrible, almost unbearable times, when he felt that death in childbed must be the logical end. Was it possible to visualise a woman, the ostensible wife of a carpenter, going about her household tasks, with complete right to call herself the Mother of God? It wasn't possible, and the only alternative was death; and whenever Joseph thought of that he plunged deep into the pit of premature bereavement. He loved her now, with a love that was completely different from the love he had felt for the pretty young girl who had caught his eye, and most surprisingly consented to marry him. These celibate months had taught him something that very few men ever guessed, or imagined, however dimly. He loved Mary as a person, not as a woman, as a companion, not as a bedfellow. And he had come to understand, grudging his own understanding, why she had been chosen; beautiful, kind, gentle, intelligent, witty at times, knowing when to speak and when to remain silent . . .

Mary said, "I am not going to die, Joseph; on that score put your mind at rest. This will be an ordinary human baby and God will know that he needs a mother to suckle him and rear him. I shan't die until I see him come into his kingdom. I shall be an old woman, with grey hair and nobbly knuckles, and very probably a sharp tongue, like my mother's."

But she thought, "A man of sorrows and acquainted with

grief," and she knew, with deadly certainty, that she would witness the death of this child who now, vibrant with new life, kicked her in the ribs. He would be human, and as a human he would die; but he would also be the Son of God, and as such immortal. Difficult to understand, impossible to communicate, but in her heart she knew.

So they moved Southwards. Every morning the old donkey set out bravely, the finished product of at least four thousand years of conditioning, from the free wild ass, stamping his hill beat, through captivity, gelding, near-starvation, into this tempered slave, this triumph of survival. But each day, when he began to sag and limp, and with any ordinary owner would have been given fresh impetus from pain, whip or stock or goad, Mary alighted. And each day she walked more heavily. Presently Joseph began to fret about the weather.

There were always a few weeks when, even as far south as Jerusalem, the rain-laden winds were chilly; about once in every three years the rain would turn to snow; even more rarely there would be frost. Such times were known as bad winters and helped to date things: before, or just after, or during the last bad winter, people would say, recalling some event. Joseph hoped and prayed that this was not to be one of those bad winters; but the signs indicated that it might be. The wind veered and came screaming down from the North, filling the sky with leaden, swollen-looking clouds. Then, in the evening, after they had found a place to sleep—and for all his anxiety he always insisted upon stopping early—he'd go out to attend to the donkey, or simply to sniff the wind; and the sky, so lowering all day, would be swept clear of clouds and the stars would shine with a frosty sparkle. There was one, particularly large and bright which seemed to look down and say "Frost tomorrow!" Frost or snow, and what would happen to the old donkey, already making such heavy going that occasionally Joseph lost patience with it.

"When he worked for Micah he carried heavier loads," he'd say. Or, "He takes advantage of you; he knows he has only to sigh and you'll get down and walk."

It worried him greatly when people passed them in the road; and it seemed that everybody passed them, even people on foot. Mary walked slowly and heavily now and easily grew short of breath.

"If all these people are bound for Bethlehem, the place will be crammed," he said.

Mary always replied, "Don't worry, Joseph; there'll be a place for us."

She said that on the last morning, just as Joseph, shouldering his bag, took the donkey's head-rope and said:

"Come on, you! We're having no nonsense today!"

And at that moment he felt, on his cheek, the first, soft, almost caressing, deadly ominous touch of a snowflake.

CHAPTER VIII

After Balthazar had joined them, Melchior and Gaspar travelled more comfortably and more cheaply. He did all their shopping, took on the menial jobs of camel-tending, fire-making, and cooking when they camped in the open, negotiated all the arrangements if they slept at inns. He could also have made the journey much more interesting and instructive, had Melchior not been so impatient. Gaspar was eager to exploit his ability to ask questions and explain things, but Melchior often acted as a buffer, saying, "We have no time now. That can wait."

The company of a third person brought the inevitable discord. Two men, however different in character, can, unless they are unreasonable, come to terms between themselves; with two there can be no taking of sides, and in an argument it is one voice against one voice. With three it is different.

Usually, as they pressed onward, Balthazar, in any argument, tended to side with Melchior who had befriended him, who followed the star, who was a man of education, the man to whom he could speak directly, the man who, except when preoccupied or bothered about time, was friendly. But when, as they came nearer to Jerusalem, their arguments were no longer concerned with such trivial things as to when to stop and where to spend the night, but devolved upon their point of destination, then Balthazar found himself siding with Gaspar.

"I know now," Melchior said, coming back from a session with his chart and his tools, "that Jerusalem cannot be the place. It is too far North. If we come to a road which branches off we should do well to take it. This road is crowded and leads to the city. We have no reason to enter the city at all."

There followed one of their awkward, three-cornered arguments.

Balthazar could recall, with complete clarity, the maps that had hung upon the walls of the counting house in Tyre. On them all the caravan routes were marked, and every city with which the Greek did business was ringed in red.

"There is no large city directly South of Jerusalem," he said with what, for him, was assurance. "South of Jerusalem there are a few villages, sheep country, then desert, and nothing else until you come to Egypt. In my dream, or my vision—call it what you will—I saw the three of us, riding into the gateway of a city, a walled city with many towers. There is no such place South of Jerusalem."

"I'm inclined to discount what you saw," Melchior said, politely, but firmly, "as I told you, clairvoyance is an inexact science. The star has guided me, unfailingly for thousands of miles. Am I now to disregard it because of something you saw in a dream or a trance? With no moment to waste, mark you."

"What is it now?" Gaspar asked, sensing contention. Melchior informed him, briefly. And with almost equal brevity Gaspar said:

"I wish to see Herod, and Jerusalem. I do not like huckster's talk, but it is a fact that you have come so far at my expense."

"That I do not deny," Melchior said sourly, "but it is of no importance." He looked at his two companions and thought how dangerously easy it would be to hate them both, the young man with his money and his passion to see things and ask questions; the black man with his chatter about visions; both of them prepared to waste time, that most precious commodity of all, by going to Jerusalem, the one to satisfy idle curiosity, the other to fulfil his dream. Yet they were both indispensable.

Balthazar looked at his two companions and thought how easy it would be to dislike them both; the young man so arrogant because of his money, the old man so stubborn about his errand. He thought of his vision, the risks he had taken. Would either of them have risked such a flogging as he would endure if recaptured? Yet, in their separate ways they scorned or were oblivious to, the thing which had made him risk his life.

Gaspar looked at his two companions and thought how pleas-

ant it would be to hate them; the old man, so physically in-
exhaustible, with all his gabble about stars and his innate
arrogance; the black man, so emasculate and servile. Yet there
they were, his left hand and his right. Without them he could
not ask for so little as a cup of water.

"What you saw," Melchior said to Balthazar, "could have been
the gateway to a palace. Perhaps, with your real eyes you have
never seen one. I have seen many, with great gateways and towers and turrets, easily to be mistaken for cities . . ."

"With my real eyes I have seen palaces. In Egypt, in Tyre
. . . places that you perhaps have never heard of. Believe me,
I know a palace from a city as you know a radish from a melon.
And I saw us, dressed just as we are and riding the camels we
ride, passing into the gates of a city. I know," Balthazar said,
with the humility that has power because, being so low it cannot
be struck down, "that you ridicule my vision. But I beg you, ask
yourself: But for that vision, which brought me to you, where
now would you be?"

"Lost and penniless, in a strange land," Melchior said with
equal humility. "That I admit, and so, when he understands,
will he. But I still say that Jerusalem is not my goal and I am
positive that to go into Jerusalem will not only be a wicked waste
of time, but, because of the waste, dangerous to the child."

"Now I beg you to consider," Balthazar said, "you look at the
stars and see a child, connected with a star. I—dreaming, or
tranced, what you will—see a star and the gateway of a great
city. In ordinary terms, which of us, I ask you, carries most
weight? He"—he nodded towards Gaspar—"has seen nothing, but
he has paid and paid and paid. And he wishes, you tell me, to
see Jerusalem. Could we not oblige him?"

"It is the waste of time," Melchior said. "That is all I deplore.
You have been useful, he has been useful. I would gladly oblige
you both. If you asked my right hand I would lay it on the block,
willingly. But for nine months now I have followed this star and
it does not, I swear, lead to Jerusalem. And time matters."

"What are you gabbling about?" Gaspar asked in the voice
that often called the Five Hundred to attention. Melchior told

him, shortly, honestly. And that gave Balthazar time to think up a really clinching argument.

"Suppose," he said to Melchior, "you had not decided to halt at that inn where you found me. There was the twilight hour left; you could have ridden on, and five miles along the road found a better inn. Then you would have missed me and by now every one of his rose jekkals would have been spent, people cheating you as they did. Is it not possible that, leaving the intervention of gods and goddesses aside, there is *something* that governs our lives? Your stars, my dreams, his . . . what has he, poor man, except his money? A wish to see Jerusalem. To see Jerusalem he has travelled far and hard. May it not be that his will has as much significance as your star and my dream? May it not be that we are to go to Jerusalem because something awaits us there?"

"I do not understand such talk," Melchior said coldly. He added, with reproach, "I thought you were a sensible man."

As he read it, the place for which he was bound was only a short distance from Jerusalem; he could travel so far without the help of Gaspar's money; what he feared was that he would reach his destination and find that nobody understood his message. Very soon Balthazar might be of the utmost importance, and he set himself to argue, to cajole, anything to win Balthazar round to his way of thinking. But in his humble, unaggressive way the black man was adamant. The fact that he had found these companions, was riding a camel, wearing the very clothes of his vision, fortified his stubbornness.

"I shall know the gateway when we reach it," he said. "And we must ride in."

Then, soon, there was another trouble; the roads became crowded, not with the ordinary traffic, designed for speed, but by slow-moving groups of people on foot, mainly men, but enough women and children to be noticeable. A few rode inferior donkeys, here and there there was a cart with slow-turning, creaking wheels; everywhere there were bundles. To Melchior they were merely a nuisance, but to Gaspar, who was interested in everything and only too willing to halt and order Balthazar to ask questions, they were a prod to curiosity.

"One would think," he said, "that they were fleeing from the sack of a city, but that they go in both directions. Ask him to ask who they are and where they are going."

The first question Balthazar could answer immediately.

"They are all Jews," he said and hoped that Gaspar would be content with that, and not insist that he stop and ask questions and thus provoke Melchior even more. But Gaspar insisted; so Balthazar gathered as much information as he could in the shortest possible time, and reported.

"They are going back to their places of birth in order to be taxed."

"By whose order?"

"By the order of the Emperor, Caesar Augustus."

Gaspar looked at the throng, moving this way and that, and gave his verdict.

"Then he is a fool as well as a rogue. What a way to organise taxation! In Jexal, when I . . ." He paused, on the brink of betraying himself. "When I lived there, the whole tax system was reorganised from top to bottom. People were ordered to stay in their homes and the officials went round. It was quiet and orderly. And all over in a day." He looked more closely at the people, finding, on the whole, little likeness to the one Jew he knew.

"A miserable-looking lot," he commented. Melchior passed this remark on to Balthazar—as he passed, almost without thinking, these days, any remark made by either man.

Balthazar said, "I think they are unhappy. Not only about the new taxing. They believe that they are being counted and that is displeasing to their God. I was once well acquainted with a Jew who told me many interesting things. One of their own kings numbered them, long ago, and their God was angry and killed many people—to put the numbers wrong again!" He allowed his voice to be tinged by ridicule, remembering the time when he had been anxious to give himself to Eliezer's God and been rejected with contempt.

"If they really believed that, or in their God," Gaspar said, thinking of the old carpet merchant's honesty over the purple dye, "they would rebel."

"Rome is mighty," Balthazar said. "Also the Jews have no leader." A long-buried loyalty to Eliezer, and the memory of the stories with which that fellow-slave had entertained him, made him say, "When they had leaders, they fought well and won many battles."

Melchior, remembering that fantastic horoscope that he had worked out at the top of his tower in the long ago spring, said:

"The child who is about to be born might lead them. If only we arrive in time. Which we may not if you insist upon wasting time in Jerusalem!"

The three-cornered argument then began again and went on until, just North of Jericho, something happened to give Gaspar a temporary ascendancy.

Lately they had abandoned any attempt to sleep in caravanserais; they were too crowded and uncomfortable. This was well-watered country and it was easy enough to let the camels drink their fill at some public watering place, and Balthazar could shop, well and shrewdly, for what food they needed; he could also cook. Sometimes the nights were chilly but an unspoken competition in hardiness prevented any one of the three from complaining of that.

On this evening, when Gaspar pointed out as he so often did, that the camels were exhausted, and the truth of that was apparent even to Melchior, they were on a narrow road which wound in and out and up and down in bare, hilly country. The road, for once, was clear—which made Melchior all the more annoyed by the necessity to halt at all; none of the three was informed enough to know that this stretch of road was notorious and that nobody in his right senses would be anywhere on or near it after sunset. Looking for a place to camp they came upon a break in the rocks which for a long time had enclosed the road like a wall and Balthazar, the one who felt the cold most, and also regarded himself as being responsible for most of their practical arrangements, pointed out that if they pulled off the road here, they would be sheltered by the rocks on either side; that he could hear the noise of one of those curious little waterfalls which in this country appeared from nowhere and disappeared again; that this would, indeed, be an ideal place in which to spend the night. Melchior, raising his eyes to the heights on either side of the little opening, agreed that it would be a good place; on either side the rocks rose sheer, unclimbable, but straight ahead was a steep incline, covered with scree up which he could make his way and so gain a clear view of the sky. Gaspar, though accustomed to flat, open spaces, relished the loneliness of the place, and looking at the hard, inhospitable terrain, felt respect for the men whom Benjamin had mentioned to him; the nameless men, the night-walkers, the rebels who had taken to the hills.

Earlier in the day Balthazar had bought some goat meat and he was soon busy, making a fire and rigging up his makeshift spit. He now carried the two forked sticks and the crosspiece with him, having learned that there were places where one could not count on finding even a bush. He was glad that the duty of provisioning the party had fallen to him for Melchior and Gaspar, though willing enough to eat when food was handy, never gave it much thought beforehand. It seemed, at times, as though they were trying to outdo one another in their indifference to it. Balthazar, for the most of his life, had been accustomed to regular mealtimes; even when the Lady's temper had resulted in a reduction of her slaves' rations, there had always been something to eat when mealtimes came round. And he had enough to contend with in the mere riding; he never complained, was never the one to suggest a halt, he had no intention of being a drag on his company; but the stiffness in his fingers had often, by the end of the day, communicated itself to every bone in his body and sometimes, when he alighted from his camel, the whole earth would swing and sway and reel around him.

He made the fire, lighting it with a little bundle of sticks which he prudently carried, and then, in the fading light began to hunt about for something to keep it going. Evidently, at some season of the year, even these barren rocks bore some short-lived vegetation; all withered and scorched and dead now, but with roots, waiting the winter rains and the soft warmth of a brief spring. He grubbed out an armful of them and carefully replenished the fire. Soon the savoury, peculiarly pungent scent of roast goat meat filled the narrow place. The camels grunted and groaned as they slept. Gaspar indulged in one of the short naps which Balthazar envied; he could sleep for a few minutes at any time, in any place and wake instantly, with all his wits about him. Melchior unrolled a chart and holding it close to the fire—so close that once the sizzling meat spat fat into his eye—studied it, gloomily.

They ate, pulling the meat apart with their fingers and passing from hand to hand the goatskin of cheap wine mixed with water which Balthazar had provided, each one careful to wipe his mouth on his sleeve before drinking, and the mouth of the container afterwards. They were halfway through their meal when Gaspar lifted his head, listened, seemed to sniff the air like a dog.

"We are not alone," he said to Melchior, and getting to his feet, put his hand to his knife which he carried thrust into the belt of his baggy trousers, under his leather jacket. "See," he said, and pointed towards the slope of scree up which, as soon as he had eaten, Melchior proposed to scramble. Neither Melchior nor Balthazar had heard anything, and looking into the darkness outside the fire's range, they saw nothing for a minute; then they did, and it was a frightening sight. Three men, all looking larger than normal, clad in tatters that fluttered as they moved, all carrying clubs, all with wild, desperate faces.

"Robbers," Balthazar said in a breathy whisper, recognising the breed. His legs had turned numb, his stomach quaked; one blow from a club like that and you'd be dead, or hopelessly disabled.

Melchior, alarmed, but still thinking clearly, said:

"The camels. They must not take the camels. Gaspar, give them everything we have. The camels they must not take." Lose the camels now and all would be wasted.

To Gaspar these were the men he wanted to see, members

perhaps of that nameless, unnumbered army of rebels who might one day be his allies.

"Do not be frightened," he said. "I am here. Melchior, tell him to speak civilly. Tell him to ask them what they want."

The men were now within hand's reach and arrogance hung about them, palpable, unmistakable. One old, frail man, a soft, flabby merchant, obviously rich and as obviously terrified, and one, younger and capable of giving trouble but prepared, from his attitude, to be placating. A hired guard, perhaps, with no intention of risking a cracked head to protect the interests of those who had hired him.

Balthazar asked the question and one of them replied:

"To begin with, a share of your meal."

"They wish to eat with us," Balthazar told Melchior, and Melchior said to Gaspar:

"Let them take the food, the gold, everything; but *not* the camels."

In the desert the rules of hospitality were strict; it came easily to Gaspar to say:

"Tell him to ask them to sit down and eat." But it was plain that these men did not know the rules. They were already helping themselves. Most unmannerly!

"I have many questions to ask them," Gaspar told Melchior. "Tell him to ask them where they come from, how many they are, how they feel about Herod and about the Emperor of Rome." Never yet in all this journey had Gaspar so much regretted his inability to speak strange tongues.

But with these men, even Balthazar's skill was unavailing. They understood his quavering questions, that was plain by the way they laughed and nudged one another and laughed again.

They gave no proper answers. One said:

"We have no names; we are not numbered. We know nothing of Herod, or the Emperor of Rome."

Wary and dangerous as wolves they squatted by the fire and ate all that was left of the goat meat and the bread which Balthazar had bought from a village bakery at mid-day, and they made short work of the wine.

One of them said, "Tell the young one to sit down and take his hand off his knife handle."

Already terrified, Balthazar felt considerable dismay in being ordered to give Gaspar such a curt command. The young man with his haughty looks and his money was still, to the slave, a figure of awe. He said to Melchior:

"The one with the most hair wishes that Gaspar should sit down and remove his hand from his knife."

Melchior passed on the words and Gaspar sat down in an attitude that any of his own men would have known to be potentially dangerous. He sat with his legs crossed and the outer edges of his feet resting on the ground. It looked relaxed enough, but the slightest pressure against the sides of his soles would bring him upright. His arms were crossed too, but in such a fashion that in a blink of an eye his hand would be back on his knife.

Such precautions were second nature to him; he felt no fear; only a burning interest in the men who looked so hardy, who gave such cautious answers; and a maddening frustration because he could only communicate with them through Melchior *and* Balthazar. How could he be certain that the questions were rightly put and the answers rightly returned. He tried again.

"Ask them their names," he said.

The answer came back from the same man who had spoken before:

"We have no names." All three laughed.

They were remarkably uncouth, Gaspar reflected; a good deal of discipline would be needed to turn them into anything like a useful fighting force. But they looked hard and tough, quite unlike the harassed, tame Jews who were hurrying about in obedience to Caesar's command. Something could be made of them, if it came to the pinch.

"Ask them if they follow a leader."

"We have no leader," the answer came back.

The wine, though watered, was still potent—Balthazar was a careful shopper; and in the hills wine was a rarity. The three men grew hilarious, laughing at nothing. One of them reached out and snatched off Melchior's hat, set it on his own shaggy head, and exercising some peculiar gift of mimicry, composed his body and his features into a caricature of the old man.

Melchior, unaffected by the mockery, said to Balthazar:

"Tell him he can have my robe as well. Anything but the camels."

And why, Balthazar asked himself, as he translated this statement, should they spare the camels? It was plain to him that these were robbers, bandits, who would take everything. They would certainly take the camels, drive them away over the hills and sell them somewhere, cheaply.

But the laughter, the mocking of Melchior's dignity, affected Gaspar; leaning forward a little from the hips he said to the shaggy-haired man:

"Stop that; and give back the hat."

The shaggy-haired one, without understanding the words, sensed the protest, and replied, mocking Gaspar:

"Yack-yack-yack! Yack-yack-yack!" And they all rocked with laughter.

"We'll have all your hats! And everything else you have!"

Balthazar said to Melchior, "These are robbers; they will strip us of everything."

Melchior said to Gaspar, "They are bandits. They will take all."

"They will take nothing! Wait. Leave this to me."

It had dawned upon him, with the snatching of Melchior's hat, that these were not the dignified, dedicated men-of-the-hills of whom old Benjamin had spoken with such respect, and whom he had come so far to see.

And there were three of them, men in their prime, armed, against him alone. At a moment like this he couldn't count upon the frail old scholar, or the easily terrified black fellow. And what could one knife do against three clubs? Strategy was called for.

Suddenly he swayed back, laughing, laughing; his teeth bared in a grin as wolfish as any of theirs.

"Laugh," he said to Melchior. "Tell him to laugh. Laugh, I said, this is important!"

Melchior, wildly distressed at the prospect of losing the camels, managed only a death's head grimace; Balthazar, trained in obedience, creased his face into a smile that was in ill-accord with the terror in his eyes where too much white was showing.

"Now tell him," said Gaspar, pretending to hold his sides with amusement, "that when I move my hat, he is to offer his turban to the one nearest him; but to loosen it first. Say this as though you were joking with him!"

Smiling pallidly Melchior passed on this order.

Still laughing loudly, Gaspar took off his hat, held it a second in his hand and looked at Balthazar who immediately removed and loosened his beautiful turban. Gaspar clapped his hat onto the head of one of the men, pushing it down, still acting as though it were a joke. Balthazar put his turban upon the head of the third and a fold fell. . . .

They were still laughing, the two temporarily blinded, when Gaspar got to his feet, drew his knife across the throat of the one who wore Melchior's hat, and in less than a breath's space, despatched in similar fashion the other two. It was done so quickly, so surely, with such deadly savagery that neither Melchior nor Balthazar could believe that it was done. One second the throats were emitting laughter and the next gushing fountains of blood.

Gaspar wiped his knife on the rags of the last man he had killed and straightened up, his face impassive.

Melchior, that civilised man, felt a single queasy heave of the stomach, but it died away under the thought, The camels are safe. He said:

"By my father's grave, you are quick."

"In my country," Gaspar said, "a man is either quick or dead."

Balthazar, who had seen blood spilt before, was far more affected; he hadn't the strength just then to stand up, so he shuffled backwards a little on his haunches and turning out of the firelight, threw up his supper.

Then something extraordinary happened. From the top of the rocky wall to the left of the enclosed space in which, by the fire, three men in grotesque attitudes lay dead, and one live man calmly sheathed his knife, and one thought of his errand, and one vomited, something came hurtling down, stumbled as it fell, recovered itself and made for Gaspar.

It was a boy, quite a small one, no more than six or seven years old, but in such a blind, murderous rage that he was momentarily as dangerous as a tiger. Had he worn shoes the kicks he aimed at Gaspar's shins would have done real damage, the will to damage was there, but he was barefoot. And his teeth, directed at Gaspar's throat, were defeated by the collar of the leather jacket. He had launched himself, made the assault in silence, but under the double frustration he began to scream. Gaspar took him by the nape of the neck and held him at arm's length, as though he were a puppy. The boy's legs and arms thrashed about and he went on screaming. Gaspar dispassionately cuffed him about the head until suddenly he hung limp and quiet.

"One of their cubs," he said, dropping the boy to the ground, and looking about. "There may be others."

But all was quiet.

"We must go," Melchior said, standing up on legs that were not quite steady. "This is a dangerous place."

Balthazar wiped his mouth and his sweat-drenched face and turned back into the firelight, carefully avoiding looking at the dead men.

The boy, who had stood, dazed and dizzied, where Gaspar had dropped him, moved and went to the side of the shaggy-haired man who had taken Melchior's hat. He said:

"You killed my father. I wish I could kill you."

Balthazar, falling into place again, said to Melchior:

"That man was the boy's father."

"The boy's father," Melchior said to Gaspar.

"A spirited boy," Gaspar said; but Melchior disregarded the remark. They must get away from here.

"You killed him," the boy said again. "He was only seeking food." He began to cry. "He was bringing me my supper. Look!"

He fumbled in the dead man's rags; and Balthazar, the only one who understood what the boy said, forced himself to watch, and it was true. Under cover of the ravenous eating, the greedy drinking, the horse-play, the man had remembered the child and secreted a good hunk of goat meat and some bread.

"He had saved some for the boy," Balthazar said. This remark Melchior considered not worth passing on.

"Come," he said, "let us go."

But Gaspar and Balthazar seemed to be fascinated by the boy. He held the food in his hand and he looked at it with a tragic expression, tears streaking his dirty face; but he was hungry, plainly very hungry, for though he wept with his eyes, his mouth began to drool like a dog's. Then, suddenly, he ceased to cry, his mouth folded in on itself, and he flung the meat and the bread straight at Gaspar's face. Gaspar, with one of his swift movements, ducked and the two missiles went over his head.

It was sad; so much Melchior admitted, in his mind. But the men were robbers and might have taken the camels and rendered his whole errand abortive. The boy had made his gesture; and probably, as soon as they had gone, would hunt for the food, find it and eat it.

He said again, "Come. Let us go."

But Gaspar said, "I like this boy. Ask Balthazar what other food we have."

Impatiently, Melchior asked, and Balthazar said that all the meat was now eaten; they still had bread and some cheese.

"Give him some," Gaspar said. And while Balthazar opened the food bag, he retrieved their headgear; Melchior's first; the old man took it and with an impatient gesture, slapped it on his head; then his own, unsullied; the extreme end of Balthazar's turban, hanging down over the robber's face, was damp and dark with blood. Gaspar, with a delicacy of feeling that nobody would have given him credit for, took out his knife, cut off the soiled portion, threw it on the fire, and tucked the raw edge back. Balthazar, returning with the food, accepted the turban with fastidious suspicion, but it looked all right. . . .

The boy took the proffered food with a look in which sullenness and something else warred for mastery.

"Ask him to ask the boy's name."

"Such a waste of time!" Melchior said. "What does his name matter?" But he passed on the question and Balthazar asked it, gently.

The boy said, "I am the son of my father. My name is Barabbas."

Melchior, moving towards the camels, tossed this piece of worthless information, as he had tossed many similar pieces, to Gaspar.

"Tell him I wish I had such a son and that I am sorry his father is dead. But it was necessary." As he spoke Gaspar fumbled in his pouch and brought out a rose jekkal. The boy took it and said something. Balthazar spoke, Melchior spoke.

"He says his father is dead but he is alive and he will be avenged."

They mounted their camels and turned them, and as the weary, unwilling animals moved, grunting and protesting, down the defile towards the road, the boy pelted them. Two crusty loaves, a piece of cheese, a rose jekkal and then lumps of rock, thrown with unerring aim, and with all the impetus of impotent fury, hit the camels' hindquarters, so that their pace, for a few moments, satisfied even the impatient Melchior, who had just realised that with all this fuss, he had failed to take his nightly reckoning.

Next day, thinking over the incident, calmly, he acknowledged that but for Gaspar they would have lost their camels; and that even Gaspar's speedy trickery could not have succeeded without Balthazar's gift of tongues. So his opposition to their desire to enter Jerusalem was rather less obdurate than it might have been. He gave in, grudgingly and petulantly. "One hour, then. That is all I can spare. And that is an hour wasted," he said.

And then, of course, when they reached the great city, with the massed towers, the many roofs showing above the walls of hewn stone, and thousands of people going this way and that, halting progress in the most infuriating way, Balthazar must choose to be difficult. He said, "This is not the one, I'm sorry," at gateway after gateway. Gaspar, all agog, was quite willing to ride all round the city, but Melchior, though the day was very cold, felt hot sweat prick out all over him, even to his eyelids as they wasted time and wasted time.

Then, as they came towards the Gate of the Fountain, Balthazar said in a tranced, ecstatic voice, "This is it! This is the gate through which I saw us riding." He halted his camel and would have sat there, staring, had not Melchior said peevishly:

"Let us ride in then, and get it over with."

Gaspar had been assessing the city with a soldier's eye. It was a strong, fortressed city which, properly provisioned and held by resolute men, would withstand a prolonged siege. Not, compared with Jexal, a beautiful city, but certainly strong.

To him, Melchior said in the same peevish way:

"I have not come so far to sight-see! There will be time to stare later."

So they rode into Jerusalem; and even Melchior was slightly pacified to find that Balthazar had chosen the gate that was nearest to the Palace of Herod.

CHAPTER IX

Ephorus, Greek by birth, and once a sailor, had been stranded in Bethlehem for eleven years, and knew that he would die there: yet there never was a morning when, blinking his gritty eyes, licking his dry swollen lips with a dry swollen tongue and throwing back the shutter, he didn't think, What a place! How did I land here? Why do I stay? The answers to both questions would pour into his momentarily sober mind, smooth as oil, and he'd take a cup, draw some wine, add a few drops of water and drink. The first drink of the day. Then he felt better, able for about an hour to make himself useful about the place. An old sailor—he called himself that, though in years he was far from old—was handy, could turn his hand to almost anything; one hour of his time, every morning, every morning for eleven years had made a great difference in the appearance of this place which, though the smaller of the two inns in Bethlehem, was much the more attractive because of the way in which he had made and mended, plastered, painted and applied his natural Greek talent and his experience to decorating.

But an hour in the morning was as much as he could bear. Then, back to the wine, this time without water; wine, more wine, and soon the real Ephorus was drowned again. Dead for one more deadly day. Sometimes, sheltering behind his own recognisable shape, but never one with it, he was a merry man, ready to quarrel and, if necessary, fight; sometimes he was a sullen man, brooding in silence. None of these men was Ephorus. Ephorus woke, took a drink and worked for an hour because after all he owed Eunice something; and then he took himself off. And what the merry, the aggressive, the sullen men did or said concerned him very little.

Once, only once, had he struggled up out his drunkard's happy anonymity and tried to talk sense and truth to a fellow being; and that was when a neighbour, a man named Josodad, suffered a bereavement and began to come to the inn in search of comfort. He'd heard himself—to his amazement—speaking in metaphors, like a poet. He'd told Josodad that there was no comfort lying in the bottom of a wine cup; and that a loss might make you a cripple but drunkenness made you a social leper. It seemed to have worked, for Josodad ceased to frequent the inn; and now, after years, still looked as wretched as ever.

There'd been a little trouble with Eunice over Josodad; they hadn't so many customers that one needed to be driven away, she said. She also said, "I heard you. Talking about that whore! After all this time! After all I've done for you!"

He said, "I was only warning Josodad not to try to drown his sorrow or he'd end as I have."

Eunice gave one of her short, rather cruel snorts of amusement, and said:

"He'd be lucky! What's wrong with where you ended, you silly drunken clown? What's wrong with this bed, eh?"

He could have told her—everything! It was a trap, a cage, a baited hook: it was the battlefield upon which he was always defeated; it was the sandbank upon which his barque lay stranded. But Eunice was not to blame for that—or at least only in a small degree—so he'd gone stumbling to the bed. At that time he'd still been able to give Eunice what she wanted, and the carping quarrelsome day often ended in reconciliation. Later on things had grown worse.

On this morning, in the middle of his eleventh winter in Bethlehem, he rose, thick-headed and tremulous, opened the shutter a crack and looked out. The sky was greyish purple and hung just above the rooftops. Snow, he thought, unless the spiteful, bone-chilling wind succeeded in driving it over. He shivered, and thought, What a barbarous country! How did I land here? Why do I stay? He looked back over his past, boyhood and youth, before he came to Bethlehem, and saw it all in sunshine, with the exception of one spell in the middle of a voyage. Byblos,

Tyre and Sidon, Delos, Crete and Rhodes, Alexandria, Carthage, Marsala, dozens and dozens of places, and always in the sun.

He was born in Byblos, born an orphan, one might say. Somebody must have fed and protected him during infancy, but he had no memory of whoever it was; he had come to self-recognition, awareness of his own identity, and to the beginning of his memory, in a hovel, with a lot of other boys, all older than he. The owner of the hovel was an old crone, and when there was anything to cook, she cooked it. It was not a home; his home always seemed to be the quayside. Somebody must have taught him a few professional begging phrases and as a small boy he had haunted the places where sailors, just back from voyages, were paid off. They were always generous. Possibly their seeming wealth and their good nature had inspired in him the desire to go to sea as soon as he was old enough. Possibly his unknown father had been a sailor. Anyway, to be one himself was his earliest, his lasting ambition. There'd been an interval when he was rather too big to beg; and during that time he'd run with the other boys, stealing if a chance offered, doing odd jobs and errands. The old woman ran things in a simple way; if you went home once with no loot and no coin she'd grumble and give you a bit of whatever there was to eat, but if you were unlucky on the second day then you were unlucky indeed, you got nothing. It was a hard, haphazard life, but he'd known no other, so he never felt sorry for himself. And somehow, he grew up to be big and strong and remarkably good-looking. Whoever his parents had been it seemed that they had both been Greek, of pure blood; there was nothing of the mongrel blur and conflict about his features or his colouring.

When he was twelve he went to sea for the first time in a very menial capacity, a fetch-and-carry boy, even his name lost. "You" they called him. Do this, you! Look sharp, you! You, get out of the way! His upbringing had sharpened his wits, and while he fetched and carried, and looked sharp and got out of people's way, he'd learned a lot. At fifteen he was a sailor. And he, too, was always openhanded with small coins for small beggars.

At twenty he was working on a ship which plied regularly between Byblos and Alexandria. From Byblos they carried the Eastern goods that had already travelled for months on the overland caravan routes; spices from the far islands, silk from China, from India jewels and a very fine, almost transparent material which women liked for veils and headdresses. To all these was added a certain amount of the precious Tyrian purple dye. Out from Alexandria they carried papyrus. Byblos and the papyrus trade were so firmly linked that the town had given its name to the books made of the papyrus; Byblos softened down to bible, meaning a book. Also from Egypt the ship brought objects made of glass, and from one of his voyages Ephorus had brought Dorcas a string of glass beads which had cost far more than he could afford, but were beautiful, curiously mottled, pink, purple, and rose-coloured. A wonderful present, but of course, unworthy of her.

Unworthy . . . that was the key word; it ran like a song theme with many minor variations, through all his dealings with her. Women like Dorcas weren't caught young and trained and schooled for the delectation of common sailors. They were the hetaira, designed for the delight of men's minds as well as their bodies; they could all converse with wit and intelligence; some could sing, some could dance or play musical instruments. They did not ply for hire, like the common prostitutes who flaunted themselves on the quayside and in the streets; they were not compelled to consort with any chance comer like the girls in ordinary brothels. Money was involved, of course, the hetaira were a luxury, but the business side was very discreetly handled; and because the girls were allowed freedom of choice and were all so beautiful, elegant, and clever an association with one of them was a thing to boast about.

Ephorus knew nothing of this when one evening he saw an open door and heard music and saw men coming and going and followed a group of men in. Once inside he knew that he was, as he termed it, off-course; but his pay was heavy in his pocket and he'd braced himself defiantly, thinking, My money is as good as the next man's. In the paved and pillared atrium, prettily arranged with urns of flowers and singing birds in cages, he'd braved some curious, some hard, some almost amused glances, and then, all at once, he'd found himself in such company, enjoying such happiness as he had never dreamed existed. He had never talked to anyone, let alone any woman, as he could talk to Dorcas.

She had never set foot on a ship, yet she seemed to be conversant with nautical terms, with sea routes. She had never been to Tyre or Carthage or Alexandria, yet she knew as much about them and a dozen other places as he who had visited them all. He was astonished and enchanted and at the same time humbled. She was so lovely, so clever that she seemed to him almost like a goddess, and at first the idea of using her as he had used other women here and there, was inconceivable. Later his astonishment and enchantment grew at finding her just like other women, but infinitely sweeter, infinitely more skilled.

She said, "What are you doing in a place like this?"

"You mean that this is no place for a common sailor?"

She laughed. "Don't be so touchy. That isn't what I meant at all. I meant that you are so young and so handsome. Why should you pay for what any girl would gladly give?"

He said, "After tonight there will never be another girl for me."

"I should have added a flattering tongue when I listed your attractions," she said.

After that his sea-going life, hitherto his whole life, his chosen life, his achieved ambition, meant nothing but enforced absence from what he loved. The voyages were vast desolate stretches between brief joys. He fretted incessantly. To whom was she talking, now? To whom, at this moment, was she opening Paradise? It was terrible to have set the private mark of one's heart upon a public thing. But he had done so, and there was no help for it.

There came a time when he could bear it no longer: he asked her to marry him.

He was not surprised that she should look amazed; he was amazed at his own audacity.

"Don't laugh at me," he begged her. "That I couldn't bear. I've nothing to offer you except my love. I know. But don't laugh."

"Why should I laugh? Ephorus, how old are you?"

"I'm not certain. If the old woman reckoned rightly, and she's all I have to go by, I'm about twenty-one."

Dorcas said, "I'm thirty. Eight years from now you will be in your prime and I shall be an ageing woman, with no beauty left."

He had never thought of her as being of any age and by this time he was not particularly conscious of her looks. There was the beautiful façade, but that was largely artifice, hair elaborately curled, white skin that the sun never touched, eyes made to look large and languorous. The real Dorcas, the woman he loved, lived inside this pretty shell and was a different person altogether. He often caught glimpses of her behind all the decoration. He tried to put this into words and failed.

He said, "If you went bald, or were pitted by pox, you'd look the same to me. I love you."

She didn't say what he yearned to hear—that she loved him, though he had sensed the possibility that she did, otherwise he would never have dared to mention marriage.

She said, "I think you are a poet, Ephorus. And that means you could be dangerous to yourself. You make statements like this inside your head, and they sound well. But you mustn't believe them."

"But it is true. Let me prove it."

"By losing my hair and getting pox-pitted? Dear Ephorus, what a thing to ask."

"I'm asking you to marry me."

She moved, restively. "Nobody marries women like me. Well, now and then perhaps; some old man, already provided with heirs. You see, we are barren. The precautions we take, the draughts we drink if they fail, offend the gods of fertility and we become barren."

"I don't want children," he said with great vehemence. "I want you."

"But my dear, you can't afford me. I am a plaything, a toy. I can neither cook nor sew. I have never in my life been in a market. Until I have it on a plate before me I can't tell a melon from a cucumber or beef from mutton. I sleep till mid-day. Just imagine what a wife I should make."

She spoke with sincerity, honestly hoping to dissuade him. In her life he struck almost as strange a note as she had struck in his, and for the first time in many years she was unsure of herself. He was young and handsome, his devotion was very touching; it would, she knew, be all too easy to love him; but what then? Poverty, ugly in itself and with an infinite capacity for making everything it touched ugly too. Could love compensate? Would it last? Could a woman of thirty, reared and trained as specially as a chariot horse, make the necessary adjustments? She didn't know; she wished he had not disturbed the nice balance of their relationships by his simple forthright question.

Ephorus said, narrowing his eyes, "Suppose, just *suppose*, that I made some money. Not a lot, but enough. Enough to hire a little white house, and to buy you a slave who could tell melon from cucumber. What then?"

Why must he mention a little *white* house? A lifetime ago, when she was young, thirteen, fourteen, rebellious against her lot, a little white house had been visible from the window of the room that had been allotted to her. It was gone now, torn down to make room for a great tenement building; but she remembered it. A small white house, a woman, several children, a man who came home every night. The woman was always busy, cooking, washing, wiping a child's nose, picking up one that had fallen, occasionally dealing out smacks all round; but the girl Dorcas, busy then with mastering the Latin tongue and the playing of the lute and how to look, how to speak, how to arrange her hands and feet, had watched, often with envy, the simple domestic life in the little white house.

A lifetime ago.

Now she said, "Ephorus, I do not know. I was taught early to avoid four things, obesity, pregnancy, boredom, and sentiment. It may be that on the last I have failed my teacher. I do feel for you what no woman of my kind should feel for any man. But I am afraid. It could so easily be as it was when Psyche lit her lamp. For us the lamp would be the light of common day; in that light what should we see? I should see a young man and count my years and be sad. You would see an ageing sloven and feel defrauded. Leave it as it is, for a time at least. Visit me when you can. And look about for a girl of your own age and kind. Teach her, if you wish, something of what I have taught you, so that kneading her dough and chopping her onions she will think of the night's joy and feel her bones melt. That way you will have a faithful wife and may remember me with gratitude. Better still, forget me altogether."

Ephorus said, "That is nonsense, and you must know it. I could *never* forget you. I told you, on that first night, that there would never be another girl for me. And it is true. You know how sailors are welcomed, set upon, wherever they go. I swear that for me the women might be apes or goats or stone statues for all I care."

And that was how she had been trained to look at men. Not as people. Her indifference had been cultivated, but she understood exactly what Ephorus meant. Out of a world populated by shadows, one person emerged, whole, real, as real and as dear as oneself. So easy to give in, to let oneself be carried away, to say yes, and yes, and yes, to pledge oneself with a kiss and begin to make plans. But there was this eight-year gap which poverty would only emphasise. Oh dear, she thought, I was taught so much, but never how to deal with such a situation.

"I know," he said, "how to make some money. Real money."

"You're not to do anything dangerous, or illegal. Please, Ephorus, I have to live with myself, and if I thought that because of *me* you had run into trouble, I should never sleep easily again."

He said, "It isn't dangerous . . ." and whether that were truth or a lie he couldn't tell; the whole thing was so shrouded in mystery and in silence that nobody knew. "And it isn't illegal. It is the one way in which a sailor can make money."

And although he had, from the first, appreciated her sharp intelligence and wealth of information, he was startled, somewhat displeased, when she said:

"The tin trade! Ephorus, no! That is suicidal. Do you want to saddle me with the responsibility for your death?"

He asked truculently, "What do you know about it?"

"More than you do, I'll warrant. Do you realise, Ephorus, that on a tin-trading ship you have not only the elements, the wind and the waves, lightning and thunder against you, but your own ship's master? The secret is so valuable, so precious, that men swear to keep it, even if it costs them their lives."

"How do you know so much about it?"

"Never mind that. I know. I could, but I won't, give you the name of a ship master who, finding that he was followed by a spy ship, marking his course, deliberately ran his ship aground. Half his crew died, drowned; he and those who remained with him, walked for a month through Iberia and many more died of starvation and exhaustion. He survived—and he was rewarded; a ship had been lost and many men had died; but the secret had been kept and that was all that mattered. I *know*," she said, reaching out and taking his hand and beginning to weave her smooth white fingers with his, "that set in the scales against possible profit a man's life weighs lightly anywhere, but in the tin trade it does not weigh at all. The tin ships are in the charge of men who set no value on themselves, much less on their crew."

He thought that she exaggerated. In his time he had known several reckless men, but they were, really, men who trusted their luck and were inwardly sure that the risks they seemed to take were not risks at all. A deliberately self-destructive man he had never yet encountered; frankly he doubted whether such a one existed. Men owned ships for profit, and other men sailed them for pay. True, the whole of the tin trade was a mystery, but he could not believe that any ship's master would sacrifice his life to preserve his secret.

However, Dorcas appeared to believe it and, to lift the look of trouble from her face, he said:

"Why are we talking about the tin ships? That may be one way to make money, but I know another, and much safer way."

"What is it?"

"That is a secret, too." And though she teased him and tried to trick him into telling her he remained obdurate. Had he been quick-witted enough to invent a believable story—believable to a woman of her intelligence—he would have told it; so he teased her back, saying that she knew too much already and that no woman could keep a secret. Then he came back to his original question; if he were lucky and returned with enough money to hire a house and buy a slave, would she marry him?

She looked at him, her eyes very clear between their artificially darkened lashes, their artificially lustrous lids.

"You are absurd," she said. "And very young, and very sweet."

"Good enough to wait for?"

"Oh, I shall be here," she said. "I shall be here when you return, and we'll talk of it then. How long will this mysterious, profitable voyage take?"

"It could be a year," he said, knowing nothing about it but feeling that in the circumstances it was better to guess at too long a time, rather than too short a one.

"A year. To me that will seem a short time. Did you know that, Ephorus? As one gathers years, each one seems shorter than the last." She put her hands on either side of his head, digging the tips of her fingers into the crisp, close curls. "Swear to me," she said, "that you are not embarking upon any dangerous or difficult enterprise."

"I swear that. It's a simple easy way of making money which would cease to be profitable if more people knew about it. And you will wait for me?"

"If, during this voyage which will last a year, you promise to think over what I have said. And promise to consider yourself free; not bound in any way to a woman who would make a bad, barren wife."

He said, "You are the one woman in the world for me. As for

children; you can buy them, you know, in any market, choosing the sex, the size and shape, the age, even the disposition that you prefer. In Delos I saw children with labels about their necks; one label read 'This boy bites if provoked.' He fetched a good price."

"Oh, why must we bother about the future?" she asked. "To go, to stay, to wait upon the morrow, which the gods hold in their careless hands. This is now, and you are here and I am here. Let us make the most of the moment that is ours."

So they made love once again, in the small pretty scented room. And then he had gone straight out and sold himself into the tin trade.

The place that one sailed for was called the unknown destination; the world's end; the hidden place. And before he was accepted he had to subject himself to a strict inquisition, ominous in its implications and very enlightening. When he emerged from it he knew why the ship master whom Dorcas had mentioned had wrecked his ship rather than allow himself to be spied upon and followed—his family was his hostage. The tin-traders had a monopoly and they guarded it unscrupulously; no man ever took ship on this enterprise without knowing that not only his life was at stake, but the life of someone beloved.

In the office where Ephorus offered himself, the man asked why he wished to make this venture; and he gave an honest answer; he wished to make money, so that he could marry. Marry whom? He gave her name, just as every other man who sailed for the unknown destination had given the name of someone who mattered to him.

"Come back tomorrow," the man in the office had said; and when, on the next day, Ephorus presented himself, he knew that there had been a check, to make sure that Dorcas existed and was there, in Byblos, easily available, to be tortured, killed, if he should fail in any way, or should utter an indiscreet word. Tin was the most important commodity, scarcer than gold, and the few Phoenicians who held the trade in their hands knew the value of the secret.

The man in the office was quite blunt, as he could afford to be.

"A complaint," he said, "or a misplaced question, a comment, a hint, an unconsidered word, and . . ." He made the gesture of a man slashing a knife across a throat. Ephorus thought, With other men, no doubt, he makes different gestures; Dorcas is particularly vulnerable in this respect. Any man with a knife could enter that house. . . .

He said, "I understand; no complaints, I promise; no question, no loose talk."

"Very well. You are hired. Take this"—he handed Ephorus a small clay tablet, with, inset on its upper side, a tiny thread of tin, not much thicker than a hair and in length the eighth of a man's thumb—"to Appolodorus, on the *Dido*."

When he handed the clay tablet to Appolodorus that stout cheerful man had said, "Oh. One in two hundred! Well, boy, if we're lucky you won't be able to buy up Byblos when we get back, but you should have what it would take you ten years to earn in any other trade."

And that was exactly what the dockside whisper had said— one voyage on a tin ship paid as well as ten in any other kind. Ephorus, settling down amongst his fellows, all for some reason desperate and committed men, thought of the little house, the busy slave, and Dorcas, enshrined.

He had known, for this was common talk in all the ports, that voyages made to the secret place were not very pleasant. Ships that went in search of tin faced unimaginable dangers, places where the sea was a sheet of flame and sails scorched; places where two-headed monsters rose from the sea and crunched a ship in their jaws; places where there were women with snakes for hair, and kisses that were irresistible and fatal. He'd heard all the stories; discounting some and believing others, he had been prepared to risk all for Dorcas' sake. When he had been aboard *Dido* for a short time, he began to suspect that old seamen were paid to sit about in taverns and tell such discouraging tales. *Dido* sailed due West, holding roughly to a course that he knew; but she did not go South to Carthage, or

North to Marsala. Soon they were in waters farther West than any he had known, but the sea was not on fire and there were no snake-haired women. Finally they came to a place of which Ephorus had heard but which he had never seen, the Pillars of Hercules as it was called, where the known sea ended in a narrow passage between high escarpments, Calpe and Abyla. This was, to sailors, the end of the world. But not to Appolodorus. He pressed on, through the straits and into the sea beyond, which was ordinary sea, though rougher than any Ephorus had yet sailed. And—this was what Ephorus, years later in Bethlehem, remembered—there was no sun. They moved now between a grey sea and a grey sky, a curious twilit world. Soon they took a northerly course and then, turning East, headed for the land which lay, tiger-coloured, on their starboard side, but they did not make port. They anchored and a swarm of little boats came out from the tawny land, boats manned by men with Phoenician faces, clothes, and tongues. This, then, Ephorus said to himself, is the unknown destination, the source of tin. But he was wrong. What the swarming boats carried were fresh supplies of perishable foodstuffs, meat, vegetables, fruit, and cheese. With stores replenished, they headed out into such a sea as Ephorus had never imagined, a sea which, by a fine irony, took away the appetite of even the most hardened. The grey sea reared and tumbled, and every wave bore a crest of white foam which often blew free and with the wind behind it stung faces and hands. *Dido* plunged and rolled and every man in her, even Appolodorus, was grimly sick; the wind flung foam and rain, and worse than rain, small pieces of ice at the sick, dizzy, reeling men who manned the tortured ship. But she survived, and so did they, and presently the seas smoothed out, the wind eased, the belly muscles ceased their spasmodic contractions, and Appolodorus, his face coloured as no human face should be, green around the mouth and purple around the eyes, said, "We've made the Bay. And that is what we're paid for."

There was still no sun; a faint golden glimmer around midday sometimes, a pink glow at dawn or sunset, but on the whole a grey, cool, sad light divided dark from dark. Spirits were low.

Even the inevitable quarrels seemed muted and halfhearted. Ephorus was the only member of the crew making the voyage for the first time, and experienced men said that often it was worse than this; sometimes the grey sky sank until it joined the sea and progress was halted and men walked about through a clammy cloud.

At last they sighted land; it rose from the sea, a blur of solid grey in the greyness, and then slowly it revealed itself in colour and shape, a red and rocky coast, with waves beating high and hard at the foot of the cliffs and creaming over the small rocks with which the sea was sown. There seemed to be no harbour, no houses, no people. The jagged, rose-coloured coast, and as they came nearer, inland a wonderful green became visible. Ephorus had never seen a green so vivid, nor quite such an inhospitable shore.

Appolodorus nosed the ship nearer, the man with the plumb line calling soundings every few minutes; then, just short of the outmost fringe of rocks, they anchored and a man ran to the ship's bows and blew a horn. Blast after blast sounded through the sunless air, apparently into empty silence.

And then, suddenly it seemed, the narrow fringes of the shore at the places where the sea had beaten the red cliffs back, there were men, running, running into the water and dragging with them dark, circular objects which floated upon the sea, and into which, once they were afloat, the men jumped, took up paddles and came, with what seemed incredible speed, towards *Dido*. Ephorus stared with interest at these boats, if boats they could be called. What brave crazy people these must be, he thought, to venture out, in such a sea in what were no more than round baskets, fashioned from boughs over which hides had been stretched. These men were not Phoenicians, as the men from the tawny-coloured land had been; they were a different breed altogether, with round dark heads and very light skins, so light that the blood showed, red, in their faces.

Appolodorus opened the chest which had lain, locked, in *Dido's* hold. There were knives, and arrow heads, some lengths of brightly coloured cotton cloth, copper bracelets and anklets, some articles of pottery of the coarsest, cheapest kind, boxes of dried figs and dates and raisins; a sack of almonds. There were only three things of any real value; one was a lump of amber on a silver chain, one a silver brooch set with a piece of turquoise, and one a highly polished silver mirror such as rich men used for shaving and rich women used for self-admiration.

The natives, very quietly and shyly, loaded *Dido* with lumps of tin, some freshly mined and shining, some grown over with moss, as green as the inland meadows, some white with encrusted sea-salt. A year's hoard at least.

It took some time since the flimsy round boats could carry only small amounts.

Appolodorus said, "This could be done in half the time if everybody dealt with them as honestly as I do. There was a time when the women used to come out too, then some wretched fellow grabbed a few, thinking they'd fetch a good price at Delos—they're very pretty. So now, when they hear the horn they hide their women and only men come out. And grabbing them, everybody knows, is sheer waste of time. They can't live in captivity."

There was no attempt at communication. When the last lump of tin was delivered a man who seemed to be the leader of the group—he wore a wolf skin around his middle and his chest, upper arms and legs were stained with a blue dye—simply spread his hands to signify that that was the end. Appolodorus with a similar gesture indicated the chest and man after man took the object nearest to hand without any discrimination.

"They share it out, later, amongst themselves," Appolodorus explained.

Carrying their payment—pitiable in comparison with the worth of what they had delivered—the men paddled back to shore; but Appolodorus did not immediately give any order. He waited; and soon the little round boats were heading out again. This time they brought fresh meat and fish, baskets of berries, some horns hollowed out to make drinking cups, ornaments of bleached bone, curiously carved. These were presented with eloquent gestures of the hands, and with the first smiles Ephorus had seen on the pink and white faces.

"They always do that," the man standing nearest to Ephorus explained. "They're very generous. Gentlemen, in a savage sort of way. It's a pity they're doomed."

"Are they?"

"It's my guess that in twenty years or less this'll be Roman territory."

"Then what about the tin trade?"

The man shrugged. "All organised and taxed! But by that time I shall be done with it. I had six daughters," he explained. "I've dowered four and married them. This trip should take care of the other two. . . ."

Heavily laden, *Dido* headed South. In the Bay the weather was rather worse and she was no longer buoyant; everyone in her was—which would have seemed impossible—more nauseated than before. Then she slipped between the Pillars of Hercules, this time so close to Apyla that one could see the apes bounding about on its rocky face, and then they were back in the known world, making for Byblos.

There was a waiting time—to the impatient Ephorus a long, an interminable time—while the tin was assessed; then, according to his term of contract, every man was paid off.

Walking so fast that he was almost running, Ephorus began to make his way along one of the narrow alleys that led from the quay, one of his childhood's haunts. And there he was accosted not by a painted harlot or a mendicant child, but by a young man, wearing the toga of Roman citizenship, neatly groomed, well shaven, but apparently exuberantly drunk. He said, barring Ephorus' way:

"Welcome home, sailor. I'll warrant you have a thirst. Come and take a cup of wine with me."

"I've no time," Ephorus said brusquely. "Let me pass."

The young man reeled against the filthy wall and hiccupped. Then he turned about and was walking as near alongside as the narrowness of the alley permitted.

"You think I'm drunk, don't you?"

"What is that to me?"

"You're right. I am. So would you be. I've just come into a legacy. All made out of sailors' sweat, so I thought I'd spend a little on sailors."

"Find one who isn't in a hurry. I am."

"Wife waiting? Ha ha! You been long away?"

"Six months," Ephorus said untruthfully.

"Tell me; did you ever see a mermaid?"

"No."

"They say there's a rock off Sicily where they sit and comb their hair. You ever been to Sicily?"

"In my time."

"Not this time? What a pity! I dote upon sailors' tales. Come and drink wine with me and tell me a tale."

"I told you," Ephorus said impatiently. "I have no time; I have no desire to drink and no tale to tell."

"Uncivil," the young man said in a maudlin, reproachful voice.

They had reached the point where the narrow alley opened into a wide busy street, and stumbling as he turned, the seeming drunkard began to retrace his steps. Within three paces Ephorus heard the change in the rhythm of the walk, and glancing back saw the man making for the quay with a purposeful and completely sober stride.

It might have been a serious attempt to get him drunk and wagging an incautious tongue; it might have been a deliberate trap, laid by the shipowner. Dismissing it thus, he hurried on.

It was still early in the day. The house was shuttered and dark and very quiet. A slave was apathetically swabbing the floor of the atrium and hardly bothered to look up as he entered. He said:

"Rouse Dorcas. Tell her Ephorus is here."

Now that the moment had come his heart beat with such excitement and exultation that it shook him to his finger-tips. All through his absence—ten months and eighteen days—he had exercised a Spartan self-control, knowing that it was useless to tantalise himself with dreams and hopes and plans. He'd gone from this place with the object of making money, knowing that he might perish in the attempt.

He was back; in a few minutes Dorcas would come; he would show her his money; assure her of his ability to provide.

He stood waiting; staring around the place which he had never before visited in daylight hours. For all its grandeur it had the sleasy, somewhat furtive look of a place devoted to the pleasures of the night. She would be glad to be out of it.

The slave came back, gave him what he called a silly look—but she had, by nature, a silly expression—and resumed the floor washing. Then, through the arch came, not Dorcas, but another girl named Lydia, known to him by sight and by name but hardly recognisable. She had just been roused from sleep and her un-painted face looked almost phosphorescent in the gloom. But she was a professional; she made an effort, said, "Welcome back, Ephorus," and laid her henna-tipped fingers on his arm.

"Where's Dorcas?" he asked. The dry-leaf rustling whisper was not his own voice.

"She's gone."

"Gone," he repeated stupidly. "Gone where?"

"I don't know."

"Then fetch somebody who does."

"Oh, if she'd told anybody, she'd have told me," Lydia said. "But she wouldn't tell me. So nobody knows."

"When did she go?"

"A little more than three months ago. I miss her very much."

"*You* miss her!" he said brutally. "I came back to marry her!"

"Oh. Then that is why she left you a message."

Stupid bitch, he thought. Of course Dorcas would have left a message for him; and anybody with any sense would have said so, at first.

"What was it?"

She closed her heavy eyes and said, like a child dutifully re-peating a well-conned lesson:

"She said, 'If Ephorus comes, tell him I wish him well and not to be unhappy because he will live to thank me.' That is what she said." She opened her eyes and blinked.

"And that is all? Think. Try to remember. Nothing else?"

"Nothing else. Ephorus, you are distressed. Let me get you a drink."

"Who'd she go with?"

"Oh, a man." The way she said that indicated what a stupid question it was.

"What man? What was his name?"

"How should I know? He wasn't my customer. He wasn't a regular. He came—twice I think. The second time he gave her a bracelet. She said, 'Look what my fat friend gave me.' He was fat. Then she told me she was going to live with him. But she didn't say where, and she gave me the message for you. Oh, and she's gone to a palace."

"How do you know that?"

"When she packed. She was in a strange mood, not like herself at all, half-laughing, half-crying. She took things out of her chest and said, 'Is this fit wear for a palace? No!' And then she'd fling them on the floor. She took hardly anything."

"And you haven't any idea where the palace is? Lydia, even if she vowed you to secrecy, tell me. I must know."

"She didn't tell me anything. It was all very sudden; and I had my own customers. She just told me she was going and gave me the message for you. What she said about the clothes told me that she'd gone to a palace. And that, Ephorus, truly is all I know. Except that it is a *red* palace."

"Red? Who told you that?"

"She did. At least, I guessed. You see she had a red dress; new; she'd only worn it once. She threw it on the floor with the rest. She said she wouldn't take it, there was enough of that colour where she was going; even the stones there were red. . . ."

She was more widely awake now, recovered from her abrupt wakening.

She said, "If you really thought of marrying her, I'm sorry, Ephorus. And I think you need a cup of wine. Come with me. She's gone, but we're still here."

Business as usual!

Repulsed, with no word spoken, simply reading the look on his face, she hunched a shoulder and said, not without malice:

"The way she went was understandable. She's gone with a rich man, to live in a palace; she wouldn't want anybody who knew her here to go seeking her out. Would she?"

Something must have happened inside his head. He had no memory of taking leave of Lydia or of leaving the house. But here he was, in a tavern, and pretty drunk, too. Folding his arms on the table, putting his head down on them and crying. Everything wrapped in a red mist.

And there was the tavern keeper saying in a quiet, tactful way, "Go elsewhere to weep, please. It is such a bad advertisement."

The man was fat. Noting this, through the red mist, Ephorus said:

"I hate fat fellows. A fat fellow robbed me. A fat fellow in a red palace. She said a year would go swiftly, but when I was sick in my belly it seemed a long time. And how many *red* palaces are there in this world? Because I shall find her if it takes the rest of my life."

The tavern keeper, experienced and reasonably honest, helped him to his feet. "You go home and sleep it off. And look out for that money."

"I shall," Ephorus assured him. "I spewed it up, every coin, out of my guts."

And so began the timeless time when he was never sober from the moment he woke until he fell into sodden sleep again. But in every day there was a time when, sober enough to be coherent, drunk enough to be confidential, he'd ask anyone who gave him a moment's attention, if they'd ever heard of a red palace. And the day came when a man said:

"That'd be Petra, surely. Red as a rose they say it is. Red as a rose."

"They say? Who says so? Have you ever seen anybody who's been there?"

"Yes, I have," the man said a little truculently. "A man I do business with. If you want to know, it's the capital of Nabatea, a very busy place, with caravan routes to Gaza and Bosra and Damascus. And it's all cut out of red rock, houses, palaces, and temples. Quite a sight to see. But it's a long way away."

Ephorus asked a few questions about direction and received unsatisfactory and conflicting answers which worried him little. It was only a question of navigation, he told himself; he had a Greek tongue in his head, and on none of his voyages—except to the tin island—had he found a place where he couldn't make himself understood. Money didn't bother him either; he still had some; less than he should have had, for he had been drunk in dubious company more than once; if the money gave out before he reached Petra he would have to earn some, or beg or steal.

What exactly he intended to do when he reached the distant city, found a red palace and Dorcas in it, he didn't know. Shock and steady drinking had rendered him incapable of making any coherent plans. He felt under a compulsion to see Dorcas again, to reproach her to her face; he wished to do some real damage to the fat man who had, he felt, robbed him. Meanwhile he walked.

He was still drinking; his hearty appetite had vanished, and at the end of a day's march he was often too tired to eat. So he drank and slept, woke in the morning with a queasy stomach and walked on. The weather was hot, and this was the first time he had experienced the inland heat. At mid-day or about then he'd buy bread or fruit, find a shady place, eat and rest a little, then on again. He was aware, in a dull kind of way, that his hitherto superb health had deserted him; there were times when he turned dizzy, times when he shook as though he had palsy, times when he lost his sight for a few minutes.

He had such a spell one afternoon, just after he had resumed walking; and the next thing he knew, he was lying on a bed and being tended by Eunice. She told him—oh, how often—how a decent honest man with two camels had deposited him at her inn, senseless and naked but for a breechclout. "Nobody but me would have taken you in," Eunice said. Over and over again.

Somebody must have robbed him, even of his shoes. And probably hit him over the head, too, for he was now disabled in a fashion which did, he knew, result from some head injuries. His left arm and leg were almost powerless, seemed to weigh heavily and were afflicted, every now and again, with a maddening tingling.

Eunice couldn't have been kinder. She was Greek, which made a bond; she was eight or nine years older than he, and not uncomely in her way. She was so sympathetic that she invited confidences, and to her he told what, drunk or sober, he had never told in full to anyone—the story of his love and his betrayal.

She said, "You're young. You'll get over it. Your mind will mend with your body."

His mind, if not mending, was clearing because for the first time since his talk with Lydia, he was sober; and he could see the sense of Eunice's argument when she said:

"Maybe it's a good thing you never got to Petra. What could you have done there? If the man's rich, he's powerful. You couldn't have hurt him, and he could have hurt you. Got you locked up for being a nuisance if nothing else. As for her, she made her choice, didn't she? She'd laugh to think of you trudging all those miles just to have a look at her. That's all you'd have had, you know. Just a look."

The room where he lay, with its thick mud roof, its thick, sun-defying walls, its vine-shrouded windows, was as cool as Eunice's reasoning.

"You just lie and get better," she said. "I'll look after you."

Getting better took a long time, and when he could stand, and had learned to walk again, the left leg still dragged and the left hand was not to be wholly trusted. He was in no shape to continue his journey and no longer felt the urge to do so. Nor could he ply his old trade again. What should he do?

He talked this over with Eunice, and she had the answer. For her it couldn't have worked out better; she had always helped her father with the inn, and he had died only a short time before the good-hearted man had brought Ephorus to her door. She'd been waiting for a purchaser for the place, since innkeeping wasn't a job for a woman alone. Why shouldn't Ephorus stay and help her?

She did not, at that point, make any mention of what she had done for him or imply that he'd owed her anything. Ephorus, however, realised that he was in her debt and felt that now he was almost able-bodied he should stay and help her for a bit.

Eunice wove her net cunningly; she made him very comfortable, and Ephorus, who had never known a home, was susceptible to domestic order and ease. She coddled him and flattered him, listened, seemingly entranced to his tales of his sea-faring days, forbade him to overexert himself; it was his presence about the place that mattered, she said.

He drifted on; and when by little signs and hints she indicated that her objective was to get him into her bed, he drifted there, too. Grateful, not unflattered. She was surprisingly good in bed. He never asked, never even wondered, where she had learned such tricks. What he did tell himself was that in the ultimate act one woman in bed was very much like another. And out of it there was nothing, not a turn of the head, not a tone of the voice to rouse an unwelcome memory or a hurtful comparison. When Eunice revealed her next objective, marriage, he drifted will-lessly into that, too.

There was no visible reason why they should not have become just another married couple, moderately happy, more than moderately comfortable; but almost immediately after the marriage their relationship deteriorated. Neither he nor she changed overnight, yet the changes came. Some obscure dissatisfaction in her turned her sour, she became a nagging scold; he sought refuge in the wine jar and in dreams, which even as he entertained them, he knew would come to nothing, of making his escape. For several years there was the bond of bed, but that failed at last. Under her nagging his indifference changed to active dislike, and that made him impotent; and that gave her something else to taunt him with.

The inn prospered, however. Eunice was a good manager, and Ephorus, though he worked slowly and only a little each day, had improved its appearance. It was known as a respectable place, and Vatinius, the centurion in charge of the small barracks not far away, always recommended it to the newly arrived legionaries, at the same time tactfully avoiding it himself since men off duty are off duty and do not care to be overlooked.

It stood at the end of the street, set back in what, before Ephorus' time had been a yard, dusty, unshaded, uncared for. He'd planted trees around it, made stands for lanterns, set benches and tables under the trees. He'd sawn old casks in half, painted them green, and in spring and summer kept them filled with flowers.

Behind this pleasant courtyard stood the house; one big public room, the kitchen, and opening off the kitchen two small rooms, one where the two female slaves slept, one where Eunice and Ephorus fought their more private battles and Eunice, when she was not otherwise busy, made and mended clothes. Above there were five rooms, one the connubial chamber, the others for letting to travellers who could afford to pay for privacy.

At the back of the house, accessible from a side entry, was a yard with a large water-trough in the centre of it. On two sides the yard was enclosed by a low platform, roofed over, and it was on this platform that most travellers slept. The third side was open to the orchard and garden; the fourth was occupied by a stable in which, in winter, the house cow and the ass, which was used for serious marketing, and for carrying firewood, lived. In summer they were turned into the orchard, often enough with a calf, a young pig, or a sheep, which Eunice, careful housekeeper that she was, was fattening up. The inn animals were never allowed to mingle with those of the travellers; transient animals had all kinds of diseases, from foot-rot to the itch; and many of them were so perpetually hungry, so accustomed to shouldering others aside in order to eat themselves that any well-behaved animal in the enclosure would have starved. Eunice had explained that to the ignorant Ephorus years ago when he had suggested that their animals should share the yard and that the stable should be floored, opened on the side facing the yard and made into extra sleeping space. That was in the days when she still explained things; now she would merely have shouted and called him ignorant; but he'd stopped making suggestions long ago.

The snow, which he had sensed when he opened the shutters, held off until almost sunset. By that time the animal enclosure and the platforms were almost full and Eunice was in a raging temper—and in her element. People who, had the weather been clement, would have hoarded their pennies and slept at small cost under the awning, came and asked for room in the house. Poorer people who, had the weather been clement, would have slept in the open, came and asked for room under the awning; the good manager, the bully who shared Eunice's hide, had enjoyed themselves hugely, Ephorus thought to himself. She had anticipated this invasion at about this time; she had heard about the new tax rule some time before, and talking about it had betrayed her latent scorn and contempt of the people amongst whom she had spent her whole life. "They'll obey," she said, "like sheep. Such a silly order, given to *our* people would have led to rebellion." She had laid in stores; enough to feed an army. She could feed all-comers, and their beasts. But space she couldn't make, though she did her best. She went to the edge of the platforms and cried, "Move along there! Move along, I said. You there, move along. You're taking up room for three. It's a bad night, shelter must be found. Take that child in your lap. Make room."

She was having a wonderful time; she came back into the house, the snowflakes melting on her still-dark hair, and went into the room where supper was being served.

"Eat up! Others are waiting. I have many more to feed. Eat up, please."

With swift competence, aided by the panting slaves, she served supper three times over, and then set about converting the big room into an extra sleeping space.

During all this haste and confusion and noise Ephorus stayed, as was his habit, inactive and apart. It was a curious thing, but never, even at her busiest, did Eunice make any demands upon him for help. She'd say, "Oh, get out of my way," in an irritable tone if she happened to pass within a yard of him, but she did not suggest that he should carry a dish, full or empty, or go out into the yard and, by shouting, pack one extra body onto the platform, or crowd one extra donkey into the enclosure. Her attitude towards his drinking was similarly negative; she would remark, hastily, that he was drunk again, would say that he had better lie down before he fell, but she never made any attempt to persuade him not to drink, seemed to ignore the frequency of his visits to the small, half-subterranean store where the wine was kept. A shrewd, impartial observer might have deduced that as he was, idle, drunken will-less, she wanted him to be.

Tonight he had no place to sit; the house was crammed; his bed and Eunice's and those of the two slaves would presently be spread in the kitchen. In every other place people, weary from travel, or wishing to make sure of their sleeping space, were lying down. Because of the weather it was impossible to have any shutters but two on the leeward side of the house open, and very soon the air was foetid, the stink of human bodies mingling with that of food. He must have air, he thought. He stepped over and around the recumbent forms on the floor of the public room and went to the wine store and poured himself not a cup but a jug of wine, and carrying it in his hand went to the door. He'd had some intention of sitting on the bench under the trees for a few minutes; but the wind was too bitter and snow was still falling; so he stood in the shelter of the doorway, braced against the jamb, staring into the night and lifting the jug to his lips every now and again.

There were lanterns on the two posts which he had set up at each side of the entry, and another hanging from a hook over the door. Each had a faint golden halo of light in which the slow, spiralling flakes were visible. Like life, he reflected, his thoughts as idle and aimless as the snow; out of the dark, a brief space in the light, and into the dark again. No permanence, and no point.

From the kitchen, where one of the shutters was open, he could hear Eunice's voice, railing away. He could catch no words, but he knew her tirades so well that he could have repeated them perfectly. She was an ill-done woman who worked her fingers to the bone and had no consideration from anybody, nor a word of thanks. Customers were demanding and greedy and prepared to be dishonest if given half a chance; the slaves were idle and clumsy. Why she should be expected to work herself to death, she really didn't know and she swore that tomorrow she'd sit down, fold her hands in her lap and see what happened then.

She was capable of expressing these few simple statements in such a variety of ways that she could grumble on for an hour.

He could hear, too, the clatter of dishes and bowls being washed and stacked; once something fell with a thud and that sound was immediately followed by that of a good smart slap.

He shivered, huddling in the doorway, and lifted the jug. He'd wait a little longer; then he could go in and help arrange the beds, and Eunice, exhausted, would fall asleep. That would be another day done.

Then, on the edge of the forecourt, the darkness between the two lanterns took on solidity, and shape, and movement. Silhouetted against the grey and the shift of the snow-filled air the figures showed up black, surprisingly clear. A man and a woman, their heads bowed against the blizzard, and a donkey, limping so badly that only the man, pulling at its head-rope kept it in motion at all. The woman had her hand on its flank, whether to support herself, or to help its sagging progress, it was impossible to say.

They stopped. The donkey dropped its head and looked as though it would never move again. The woman walked to the end of the bench and sat down as though she, too, had expended her last bit of strength. The man came towards the door, walking with a step that told of weariness and haste.

He was quite near the door when he realised that Ephorus was standing in its shelter.

He asked, in a deep, pleasant voice, "This is the inn?"

"It is. But you're too late. Not an inch left."

It occurred to him that he had never seen a more worried-looking man; no ship's master, in the most hazardous situation, had ever looked more anxious, more eaten up by fearful concern.

"Oh, please," the man said. "Just room for one. For my wife. That's all I ask. I know we're late; the donkey went lame. But you could find room just for one, surely."

"We're full," Ephorus said. "Packed like fish in a barrel."

He saw the expression of sheer despair wrench the man's face and in a laconic, wine-muffled way, he was sorry for him; but he thought, We all have our troubles. Still he roused himself enough to say:

"There's another inn on the other side of the town."

"I tried there. We came in that way. They were full. They suggested a private dwelling. I've tried dozens. All full. My wife"—he looked at the woman on the bench, and back, pleadingly at Ephorus—"she can't go farther. She *must* have a bed.

"I can pay. I'll pay anything." He was prepared, tomorrow, to go and sell himself into slavery; anything so that Mary should have shelter and a bed tonight.

His insistence exasperated Ephorus.

He said, "Well, I'm sorry; but I tell you, we're full. No room for a dwarf. We've been turning people away."

The man said, "Oh God! God!" It sounded as though he were praying; and Ephorus thought sardonically that he was wasting his breath; it'd puzzle even the Jews' God, that powerful Jehovah, to find a spare bed in Bethlehem at this time of night, on such a night. With that thought he turned himself and took the handle of the door in his free hand, which was his infirm, left hand, so he fumbled and was about to shift the jug and lift the handle with his good hand, when the woman stood up and came forward. She said, "Joseph," and the man turned and said in a terrible voice:

"There's no room here, either."

She said, "Don't fret. I'm rested now. We'll find a place . . ."

And by that time she was within the radius of light cast by the lantern over the doorway; and Ephorus' heart, quiescent for so long, gave a great jump, and seemed to stop. He had to put out his right hand and catch at the door jamb to save himself from falling, and the wine jug, entrusted to his untrustworthy left hand, did fall and break.

The face inside the blue hood was so like that of Dorcas—not the Dorcas he had known, but a younger Dorcas, untouched, unsullied, the girl whose existence he had always sensed, under the paint and the fine clothes.

It seemed a long time before he could find breath to speak. Then he said:

"Wait here. I'll see what I can do."

In the kitchen the dishwashing was finished; the slave girls were laying out the makeshift beds; Eunice, having talked herself to a standstill, was rubbing her mixture of honey and rosewater into her hands. She looked hot and flushed and formidable.

He said, "Eunice. There's a woman wanting a bed. Do you mind if she has my place?" Before she could protest he added cajolingly, "That way you'd be all females together. Better so."

"And where," Eunice asked, "do you propose to sleep?"

He had not given that a thought, but he scrambled about in his mind and found an answer.

"In the stable," he said. "Her husband's with her. We'll sleep in the stable."

"Alongside the donkey!" Eunice's voice took on its sharpest cutting edge. "Very right and proper. You and a fellow with a wife, hunting a bed at this time of night. You and him and the donkey—and the donkey with more sense than either of you. Well, if you don't mind, why should I? They'll pay. But I want to take a look at her first."

They went to the door. The man and the woman stood under its shelter, the donkey had hobbled forward and joined them.

"The best we can manage . . ." Eunice began, and then she rounded upon Ephorus. "You great fool! I knew you were a fool, but I didn't know you were blind! It isn't a bed she needs, it's a place to give birth in. And you'd have landed me with her, in my kitchen! You daft drunken sot!" She drew in her breath with the peculiar hissing sound that punctuated her worst tirades. "We have no room here. No room at all!"

Ephorus began to shake. Amongst all the other thoughts that battered him at that moment, a horrible memory came. Once, at Byblos, there'd been a beggar woman, one of those who came, purely to beg when a ship was about to sail. Women who met an incoming ship were all intent to sell themselves; those who begged from an outgoing ship were old, with no shadow of attractiveness left; they simply hoped that men with a few remaining coins, men who had just left wives, sweethearts, mothers behind, would be generous. This particular woman, holding out her hand with an imploring, ingratiating smile, had suddenly taken on an agonised expression, bent over, groaning, and dropped to the gutter. Most of the other women had drawn aside, but two old hags had gone to her aid, and there in the gutter, she had given birth. Ephorus, fifteen years old and safely aboard his ship, had watched it all; and it was that experience as much as anything else that had made him glad when Dorcas had said that she was unlikely to bear a child. If Eunice, on the other hand, had ever fallen pregnant he would have been pleased. But how a man could knowingly doom a woman he loved to such agony he could never understand.

And now, here was this woman, with the face of young Dorcas, about to face that ordeal, with no roof, no shelter.

He said, "There is room. There is the stable."

"Shut your mouth!" Eunice said. "Once get her on our premises and who can say where it'll end? Childbirth fever. Milk fever. She might lie in our straw for weeks. I ask you, would any decent woman be in such a pass? Let her bear her child in the ditch, where, like as not, it was begotten."

He said, "You shut *your* mouth! I've done with you. D'you hear me? Done!" He lifted his hand, which shook like a leaf, and unhooked the lantern from over the door.

"Allow me," he said, "to conduct you to the stable. It is at least sheltered and warm."

"And it's mine!" Eunice shouted. "So is that lantern and I absolutely forbid . . ."

He said, "Eunice, I never yet have struck you; but another word and I will hit you, hard!"

Both he and Eunice were completely bilingual, switching effortlessly, sometimes even in mid-sentence, from Greek to Aramaic, from Aramaic to Greek. Ephorus, assuring Joseph that there was no room, had used Aramaic; Eunice had spoken the same language when she said, "The best we can manage . . ." But the altercation between them had been in Greek. Joseph, the much-travelled man, had followed it, and in his heart been deeply affronted; but the innkeeper had mentioned a stable, and even the shelter of a stable would be welcome now. So he had held his tongue, tried to control his face and been thankful that nothing this horrible woman was saying meant anything to Mary.

Eunice, quelled by the threat, opened the door and went in, banging it behind her; and the three of them, with the donkey, were left in the wind and the snow.

"If you will come this way," Ephorus said, and holding the lantern in his quaking hand, led the way to the side entry and the stable door. It was a low building, but deep and wide, with a manger along one side. To the left of the doorway were some neatly ranged tools, to the right a great heap of straw. A cow and a donkey stood by the manger, and their bodies had heated the place so that coming in from the night, it felt warm. It smelt sweet too, of straw and the breath of the non-carnivorous animals.

"It isn't much," Ephorus said, "but it is the best I can do. It's quiet," he said, consoling himself, "and you'll have it to yourselves."

The woman turned to him with a smile, which, because it reminded him of Dorcas, he tried to analyse. If you said it was sweet, he thought to himself, you'd wrong it, because sweet sounds insipid; yet there was a sweetness about it, and a radiance which lit up her pale tired face.

"We're extremely fortunate," she said. "And you are very kind."

"I meant it all to be so different," the man said. "I aimed to get here yesterday, or the day before. But we're thankful to be under cover."

Ephorus' desire to serve outran his caution.

"I'll bring you a blanket," he said. "And what about supper?"

She said, "Thank you. We have some food left."

"Cold food," he said. "You need more than that on such a night. I'll be back. . . ." He looked round for a hook on which to hang the lantern, and hurried away, his lame leg dragging a little less than usual.

When he had gone, Mary said, "I knew that somehow a place would be found for us."

"But what a place!" Joseph looked around him with distaste. "Suppose your time should come, here on a bed of straw."

She said, "It must be the right place, the place God chose. The pains began hours ago, and they're getting harder now. He'll be born by midnight."

Something seemed to burst in his brain. "You didn't tell me!" he said, almost angrily. "You walked and walked. And all on account of that damned donkey! I didn't want to buy it in the first place. It's ruined all my plans. What baby was ever born in a stable . . . let alone such a baby as this. . . ." And his thoughts ran about; in a crowded inn there must be some kindly, experienced woman who could help; and how curious it was that they'd been without any shelter until he'd said "Oh God, God!" Then the innkeeper had relented and he'd thought that God had them in His keeping after all. But the end was a bed of straw, in a stable. Mystery added itself to mystery, enough to make a plain, ordinary man run mad.

"It is the right place," Mary said confidently. "For me, for *Him*. Look at that!"

Their old donkey had limped in behind them and made for the manger, snuffing eagerly. It had made for the manger and Eunice's well-fed animal had edged away, making room for the newcomer at that portion of the manger that contained food.

"He's prepared to share," she said. "And the man is kind. Where better could a child be born?"

She'd tell Him, she thought, when He was grown and Lord of the world, just how He had been born, and ask Him to look out for humble people and animals.

In the kitchen the two slaves were abed and asleep. Eunice was abed, but not asleep. When Ephorus entered and went towards the great black pot which held the remains of the mutton stew she reared up and said:

"Oh, so you've done with me, but you come crawling back for your supper!"

He heard only the chiding, not the relief in her voice. He said, "I don't want your supper! It's for her . . . for them. They're customers, aren't they, like all the rest. They're entitled to supper. They'll pay, don't you fret about that."

Ordinarily he defeated her by his apathetic silence, the best buffer a man could rear between him and a nagging woman. Now he was answering back. Happily she threw herself into what promised to be their first real quarrel in years.

"That's right," she said. "That's just like you. Stand like a stuffed man when I'm serving proper people, then hop about like a flea to serve a couple of feckless no-goods that turn up late and happen to take your fancy. Threatening to hit me, too; after all I've done for you. And that's about all you're good for, biting the hand that's fed you all these years."

He moved the black pot onto what remained of the fire, took two bowls and two spoons.

He said, "You can stow that talk, Eunice. I've had about enough of it. You've fed me and housed me, but you did it because you wanted to. Don't deceive yourself about that. Out there, just now, you said things no man could bear. *Your* lantern, *your* stable. Try that in a court of law and you'll soon learn whose this place is, down to the last spoon! But I want none of it. It's all yours . . . I give it to you, with a glad heart and you can enjoy it, all by yourself, tomorrow. But tonight I'm dishing out *my* mutton stew and I'll also have *my* blanket."

Astonishingly, she was silenced. In silence she watched him dish the stew into the bowls, cover them with a cloth and set them on a serving tray. In silence she allowed him to take the blanket, fold it over his arm and go out. When he had gone she turned on her pillow and cried into it. She cried and cried, weeping for the man whom she had seen in that stripped, unconscious body, the man who had eluded her, never coming to life, however coaxed or provoked, until now, when after eleven years of skirmishing, he was about to elude her forever.

She was still crying, and her candle was still burning, when Ephorus came hurrying back. His face was bleached and distraught. He spoke her name, "Eunice," in a way he had never said it before. Ha! she thought, he's had time to think things over, and has come back to apologise. She steeled herself. Never let him think that he had got the better of her!

"What is it?" she asked coldly.

"I want you to do something for me."

As she had guessed; he wanted to be forgiven and taken back, fed, sheltered, kept in idleness. This was what she wanted too, for him, but it would never do to relent too quickly.

"Things'll have to be very different around here," she said.

"Oh, they will be," he promised hastily. "I'll do anything you want me to, Eunice. I'll work, I'll stay off the wine. I'll do everything I can to repay you, if you'll do this one thing for me. . . ."

She was tired, she had been upset, she had been crying, and her ordinarily sharp wits weren't at their best. She could only think of times in their earlier life when quarrels had been mended in bed. Tonight, for the first time in several years, they'd had an open quarrel, and he had been angered; he was now seeking what had formerly served as a remedy. A deep satisfaction moved within her; she had won after all! She had known from the first that their unions had meant more to her than to him, that she, in a fashion, had always been the suppliant, he the obliger. And when the bed bond had been broken under her nagging and his apathy, she had been, very decidedly, the loser.

Even his threat to strike her, earlier in the evening, helped now towards her self-deception; so did his behaviour over the stew and the blanket. That was real man's behaviour. So was this.

She cast one look at the slaves; they were sleeping soddenly, worn out by all they had done that day. Her sense of propriety was satisfied, and desire, the more powerful because so long unappeased, began to move in her. She gave in. She smiled and lifted the blanket.

"Come, then," she said invitingly.

He recoiled as though she had spat in his face.

"Not that," he said, "I want you to *do* something for me. A favour. I know it's a lot to ask. The woman out there—you were right; she is having a baby; it's started. And Eunice, she's so young; it's her first. She'll need a woman's help. . . ."

It was her turn to recoil.

"I never had a child," she said in a small, bitter voice.

"But you'd know what to do."

Her eyelids were swollen, still damp from her tears, but between them her eyes were stony.

"I know nothing about it," she said.

"I'd tell you what to do," he pleaded. "I'd help you. And the man carries carpenter's tools, so he's a handy man, too. We'd help."

"If you're both so clever, do it yourselves. Why bother me?"

"A woman should be there; for decency's sake." While he pleaded he reckoned the alternative; there was a woman, in the crowd on the sleeping place beside the yard; a woman with a child. But to rouse her he'd have to wake a score of people; and he had no idea what kind of woman she was. Then there were the slaves, young, silly, heavy handed. Eunice, with all her faults, was sensible and competent; he thought of how well she had tended him when he was helpless.

"Eunice, *please!* If you'll just do this one thing for me, I'll . . . I'll love you forever. I know you've had a bad bargain in me, but I'll be different I swear. I'll *love* you, Eunice."

Her whole life had been spent in trading one thing for another; you handed over so much money and bought so much wine, so much food and fodder, then you parcelled them out into smaller portions to be exchanged for smaller coins. Only once had she given something for nothing, and that was when she nursed Ephorus—and she'd received exactly nothing in return. Upon that thought, her sound good sense halted; she hadn't cared for the stranger for nothing; ill as he was, starved as he seemed and poor, she'd seen possibilities in his youth and good looks; so that had been a bargain, too. All the same, she had dreamed of something that wouldn't be mere payment, of something that would have been an offering, a flower laid in the lap. It had never come.

Now here he was, promising what she had dreamed of, not as a gift, another bargain. But as things were, and at her age, a sensible woman must compound for the best she could get. She pushed the blanket aside and heaved her weary body to its feet. As she reached for her outer clothing Ephorus gave a great sigh of relief.

"I've heard plenty of talk," Eunice said. "There's nothing much to birthing a baby, really."

"And you're so clever," he said. "There's nothing you couldn't do if you tried."

She gave him a sidelong, sardonic look, intended to let him know that she wasn't taken in by his flattery; and she was startled by the expression on his face. Never, not even in the early days, when he had most reason to be grateful to her, had he looked so grateful, so admiring, so almost . . . almost adoring.

"It's cold out," he said. "You'll want this." He turned and unhooked her cloak from the door and held it open for her. As he folded it around her, his hands lingered for a second, touching her; a middle-aged body, a trifle too solid, but a good comfortable armful of woman still.

She bustled into the stable, with all her vigour and energy suddenly replenished.

"Well," she said briskly, but not unkindly, "this is a fine to-do. But don't fret. We'll manage. I don't want you, or you," she said to Joseph and Ephorus. "Go in the kitchen, make up the fire and heat some water. I'll call when I need it. Better warm some wine, too."

In a momentary respite Mary unclenched her teeth and said: "You are kind. God must have sent you."

Eunice, the Greek, thought, What a typically Jewish thing to say! She felt like retorting that Ephorus had sent her. But if faith in her God was a help to the girl, let it go; she was going to need all the help she could get.

"I don't think this will be a long job," she said. "And if you want to yell, yell. There's nobody to hear except me."

CHAPTER X

This would be his fifth winter of tending another man's sheep —and to that he was not resigned, and never would be. This would be the fifth winter since his bereavement—and to that he was not resigned, and never would be.

People, meaning well, had said, "You have other children; another son." But a heart once given is given and cannot be retracted and bestowed elsewhere. People, meaning well, had said, "Time is a great healer." So it might be, for small wounds; but had time, he asked himself, ever enabled a man to grow a new limb to replace one sawn off? People had also said, "It was a hero's death." And the reply to that, in the depths of his heart, was always, "It was the wasted death of a fool."

The would-be consolatory remarks had ceased within a year. It seemed to him sometimes that he was the only person who remembered at all; and he thought that even he might have remembered less, had he taken on a job where he had to be busy and bustling. A shepherd, even a good one, giving the flock every care, could think with a part of his mind, and on the journeys from pasture to pasture, and between watering holes, he must dawdle along with little to do but think.

On the other hand, what could he have done? Nobody could learn a trade overnight; to set up in business one needed money. He was forty-three when ruin came upon him, a big, slow-moving, seemingly slow-thinking man, marked by weather and a scar or two—not everybody's idea of an employee. Except as a shepherd. Sheep he knew about. He had lived with them and for them since he was seven years old. Also, he had wanted to stay in the district where Martha, his wife, had family and friends. Being a shepherd's wife could be a lonely business.

He had not been forced to the humiliation of actually asking for a job. He had sold his flock—a magnificent one—to a man named Ezra, and as soon as the transaction was made, Ezra asked:

"And you, Josodad, what will you do now?"

"I must get to Jerusalem, and move heaven and earth to save the boy. Beyond that I can't think."

Ezra had been the first, or almost the first, to remind him that he still had a family.

Josodad said heavily, "I know." He was fond of them all, two little girls and a boy of two, but he had never felt and could never feel for them the wholehearted love that he felt for Nathan, his firstborn, who had for a long time been his only child, who had toiled beside, watched with him, through at least twelve lambing seasons, who was at once like him, often so much like him as to seem his other self, and yet endearingly unlike, being merry, and musical, and gregarious. The girls and the little boy were his children. Nathan was his son.

"They must eat," Ezra reminded him.

"I shall leave their mother enough for their needs," Josodad said, and was turning away. Ezra understood that at the moment the man should think only of his errand—in Ezra's opinion about as hopeless a one as any man ever set out upon; but he was thinking of himself, too, and what a pity it would be if, when Josodad was trudging, defeated, home, somebody else should step in and offer him a job.

"If you want a job with sheep, I can offer you one. Be glad to."

"But I can't say when I shall be back."

"I can wait," Ezra said, with apparent generosity, knowing that the waiting time would not be long. "So long as I have your word."

"You have it," Josodad said.

He came back, in just about the time that Ezra had reckoned, with his empty purse, and his empty heart, a lie in his mouth for the boy's mother—that was how he thought of her, the boy's mother—and a memory like a white-hot iron in the brain. And without wasting an hour he had gone to work tending Ezra's sheep.

He knew, almost at once, that he had been forced into the wrong job. For twelve years he and Nathan had worked together, so everything was a reminder. And there was so much time. . . . In the morning you looked the flock over. One not getting to its feet? One coughing? One walking on three legs? Any sign of fly-blows? Should there be anything wrong, you dealt with it, glad of the break in the routine. Then there was the nice judgement of pasture, of water supply, and in winter, where the wind lay. But there were great tracts of time when there was nothing to do but wait and watch, listen to the monotonous bleating, and think, and remember. . . .

He was working with other men now, he who had worked only with his own father, by himself, and with Nathan. He worked with two young men, Arad and Ibri, hirelings, as he himself was now a hireling, but of a different kind; men who had never been anything else. For a week or so they had borne his gloom and his silences. They were local men and they all knew his story and what had happened to Nathan. Everyone in and around Bethlehem knew. Nathan had been crucified. Josodad had come home and given Martha his carefully prepared lie, "It was all over in an hour." It had lasted for sixty and all that time Josodad had stood by the foot of the rough-hewn cross and prayed a single prayer, "God, of thy mercy, let him die!" and even as he prayed, had had flitting memories of the things he had done to make this boy strong, solid of bone and muscle. More than once, when Nathan's plate was empty and clean he had said, "Have this; I've made my growth." And more than once in summer he'd said, "Go and swim. I can manage." In winter he'd been careful to see that Nathan's fingers were not frost-bitten, as his own had been. And the end of all his care, his occasional self-denials, had been a strong body, dying slowly and inevitably.

Arad and Ibri had tolerated him for a time; then they had decided that he was surly and unsociable. And that mattered little to them, they were company for one another. Then he made himself unpopular with them.

In any flock, however tended, there were losses, but to Josodad, the former owner of the flock the attitude of his fellow-hirelings was shocking. A lamb was lost, and Arad said:

"The kites'll find it." He settled down to trim his nails with his knife.

"That is a sure thing," Ibri said, and settled down to play with his five stones. Five stones, polished from much handling, which he held in his palm and then threw upwards, and tried to catch all five on the back of the hand which he had turned palm downward; never yet had he caught all five, but four, on the few occasions when he caught them, made him jubilant; three was fairly good, two disappointing, and one a mere inducement to try again.

On that occasion Josodad had gone to hunt for the lost lamb and found it straddled over a rock which it had failed to jump. It was exhausted and he had lifted it, set it across his shoulders and carried it back to the flock.

Then there'd been the time when three ewes, old enough to have known better, had gorged themselves on a patch of vetchling and blown up, huge, helpless, lying on their sides and gasping with glazing eyes.

Arad had regarded them dispassionately. "All old; they'll be tough eating."

"You'd let them die?"

"They always do," Ibri said.

"Not in *my* flock," Josodad said, with a vicious snap in his voice. He drew his knife and went to the nearest ewe, set his left hand like a fork over her neck and with his right made the small incision in the blown-up belly. The gas had rushed out with an audible hiss; the ewe struggled and Josodad helped her to her feet before turning swiftly to operate upon the other two.

Ibri said, "I never saw that done before." But a few seconds later Arad said, "Did you hear that? *My flock*, he said. He looks on these as though they were his."

"You'd think," Ibri said, catching Arad's mood, "that he was *married* to them!" And in that remark lay the germ of a joke. "Old Tup," they called him, behind his back, but as such things do, the nickname reached Josodad's ears, and hurt and was resented.

But for a long time, surly, resentful, scornful of their attitude as he was, he tried to be tolerant; but the time must come, and it came, when he was bound to think, They are rubbish; they work for pay and whether they earn it or not is a matter of indifference to them. My boy, a shepherd born, is dead. They flourish, and hundreds like them. Maybe this is a world where only rogues flourish.

There were other petty annoyances, too. Ezra, once he had him safely hired, seemed to enjoy putting him in his place, in opposing him, senselessly, in small things which merely said, *my* flock. Lambs that he, with his knowledgeable eye, had marked as good breeders were sent off to market or to slaughter, others, of less potential value, retained. And there was a constant running warfare about the amount of pitch needed to treat fly-blows.

"You must be heavy-handed with the stuff," Ezra said. "A quarter of the amount served in the old days."

"Because half the blows were left untreated," Josodad snarled.

The little he had of home life was no happier. Martha had vented her grief over Nathan noisily, for a day or two, maybe three; then, exactly as she would have drawn together the edges of a torn place in a garment, she had set to work to mend her life. Nathan was gone. Martha, named for her, and Mary, and young Lazarus remained. The girls were the cleanest, the most tidily dressed, the most well-brushed of all the girls in the village and the boy was being spoiled rotten, in Josodad's opinion. "You are fortunate; you still have a brother," Martha had said to the girls once, in his hearing, "you must cherish him." Josodad had recognised it as a back-handed slap at him, the father who had failed to take comfort in his second son. He had tried; he had waited, trying not to make comparisons. But the boy was seven now, afraid of the dark, afraid of a thunderstorm, afraid of his father, a timid shrinking creature, liking to sit in his mother's lap, to play girlish games with his sisters. When Nathan was that age, Josodad had fashioned a miniature shepherd's crook for Nathan who was stamping with impatience, and then watched, how proudly and happily nobody would ever know, how the boy had mastered the use of it.

These thoughts, and the memories of Nathan's final hours, occupied his mind during the long days, the even longer nights. He would wake, abruptly as though disturbed by something, lift his head and listen, as he was paid to do. Arad and Ibri, Arad or Ibri, according to rota, similarly paid, slept on; and Josodad would stand up, survey the sleeping flock, humped shadows and know that all was well and that whatever had roused him came from within his mind. Then he would know that the torture hour was about to begin, and he would do his best to fend it off. In winter he would mend the fire, but winters were short. He would walk, with a shepherd's slow, noiseless steps around the sleeping flock; he would wet his finger on his tongue and hold it up to find which way the wind was blowing. He'd look at the sky and forecast the next day's weather. And all the time he knew that he was doing these things in a completely futile effort to avert the evil hour when in the hollow, the sharp-thinking night he must face his memories, and his God.

He'd been a happy, a most fortunate and blessed man until the season of the Passover when Nathan was seventeen. It had been arranged, far ahead, that Nathan should then go to celebrate the Feast in Jerusalem. He was to travel with others of his age, and older people who had either never been before, not being able to afford it, or a few who were going for the second or third time. Josodad had been once, and so had Martha; they had remembered it and spoken of it often. Then she, busy with house and children, and he, busy with the sheep, had kept the Passover at home. Nathan had been very much excited by the project.

Non-Jews, of whom there were a few in the neighbourhood —the innkeeper was a Greek, the blacksmith a Roman veteran who had learned his trade in the army—had the wrong idea about the Feast of the Passover; because it was solemn they thought it dull and dreary, and thought the word "Feast" misapplied. But it was a feast, even for those who stayed at home, and for those who went to Jerusalem it was an expedition, a sight-seeing visit, a holiday and often a family reunion as well.

That year Josodad had enjoyed the Feast a little less than usual. Martha had put all the traditional things on the table, the unleavened bread, the mutton, the eggs, lettuces and radish, and the sweet dish made of raisins and nuts and spices; all the traditional things had been said; but Josodad's mind, instead of being fixed on the Escape from Egypt which the Feast celebrated, had been all the time marking the vacant place and wondering how Nathan was faring, whether he had fallen in with congenial company, whether he were being robbed or cheated by the rascals who haunted the outer precincts of the Temple, battening on inexperienced pilgrims.

Nathan had come home changed in some subtle way. He was still merry and lively, but with thoughtful spells. He seemed older, which was right, he was growing up; and perhaps, the father thought, the Temple had impressed him. His mother had produced the obvious feminine reason for the change; somewhere a girl had taken his eye; and she hoped that it would be a daughter of one of the family's friends or distant relatives to whom he had been charged to give messages, should he see them.

This explanation Josodad could not accept. Nathan would have told him. He was not the kind of boy to cast his eye on an unacceptable girl, and he knew that all he had to do was to mention his preference to his father who would at once begin to make inquiries and approaches. Then they would build an extra room onto the house, prepare for and celebrate the marriage, and as a gift Nathan would receive part of the flock. Josodad had already selected the breeding animals whose progeny in a few years' time, would form the nucleus of a new flock. That was how it had been in his family for generations, ever since the return of the Jews from the Babylonian captivity; Josodad

hoped that so it would also be. He was a Jew of the old-fash-
ioned, orthodox kind.

But although their relationship was as sound and easy as it
had always been, there was no mention of any girl. What there
was a good deal of talk about was a young man named Dan whom
Nathan had met in Jerusalem and who had proved to be almost
a neighbour, coming from Tekoa, a village within an easy walk
away. Dan played the pipe, too; he made songs; he was altogether
congenial. His father was a shoemaker and he himself had
learned that trade.

All through that summer Nathan, whenever he had any spare
time, set off for Tekoa to visit Dan. Martha said, "You must
invite him back." Nathan said, "I will," but never did so until she
began to nag. "Why must you always go to him? Isn't your company worth a walk?" "Are you ashamed of your home?" "Do I not
cook as well as *his* mother?"

Thus pressed, Nathan had issued the invitation, and Josodad
and Martha, without knowing exactly what they had expected,
were disappointed in Nathan's new friend. A hulking, awkward, dumb young man who seemed at first painfully shy, and
then suddenly, over supper, came to life when he began to talk
of the iniquity of the Roman occupation and the even greater
iniquity of the Jews' apathy. Once his silence was broken, words
poured out of him; he spoke bitterly about the Hippodrome that
Herod had built in Jerusalem, and of the Jews who attended it.
"In ten years' time," he said, "you won't be able to tell a Jew from
a Roman or a Greek."

Nathan, looking very uncomfortable, listened, and when Dan,
from lack of breath, not invective, paused for a second, said:

"Don't talk politics over supper, Dan. It spoils the taste of the
food."

Then, for some reason, Dan had looked contemptuously at
Josodad and given a little grunt and relapsed into silence.

Next day, out with the sheep, Josodad said, "Your friend, Dan,
is a Zealot."

"He is that way inclined. I think he'd be in the hills by now, but his father's sight is failing and he has several sisters. So he's needed at home."

"Then I hope he doesn't say in the open what he said last night in our house. Such talk is dangerous."

"Maybe. But everything he said was true. And such things should be said."

"That I doubt," Josodad said mildly. "I've never known talk like that do anything except stir up trouble."

"What would be your remedy, then, for our present situation?"

"Patience; faith in God; and the strength to survive, holding to the law and keeping our blood pure."

"You think that is enough?"

"It has served, in similar situations in the past. We were slaves in Egypt, but we came out as a people; we were captives in Babylon, but we came out as a people. Now we have the Roman heel on our necks, but we shall emerge, as a people."

"How long is it since you were in Jerusalem, Father?"

"Eighteen years."

"Then forgive me if I say that you can have no notion of the changes that have taken place. Life here goes on the same, so you think it is the same everywhere. Do you know what Dan calls people like you, Father? Happy-do-nothings."

"But what is there to do, except what I have just said? Wait. In His own good time the Lord will deliver us."

"With what? That is what Dan asks. Who could free a whole nation of happy-do-nothings, and worse?"

All around them the sheep were quietly grazing and Josodad jerked his crook towards them.

"My boy, if God so willed he could turn that flock, in a blink of an eye, into an army, ready and girded."

With some awe, but also with some curiosity and a slight disdain in his voice, Nathan said, "You really believe that, don't you?"

"If I didn't I should not have said it."

"No. You are a man of integrity," the boy said. "And you are happy in your faith." It was as though, suddenly, their ages had been reversed. This thought stung Josodad and he summoned all the parental authority which in families like his seldom had to be called upon because it was so implicitly acknowledged.

"Look here," he said, "I don't want that boy to go putting crazy notions into your head. Talk of resistance and of guerrillas is all very fine, but what do they *do* except make things worse for ordinary people? So, they kill one Roman, or they steal three horses. The Romans can spare what they lose, but in the subsequent inquiries in all the nearby villages we lose what we can ill spare. The lesson taught at Sepphoris wasn't wasted on sensible people, and on a smaller scale, every bit of revolt is similarly punished. If I thought that you," he said, very confident of his power over this beloved boy, "went to Dan's house to listen to such inflammatory nonsense as he talked last night, I should forbid you to go."

"Often enough," Nathan said, "we hardly talk at all. We make songs and sing them. He has many friends. And he plays the harp. It's easier for us to go to him, carrying our pipes."

Hundreds of times later Josodad was to reproach himself for being overconfident, too easily satisfied, blind. It hurt him sometimes, even now, to remember that in her unwitting, female, jealous way, Martha had been nearer the truth than he had. The little group of musicians had achieved a certain local fame and been asked to make music for a wedding in Zilgah.

"Oh," Martha had said sharply, "he can carry his harp so far!"

"There is a harp in the house of the bride's father," Nathan said.

On that occasion he had been absent for two days and a night —and why not? He was young, and when he worked he worked; he was entitled to his recreations.

For two years it had gone on, had become part of life; a wedding, a *bar mitzvah,* a circumcision feast, all in need of music.

Looking back, in the light of hindsight, that most vivid and dreadful illumination of all, Josodad could see that often, around the times of Nathan's absences, there had been incidents. But what was there about them to make a connection with a boy who was always home exactly when he had said he would be, who never had a mark on him, who never showed any sign of excitement, or of interest in the incident; and who could always supply, in the detail so dear to women, exactly what had been worn and eaten at the wedding or whatever it was which he had witnessed?

In the end what had happened was plainly the result of a thought-out plan, a carefully laid trap.

Rachel's sepulchre lay to the North West of Bethlehem. It was regarded by pious Jews not exactly as a holy place, there was only one holy place and that was in the heart of the Temple, but as a place of reverence, a landmark in their history. There the patriarch Jacob's favourite wife had died in giving birth to Benjamin, his favourite son, and he had buried her and reared a pillar over her grave as a memorial.

A small contingent of Roman soldiers, out on patrol from the subsidiary barracks just outside Bethlehem, had chosen to camp by Rachel's tomb—there was water and firewood handy. They had leaned their standard against the weather-worn pillar and two of them had succumbed to that perpetual disease of soldiers, the necessity to leave their mark, to carve their meaningless names. The rabbi of the nearest village, accompanied by three elders, had gone out and asked civilly that the standard should be shifted and that the pillar should not be further defaced. Some of the men had not understood a word, but one had, and he had said, "Old men, go shave yourselves!"

How had the ill word spread? Tekoa was even farther from the sepulchre than Bethlehem was; who had carried the news? On what swift and fatal feet it had travelled, how instant and unthinking had been the response.

Nathan, Dan, and a third boy had taken axes and hacked the standard to pieces. The Romans had pounced; two had been killed and one injured. The boys, outnumbered four to one, had been hauled off.

For Josodad the time immediately after had been a blur of misery, self-reproach, and conflicting advice. Had he been able to feel surprise he would have been surprised to find how many people in the immediate vicinity had known what was going on under the pretence of music-making, and believed that he did, also. To the remarks of such people, knowledgeable after the event, he paid no heed at all; but he did listen to the wildly varying bits of advice.

There were those who said, "Do nothing. To take any action now will be to inculpate yourself." Those he ignored.

There were those who said, "The Romans are great on law; even boys like this will be properly tried. Go to Jerusalem at once and hire a good lawyer, one who will plead that the boys were taking a short cut home and that the Romans, alarmed, attacked them first."

"Does such a lawyer exist?"

Dozens, they told him, men who would stand up and plead any cause, with eloquence and passion, for a price.

There were others who said that in such a crisis the only possible hope lay in the High Priest. He was very powerful; even the Romans, even Herod the King never wittingly went against him. And the only way to his ear was through a venal priest named Ephraim.

There were those who said, "Keep religion out of it. Once mention religion and you're done. Hire a lawyer who will plead that Nathan is younger than Dan, completely subservient to him and simply did what he was told."

In any other circumstances Josodad would have questioned the ethics of such pleading. But he knew that he would sacrifice a dozen Dans to save Nathan. A dozen? A hundred. A thousand.

Plainly the one thing that all the advice had in common was the need for money; money to buy, money to bribe. So he'd gone to Ezra and sold all that he had to sell, his flock.

Often now, in the slow-dragging nights, he could see that in love, in panic he had rushed into folly. On the day after Dan's first visit he had to Nathan decried desperate action and praised patience and trust in God. But when the moment came when he must choose between the two, he'd gone into action that was just as futile as anything those boys had ever done. And so he had injured his cause with God.

He had offered bribes, thereby breaking the law against not causing another man to stumble. They'd stumbled very eagerly, taken his money, promised impossible things. He'd lied too, borne false witness, sworn that Nathan was a near simpleton, completely under Dan's thumb.

It was unavailing. Afterwards, when he came to his senses, he realised that men who had taken his money and given him promises and hope, had known how it would end. Had Nathan not been concerned he would have known himself. The boys were guilty, the Romans could have killed them, there by Rachel's sepulchre and committed no outrage; the meticulous mockery of a trial, with its inevitable end was designed as a warning. Nothing was left but to go to the Wailing Wall and ask one favour of God—that the boy should die quickly. And even that had been denied.

These had been his memories for almost five years as he walked about by day, or woke, with that abrupt jolt, in the night.

What followed the memories, grew out of them and seemed inseparable from them, and were even more torturing, were the doubts which the whole business had bred. He'd always been a devout Jew, with the religion of his fathers woven, firmly he would have said, into the fabric of his life. But he'd prayed that agonised prayer for one last small mercy for his son, and the prayer had not been answered. Had God no mercy? Was there no God? And if no God, then no life hereafter; which meant that Nathan was not gathered to his fathers, safe in Abraham's bosom, but a dead thing, rotting in the ground. To think thus meant despair.

Night by night he fought that thought. He would remember that psalm of David's known as the Shepherd's Psalm. . . . There was a passage in it that ran, "Lo, though I walk through the valley of the shadow of death, I will fear no evil." That seemed to imply that death was only a phase. Then, not far away, was a place called Endor, where in the distant past a witch had summoned up Samuel's spirit and Saul, who had known Samuel well, had recognised him. If that wasn't proof of a life hereafter, what was?

Hopes and questions and speculations spun round and round in his mind until finally he reached the most dreadful thought of all. That over the years the poems and the stories and the whole business of belief had been invented by men, bereaved as he had been bereaved, who could find no comfort on earth.

In the quiet dark the stars so far away, so uncaring, the night wind blowing, it was dangerously easy to harbour such a thought; to see men as sheep, of no real importance, born only to die.

Sometimes from exhaustion, he would reach this point and sleep again; sometimes the torture lasted until the stars faded and the darkness paled and the dawn lay rosy in the sky. And never once, no matter what dark paths he had trodden through the night—and might tread again, two or three times during the day, had he ever failed to make the good Jew's first prayer of the morning—"Blessed art thou, O Lord our God, King of the Universe who hast sanctified us by thy commandments."

In part this was habit, but it was a great deal else besides. Truth for one thing; by the commandments of God the Jews who observed them were sanctified. Nathan's friend might say that Jews were being corrupted and absorbed and that might be true of a few, in cities; but the great majority of them resisted the temptation to run after strange gods, attended the simple, clean service in the synagogues, believed that God was a spirit, kept the Law and were the Chosen people. Josodad, even in his despair had no wish to cut himself off from them. There was a certain amount of caution, too, in his attitude; no man could fully understand God's ways, and despite everything—and by that he meant his doubts, his unanswered prayers—it was possible, more than possible that Nathan was with his fathers, and there, when he himself died, Josodad hoped to join him. So all day and every day, he still lived exactly in accordance with the Law, just in case his thinking had gone a little awry through grief.

So, day followed day, and now it was winter again, his fifth of tending Ezra's sheep and the flocks were in their winter quarters, near enough to Bethlehem so that should snow fall and

cover the ground for any length of time, they could be fed from
Ezra's well-stocked barns. Josodad did not appreciate, as Arad
and Ibri did, this proximity to the little town; it meant that he
could make frequent visits to his home. The boys—as he called
Arad and Ibri in his mind—were rigorous about claiming their
free hours, and if he abjured his, always thought he was doing
so from the intention of presently cheating them; and everyone
knew where the flock lay, so if he didn't go home there would be
talk.

So on this particular day—very cold he noticed as he climbed
down from the sheltered place where the sheep were—he had
gone home. And he had had a very miserable visit.

He blamed himself. Something like hostility had long existed
between his wife and himself. She had, very sensibly, mended
her life and unconsciously blamed him for not mending his, and
read into his not-mending a criticism of her for having made
almost a perfect job of hers. She was wrong there, he was glad
to see her happy; but he could never bring himself to say so. The
children, awed perhaps by his face which grief and the constant
thinking had scored deeply, or perhaps warned by their mother,
were always too well-behaved in his presence. He was the stranger; the father who came and went; came—they must sense it,
without joy—and left without regret. And for him the small,
comfortable house was haunted by Nathan's invisible presence.
On the door jamb were the marks which Josodad had scored
with his knife, measuring Nathan's height from time to time.
He had said, "Yes, you shall sit up with me through a lambing,
when you are so high!" And he'd marked the height, against
which the boy would measure himself, standing on his toes,
stretching his neck. And hanging on a hook in the wall there
had always been, until this day, Nathan's pipe. There were other
reminders too; but on this cold day, entering by the door he had
looked at the notches and then towards the pipe. He always did,
he always would. But on this day the hook was empty.

He greeted his wife, and his elder daughter, named for her
mother, who were in the room; the girl her mother's very image,

even to the way she stirred a savoury smelling pot on the hearth. Then he said, "Where's Nathan's pipe?"

His wife said, "Oh, the pipe, Lazarus has it. Mary went along with him to Ebenezer; he is going to teach him to play."

"*Teach* him!" Josodad said. "Nathan taught himself to play. What is more he made that pipe himself. If Lazarus wanted a pipe he should have made his own!" And then, all at once, knowing that nothing but disharmony could result, but feeling something beyond his power to control, a mental scab which itched and must be scratched, he said, "And Mary must go along, to guard a boy of seven. Two hundred yards along a village street. What did he think would get him? Wolves?"

The elder Martha said to the younger, "Go and see if the little brown hen has laid yet. She's our only hope today. If she hasn't and is on her nest, stand by her."

"You must watch this pot, then," the young Martha said, "its bottom is wearing thin and unless you stir the beans stick."

"That's my good sensible girl," Martha said; and she took the long spoon her daughter had been using, but did not employ it. Instead she pulled the pot to the side of the hearth and squared herself, facing Josodad. She said:

"You are my husband; but I have had enough of this!"

"Enough of what?"

"Many things," she said. "The constant criticism of Lazarus for one. So, he is seven years old, and at that age, we all know, Nathan was a shepherd with short legs and a short crook and he wasn't afraid of anything. I know, I'm tired of hearing it said, by word or by look. Oh, you may think I cannot read your looks, but I can. And every time I think, One family could not expect to breed two such wonders. One we had, and we lost him— through his own folly. Now we have one ordinary little boy who happens to be timid. Remember, to get to Ebenezer's he must pass the inn, and that Ephorus is always drunk. Nathan thought him funny, but Lazarus is scared of him; and I for one see nothing wrong with that. Nor with his taking the pipe. Nathan made it; but since there it is, made already, why should Lazarus risk cutting his fingers making another? Tell me that."

And then, before Josodad could frame an answer, if there was one, she ran on:

"There's another thing, too. And that is why I sent Martha out of the room. . . ." The mention of the good sensible girl reminded her of her duty to the cooking and she turned, gave the savoury mess a perfunctory stir and went on, her words hitting Josodad like little hailstones.

"You may not have noticed," she said, "but the girls are growing up. Martha is fifteen, and if she isn't betrothed soon she never will be; Mary is almost fourteen. Have you ever asked yourself what will become of them? In the old days men came to the house, asking your advice, wishing to buy your sheep; anyone with a flock which he wished to improve might very well have taken one of your daughters and a few choice sheep as dowry. But it is very different now. . . ."

He said harshly, "I know that!" He'd realised on his return from Jerusalem, that it had been a mistake to sell the whole of his flock outright; he should have sold them and then raised money on the rear, bear, shear and share basis by which he would have been able to claim one lamb out of two, and half the price of the fleeces; but he'd thought of nothing except laying hands on the money and getting away to Jerusalem as quickly as possible. And this woman, fluffing herself out like a hen defending chicks from a hawk, was right to reproach him. He had sacrificed three to one. And uselessly.

"So," Martha's voice was relentless, "you know. That at least is something. What I am asking is, what do you propose to do about it?"

"What can I do? You know my wage. You know what it costs to live."

"Who better? So there will be the girls without dowry and they'll die unwed; Martha my true daughter, who would make an excellent wife, and Mary, less good in the house, but sweet and gentle. And then," she said, her voice sharpening, "you blame me for treating Lazarus as I do!"

There must be some connection, Martha, even in anger did

not talk incoherently, but he could not see it, and was obliged
to say:

"What do you mean by that?"

"That I want him to stay alive; to recognise danger, and be
careful." Then she added, "*You* reared Nathan!"

In the three final words he recognised a twenty-year-old jealousy. Justified, in a way; from the time that he could toddle the
boy had always wanted to be with his father, had been, as Martha
said, "a shepherd with short legs." And that would have mattered
less if another child had been born, or on the way. There was a
gap until young Martha was born.

Alongside the jealousy there was blame. *He* had reared Nathan to be hardy, to minimise risks . . . and so, indirectly, he
was responsible for what had happened. A dreadful accusation,
and one he could not accept, but the idea added one more twist
to his misery.

Young Martha returned, cradling an egg in her hand. He
viewed her from the aspect to which her mother had drawn attention. It was true, somewhere, imperceptibly, she had passed
the borderline between childhood and womanhood; and what
was going to happen to her?

"Good," his wife said, seeing the egg. "Put on the pan and
begin to cook it when your brother comes in."

"Is the boy sick?" Josodad asked, knowing that the question
was a return to a sore subject, and yet unable to hold it back.

His daughter answered, saying gravely, "He isn't sick, but he
would be if he ate that." She indicated the bubbling pot. "I think
the grease upsets him." She took the long spoon and stirred. "He
has a delicate stomach," she said.

Then Lazarus and Mary came in and Josodad eyed them as
though he were seeing them for the first time. Mary, only a
year and a few months younger than Martha, was still a child,
thin and angular with beautiful, dreamy, almost sleepy eyes.
The boy was tall for his seven years, taller than Nathan had
been at that age, but fragile looking; and, at the moment, wearing a sulky look.

Josodad roused himself and made an effort.

"Well," he said, "and how did the lesson go? Can you play the pipe, Lazarus?"

"No. Ebenezer was horrid to me. He said I had no ear."

Why that report should please him Josodad could not have said, but it did; and the fact that it did proved that there was something very wrong with him.

"I tried," Mary said. "When Lazarus had done." She glanced at her mother as she made this explanation. "And *I* have an ear. Ebenezer said so. And he said it was a pity because pipe-playing is not for girls."

"I should think not!" her mother said.

Martha boiled the egg, cracked it and put it into a small bowl and set it before her brother. Her mother began, rather slowly, Josodad thought, to dish the savoury mess of mutton, onions, and beans into the plates. Then, with a plate in her left hand and the spoon in the other she turned her head, looking at the door and listening; it was all right, her expression said; and in a few seconds in walked her brother Lazarus, the one for whom the second boy had been named. He was a big, handsome, jovial man who up to four years ago had made a humble but adequate living as a weaver. Then his wife, a childless woman, had died and soon after he had married a widow who owned a prosperous vineyard. Upon her he had begotten a child, but she was too old for successful breeding; she and the child had died, less than a year ago. Since then he had eaten, several times a week, at his sister's house, and once he had said to Josodad that he now knew that it was God's will that he should be childless, "So I look on these as my own," he had said, indicating his nephew and his nieces. Josodad had known a moment's envy for the cheerful man who could suffer two bereavements in a short time—three if you counted the still-born boy—and find comfort where it was to be found. Lazarus, like his sister, was sensible; they mended up the holes in their lives and didn't go about with great, raw-edged wounds in their hearts.

For the first time Josodad noted, but without the least feeling of envy, the difference in the quality of the welcome extended to the uncle and that which he, the father, had evoked. His own presence cast a gloom, with Lazarus the sun entered and they all basked in its radiance.

The boy recounted, for his uncle's benefit, his unsuccessful attempt at pipe-playing and Ebenezer's verdict; and Lazarus said:

"No ear? That can't be right. You have two; I can see them. One, two!" he said, pulling each ear in turn, and the boy's sulky expression lifted and he laughed.

Then Mary made her report, and Lazarus said, "Well, there I agree with the old man. You know why? To play the pipe properly you have to screw up your lips and in time that'd spoil the shape of your pretty mouth."

To the younger Martha he said, "Something tells me that you had a hand in this delightful dinner, my dear."

Josodad's wife said, "She did; she was almost entirely responsible. How did you know?"

"By the seasoning," he said. "It is exactly how you used to cook, Martha, when you could think of the taste and not how long the salt and herbs must last."

He pleased them, effortlessly. Josodad, eating his own tasteless portion—all food tasted the same to him these days—felt like a stranger in his own house. And the worst of it was that he didn't mind at all. They were happy. They gave the impression of being a happy, united family with the uncle as its centre. And that, even if he had resented it, was so natural that resentment would have been absurd and unworthy. Of course children clung to those who amused and approved of them and made simple little jokes. And of course a woman like Martha, who had mended her own life, felt more at home with her brother, who had mended his, than with a man whose grief was unassuageable.

It occurred to him suddenly, just as the elder Lazarus said:

"It will snow before sunset; of that I am sure," and he himself had said:

"Then I must be getting back," and sensed that his going would be a relief, I might as well be dead!

He regarded that thought for a minute and then revised it, They'd all be better off, if I were dead.

Lazarus, a good brother, as well as a pious Jew would do his duty, take his sister and the children into his house, exert himself to find husbands for the girls, leave his vineyard to the boy. And when some time Uncle Lazarus said—as he surely would, being a man of sense— That is a ruinous way to bring a boy up! the mother would take heed. She couldn't turn on her brother with the unanswerable words, *You* reared Nathan!

He left them. Uncle Lazarus was in no hurry to get back; there was nothing he could do about the snow if it fell, except be thankful that it had come instead of frost. His winters now were easy and leisurely and he was prepared to spend the rest of the day in the cosy house where young Martha had mended the fire and they were all about to roast apples. There was nothing wrong with the leave-taking, he was their father and the children were reared to be mannerly; Martha asked when he would next be home and he told her truly that he did not know; much depended upon the weather. Lazarus said the snow was certain but he hoped that for Josodad's sake it would be a light fall.

Then he was out in the cold air, alone; but no more alone than when he sat amongst his family.

His house stood a little apart from the village and he had to descend a slight slope, cross the end of a street and then mount again to where the flock lay in a sheltered valley between two hills. The last of the houses in the street was the smaller of the two inns in the town, the one kept by Ephorus the Greek, if the word "keep" could be used in connection with Ephorus who, as Martha had said, was usually drunk. It was curious, and ironic, but it was true that the idle, drunken sot of an innkeeper, Greek by birth, was the only person who had ever come near seeing the depths of Josodad's desolation. He had also, by a timely word, prevented Josodad from becoming a sot, too. For there had been a time, during the first autumn after Nathan's death, when Josodad, having tried every mental form of self-consolation, faith in God, prayer, joy in his living children, and dismally failed to find what he sought, had experimented with drunkenness and found that to lie down with one's head spinning, one's stomach slightly sickened, did at least mean that one slept. Then, when one waked, grief, denied its nightly outlet, clamped down more fiercely, and a feeling of guilt because one had slept and forgotten, mingled with the sorrow; and the only remedy was more wine.

But one evening, Ephorus, quite drunk himself, had said, "Don't do it, Josodad. Comfort is not to be found at the bottom of a wine cup. I know. I sought it there myself." And Josodad, so lately a flockmaster, and still a respected member of his own community, had been shocked back to sobriety by the thought that a drunken Greek innkeeper should feel compelled to speak to him like that. That had been his first reaction. Then Ephorus said, "We all have our losses, you know, and they cripple us. But a cripple would be a fool to invite leprosy as well. I know," he said, "I did it. Grief made a cripple of me and then I made myself a leper—I'm speaking metaphorically, of course, and I'm a fool to do it. You Jews don't understand metaphors."

"We call them parables," Josodad said, thinking of the prophet Nathan . . . Nathan . . . Nathan . . . who had rebuked King David for taking Uriah's wife by telling him a parable of the man with the one ewe lamb.

"Use your own word," Ephorus said, concentrating so fiercely that he was almost cross-eyed. "And don't go saying I'm a leper. I'm not a leper; nor a cripple as anybody about here understands the words. I'm just trying to tell you, because I feel for you, Josodad, I feel for you. I had a loss and it crippled me, I lost Dorcas and then I took to wine-bibbing and so I'm a leper, socially. Don't you travel the same road. I'm just warning you . . . warning you." He'd tossed off another cup of wine and relapsed into his usual silence. And Josodad had left his cup as it was, and had not, as he had intended, asked to have his flask filled to buffer him against his night thoughts.

He'd never been inside the inn since, but he'd always remembered Ephorus with a kind of affection; the one man in Bethlehem who understood what a loss was, an amputation that could cripple a man.

On this evening, so busy with his own gloomy thoughts, he

noticed, with a distant, impersonal satisfaction on Ephorus' behalf, that the inn was very busy. Bethlehem-born men coming back in accordance with the new order, to put their names on the tax register. He'd registered that morning, before going home.

Name? *Josodad, son of Nathan.*

Occupation? *Hired shepherd.*

Place of residence? *Bethlehem.*

Age? *Forty-eight.*

As the questions were rapped out, the answers given, he'd thought, Nathan should have been here beside me, and the answer to the second question should in both our cases have been, "Flockmaster."

Thinking about the tax register had been some slight relief and carried him on, in the teeth of the biting wind, to the top of the hill from which point he could look down upon the sheep, just visible in the gathering dusk. They were huddled together and he thought, They know. Lazarus was right; it will snow before dark. And almost instantly a few flakes, slowly, indecisively, seeming sometimes even to ascend, filled the air.

He thought, I chose the spot well. If I'd listened to Arad or Ibri we should now be lying nearer the town, with nothing between us and the snow-bearing wind. Not that I was thinking of snow, only of the wind; sheep don't like the wind from the North.

Arad and Ibri had collected plenty of fuel and made a good fire. They were playing with Ibri's stones, the light danced on their moving hands, and on their laughing faces. He could hear the laughter and the loud talk as he approached; but when he joined them they fell silent and took on glum expressions, as though his presence were a rebuke to their merriment. He thought, Here too I cast a shadow. He tried to think of something to say and could only think of a question, "Is all well?" And that, he knew, would strike a wrong note, as though he thought that in his absence things were bound to go wrong. Yet he could have asked Nathan that question as unthinkingly as he breathed. So he thought again, and produced a remark about the weather.

"It looks as though we're in for a nasty night."

Ibri—recently married—said, "All nights apart from Ruth are nasty for me." Then he said, "Your turn, Arad," and the game went on, but in a muted way.

A kind of contrition made itself felt in Josodad; he thought, I have resented them because they are alive while Nathan is dead. And he remembered the perverse pleasure he had felt over Lazarus' failure to manage the pipe. He thought of wounds: some healed, leaving no mark, or only a dry, healthy scar, some went festering on and on until they had poisoned the whole body. That was what grief had done to his mind, to his very nature, poisoned the whole. He was now fit company for nobody, not even himself.

He opened the bag of food which the two Marthas had packed for him, small loaves of sweet crusty bread, some fresh cheese, some of the salted, smoked mutton which the Jews prepared in the same way as unbelievers treated pig meat. And as he opened the bag he saw that the food was exactly the same as that which Nathan had carried with him on the fateful journey during which he had fallen in with Dan. So although he had intended to offer the food in a pleasant, conciliatory manner, his voice, when he said, "Help yourselves," came out harsh, offhandedly as though he were offering food to animals.

Arad said, "But if we eat this, what'll you do tomorrow? And the day after?" He was reminding Josodad that he and Ibri both had their home visits to make, and he must be on duty.

"There's more than I shall need, even if you eat your fill." And he thought, Never to be obliged to eat again, mumbling the tasteless stuff! Never to think again; or to remember. . . .

He knew then what he meant to do. The thought, I might as well be dead, had fallen, like a seed, into fertile soil. The first sign that it had rooted had been the next thought, They'd be better off if I were dead; and now, springing to full life the growth had revealed its nature, a determination to be dead. To end it. To have done with everything.

There was plenty of time; he must wait until Arad and Ibri were asleep. He felt restless and would have liked to say, I'll just walk round; but if he did that they would misinterpret his motive, think that he suspected some neglect on their part. So he sat down, within the fire's radiance, but a little apart, and watched the snowflakes spin down.

It would be, as Lazarus had wished that it should be, a light fall. Already in the West the low clouds were breaking up.

He sat, wrapped in his thick brown cloak, and thought of what he intended to do; he thought of it from every aspect. Family first. He was sure that they would be better off. His brother-in-law was a good man, and his business brought him many contacts. The girls would be seen, admired, spoken for; the boy would take kindly to his uncle's business, there being nothing in a vineyard to frighten him, as a ram had once frightened him when Josodad had tried to introduce him to the flock. Martha would be happy.

He then thought about God, who, though He had failed him, could not be ignored without condemning Nathan to oblivion. (And the strange thing here was that though for himself he desired nothing more than complete oblivion—Let Josodad be blotted out as though he had never been!—he couldn't accept oblivion for Nathan, that merry laughing boy.) There was nothing in the commandments against killing yourself. He ran them through in his mind, and there was nothing. He then called to mind such of the stories of the past as he had heard and could remember. After his defeat on the Mount of Gilboa, Saul had fallen upon his sword. But Saul had been mad, deserted by God. Then there was the story of Elijah the prophet and how he had gone into the wilderness and sat down under a juniper tree and prayed, "Now, O Lord, take away my life." His life had not been taken, because he still had work to do; but the prayer had been suicidal, and he had never been rebuked for that. And there was an account of somebody—the name escaped him—turning his face to the wall and willing himself to die.

He considered it all, quite calmly, and reached the conclusion that if Nathan were now in the safekeeping of God, his own self-destruction would be no barrier against their reunion.

And what was the alternative? Years and years more of this

life, days during which he would steadily alienate himself from his fellows, nights when he would doubt his God.

But he would, he thought, give God one last chance! And then, for all his doubts, his orthodoxy rose in protest. A blasphemous thought. He'd ask God one last favour.

So he made his evening prayer, "Blessed art thou, O Lord our God, King of the Universe, who at thy word bringest on the evening twilight . . ." and then he added his special request; that he might die as he slept.

It was usual for shepherds to draw lots for the order in which they should watch; but he and Arad and Ibri had long ago abandoned that custom. If he slept at all it was always in the first watch, then he'd wake with that jolt and spend most of, if not all, the rest of the night awake. His two companions, after a very short time, had turned this to their advantage. No need, they said, for two people to stay awake. So one of them, or both of them, officially stayed awake and watched while he slept the brief sleep of exhaustion and then he watched for the rest of the night. Most often, when he woke, they were both asleep. In winter there was danger from wolves that would sneak down from the hills, and always there was danger from sheep-stealers, and these were not all men-of-the-hills, hungry and stealing for food. There were professionals, very skilled and soft-footed, who could snatch a sheep from the edge of a flock—the more easily if it were a large flock, like this, smother its head in a cloth and bear it off and sell it to a butcher.

There was no outcry, no trail of blood. In the morning there was a sheep missing, and somewhere, far away, an unidentifiable carcase on a hook.

Tonight, however, there was little danger from thieves. Men who lived by sheep-stealing were, fundamentally, men who liked ease and comfort without working to earn either; the cold and the snow would deter them. A visitation from wolves was unlikely, too; with the flock lying so near to Bethlehem, it would take a prolonged spell of bad weather to make them desperate enough to venture so near a town. As for the men-of-the-hills, their raids had in the past two years been so infrequent that it seemed to Josodad as though the resistance movement which had cost Nathan his life, was dying down. So the flock was safe, and it wouldn't matter if he died in his sleep and Ibri and Arad slept on, as was their habit.

As he thought these things he was aware of the absurdity. At this crisis of his life, what did the flock matter? If the flock were stolen or ravaged, he'd be out of reach of any blame or chiding. Still, even now, he reckoned the risk to the flock carefully, because at heart he was still the good owner shepherd, not a hireling, like Ibri or Arad. And when, dead to this world, he woke in the next—if there was another—and faced the judgement of God, he hoped that it would be taken into reckoning that though as man, as father and husband he was a failure, as a shepherd he had been reliable.

So he looked over the flock before he lay down. All was well. The fire was bright, and beside it the two young men were still engrossed in their game.

He couldn't, in the traditional manner, turn his face to the wall, but he turned it towards the rock, under whose overhanging edge they had made their little camping place. And as he lay down he thought, with a profound feeling of relief, that now he had done with it all, done with the grief and the toil, the searing doubts, the consequent self-recrimination. As he composed himself for sleep, faith came flooding back; he had prayed and he believed that this prayer would be answered. So he began to sink down into darkness and softness and not-knowing as gently as he had done in the happy days. His last thought was that he had not approached sleep by such a pleasant path since he had shared a night watch with Nathan. . . .

Shortly before midnight he woke, with the old familiar jolt, Something wrong? He raised his head and listened and, as usual, knew that with the flock all was well, with him all was wrong. The feeling of loss and disaster fell upon him again. Not dead. Alive and wide awake, back with his misery.

He stood up and looked around him. The snow had ceased; the sky had cleared and overhead the stars were brilliant. Arad and Ibri were sound asleep beside the fire which had died down to a pinkish glow under a shroud of ash. The sheep were sleeping too, lying close like the boulders in a dry riverbed. It was all as usual. He thought, God has failed me again; and this time felt no self-reproach. It was simple truth. God had failed him, all along. He'd kept the Law, done his duty, paid his dues, made his prayers, and never, until tonight, asked a favour for himself. On Nathan's behalf he had prayed for an acquittal, then for swift death; both denied.

He thought, in plain peasant fashion, that if you knocked on the door of a human friend, once and again and again, and had no answer, you'd conclude that he was not there, or that he was, for some reason, no longer your friend. Did not the same apply to God?

The wind blew coldly and he stood there between the great empty space of earth and the great empty space of heaven, between a vast flock of senseless sheep and a vast flock of unheeding stars and knew the ultimate loneliness. He faced—for the first time without recoil or protest—the fact that Nathan had gone forever, the strong, merry, bright-eyed boy who had made music and cracked jokes and loved his food, was now just a dead thing, rotting; what he had been had vanished into darkness.

And I will follow, Josodad thought. I will make an end. He knew just how to do it. His knife was sharp; one firm slash across his left wrist would suffice.

Even now, in this moment of no faith, of dead belief, his mind reverted, from habit, to the Law by which he had lived all his life. Thou shalt not kill. That was plain enough and any believer in the Law would understand that suicide as well as murder was forbidden. Yet it was never held against Saul that he had thrown himself on his sword after his defeat at Gilboa. His suicide, indeed, had inspired one of the most beautiful of David's songs. But Saul had long before lost touch with God. Like me, Josodad thought. He drew his knife and saw the starlight sparkle on the clean bright blade.

Then he paused. He had lost touch with God, but not with man, and not with sheep. Arad and Ibri didn't like him, he knew that; to his face they were sullen and suspicious, behind his back they laughed at him and called him Old Tup; but it would spoil their breakfast if they woke and found him here by the dead fire, lying in his blood. And the sheep would be upset, too. All animals were sensitive to blood; carnivores liked, were excited by the smell of it; sheep, oxen, horses abhorred it. So he must go away to do what he had to do.

He began to scramble, making as little noise as possible, over the sheltering rocks. At the top he walked a hundred paces and then looked around for some hidden niche in the broken ground where he could lie. The boys would wake in the morning and look over the flock in their casual fashion, have their breakfast, remark upon his absence, and wait. Eventually one of them would report to Ezra and a search would be organised. Maybe by that time the kites would have picked his bones clean. His death would cause nobody any bother, or any grief.

Up here the stars seemed even brighter and there was one, very large, very golden, hanging low in the sky, a star which he had never noticed before in his sleepless nights. Once he had thought of the stars, as of the sun and the moon, that they were all part of the miracle of creation, the result of God's order, Let there be light! But tonight the courts of heaven were untenanted, and the throne was empty.

Searching for what was to be his last bed he turned his eyes from the sky to the ground and was startled to see his own shadow very black and sharply defined, stretching ahead of him. No amount of starlight could cast such a shadow. He turned and saw that behind him the sky was luminous, filled with light that was not of the moon or the stars, light without origin or focus, visibly brightening. It was, he thought, as though the sky were opening.

A fearful terror came upon him, terror so complete that he could not move, or breathe, or even tremble though the marrow of his bones vibrated. The light grew dazzling, and shifted, and took shape. Then suddenly, brighter than the light, more beautiful than anything ever seen or imagined, there was the angel, leaning down along the shafts of radiance and speaking with a golden voice.

The angel said, "Fear not; for behold I bring you tidings of great joy, which shall be to all people. For unto you is born this day in the city of David, a Saviour which is Christ the Lord. And this shall be a sign unto you; ye shall find the babe, wrapped in swaddling clothes, lying in a manger."

The Saviour. The Messiah. Something in Josodad's mind shouldered fear aside. He said in a loud, almost angry voice, "Didn't I tell him so? Didn't I say that in His own time, in His own way, God would deliver His people. He had only to wait. The waste of it!"

He had felt that his misery was absolute, that nothing could add to it. But he had been wrong. There was this extra bitterness to come. "Too late," he said. "This is too late for Nathan who is dead, and too late for me, who have denied my God."

Then he saw that the angel was not alone. Around him there was a multitude, a great host, all with bright, beautiful faces. But of the host Josodad had eyes only for one familiar, beloved face; and in the chorus of voices singing, "Glory to God in the highest, and on earth peace, good will toward men," he heard only the voice of his own son.

They vanished and he was alone in the starlight. He stood there knowing that Nathan was not a dead thing in the ground, but alive, recognisable and happy, part of some inconceivable glory. He was filled with joy, and mingling with the joy was remorse because he had allowed grief to sour him, to estrange him from his family, from his fellow men, from life itself. All those years wasted in grief and bitterness, with Nathan, young and beautiful, safe in the hands of God all the time. He said aloud, "Oh God, maker of the Universe, forgive me. How could I know?" The answer came from his own mind: no man could *know*, but a man should have faith.

He began to shake then, realising how nearly he had escaped final calamity. Moving like a palsied man, he hurried, not caring how much noise he made, over the rocks and down into the sheltered place. Arad slept the sleep of the carefree single man, but Ibri was awake, blinking and bemused.

"I saw a great light," he said. "I heard voices." He spoke as though the light and the voices had been things he had dreamed.

Josodad said, "Come, let us go to Bethlehem."

CHAPTER XI

Except on state occasions, when he must appear as a King, it pleased Herod to wear the simple toga that was the mark of the Roman citizen. This he was entitled to do, for the first Caesar, Julius himself, had conferred full citizenship, with all its privileges, upon his father, Antipater, forty years earlier.

On this day, however, he wore his kingly, almost Oriental, robes, with jewelled clasps and a jewelled belt, a coronet of emeralds on his head, where the hair was still plentiful and crisp, the black only just frosted with white at the temples; on his wrists he wore bands of gold, set with other emeralds and rubies and sapphires, and his fingers were stiff with rings.

He was about to go out and show himself to his people, so that those who loved him, and those who hated him, might see for themselves what rumour was worth. His friends had been grieving, his enemies rejoicing, over the state of his health; and both had had good cause. He had been gravely ill: but he had made a most painful journey by litter, across the Jordan, to a place called Calirrhoe, and there he had taken medicinal baths and drunk immense quantities of revolting, bitter-tasting water, and been not only restored to health, but rejuvenated. The pain that had gnawed, a wolf in his belly, had gone; his ravenous appetite was now normal, and his complexion, lately the colour of beeswax, had regained its smooth, faintly tanned Idumaean hue.

He had come back, jubilant, just in time for the Feast of Saturnalia, and inside his palace he had celebrated, merrily: but he was far too cautious, far too wary of the High Priest and his following, and of the orthodox Jews, to make any public appearance during the Festival. So on this day he intended to ride out.

The gentleman-attendant, whose duty it was, held open his cloak, purple velvet, lined with fur and embroidered with gold thread. Parosh was a Jew, of the Hellenised kind whom Herod found tolerable, so to him he could say, "Solomon in full glory could not have been better clad!" and be sure of provoking a smile.

"I am ready, now," Herod said, shrugging his shoulders into the cloak. "And if Archelaus keeps me waiting, I shall disinherit him."

The threat to disinherit was one of his slightly sour, self-mocking jokes; he never for a moment deceived himself about the extent of his power. He was King of Judea because his father had been a friend of the Romans and because his own personality and abilities had recommended him to Mark Antony and Octavius while they were still friends and shared the government of Rome. He had remained King of Judea because he had been wily, and because even when Antony and Octavius had fallen out, and Antony was dead and Octavius supreme, the latter had had the good sense to see that there was nothing to gain and much to lose by deposing a man who was managing well, who had put down civil war in Judea with a heavy hand, who was a good friend of Rome, whose half-Jewish blood made him acceptable to at least part of the nation he ruled. But when he died, even though he made a will and showed clearly which of his sons should succeed him, there was no certainty that Archelaus or any of his other sons would be chosen by Octavius—now Caesar Augustus—to occupy the throne.

Of his five remaining sons, Archelaus, the youngest, was his favourite; most like him in appearance, and, though only sixteen years of age, most compatible in mind. Unless something very regrettable happened, Herod intended to use all his influence, even his posthumous influence, on behalf of this boy; and with that in mind often appeared with him in public, frequently sent him on visits to Rome, and while he was in Jerusalem never failed to bring him to the notice of any visiting Roman.

Archelaus was punctual and Herod, looking him over, was satisfied by his appearance; he was dressed as befitted a prince, but not in such a way as to offer any competition to his father. Herod, who had on at least three occasions placed policy before paternal feelings and murdered his sons as though they were enemies, was fond enough, at this moment, to say:

"No cloak? They tell me the wind is very cold."

The escort waited; six members of the palace guard, a body of men whom Herod had organised very much upon the lines of the Emperor's Praetorian Guard in Rome; imitation, so long as it was not tainted by competitiveness, was a useful means of flattery. It often seemed to Herod that many men of intelligence failed to succeed because they lacked knowledge of human nature. In one of the long, rambling complaints which the priests were always sending by delegation to Rome, one charge was that Herod copied the Emperor; and Octavius had given the reply that any sensible person could have expected. "Whom better could he copy?" Octavius had asked.

Herod had felt well when he wakened, well as he was robed; now with a horse between his knees again, he felt even better. Before his visit to Calirrhoe he had been able only to ride in a litter, and even that was painful. Now he rode a superb horse, one of Arab breed, brought up from his native Idumea.

They rode through a wide courtyard where the grass was always green, even in the height of summer, because it was intersected at regular intervals by small irrigation streams. There were many fountains, too, bronze or marble figures of boys and girls, holding bowls or torches out of which the water spouted, horses and deer and strange mythical beasts with water pouring from their mouths. Such things were detestable to the pious Jews who took the first commandment literally. But there was no need for any Jew to enter this way; there were other entrances, some containing nothing likely to offend. In this, as in other things, Herod had been willing to compromise between what he wished and what was acceptable. About the water supply, so essential in a civilised city, compromise had been impossible; one could not build an aqueduct secretly, nor cheaply, and there had been a short, sharp rebellion when it was discovered that some of the Temple funds had been appropriated for the aqueduct. But to balance that, Herod could point to the immense amount of work he had done to embellish the Temple itself. It was now finer than the one that Solomon had reared, which had been destroyed by the Babylonians. At the return from exile, the Jews under Ezra had rebuilt it, but small and plain. Herod had greatly enlarged and beautified it.

Behind him, as he rode out this morning, was the Palace, upon which he had lavished money and planning genius, and across the huddled roofs of the city, as he gazed ahead, he could see the Temple.

He said, "I intend to do something generous and spectacular to show my gratitude to Calirrhoe. The waters there are as good as any in the Empire, but the buildings are nothing, and the place is amateurly run. I think I shall build a great new bath with a musicians' gallery and a library and rooms for massage and amusement. To make the place popular would be an investment. As the roads improve more people will travel. That fellow Quintilius, who dined with us the other evening, was on his way there."

The old man talked as though he had years of life ahead of him, Archelaus thought; and really since his return from the baths, he looked as though he had.

Aloud he said, "Now what did you make of *him,* sir?"

Herod thought, I could tell you exactly. He's an independent observer, in other words a spy. Augustus had heard of my illness and was beginning to plan ahead. Reports from officials are always biassed. . . . But it was unwise to be too open, either of mouth or heart, even to your favourite; so he answered by asking:

"I don't know. What did *you?*"

"It struck me that either his gout was very mild, or he has found some very powerful opiate. He ate and drank everything that was put before him."

"That was very observant of you."

"Also," Archelaus said, "his appetite for information was as insatiable as his greed. He seldom asked a direct question, though. I noticed that. He had a way of bringing the conversation round, so that the way was open for you to *tell* him things."

"Did you tell him anything? I saw you in conversation for a considerable time."

"I told him nothing—at least nothing he wanted to know. He told how badly he and his brothers agreed when they were young; and the way was wide open for me to tell him how Antipas and Antipater and I hate the sight of one another. But I did not do so. In fact, I think, sir, that I left him with the impression that I was somewhat slow in the uptake."

"Never fear that! It's the slow-witted ones who gulp down the bait, my boy."

From under their hooded lids his bright eyes looked at Archelaus with something like approval. The boy had his wits about him. From Herod's point of view there was only one thing wrong with him—apart, of course, from what was wrong with every human being, untrustworthiness—he was the son of the wrong mother! Whenever he approved of Archelaus he was bound to reflect that if he could breed such a boy upon an ordinary woman, how exceptional his sons by Mariamne would have been. They, however, Alexander and Aristobulus, had allowed their untrustworthiness to become blatant, and he had been obliged to have them murdered.

This, however, was no moment to think of Mariamne or her sons. He gave his attention to his capital.

Most of the streets they rode along were narrow and steep, presenting, under the heavy grey of the sky, a dull, ancient, rather grim appearance. The people, huddled against the cold, looked dull too. In many places the sullenness of the sky was reflected in the faces turned towards the clattering little cavalcade. To many Jews Herod was a semi-barbarian, a usurper, a man who endeavoured both openly and secretly to bring them, their city, their way of life into line with the pagan ways that masqueraded under the term "civilisation."

"I often think," Herod remarked as they passed a group of men who stared, silent and hostile, "that of all rulers, he who governs a theocracy has the most thankless task. People are so busy praising God for his mercies—mainly invisible—that they can't be ordinarily grateful for tangible advantages."

Archelaus privately decided that when he was King—as he fully intended to be, by craft and corruption if qualification was not enough—he would do something about these surly, stubborn people. If they wouldn't smile and cheer from loyalty and gratitude, they should do it from fear. He looked at his father and thought, with some bewilderment, that you couldn't honestly say that he was a soft man; he'd killed hundreds and would not hesitate to kill again; but he was oddly careless about the attitude of the ordinary man towards him.

Once, on a similar ride, a man, safely anonymous in a crowd had flung a taunt; "Son of Esau!" he had shouted, referring to Herod's ancestry. Herod had turned in his saddle and laughed and shouted back, "Thank you!"

Archelaus, younger then, had said, "But sir, that was an insult."

"From a Jew, a compliment," Herod said. "If you must go picking over your pedigree like a race-horse, who wouldn't rather be a descendant of Esau, the firstborn, the good hunter, than that lying, cheating, mother's darling who spawned this lot?"

Archelaus remembered that incident, and thought, Well, that's one way of looking at it; that's one way of governing, so completely to despise those you rule that whether they cheer or not doesn't matter: all the same, when I ride these streets as King, people will cheer or I shall know why!

In places they were cheered. Anywhere where there was building going on. Even a Jewish builder knew the value of full employment and over the rebuilding of the Temple alone, ten thousand workmen had been employed steadily for six years. There were loud acclamations, too, from people about the theatre, the amphitheatre and the hippodrome where the workers were mainly Greeks or half-breeds of one kind or another, with some Jews who were prepared to accept civilising influences in the proper spirit. In places where the reception was warm and friendly Archelaus responded with a guarded enthusiasm. To be popular for yourself alone, and to endeavour to foster popularity was not a safe thing, if you were Herod's son. Antipater, at the moment, enjoyed great popularity, simply because he and his father were always quarrelling. They would have a row in the

Palace overnight, and somehow the word would spread and be all over the city by morning and on Antipater's next appearance he would have a tumultuous greeting. But that kind of thing merely worsened the situation between father and son, and Archelaus was clever enough to realise it. He was risking nothing; after all, Herod was seventy, and the Romans had enough respect for his judgement, and enough awareness of all he had done to keep this province of the Empire peaceful and prosperous, to take some note of any wish he expressed on his deathbed. Archelaus intended to wait.

When, with the wind growing colder and the grey sky darkening towards twilight, they passed the Royal Portico of the Temple, on their way back to the Palace, Herod said:

"I have the High Priest and five other Sanhedrin members dining with me this evening. It's amusing to think that they have probably spent most of the day composing a complaint to send to Rome because I allowed Saturnalia to be celebrated. Unless Octavius lost his sense of humour when he became Augustus, he must often have a good laugh over these deputations."

"They show such poor judgement," agreed Archelaus who had once been in Rome when such a deputation arrived. "One deputation, I remember, complained, hardly pausing for breath between, that three men had been unjustly tried and sentenced to death and that you wore the toga. Augustus did smile—he seldom laughs outright—and he said, 'Which of these is a serious crime? One I commit regularly myself!' "

"They have too much money; too much money by far," Herod said darkly. "Jews scattered all over the face of the earth, prosperous some of them, many poor, but all sending back money, sending back money for the Temple funds. But when the harvest failed—oh, long before you were born—and pestilence broke out, did the damned priests lift a finger or give a sesterce to help the people? Did they even remit their tithes? They did not. I remitted my tax, my income, for a whole year. I also sold treasures from my Palace that I have never been able to replace. My best gold candlesticks ended up in Pontus, I believe; and there was a table of lapis lazuli. . . . I bought corn from Egypt, they'd had a good harvest, and I gave it away, free. And what thanks did I get? I was trying, they said, to pauperise upright Jewish citizens by imitating the dole-giving in Rome. They said that with their mouths full of my bread. Ingrates!"

There again, Archelaus thought, the contradictory streak; if when he ruled a year of famine came, he wouldn't sell a candle to help, let alone a candlestick!

"Well," Herod said, "that's over. They know I'm alive and well, and early next week I can go to Caesarea."

That was a new town, his own creation, a beautiful place. It was cosmopolitan too, and the heavy leaden hand of the Jewish faith lay there so lightly as hardly to be felt at all. There he would not be expected to dine with six priests and spend the evening in solemn conversation.

Archelaus said, "Can I come with you?" eagerly.

"It's about time you went to Rome again," Herod said. "You can do a double errand there. You can give Caesar a firsthand account of my health. I think you'll know what to say about *that!* And you can find out his favourite sculptor and his favourite pose and order a statue, twice life size, to go in the atrium of the new baths at Calirrhoe. I owe my throne to the Emperor and my life to Calirrhoe, and that would be a suitable way of combining my expressions of gratitude. You can let that information fall in a casual way. Even flattery profits by a touch of subtlety; always remember that, my boy."

"I know exactly what you mean," Archelaus said, thinking, That's clever!

"I believe you do; otherwise I should not be sending you. You can come to Caesarea and take ship from there. Now I will go and don my detested toga, so that the High Priest's disapproval lends *some* flavour to this dismal meal."

It would be, as always on these occasions, as nearly meagre as could be served at a King's table. The Jews had all these ridiculous rules about what could and what could not be eaten or drunk; let them abide by them. The meal this evening would be just that served in any well-to-do Jewish family's household; mutton and beans, onions and horseradish. And the wine would be cheap local product, from grapes grown on Jewish soil, gathered by Jewish hands, the wine of *Kiddush*. Herod himself much preferred Falernian.

There would be one bright spot in the evening, too; sooner or later the priests were bound to mention the new taxes and the census; and there Herod would be on very sound ground. He could say, "Caesar gave that order; I had nothing to do with it. You should have sent a deputation to Rome if you had any valid objection."

There was another comforting thought. On the last occasion when he entertained the Sanhedrin members, he'd been in the throes of his illness; ravenously hungry; the miserable meal had done nothing to appease the wolves gnawing in his belly and he had hardly been able to wait until the priests left and he could order another, better meal, knowing all the time that it would merely feed the wolves and strengthen them for tomorrow's assault. Tonight he would be able to eat normally.

He was hardly inside the Palace when one of the stewards came bustling up to say that three travellers arrived and humbly craved audience. They were insistent and were waiting.

"From Rome?" Herod asked, instantly alert.

"No, my lord. From the East. Only one of them speaks a recognisable tongue."

The East? Parthia?

"Who sent them? What credentials do they carry?"

"None, my lord."

"You are sure of that?"

"Dumah questioned them and is certain they have no mission, except their own, which is a wish to see you, my lord."

"Then why should they imagine that I should receive them? If I opened my door to every chance traveller I might as well be on show in the menagerie! Send them away."

"My lord, Dumah did gather that a prince is concerned."

Herod made a sound of exasperation. Antipater again. Women? Debts?

"Is one of these a merchant?"

"So Dumah thought. A black man; better dressed than the others, and the spokesman."

Herod could guess what had happened. In one of their recent quarrels he had absolutely forbidden Antipater to obtain credit in any city under his jurisdiction; he had a generous, a wildly generous allowance, and he must keep within it. But Antipater had simply taken advantage of the words "within my jurisdiction" and had gone to the free cities of the Decapolis and there run up debts. Now a black-faced fellow, probably a freedman—and they were the sharpest traders in the world—had come, with two witnesses, to ask payment. And his daring to come showed how highly those citizens of the independent Greek cities valued themselves. Insolent upstarts! He was on the verge of saying that the men should be hustled off, roughly; then he remembered that the Decapolis was under Roman protection. The next thing he knew *they'd* be sending a deputation to Augustus complaining that Herod had no control over his own son.

He said, "Tell the Treasurer to deal with it, whatever it is," and strode angrily along to his own apartments where the attendants waited to disrobe and dress him again. But his anger with Antipater had opened the old wound in his heart: his true sons, his real heirs had been Mariamne's sons, and they were dead. So was she. And the fact that he had been responsible for their deaths, planned and ordered the executions, did nothing to lessen his grief. A man with a rotting limb might be driven to cutting it off with his own knife, that he performed the operation himself would not lessen the pain, nor the loss.

Brusquely he waved aside those waiting to serve him and went to the high, bronze decorated door that separated his rooms from those of Mariamne.

Her sleeping chamber, a large room with a silver and ivory bed on a dais, was warmed by braziers that gave off sweet scent as well as warmth, and the air was also full of the scent of roses. A slave had already lighted many candles, at the sight of Herod he scuttled away. The light shone on the flowers and on the dressing table with its silver mirror, its flasks and pots of rose-crystal, jade and alabaster; it was just as she had left it. Easy enough to delude oneself that this room's occupant, a fastidious woman, superlatively served, had just been robed, had painted her face and dressed her hair and gone out of the room for a moment and would, in a moment, be back.

His attitude towards his murdered wife was the most evident sign of that contradictory streak in Herod which those close to him had noted. He had loved her, distrusted her deeply, and had her killed. Immediately after he had given orders that her rooms were to be kept exactly as she had left them, that she was always to be spoken of as though she were alive. He had never cancelled the order for the daily delivery of roses; during roseless seasons in Jerusalem they were brought from far places, cut in bud, wrapped in damp cotton fibre, transported by the swiftest means, and arranged. On any occasion when, alive, she would have shared a meal with him, her place was set; he visited her apartments once every day as a matter of routine, and frequently at other times when he was worried, puzzled, exultant, or sorry for himself. Often he spoke her name, a thing to which his courtiers and staff were accustomed but disconcerting to strangers.

There were some who worked in the Palace who were not so sure that the whole thing was a mere foible. When Herod called "Mariamne" there was no answer but an echo; her wraith was never seen, but occasionally someone walking a hall or a corridor where there were no roses would become aware of the sweet scent which had been her favourite. Once a slave, dusting the table where Mariamne had been used to sit, beautifying beauty, had dropped and broken a glass phial and then reeled back, her hand to her face, screaming. Later she had a bruise to show to corroborate her story that she had been slapped. Night watchmen, too, told uneasy stories of the behaviour of the hounds which made their rounds with them. Over the years the Palace had become a place where few men willingly walked alone after sunset.

Herod was as jealous of these hints that other people as well as himself were aware of her as he had been jealous of anyone who approached her when she was alive. He, the sceptic, the murderer, the extremely rational man, liked to believe, did

believe, that somewhere she lived on, entirely his at last, understanding why he had done what he did, and full of sweet forgive-
ness and deeply concerned with his well-being. This imaginary
Mariamne bore little resemblance to the haughty, intractable
Asmodean princess whom he had married from expediency and
who with a glance or the movement of a hand could convey her
scorn of him, a half-breed upstart and usurper. In her lifetime
she had never forgiven a misplaced word, much less a wrong, and
when he had killed her brother, who was High Priest at the time,
she had immediately turned to plotting, with her mother, the old
Queen Alexandra, and then with Cleopatra of Egypt, another
deadly enemy of his. Yet their life together had not been without
its good moments; there had been times when his passion had
seemed to evoke an answering passion in her; and it was around
these rare and lovely times that he had built his fantasy, softening and changing the character of his love into what he would
have wished her to be.

He invariably came to this room and laid his problems before
her; he sat on one particular couch, emptied his mind, called on
her name and waited.

He did so now. "Mariamne!" he called; then he told her that
he was angry with Antipater, stared at the nearest bowl of roses
and waited.

To his attendants the waiting time seemed long; to Melchior,
his nerves shredding with impatience, it seemed interminable.
But finally Herod emerged, moving briskly, a slight, puzzled
frown on his forehead.

"I've no time," he said to the man who moved forward to begin the disrobing. "Three strangers asked to see me. Run, tell
Dumah I will receive them; in the small Silver Room. If they've
gone, they're to be followed and brought back. Run!"

To a second attendant he said, "Find Prince Archelaus and
ask him to receive and entertain the High Priest and his staff
until I can join them. I won't keep them long."

To yet a third he said, "I want no attendants at this interview."

That was unusual; when Herod received visitors he liked to
do so in pomp, surrounded by his lords.

"With guards at the door, my lord."

After a second's thought, Herod nodded. The room was called small because it was so compared with other audience chambers, but it was sixty feet long, and whatever these strangers had to tell him could not be overheard by the guards in the doorway.

And what, he wondered, as he strode, rustling, towards the Silver Room, could three strangers, without credentials, one a merchant, have to tell him of such importance and urgency that Mariamne had seemed to persuade him to change his mind and receive them? That it was urgent and important he was sure. Only once had he acted against the inspiration which seemed to flow into him as he sat in that quiet, flower-filled room, and then the result had been regrettable.

As he crossed the shining tesselated floor upon which were portrayed the seasons of the year, and took his seat in the great silver chair under a purple canopy, his mind reverted to Parthia where there were scores of petty kingdoms, loosely knit, some of them chafing under the Parthian yoke. It could be that these men "from the East" were emissaries of so secret a kind that they carried no credentials. He was known to be Caesar's friend and an intriguer with skill and experience; somebody might have had the idea of making an approach to Rome through him. If so it was fortunate that Archelaus was about to go there and could be entrusted with a verbal message. And then, thinking of Archelaus, he was reminded of a tale the boy had brought back from his last visit. From somewhere farther away, Eastward even of Parthia, some fellow, Pella, Pelli, Pello, no matter, had appealed to Augustus for help in regaining a throne he had some kind of claim to. Archelaus had recounted how Caesar had called for maps and studied them and then said, "The place is not even marked. . . ."

The three men were brought to the door and there left to make their own way towards him.

Certainly two of them came from some very distant place; their clothes were most outlandish.

There was an old man, frail and brittle as an autumn leaf, wearing a curious black hat, like a pent roof, and a stained coat of quilted cotton cloth, with wide sleeves. He looked neither to right nor left as he entered and he was the first man, in Herod's experience, to enter this room with the beaten silver panels on the walls, and the beautiful floor, and not to show either admiration, envy, disapproval, or awe. He walked straight forward, moving swiftly, his eyes fixed upon Herod's face. A King paying a visit to a King was the thought that flashed through Herod's mind before he turned his attention upon the second man. He was younger, a man in his prime, just as freakishly clad, but with an air of arrogance. He showed more awareness of his surroundings; as he walked his glance took in the room and its furnishings, and Herod under the canopy, as though he were summing them all up. And then, into his eyes, very blue and bright, there came an expression which suddenly and sharply reminded Herod of Mariamne at her most scornful. This man walked with the gait of a man who spent more time in the saddle than on foot. The third Herod summed up and dismissed; black, emasculated, well-to-do, typical freedman.

Melchior halted when he was within about six paces of the chair; the others took their places, one on each side. Melchior put his right hand into his left sleeve, his left in his right and made a slight, formal bow. Gaspar, stiffly upright, raised his right hand in the desert horseman's salute which Herod, the Idumaean recognised. The open palm, turned to face the one greeted, said, "See, I come in peace, unarmed." Balthazar, very conscious that he was in a Palace, in the presence of a King, and that he must do the talking, bowed his head and bent his knees as he was accustomed to do when entering the Lady's room.

Herod, with the cordiality which endeared him to people who were not on personal or political grounds prejudiced against him, said:

"You wished to see me? What is your errand?"

Melchior put his hand on Balthazar's sleeve. "Briefly now. Just ask where the child is and the quickest way to get there."

Herod leaned his hands on the elaborately wrought arms of the silver chair and said:

"Ask me yourself! Your Greek is like mine or near enough,

learned from a book and not much used. Where do you come
from?"

"Pyongyang; but that does not matter. Where is the child?"

"What child?"

"The child whose horoscope I read, nine months and more
ago. I am an astronomer. He is of ancient lineage, royal, and will
be born, if he is not, as I fear, already born, no more than ten or
twelve miles from where I stand. I assure you that it is of the utmost importance that I should have speech with his parents."

Herod rapidly reviewed his family, his household. Two sons
named Philip, Antipater, Antipas, Archelaus . . . secret liai-
sons? Ancient lineage? Had he overlooked some Asmodean
princeling who had gone into hiding and spawned?

He said, "There is no child here."

"What did I tell you?" Melchior said, speaking to Balthazar
but sharing his look of malice between him and Gaspar.

To Herod he said, forcing himself to courtesy:

"We are sorry to have troubled you. It was a mistake. My
friend here was under the delusion that the child would be born
King of the Jews."

"Nobody can be born to that title. I hold it by favour of Caesar
Augustus, who will choose my successor." And even as he said
the words something clicked into place at the back of his mind.
Ancient, royal line, King of the Jews . . .

His attachment to the Jewish faith was purely formal and
expedient; in public he kept the law, in public he observed the
rites. Of Jewish history he was ignorant, and of Jewish literature.
His mother had been a Jewess, but he'd spent no time with her;
his father, a brilliant soldier and a shrewd politician, had been
his hero, and from the moment that he was safe on a horse he
had been his father's companion. Mariamne, however, was as
learned as any scribe, and she had often entertained him with
stories; it was she who had told him about Esau and Jacob, about
Solomon whose glory had stunned the Queen of Sheba, about
Samson slaying a lion bare-handed, and Baalam's ass which had
spoken with a human tongue. He had always welcomed such

stories because Mariamne had related them in moments of friendliness.

What he remembered now was not a story and it had not been told in a friendly mood; it had been flung at him, in the middle of one of their quarrels, like a stone. Something about a Messiah, of the house of David, who would deliver the Jews from their enemies, "of whom you are first and foremost!" Mariamne had said.

Melchior said, "If you will excuse us. Time is of importance, and we still have some distance to travel."

"Wait," Herod said. "It is possible that I may be able to help you."

Experts were handy. By this time the High Priest and his companions would have arrived, been received by Archelaus, and be waiting for their dinner. They would know all about the legend, or the prophecy, as Mariamne had called it.

He was about to clap his hands and call and attract the attention of the guards when caution intervened. Mariamne again?

The priests were all sensible, hard-headed fellows, as professionally priests as he was professionally King; but you never knew; there might be one amongst them who was susceptible to Jewish myths, who might go out and talk, who might even see some way of turning this information to his own advantage. It would be far better to keep this trio and the priests apart.

There was another thing to consider, too; the High Priest's dignity, the respect that he considered due to his office. He might very well already be offended at being received by Archelaus, instead of Herod himself; he would almost certainly be incensed to be sent for. Hating the High Priest, and all his works and ways, liking to annoy him as far as it was safe, Herod was never blind to the fact that the man had power. Everywhere that the Romans went they liked to use the existing mechanics of government and they had recognised that to a very religious nation like the Jews, the priesthood was a source of authority. Twice during his early reign Herod had asserted himself against a High Priest, and though he had survived, he had learned to be careful. Cold, formal, just-sufficient civility cost nothing.

"I shall not delay you long," he said to Melchior, and rose to his feet and rustled away; his wily mind already busy with the question of how to extract information without giving any.

"Perhaps we have not, after all, wasted time," Balthazar said. He spoke timidly, still feeling guilty about his obstinacy over the gateway, and also deeply disappointed because nothing had happened. He had recognised the gateway as surely as he had recognised Melchior and Gaspar, and the robe and the turban and the sandals. And he had seen the star, with which Melchior's errand was involved. All the ingredients were now assembled and yet nothing had happened. And—with shame he admitted this—he was terribly hungry again.

"We shall see," Melchior said non-committally.

Gaspar said, "I shall give this man no gifts; he is already decked like a kept woman, and he smells like one. Also he is ignorant. Water was not offered us. Nor food!"

All the time that the incomprehensible talk had been going on he had been watching Herod, and like many other men, far more sophisticated and experienced, had been deceived. Another dressed-up jewel-hung figurehead, with soft hands and nails trimmed like a woman's, he had thought; no ally for a man like me. His thoughts had reverted to the wild men of the hills, of whom he had so far seen no sign at all.

"To wash, to eat, would have wasted more time," Melchior said.

"Not if food and water had been offered, as they should have been, when we arrived. Of all that talk, I understood one word. Caesar Augustus, he said. What did he say of him?"

Melchior dredged up the remark, unimportant and therefore already half-forgotten.

"Oh, he said that he held his throne by favour and that the one who follows him will be chosen, not born to rule. Which confirms what I said; this is not the place and we should not have come here. How long is he intending to keep us waiting?"

Gaspar began to prowl about the room, noting the great urns of jasper, the braziers exuding scent as well as heat, the marble troughs, the hanging baskets, filled with flowers, the silken draperies, the soft—he prodded them with a stiff finger—cushions in the silver chair. All familiar, all contemptible. Jexal all over again. The city rot, the city stink! He swung on his heel and turned to Melchior.

"Ask him one thing for *me*. How many rebels are there in the hills?"

"Three less than there were," Melchior said with his thin smile. He really must remember not to allow his exasperation with Gaspar to show; but for him the camels would have been lost. Balthazar had his uses too; but Melchior wished once more that it had been possible for him to make the journey alone . . .

He began to twist his hands together, pulling at his fingers so that the joints gave off little brittle snapping sounds.

"They were not the true men," Gaspar said. "They were robbers, and witless ones at that." His lips moved in a smile as he remembered the speed and efficiency with which he had done the killing.

"I shall now count up to a hundred," said Melchior who had spent his youth in an ordinary house and the rest of his life in a room twelve feet square and had no notion of the distances in palaces, "and then I shall leave. No information he can give is worth this delay. The star is my guide." He began to count and had reached twenty when Herod came back.

Neither Melchior nor Balthazar noted any change in his appearance, but Gaspar knew the symptoms of fear as well as any man alive. He saw that just at the base of Herod's strong, arched nostrils there were tiny white patches as though fingers had pressed there and been withdrawn. He thought, Something has frightened him, and he is a man who might be dangerous when frightened. He changed his stance.

Herod had wasted no time. He had taken a short cut to the opposite side of the Palace, the side entered from a court in which there was nothing likely to offend the most fanatical Jew. The room in which he always entertained members of the Sanhedrin was likewise void of anything offensive. The tiles on the floor were plain, the walls lined with cedarwood and un-decorated, the candlesticks of solid, unchased silver. There were three low tables of green marble, arranged to make three sides of a square, and on the outer side of the tables were divans cov-ered in green velvet. Herod had learned in Rome that the ideal number for an intimate dinner was nine; tonight there were the three priests, himself and two government officials, both Jews and both from priestly families.

In Roman fashion, too, this dinner was beginning with wine and a selection of small delicacies at which early guests could nibble while awaiting later arrivals, but the wine was sweeter than any Roman of taste would have drunk before a meal, and the variety of titbits was limited because of the dietary rules.

The greetings on Herod's side were a shade more cordial than usual because he had kept them waiting, and must keep them waiting again. Time mattered, but he must not appear hurried. So he sat down in the place which Archelaus had vacated and accepted the cup of wine which the boy, forestalling anyone else, poured, asking as he presented it, "May I go now? I have an engagement of my own."

"Yes, go. I'm sorry you have been delayed. I apologise to you all for this delay. Three men arrived, unexpectedly. They are on their way to the Essenes at Qumran." That was a cunning touch. Mention the Essenes to an orthodox priest and he flinched as though touched by a red-hot iron. The Essenes lived apart, were celibate, owned nothing, everything being the property of the community; in many ways their beliefs and their ritual did not conform to the Law by which ordinary Jews lived; they claimed to be at once better informed and more holy than secular priests. Herod disliked them every bit as much as the High Priest did, but he had hit on the use of their name both as cover for his question and as a means of quelling before it arose any interest the priests might feel in his visitors.

"These three," he said, having watched the effect of the word, "are argumentative amongst themselves; only one speaks Greek; they have no Latin, no Aramaic. So far as I can make out they are arguing about the Messiah and his prophesied birth-place."

As he had aged the High Priest's face had dropped into jowls below his jaw, small, well-filled pouches which at the word "Messiah" seemed to fall lower and go limp. Other faces altered in other ways. They were all Jews, all, in theory at least, believers in the prophets and their prophecies, but the word inspired no welcome. Consternation rather. They were professional priests, very comfortably situated, enjoying less authority than they considered to be their due, but protected, respected, provided for, easily performing their set duties, happily collecting their set dues. The actual arrival, on earth of the promised Messiah, the Son of God, could only disrupt their lives.

The High Priest recovered himself quickly. The mention of the Messiah, made by, of all people, Herod, had disconcerted him for a moment, but it was, he reflected, just the kind of thing which curious strangers, bound on a visit to an Essene community, would wish to discuss. He said:

"The place, by tradition, is Bethlehem." His voice took on the note of one who quotes, knowledgably. "And thou Bethlehem, in the land of Judah, art not the least among the princes of Juda; for out of thee shall come a Governor that shall rule my people Israel. That is the prophecy; does it settle the argument?"

Herod remembered the certainty with which the old man in the curious hat had said, "No more than ten or twelve miles from where I stand." Now the High Priest had said the place was Bethlehem, the city of David. It was at this moment that the white patches made their appearance beside his nostrils and they were not, as Gaspar was presently to suppose, the brand of fear, they were signs of a deadly determination.

He said lightly, "Armed with that information from the highest authority, they can go and argue with the Essenes." He took a sip from his cup and set it down. "I shall be with you before the first dish is served." He rose and rustled away.

The priests began to talk among themselves, about the Essenes, and then, free of Archelaus' presence, about Herod. Only one of them took no part in the conversation, but sat brooding.

He was a friend of Zacharias, had actually been on duty with him in the Temple when the older man had stiffened and stared and seemed to go into a cataleptic trance from which he had emerged completely dumb. Some time after that Zacharias' wife, a woman far past child-bearing age, had become obviously pregnant, and in the previous mid-summer, she had borne a son. On the eighth day after the birth the child had been circumcised and named, and Elkanah had been invited to be present at the joyful ceremony. And a very curious thing had happened. Everybody had taken it for granted that the boy should be named after his father, but when the moment came, Elisabeth, a very quiet and retiring woman, had suddenly raised her voice and said:

"Not so; he shall be called John."

The fact that at her age she had borne a child at all had attracted attention and there had been many neighbours present and practically every relative on both sides of the family except Mary, a cousin married to a carpenter in Nazareth, who was pregnant herself, and when Elisabeth said "John," all the families had burst into protest. In neither family had there ever been a man of that name. Boys were always named for their fathers or some respected elderly relative or friend. Why John? everybody asked. But Elisabeth was adamant, the child must be named with the name which she had chosen. It seemed arbitrary and someone had suggested that Zacharias should be asked. They had made signs at him, assuming, as everybody always did, that a dumb man must necessarily be deaf as well. Zacharias had written upon one of the prepared tablets which since his affliction he had always carried, and he had held it out to be read by the nearest literate person, who happened to be Elkanah; and what Elkanah had read out was, "His name is John." Not should be, or will be, or even must be, just, "His name is John," as though in another place the child had already been named.

So the alien-sounding name had been given, and that was no sooner done than Zacharias recovered his power of speech and burst into a chanting song, declaring that this child should go before the face of the Lord to prepare his way. That was six months ago. Now there were men asking where the Messiah should be born. Elkanah had a great deal to think about. . . .

To the three waiting men Herod said:

"I have wise men in my household. I have consulted them and there is a general agreement that a child of some importance may be born in Bethlehem."

"South of here," Melchior said, not asking a question, stating a fact. "Thank you, we know now what road to ask for in leaving the city. That will help." His hands moved towards his sleeves, he was about to take hasty leave when Herod said, "Wait," and at the same time Gaspar said, "Ask him *my* question!"

"This one," Melchior said, past all patience, "would be a good companion were he dumb. Now before we can leave he must ask, how many unruly men live in the hills?"

Momentarily diverted by this inconsequent question, Herod said:

"Six hundred; debtors hiding from their creditors, men hiding from their wives."

"Six hundred," Melchior said to Gaspar in the tongue they shared. And again he made the preliminary gesture of polite leave-taking.

"I wanted to ask you a favour," Herod said. "If this child is as important as you say . . ."

"Nothing that I could say would tell you how important," Melchior said. "And for that reason I must go."

"Go," Herod said, "go swiftly; search diligently; but when you have found him, come back and tell me where and in what condition you found him. Of such importance and born in my realm, it would be only right that I should make some sign of recognition. You will, in any case, be returning this way."

Something in this speech struck Melchior as being very odd. If the man had his own soothsayers, Chaldeans or whatever they were, who could pinpoint the very place of birth for the child, why should he make that request? It didn't make sense; and all his life Melchior had dealt with things which, properly regarded, did make sense. This man, he thought, consulted nobody; he looked at a map, came back and gave me a name within the right distance, and is now relying upon me to return and tell him where the star led me . . . And the baby is not of his lineage, or he would not need to be told. Such a pity, the old man thought, looking at Herod with his study-dimmed eyes; I have never yet deceived anyone, even myself, but this man could be dangerous, and to him I must lie.

He did it as evasively as he could. He said:

"That is indeed little to ask in return for the help you have given us." The sad truth was that once you came down from your tower you had to deal with people, and in their own currency. He had made what sounded like a promise, while privately determining that neither he nor either of the others would come back this way.

Then Herod, all unwittingly, confirmed Melchior's worst suspicions. Anxious to ingratiate himself, he belatedly offered refreshments.

"Thank you, no!" Melchior said. "We must be on our way."

Time was now more pressing than ever. If Herod had looked at a map, pinned one leg of the compass on Jerusalem and set the other leg at ten or twelve miles, he would already know roughly where that baby was. And Kings had enormous re-sources, men on horseback, men on foot . . . Then why ask us to return? Oh, I see, because I know; I might be dangerous too . . .

"We thank you," he said, making his bow. "Come, we must go."

Outside the brisk cold wind had cleared the clouds and their star shone, with a myriad others, lighting the night.

Melchior said, "We must ride now as we have never ridden before."

Balthazar, very humbly, said, "The visit was not all wasted time. We know the place now."

"We know what place he named," Melchior snapped. "I place no faith in that man. I shall go where the star leads; and by the shortest road." He slapped his camel with a hand that trembled a little more than it had done.

Herod sat for a little time in the great silver chair in the room where never before had he been alone. He said softly:

"Mariamne. Mariamne." And when he felt, in that inexplicable way, that contact had been established, he said, "I thank you!" The danger had been so narrowly avoided. If he had sent that old man, with all his dangerous knowledge, away, to go blabbing about royal lineage and great destiny . . . If he hadn't remembered, as willingly or unwillingly he remembered every word that Mariamne had ever said to him . . . what might have happened was horrible to contemplate. If that story had once reached, in however garbled a fashion, the ears of the religious patriots amongst the Jews almost anything could have been expected. More than once during his reign Herod had seen what religious frenzy could do to a crowd. Unarmed, they had lain down in the streets and allowed themselves to be trampled to death in the attempt to hold up the progress of something obnoxious to their faith. Give them a fulfilled prophecy, a glimmer of hope in Jehovah's direct intervention, and they would rise in full-scale revolt; and that would mean military action on the part of Rome, a proconsul established in Jerusalem, the end of Herod.

However, thanks to Mariamne, that had been avoided. The child would be identified and as soon as identified, slain. The three men would return, and once they had entered the Palace they would never leave it again. Herod, who had never shrunk from killing even his nearest and dearest when policy dictated such action, would think nothing of adding four more murders to his score. Killing was effective. Once, long ago, when he had seen Mark Antony falling under Cleopatra's spell, he had advised him, "Kill her!" If that advice had been taken, how differently things would have turned out.

He realised that he must not sit here, thanking Mariamne and inviting her approval of the way in which he had handled things; it would be injudicious to keep the priests waiting any longer.

So, ruthless and determined, Herod went in to his dinner. Melchior, Gaspar, and Balthazar, pressing their camels hard, rode through the starry night, the old man turning every now and again to make certain that they were not being followed. In and around Bethlehem little children slept in their beds, or in their mothers' arms.

CHAPTER XII

By Balthazar's reckonings—he had inquired in the city which gate of exit and which road to take, and how far to Bethlehem—they had done three quarters of the last lap of their journey when Melchior, who had been constantly urging his camel, halted it and made a moaning noise, like an animal in distress.

"Are you ill?" Balthazar asked. It seemed likely to him that the old man's frail body, so ill-fed and subject to such strain, might at last have given way.

"This is the wrong road," Melchior said. "Look!"

The star was now low in the sky, and did appear to be to the left of them, while the road ran straight ahead.

"But there is only the one road. I inquired most carefully. I asked in the city which gate, and at the gate I asked again. This is the road to Bethlehem and all we can do is to follow it and then turn left to seek the indicated place."

"I can go across country," Melchior said and began to edge his camel towards the bank which divided the tilled land from the road.

"That is cultivated land."

"Nothing grows in mid-winter."

"I was thinking of fences and irrigation ditches, and hard going over the ploughland."

"And I am thinking how little time is left." He struck his camel, which baulked at being asked to mount such an obstacle, but, guided inexorably, gave in and scrambled awkwardly up the bank, balanced at the top of it for a precarious second and then plunged down. The others followed.

Gaspar had understood no word of the talk, but its tone had been argumentative and he guessed that his companions were once again wrangling over direction. He was indifferent. He'd come out to see what was to be seen and though his observations had been impeded by Melchior's impatience, and by the need to have every question, every answer twice translated, he had learned a lot. He would have been willing to have turned back towards Jexal upon leaving Jerusalem; but two things held him fast to Melchior. One was that without him he would have been as helpless as a stray dog; in this country he could not ask for a bite of bread or a cup of water, he the leader of the Five Hundred, the ruler of Jexal. His second reason for sticking to Melchior was that he had been impressed by the old man's powers of navigating; far away in Jexal he had spoken of Jerusalem as a possible destination, and with a few tools and his charts, he had found Jerusalem, grumbling all the time that that city was not, in truth, his destination; and in that he seemed to have been right. In Jexal he had said that he was seeking a child, and if— as Gaspar was now inclined to believe—there was a child at the end of the journey, he would know that Melchior had the ability to use the stars in two ways. Such a man could be vastly useful to a ruler. Melchior was penniless, and far from home; it was reasonable to suppose that he would welcome an offer of honourable employment. Nonetheless the proposition would have to be put tactfully; the old man had a tough character. Gaspar remembered how, when the robbers came, he had shown no fear for himself; he hadn't cried "Save me" he had said "Save the camels." The members of the Five Hundred wouldn't laugh and jeer at him, as they did at the scholars and so-called wise men of Jexal.

The black fellow could be useful too. Amongst other things that this trip had taught Gaspar was the disadvantage of knowing only one language in a multi-lingual world. Suppose the worst came to the worst, and Rome, by supporting Pella, provoked him to strike first, if he could, and he came this way again, with his Five Hundred, strings of spare horses and an abundance of arms and tried to make contact with the men-in-the-hills. (He still had faith in them; and if Herod, the fop, admitted to the existence of six hundred you could safely double the number.) What use would it be if nobody could speak to them? He wanted

Balthazar to go back to Jexal with him too, and give lessons. The lessons should be compulsory for the young; older men could please themselves, but he himself would set an example by trying to learn, and he knew that every man of the Five Hundred who valued his good opinion—which meant five hundred—would follow.

Balthazar was keeping close to Melchior because it never occurred to him to do otherwise. Events in Jerusalem had disappointed him, and he was conscious of a great gulf between what the star meant to him and what it meant to Melchior; what connection could there be between a flashing vision of a whole new world and a child, however famous that child might live to be? Yet behind all the confusion something glimmered. His insistence upon entering Jerusalem had proved useful; muddled as things seemed some pattern might yet emerge. And even without this hope he could not have left the pair who without him couldn't have managed; Melchior often spoke sharply to him; Gaspar, he knew, despised him, but a lifetime's slavery had inured him to sharp speaking and dis-esteem.

So they rode close; and presently as Balthazar had foreseen they came to a thick-set thorn fence, a living wall, as high as a man. As far as they could see in the bright starlight it stretched across their path. Melchior said, "To the right," and they skirted the fence which presently, at a corner, ended. From somewhere within the closed space a dog barked, geese cackled, and a man's voice shouted.

They rode on, and there was a drystone wall, built of stones picked from the fields it divided. In many places it was bound and reinforced by leafless brambles.

"Right again," Melchior cried, and they followed the wall until presently they reached an opening, closed by a stout hurdle held in place by ropes tied to the thickly thorned bramble stems.

Without hesitation Balthazar made his camel kneel, and while the other two were struggling to keep their animals on their feet, he untied the rope, scratching his hands, opened the makeshift gate, held it while Melchior and Gaspar rode through, led his own camel through, and tied the hurdle in place again.

After that they came, in quick succession, to two irrigation ditches, one narrow enough to be crossed by a camel's stride, the other wide. But the camels were unaccustomed to water except as something to drink. At the first ditch they drank, against Melchior's wishes, but Gaspar said, "Be reasonable; a drink will keep them going." At the second ditch the camels sidled and danced grotesquely and had to be cajoled and forced into crossing.

But after that it was remarkably easy going, a flat, hard, uninterrupted space at the far edge of which there were lights.

"There, you see. We have saved time. There is the star and there are the lights of Bethlehem!"

But Balthazar had his doubts. The lights were indisputable but he had never yet seen a village where every lighted window was exactly in line with its neighbour and exactly the same shape and size. Village lights were haphazard; poor men had low houses, rich men higher ones; on the ground floor women cooked supper at about this time, on upper floors ladies dressed their hair.

He said tentatively, "This might not be a village. Only Romans build so straight. And it's all one building, I think. It could be a barracks. We should do well to avoid it."

"Look how low the star is now. We have no time to make a detour. Even if it is a barracks we can ride past it."

"Not if we are on their ground," Balthazar said, arguing as he had argued about fences and irrigation ditches, from his greater knowledge of the country. "I think we are already trespassing. This flat ground is where they march and exercise. We had better turn back to the ditch and seek another path."

"I am not going back," Melchior said stubbornly. "I have come from Pyongyang to deliver a message and I have hardly any time in which to do it."

"What is it now?" Gaspar asked.

"He thinks it is a barracks, a place for soldiers. Romans."

"Oh," Gaspar said, his interest quickening, "that I should like to see."

"By the grave of my fathers," Melchior said, forgetting absolutely that Gaspar had paid for his journey from Jexal and dealt with the robbers, and that Balthazar's insistence upon entering Jerusalem had enabled him to pinpoint the source of the threatened treachery, "I am tired of you both! I care nothing for his caution, or for your wish to see things. I go where the star leads and you can please yourselves whether you come with me or not . . ."

He slapped his camel and rode headlong into a sentry who cried, "Ho. Who goes there?"

It was Latin, it meant nothing; no more to Melchior than the voice of the man shouting above the noise of the dog's barking and the geese cackling inside the thorn fence. With one hand he guided his camel to avoid the man who shouted, with his other he slapped it, to hasten its pace. But the sentry had resources that the old man hadn't dreamed of. He let out another, louder, roaring shout and suddenly the night was full of men, of bobbing lights, noise.

After that it was all confusion. Balthazar was prudent enough to make his camel kneel immediately, so he escaped rough handling; but his heart sank. Romans had a passion for law and order; they'd ask who you were and where you came from, they'd inspect your papers, if you had any.

Gaspar thought, They're alert, which is as it should be; and we have done nothing wrong; this will enable me to see them at really close quarters.

Melchior said, "Take me to your chief. Your khan. Your head man," and realised with a lurch of the heart that nobody understood him. Once again dependent upon Balthazar whose advice he had disregarded, once again wasting time. He looked at the star, moving, moving . . . In a thin voice he said, "Balthazar, speak to them. Ask for the head man."

Balthazar said, "We ask to have speech with your officer."

"You shall have it," one of the soldiers said. "Here he is, now."

Caepio, who, with his century, had come to do a two-month tour in Bethlehem and had arrived a few days before, came out, treading heavily.

He was in a cheerless mood, missing his drinking companions, the lively girls he knew, the opportunities for amusement that

Jerusalem offered. Here there was nothing except duty, boredom and Vatinius, the permanent centurion-in-charge who acted as though he owned the place. Caepio knew all the gossip about this man; he had a blunt tongue and an inflexible nature, and so, though an experienced and reliable soldier, had missed the aim of all centurions—to be *primus pilus*—and had instead been promoted downstairs and put in charge of this dismal backwater. Caepio had expected to find an embittered, disappointed man, and since he himself was a man with a grievance, he had expected that they would have a good deal in common. But he found a contented man, apparently unaware of how he'd been pushed into a backwater, apparently pleased with himself and his job, holding himself a little aloof, and on good terms with several Jews. There'd been, so far, none of the long, grumbling sessions which Caepio had anticipated; nor had there been the one thing that compensated for the dullness of the place, leisure. Vatinius went about finding jobs to keep everyone busy, and if he couldn't find one, he'd invent one, like a captious housewife.

That was bad enough; but this evening Caepio felt that he had been insulted. A visitor had arrived, not a Jew, a Roman, with a train of slaves, including a skilled cook, and Vatinius had not invited Caepio to join them at dinner.

So the centurion was in no mood to be sympathetic to three men who had come, after dark, and from the rear, on to barracks property. Balthazar did his best, explaining how they came to be trespassing, assuring Caepio of their harmlessness, begging to be allowed to proceed. He was lavish with the word "sir" and when that did no good, substituted "lord." All to no avail. Had they been three stray sheep Caepio would have impounded them, if only for the pleasure of proving to Vatinius that while he was feasting—the gentleman's dinner had smelt delicious—*his* sentries had been alert, *he* had been available and prompt to act. He could see himself, in the morning, saying, "Oh, by the way . . ." and relating what had happened. Vatinius would be almost certain to ask, "Why didn't you inform me?" and the answer to that was civil and correct, yet conveying a slight rebuke, "I thought you would not wish to be disturbed, *sir*."

He issued his order:

"Search them."

Melchior, who had nothing to hide, only understood the order when he saw a soldier advance upon Balthazar; then he cried:

"This is intolerable! Even the cow-worshippers and the mare-milk drinkers never treated me thus."

Gaspar did not understand the order either, but the action spoke for itself. His knife! He carried it, in its sheath, stuck into the waistband of his baggy trousers, inside the belt. He drew in his stomach muscles sharply and under pretence of a willing raising of his hands, knocked his wrist against his leather jacket and the knife fell into the pouch where his trousers overhung his boots. He had been standing watching the soldiers with an unwilling admiration; they seemed well disciplined, they looked hard and tough and clean. But when the soldier slapped his hands under his arm, around the waist and at the knees and said, "Nothing, sir," he thought, These people can be fooled, too! And he felt happier.

"What about the camels?"

"Fodder bags, sir. And . . . these."

"Balthazar," Melchior said, "tell them not to touch my possessions. Is there no law in this country?"

Balthazar said, "Lord, they are the humble tools of his trade. Without them he is ruined."

"You'll all be ruined in the morning," Caepio said. "All right; take them away. Lock them up, separately."

Melchior cast a despairing look at the star and began to protest, angrily, in his own tongue. Gaspar said:

"There are too many of them," and he was speaking to Melchior and to himself. He had quickly calculated their chances of escape by violence and seen that there was no hope even had his knife been ready in his hand. A good soldier must take chances of course, but part of being a good soldier was knowing when you were hopelessly outnumbered. And to give no sign of dismay; so he stalked, a little more arrogantly than usual, as he was led away. Melchior went on protesting until he realised that by doing so he was inviting rough handling; then he subsided,

knowing that a wise man bows to the inevitable once he knows
that it *is* inevitable. And this, he had, in a way, brought on himself; he had insisted, against advice, in riding across country. He
called to Balthazar:

"You were right, I was wrong. I am sorry."

Balthazar let himself be led away like a sheep.

Even the indignity of being searched had not prepared Gaspar
for the sheer horror of what happened to him next. They pushed
him into a tiny space, nothing more than a hole in the wall; six
feet wide, less than six feet long. It was built of brick and whitewashed, and along its length there was a ledge, also of brick upon
which a man might lie or sit. Nothing else at all. When the
door was closed he was walled in, and once he realised it he began to go mad. His own simple language had no word for the
peculiar thing he suffered from, the mental quirk which made
him feel uneasy when he rode into Jexal and even more uneasy
when he entered the Palace, that made him prefer the Balcony
Room to any other apartment, made him sleep—once he brought
himself to sleep there—with the door and window of the bedchamber wide open. There was no torture that the Romans
could have thought of that would have hurt, hurt, hurt so much
as being shut in, in this tiny airless space.

For a time he went frantic, behaving much as a newly captured wild bird thrust into a small cage will behave. He tried to
break out, throwing himself against the walls, against the door,
against the built-in bench. He emitted loud hoarse cries. He
beat his hands bloody, he bruised his shoulders, his elbows, his
thighs. Then, spent, suffocating, about to die, he thought of his
knife; better to slit your throat and die quickly than to suffer
this torment and be stifled. One small remaining grain of sanity
told him that this was a desperate remedy, was there no compromise? High up in the door was a grating, could he jump and
set his fingers in it and push his nose close, breathe, control his
panic, and live? Could he?

The grating was set at a level from which anyone in the passage, which was higher than the cell, could look in upon the

prisoner. Gaspar jumped and jumped, several times missing his hold; but at last he managed the jump-and-clutch that was necessary and had his fingers through the grating and hung for a moment against the door, like a carcase suspended from one limb. Then he tautened his bruised muscles and had just succeeded in bringing his face level with the grating when the guard, attracted by the noise, noticed the protruding, clutching fingers and dealt them a paralysing blow with the flat of his sword. The fingers loosed their hold and inside the cell Gaspar fell like a sack, striking his head on the floor.

And he was back in Jexal, easy in the saddle, riding in with Kalim and Lakma and several others, on a sunny morning along the wide street, dappled with shade from the trees, all in flower. Their water bags were empty and he was thirsty, looking forward to a long cool drink. They came to the Fountain of the Maidens, and there Ilya was waiting, with a great, two-handled silver cup in her pale hands. As he came level with her she offered him the cup, and this time there was no accident; he took the cup in his hands and drank and drank and drank . . .

Outside, the guard thought, That was the noisy one, and I've quietened him.

Balthazar, pushed into an identical cell, went and sat on the built-in bed, and thought, This is the end!

The soldier who had searched him had either missed, or not been interested in, the manumission paper which he carried inside his robe. But tomorrow it would be taken out and studied and its falsity would be detected. Tonight's search had been perfunctory—they had missed Gaspar's knife. Balthazar knew, from his experience in Metellus' household, how meticulous the Romans were about property and ownership; if they had the slightest suspicion about his forged paper they would get in touch with the Lady and she would claim him, and punish him so severely that he would die.

He looked back, calmly over the events that had brought him to this situation, and finally he thought, I deluded myself. Once and once only did I truly see the future, and that was in Cleo's black ball, after she had conjured up the vision. She was a real seer, what she saw was the truth; she saw the Greek dying, and I, for a moment, shared her vision. What I saw afterwards was what I wished to see; a waking dream, of no more substance than the dreams of sleep. I wished myself free, finely clad, in the company of free men. So I saw what I wished, and it meant nothing . . .

Wait a bit, he said to himself; and he remembered that Metellus had always said that every bit of evidence must be weighed. And against this theory of self-delusion, he must, in fairness, set the fact that he had found Melchior and Gaspar, he had found the very clothes in which he had seen himself; in Jerusalem he had recognised the gateway. . . .

But all to what end? The star had been the link between him and Melchior, and now, outside in the night it was dying, while in one little brick cell Melchior fretted over his wasted errand, and in another Balthazar saw his vision as nonsense and faced the possibility of death. And he thought, It might be that it was death that I came out to seek. I thought it was the death of the world, but it might be only my own. I thought I saw an end to slavery, and death would end my bondage. When I die, under the lash, a whole world will die with me; my world; my youth; my mutilation, my ability as an accountant, my gift of tongues, everything that made me *me,* and not the other fellow, all my thoughts, my hopes and disappointments. The death of a man is the death of a world. And in death my dream will be fulfilled, for death does put a slave on the level with a soldier, making all men equal, death does stop the mouth of hunger, and puts an end to heartbreak and homesickness.

Thinking these and a multitude of other tumbling thoughts Balthazar was quiet and gave no trouble.

With Melchior it was otherwise. He sat down thankfully, and he was glad to find himself alone in a quiet place, conducive to thought. He cast back, in his mind, to the moment when, at the top of his tower he had seen this journey as something that must be undertaken, and for the life of him he could not see that he had at any point made a miscalculation of such immensity that it resulted in his being incarcerated here while the star moved on, came to its appointed end and the whole thing was made nonsense. In every circumstance he had been sensible, reasonable, and meticulous. In turning off the road perhaps a little impatient, but surely impatience then had been justified.

He sat very still, but his heart beat so fast and so hard that he could only breathe in little shallow gasps and his whole body quivered. There must be some way out. There always had been, hitherto. He thought of how he had arrived in Jexal, penniless on a spent camel—and there had been Gaspar. Then, when he arrived in a country where nobody understood him and Gaspar's money was dwindling at an alarming rate, there'd been Balthazar. True, outside the walls of Jerusalem he'd wished he'd never seen either of them, but even that waste of time had been justified. Now this!

Inside his distressed old body the trained, obedient mind worked on. He thought of his own attempted protests in the faces of the grinning soldiers, the hard-eyed officer; of Balthazar's pleading voice and subservient manner. Something had been missing, one decisive, propulsive word. A catalyst. There must be one. There must be something, and it must be a word, since there was nothing to be done. A word known to him, and recognisable to these barbarian men.

Of course; he had it. Herod!

He took off his shoe, stood up and went to the door and rapped smartly on it, just below the grating so that the sound would carry. He had a little trouble with his breathing, but he mastered it, drawing a deep breath, counting while he held it, ten the first time, then twenty. And when he felt sure of producing a firm clear sound he said:

"Herod."

Then he rapped again, breathed, repeated the word. The name sounded and died along the whitewashed passage much as the name of Mariamne sounded and died through the halls and corridors of Herod's palace. Even in this extremity Melchior realised the absurdity of calling the name as though he expected Herod himself to answer; so he began to make sentences.

"Herod will be very angry," he said in his abominable Greek. "I was with Herod this afternoon. Herod is expecting a report from me. I am on an errand from Herod. Herod is waiting for me. Herod, the King in Jerusalem. I was in Jerusalem with Herod this afternoon."

He rapped with his shoe, waited, repeated his simple, uninformative sentences, resolutely keeping his voice steady; it would never do to sound hysterical.

"Herod will be angry. I was with Herod this afternoon . . ."

The soldier on duty at the end of the passage said to another, "The old one is carrying on now. Listen! All gibberish, but it sounds to me as though every now and then he says 'Herod.' What do you think?"

"I am on an errand for Herod. Herod is waiting my report . . ." Melchior chanted.

"Right enough. It's Herod he's talking about."

"I reckoned they looked a funny lot the minute I clapped eyes on them," the one on guard said. "And Herod's pretty touchy. Think *he* ought to be told?" He nodded his head in the direction of the place where Caepio might be expected to be at this hour.

"If I was you, I would."

Caepio came out and listened, and for a moment there was no sound, Melchior was drawing breath. Then he rapped and resumed his chant. Caepio recognised the one important word and it occurred to him that if the King of Judea was in any way, however remotely, concerned with these mysterious men the responsibility for retaining them had better be shuffled, as soon as possible, on to Vatinius. So he turned, and went quickly, though still heavy-footed, towards the little room which Vatinius regarded as his own, his home.

CHAPTER XIII

Earlier that day, just as the daylight was fading, a very elegant litter, borne between two mules, had come to a standstill before the small barracks from which Eunice and Ephorus drew so much of their custom. The litter's occupant was obviously a well-to-do man who travelled in style; there were three pack mules and four slaves in his train. The mules were all plump and sleek-coated, the slaves, young, plump, and well-dressed; and when from inside the litter a hand moved and pushed back the bronze-coloured velvet curtains, it was seen to be a plump hand with a large ruby ring upon the forefinger.

"Ask," said a voice, well-used to issuing orders, "for the centurion, Vatinius; and say that Quintilius is here."

Vatinius was inspecting stores. The last day of December had seen a fresh century of soldiers come marching down from Jerusalem to occupy the barracks for three months, and the stores had, as usual at the change-over, been delivered. As usual they had been stored, all in confusion, and Vatinius had waited, tactfully, until Caepio, the centurion who had come with his men, had had time to settle in and get things into order. Like many before him, he had done nothing, so then Vatinius had said, "This is a filthy mess and muddle; you can't tell wine from vinegar, honey from oil. Set a couple of men to put it straight." Caepio had heard something of Vatinius' fussy ways—and his other peculiarities—before he came to Bethlehem; he had given the order, muttering to himself that he was a soldier, not a housewife. Now Vatinius was viewing, with only mild approval, the job the two men had made of the storeroom. The point was, he said to himself, that in an orderly storeroom any depredation was so much more quickly detected.

When the message reached him, he exclaimed, "Quintilius,

here?" and not waiting even to snatch his cloak, had gone out and stood by the litter. The curtains parted more widely and in the failing light the two men, once comrades-in-arms, closest of friends, had looked one another in the face for the first time in sixteen years.

Quintilius said, in an easy, jocular way:

"You seem dumb-struck, Vatinius. I assure you, I am no apparition. I am bound for the baths at Calirrhoe—for my gout. Being in the neighbourhood and hearing that you were here, I proposed to spend an evening with you, and cadge a night's lodging."

"A barracks is not a hostelry," Vatinius said; "but there is one, a good one, kept by a Greek, only a short distance along the road. I'll send a man to guide you."

"But this, I understand, is your *home*. I have come to visit you in your home. Is this a way to receive an old friend?"

"I told you, long ago in Areta, that if you did . . . what you did . . . you were no friend of mine."

Lowering his voice a little, Quintilius said:

"I am now Caesar's friend. I *think*, that if I needed to, I could commandeer this barracks. But I would prefer to be invited."

After a perceptible pause Vatinius said, "You are invited."

"Good!" Quintilius said and snapped his fingers. Two slaves ran forward, and with tender care, unlashed the litter, lowered it to the ground, then lifted it—the other two slaves having led the mules out of the way—and staggering a little under the weight, carried it to the entry and there set it down, and assisted their master to alight.

Quintilius stood up cautiously, his left foot, swollen and bandaged inside the soft velvet shoe, barely touching the ground.

"That will do," he said. "Hand me my stick. Now, Vatinius, if you will lend me your arm, I shall manage very well."

With obvious reluctance Vatinius bent his weathered, heavily muscled arm, and held it stiffly, keeping as much distance as possible between him and the weight, the warmth, the scent of this man, beside whom he had once marched and drilled, sweated

and laughed and slept, and swum in the waters of a faraway
river called the Rhone.

"Gout," Quintilius said, "is not a contagious disease."

Damn you, Vatinius thought, you miss nothing; you never
did.

They made slow progress along a straight, lime-washed passage towards the rear of the building where Vatinius had his
quarters.

Quintilius said, "I am well-provided; if my fellow can have the
use of a hearth he will prepare a meal which I hope will please
you—unless you have fallen victim to this Oriental nonsense
about only breaking bread with your friends. Not that I have
ever entertained any but friendly feelings towards you, Vatinius.
Every word you said was fully justified; I knew that at the
time. . . ."

"If you don't mind, I'd prefer not to hark back," Vatinius
said. He made the opening of a door an excuse for releasing his
arm. "These are my quarters," he said.

It was a fair-sized room, with walls of whitewashed brick.
There was a heavy wooden table, a chair, and against the wall
a wide bench with curved ends, upon which, from time to time,
a soldier lay to submit himself to such rough surgery as an experienced centurion could perform. There was a set of shelves
upon which maps and rolled records were ranged with precision,
and there was a row of hooks which held weapons and equip-
ment. An oil lamp, just lighted and emitting a faint, disagreeable
odour, stood on a wall bracket, and a candle burned in an iron
stick on the table. An uncurtained alcove in one side wall was
furnished with a hard-looking bed and an iron tripod holding
a basin and ewer. In the outer wall a shutter rattled in the wind.
The general effect was neat, soldierly, and cheerless.

"How familiar it smells," Quintilius said. "So this is your
home."

It had been his home for a little more than three years, and
Vatinius had never before entered it without a small secret feeling of satisfaction. His ultimate goal, to become *primus pilus*,
he had never achieved, but out of the shifting, homeless thing

that was army life, he had made this little niche for himself, and for three years he had enjoyed more independence, more privacy and more authority than most of his kind could hope for.

Tonight, however, viewing the only home he had through Quintilius' eyes, he saw it as stark, devoid of comfort, and impermanent. It was not his own; it was government property and his tenuous hold upon it could be ended tomorrow by a word spoken by a man he had never seen, and to whom he, Vatinius, was not even a name.

He said, "You'll need a cushion, even on the chair."

"I shall need three," Quintilius amended, glancing at the bench where Vatinius had pulled aching teeth and set broken bones. Two of the big cushions from his litter along its length and one between its head and the wall and it would be converted into a couch of moderate comfort.

"I'll have them fetched," Vatinius said. As he went into the passage to shout the order, he thought, He's had a long experience in making himself comfortable. Unwillingly he remembered various occasions in the past when Quintilius' genius for finding the easiest way, the best place, the little bit extra, had contributed to his own well-being.

Propped on his stick, leaning his hip against the table as he waited for the cushions to be brought, Quintilius said, when Vatinius re-entered:

"So you are in charge here? Permanently?"

"You should know that in the army nothing is permanent. I've been here rather more than three years. The place is occupied by one century, for two months, turn and turn about, and there was always trouble about the state it was left in, or a discrepancy in the stores. So the tribune decided that it would be best if one man was made wholly responsible, and stayed here. I was chosen."

Quintilius remembered the gossip in the Antonia in Jerusalem; blunt tongued, inflexible by nature, and thirty-five years old, *and* without a single black mark on his charge sheet, Vatinius had been steered into this backwater by very willing hands; and here would stay, if authority had its way, until he reached retirement age, or became infirm.

"If the appointment pleases you, my congratulations," he said. "And I think it does please you. You have the look of a contented man."

Vatinius realised, with a slight shock, that up to the moment of Quintilius' arrival he had been contented. Too easily contented?

The entry of an orderly bearing the three cushions, gave him an excuse for making no reply. The cushions were placed and Quintilius arranged himself. Then one of the slaves came in, soft-footed, to say that the meal would be ready in an hour; another brought in a tall flagon, made of glass, in a filigree net of silver and two wine-cups, silver, decorated with a pattern of vine-leaves, the tendrils making the handles. A third brought a flat silver dish containing salted prawns, sardines and anchovies, olives and almonds, delicacies calculated to provoke appetite without allaying it, and to keep thirst lively.

"I have brought you a really prime Falernian," Quintilius said to Vatinius. To the slaves he said, "Bring the table nearer to me, then you can go and I will pour. Now, Vatinius, turn the chair about and make yourself comfortable."

He reached out his plump, beringed hand; and Vatinius saw the lean, brown callused hand of his young fellow legionary. The mental vision shifted and expanded, and he saw two young men, walking back from the Games in the arena at Areta; heard himself say, "Then you choose between him and me. Nobody's boy-wife is going to be a friend of mine. If you take up with that turd, Marius, I shall never speak to you again!"

All long ago and far away. And it was crazy to think that now, by eating and drinking and talking with him, one was condoning. It was crazier still to feel that in some subtle way the food and the wine were contaminated. He'd eaten, in his time, what was practically carrion, drunk out of filthy ditches.

There was also—and this he must face, rationally—the practical considerations. Quintilius had said something about falling victim to Oriental nonsense; and Vatinius knew what was said of him in Jerusalem—"as near Jew as a non-Jew can be." It needed only one malicious remark, which Quintilius was capable of making, and somebody was going to say, "It's high time Vatinius was shifted." On at least two occasions, when soldiers had come into conflict with the natives, he had tried to be impartial; that would not have escaped the sharp eye of authority, or done him any good. Better be careful. He took up his cup and deliberately chose one of the salted prawns.

Quintilius, before drinking, tilted his cup a little and spilled a few drops, a libation to the gods.

"Good fortune, Vatinius! Now, let me look at you. You have worn very well. Very well. I swear that had I met you in Sabatra, I should have recognised you. You could hardly say, I fear, the same of me."

"I might have blinked twice. But I should have known you. Inside every fat, middle-aged man, if you look close enough, you can see the young man he once was."

"You never learned, did you? That blunt tongue of yours! Fat, middle-aged. True, most regrettably true; but such things should not have been *said*. You should have remarked that my hair has not receded, and my teeth are sound."

The words, though a rebuke, were spoken with such charm, such good nature, that something in Vatinius wished to respond and say that indeed the hair, the teeth were as beautiful as they ever had been; but he stiffened himself and said:

"I'm too old to learn such civilities now."

"You were always," Quintilius said, "the most honest man I ever met. I fear you always will be." His bright glance cast about the bare room and made a silent comment, This is where an honest man lands!

"Yes," Vatinius said, "you are right. Not about the honesty; if I'm honest it's no more to my credit than the length of my foot. I have, all along, tripped over my tongue."

"Not for lack of warning."

That was dangerously close to harking back; so Vatinius said, again gruffly and bluntly:

"What exactly are you doing here? You spoke of Caesar's

friendship—but even that would not empower you to commandeer barracks, unless you had some special errand."

"How very indiscreet of me to have said that! The sight of you, after all these years, and wearing such an unwelcoming look, must have disarmed me. Still, between old friends . . . Or is *that* harking back? . . . here and there along my route I have paid more attention to Caesar's business than to my own. Gout, oddly enough, is a most useful travelling companion; it comes and goes. There are days when even the jolting of my litter would be intolerable. So I can always halt when I'm interested and move on when I'm bored."

Vatinius was on the point of asking what there was of interest in a subsidiary barracks just outside Bethlehem, but that might be twisted by Quintilius into sounding self-important. He'd find out in another way, if he could, if there was anything to find out. Quintilius, as he remembered him, had a better appetite than head for wine; and he had already emptied his cup and refilled it.

"Let me not be egotistic," Quintilius said. "Tell me something about yourself. You were at Colenus, were you not?"

Nobody ever spoke of that engagement as a battle; rightly so; it had been a bloody massacre of trained Roman soldiers by ill-armed barbarian Germans.

"I was there. Of our maniple fourteen survived, all wounded. And of that fourteen I am the only one still serving."

"I heard of it, and wondered about you. It was quite a time before I learned that you had been fortunate and that I had wasted my grief."

Vatinius remembered the nightfall on that green meadow, where the grass had slowly shed its round flowers of blood; and how, as they counted their dead and did what they could for the wounded, he had wished Quintilius among the dead, a friend who could be rightly mourned and remembered with respect. A curious thing to remember now, with the man so sleek and prosperous, here in his room. He made no comment upon Quintilius' mention of having grieved for him, though he believed it. He sat looking at the grain in the scrubbed table top. The silence grew.

"I went to Alexandria, and to Corinth, to Rhodes, Crete, and Cyprus. Marius died there, poor man, at Paphos. Apart from a tactful, token legacy to Caesar, he left me all he had; he was richer than anyone guessed. But, as I explained to you at the time, mere money was never my objective."

That was true, Quintilius had said at the time, I'm not doing it for money; I'm doing it to escape, to have some pleasure and comfort and status. What have we to hope for if we aren't killed? To reach centurion's rank, and be honourably retired and granted a few acres of land to grub a living out of, like a peasant. Straighten out your ideas, Vatinius, and as soon as I am established I'll find you a rich gentleman friend in Marius' circle, who'll do as much for you. And to that Vatinius had replied, I can tell you where *you'll* end, with a painted face, soliciting outside the baths!

He now said, "Did you break your journey here for the purpose of showing me how well things had gone with you?"

Quintilius said pleasantly, "Well, I thought that if the years had brought you tolerance you might like to know that your *direst* predictions had not been fulfilled. And if they haven't you might be interested to hear that I have rehabilitated myself. The means was to hand. A widow, very well connected. Her husband—as I have reason to know—was impotent; can you imagine a woman married for twelve years and still a virgin? There's not the slightest doubt in my mind that, tiring of her state, she poisoned him. She was not young, and she died in childbed. No condolences are necessary, she was not of an amiable nature. The boy is all I could wish, almost thirteen years old. Handsome and intelligent. And though his father was merely rich, his mother was a Flavian, so he'll never have the troubles *we* did."

"Upon *him*," Vatinius said, "I congratulate you."

He was not—or at least not consciously—envious of this success story; but as Quintilius told it he seemed to realise something that had hitherto escaped him. The job in which he had been so happy and satisfied, was virtually a sinecure; he was nothing but a figurehead. Each century that marched down the road brought its own centurion with it; every duty was known and assigned;

he was treated with respect, he was in charge but he was nothing but a caretaker, a stockkeeper. There wasn't, for example, a single thing which he could at this moment claim called for his attention so that he could get away from this man, out of this room. If fire broke out, or a wall fell down, or twenty men fell sick at the same moment Caepio would deal with the crisis and report it in the morning. By this time everybody in the place would know that he had a guest; they'd say, A Roman, *for a change!* and respect his privacy all the more for that.

So here he was, stuck with Quintilius, and the endless evening stretched ahead.

"I had a very interesting stay in Jerusalem," Quintilius said, moving to another subject with the skill of a socially expert man. "Herod has made vast improvements. The Hippodrome is one of the best I have seen. Well patronised, too. A surprising number of Jews seem to have come round to the idea. Of course, at the gateways an even greater number were expressing disapproval, groaning and making peculiar hissing noises. Strange people, don't you think? Or are you, like most Romans, oblivious to them so long as they behave?"

"I know several Jews. The ones in this district are simple people, inclined to credit me with powers I don't possess, so they come with complaints and pleas. If I can deal with the matter I do so, if not I explain, or advise, and I must say I've always found them very reasonable and responsive."

"You have friends amongst them?"

"So that's it!" Vatinius set down his cup with a jolt which slopped the wine. "That's why you came. To spy on me. By the blood of the bull, who'd have dreamed that I warranted so much attention. Very well then! Ebenezer's cabbage field *was* ruined and I said so in my report; and that lout Crassus *did* attempt to rape Caleb's daughter, and I punished him to the utmost, not for the attempt, which could never be proved, but for being late back, for being improperly clad, for dumb insolence and everything else I could find against him. *I* know what stories get back to Jerusalem, and I don't care. We're supposed to be an occupying army, not an invading rabble."

"You sound very heated," Quintilius said. He leaned over and filled Vatinius' cup. "As for spying upon you, my dear man, you must know there is no need. A hundred men and a centurion go back to Jerusalem six times a year. Clever as I am, could I learn in an evening what they had failed to see in two months?"

"Yes; that was absurd. The thing is that over the cabbage field and the girl what I did was extremely unpopular. I have made friends here. Ask yourself what my life would be if I hadn't. A hundred men come, after two months they go. I can't consort with the men and every single centurion who has ever come here has resented me, openly or covertly. So they go away and call me a Jew-lover."

"I sympathise with you," Quintilius said, and he sounded sincere. "It's strange, isn't it, how unpopularity centres around nationality; in Jerusalem they still call Herod *'that Idumaean.'* He's a character, if you like. I dined with him one evening. He complained bitterly of the Jews ingratitude towards him; he knows he is unpopular, yet he never does anything to endear himself to his people."

"What could he do? A murderer many times over." Vatinius remembered the light way in which Quintilius had accused his late wife of murder, and felt bound to explain. "Jews—the pious sort—have respect for human life; that is why they don't like the Games or the chariot races."

"At least Antipater is popular."

"Is he? Is he? I should say that most people cheer him as a means of knocking Herod on the nose. And it's dangerous for him. My friends never expect to see him on the throne."

"Indeed; why not?"

"To be popular isn't healthy, if you're Herod's son."

"About that, I must tell you a joke." Quintilius poured wine. "Caesar made a pun, in Greek—Better Herod's pig than his son, meaning that Herod would kill his son, but being half-Jew, wouldn't touch a pig. The point is that when Herod has no Jew at his table, he eats just as you and I would. And what do you think his *favourite* food is? This is true, he told me himself. That hard, pork-and-garlic, Danubian sausage that you and I used to carry to supplement our rations."

Sliding back, Vatinius thought, back to the pleasant, rambling talks that we used to have, the kind of talk I've never had with anyone else. He was always so interested in everything. And it was his mind I loved, not his body, splendid as it was. Yet when he sold his body—for that is what it amounts to, and he sold it twice, to Marius for money, to the widow for position—I cut him off, disregarding his mind.

"If your friends don't expect to be ruled by Antipater, what do they look for?"

"How should I know?" Vatinius asked, with a return to his old gruffness. "The Jews I know are not politicians; they're poor simple men whose main concern is to make a living. And if they had political opinions they would conceal them from me, out of courtesy. I can tell you this. It'll interest you. Their main hope centres around a bit of folk-lore. They believe that their subjection is the result of their god's displeasure and that in his own good time he will deliver them by sending them what they call a Messiah. But neither Caesar nor Herod need tremble, because this Messiah is to be born of a virgin. So by my reckoning they have a long time to wait."

"Oh well, how was Minerva born? Or Mithras? He was born of a rock we are told. As a putative parent, rock or virgin, I'd wager on the latter, wouldn't you? Remember how we toyed with Mithraism? In those days I thought that the rock birth was symbolic. One says, sound as, solid as, immovable as a rock. Qualities that make Mithras superbly suitable to be a soldier's god. I understand that more and more go over to him every day. Now a god born of a virgin sounds unlikely to be a deliverer of a subject people, don't you think? Very innocent, pretty, pure, and sentimental. I've noticed that at the Games the Vestal Virgins— though their virginity is largely a matter of nomenclature—are always the first to turn *up* their thumbs and lead the crowd to spare the defeated. If symbolism counts this Messiah would be a curious kind of god."

"Ah," said Vatinius, throwing himself into the argument,

"according to my friends, he'd also be the son of Jehovah; and about him there is nothing pretty or sentimental. He's a god of battles, and he laid down a code of behaviour, stricter than any . . . I ever heard of." He had paused and added the last four words in a trailing voice, for he had remembered what one of his Jewish friends had said about Jehovah and men like Marius and Quintilius. "They shall surely be put to death." And when Caleb had told him that Vatinius had thought—well, that would be a way of putting a stop to it, this thing, which like a disease was spreading rampantly, was no longer disapproved of, was used as a ladder by ambitious young men.

And here he was, with the man to whom he had sworn never again to speak, succumbing to the old charm. He folded his hands into fists and pushed the knuckles together, wishing with all his heart that something, anything, might happen that Caepio couldn't deal with and that he might be called away.

Relief was at hand. The slaves came in and began to reset the table. Quintilius reached for his stick and stood up.

"The bog," Vatinius said, "is next on the right." Without thinking he had used the old army word. "And if you want to wash" —he indicated the tripod in the alcove—"I'll get a clean towel."

He made no attempt to help Quintilius along the short length of passage to the latrine; he laid the clean towel on the edge of the bowl and then made a rapid survey of his small domain, still hoping against hope that there might be something that would give him an excuse for not sitting down to eat with his self-providing, self-invited guest. Too many memories were involved; all the meals he had eaten with Quintilius; hasty meals on the march, dull regulation meals in barracks, and those happy times, when, their free times coinciding, they could take a loaf, some cheese or meat, a little fruit and if Quintilius had succeeded in one of his little schemes, some wine, and walk away and find a place, sheltered in winter, shaded in summer, and throw themselves down and eat and drink and talk, and be not soldiers, rigid and purposeful, but two young men, interested in everything and involved in nothing.

But in the whole of the little barracks there was not one thing which justified a moment's absence. He went back to his room, and saw Quintilius drop the used towel on the floor and begin to hobble back to his couch, and then the slaves, with nice timing, brought in the first dish.

"These mullet," Quintilius said, "were alive this morning in a pool not far from the Antonia. And if Plautus, my flat-foot, has smothered their delicate flavour with a sauce too highly spiced, he'll smart for it."

Fresh fish, as opposed to the salted and smoked kind upon which inland places were bound to depend, offered Vatinius an impersonal subject for talk. He had theories about diet. He said that he was certain that the irritable skin lesions, the softening of the gums which so often afflicted soldiers—and it was said, all sailors—was caused by too much eating of preserved, easily portable food. It could be cured, he said, and he had proved it time and again by the eating of fresh meat, fruit, vegetables. Especially cabbage.

"To my mind the least pleasant vegetable; but as a medicine, maybe acceptable," Quintilius said. "Tell me, are you much bothered by guerrillas?"

"Very little. There have been incidents. Fewer of late."

And he thought, Curse you for bringing that subject up, ruining what little appetite I had. He saw that in becoming the friend, the near-intimate of a few Jews, he had put himself in a well-nigh untenable position. Ebenezer and Caleb and Reuben were tactful in the extreme, but there had been mention of a man called Josodad whose son Nathan, a wild young man, had with other wild young men, been convicted and executed for the killing of a Roman soldier. It was impossible for Vatinius, a soldier and a Roman, not to feel that the sentence had been just and right; it was equally impossible for anyone who was a friend of the Jews not to see the whole thing as a tragedy. There was no doubt about it, life was easier if you ran on the orthodox lines; you could then say, I am a Roman and whatever the Romans do is right. Vatinius had once held that view; but a ruined cabbage field, a nearly raped girl, had opened his eyes. He'd come to know the people of the countryside, and sometimes he had asked himself, What are we doing here? In Gaul, and by the banks of the Rhine, by the banks of the Danube you could at least give yourself the answer that you were a civilising agent; but here, no. The Jews were civilised. Caleb had once said to Vatinius, "My friend, Jerusalem and Jericho were orderly cities when Rome was a haunt for wolves." Vatinius had reputed that with a sturdy answer. "Age had nothing to do with it. Babylon was an orderly city when your people lived in tents." Then Caleb had retorted, "In the tents the Law was kept."

"How many are there?" Quintilius asked.

"Nameless ones? The official reckoning is, I believe, six hundred; but you could treble that and still be short of the mark."

"How would you, or your friends, give their numbers?"

With a brusque return to caution, Vatinius said:

"How should I know. I'm acquainted with four or five Jews, all respectable, settled men. None of them is a guerrilla, or related to one, or likely to become one, so far as I can judge. They're just ordinary fellows who do what they're told—and pay their taxes."

"And await a miracle, eh?"

"Not entirely without reason. They have, more than once, been saved by what they call miracles and you and I would term lucky accidents. Once they were besieged by the Assyrians, and plague broke out in the camp. They were slaves in Egypt, and in Babylon, and both times, for some reason, set free and sent home. But you see, the orthodox Jew, from the moment he fastens his shoes to the time when he takes them off again, in everything he does, down to killing a chicken, is in the hand of his god; to him there are no lucky accidents. All is Jehovah's will."

"As Herod said, fanatics. So according to you, the worst thing he, or Caesar, has to fear is some simple Jewish girl who had, shall we say, an *unlucky* accident and couldn't or wouldn't name her seducer and claimed that her conception was Jehovah's will."

"I don't think that could happen. For one thing the genealogy of the mother is known, and girls who are eligible belong to good families, and are not only well guarded, but extremely prudish.

That I know for a fact. I was four years in Jerusalem, and I've been here three, and in all that time I've hardly seen a *loose* Jewish woman, who wasn't left without a single male relative. Take my friend Caleb; he's a shoemaker, he earns pitiably little, but as well as his own family he supports his own mother, his wife's mother and his widowed sister, and thinks nothing of it. It is the Law." Vatinius thought, too, of Ebenezer, with his two poor fields; when he grew corn every ear counted, yet he always left some to be gleaned by those who had no field at all; that was the Law.

"Very admirable. I think you do admire them."

"For those I know I have profound respect," Vatinius said. He could not tell Quintilius, he could not tell anyone, that when his time for retirement came, he hoped to settle in this country, have a small white house, an orchard, and a vegetable plot. A typical old soldier's dream, except that most men dreamed of returning to their homeland, not of staying in the place of exile.

The slaves came in with the next dish; breasts of pheasant cooked in wine. When the door was open Vatinius lifted his head and listened, his trained ear seeming to catch the sound of some faint commotion somewhere. Then he heard what was certainly Caepio's tread. Better not to interfere. Caepio had resented the storeroom incident and would need tactful handling for a few days. So he sat still and Quintilius chatted on, saying how highly Herod had spoken of the waters of Calirrhoe, and what a beautiful city Caesarea was. Seemingly aimless talk which yet persisted in returning to the Jews. Once Quintilius, who seemed to have wasted no time in Jerusalem, mentioned the Sanhedrin. "They struck me as being mercenaries," he said of its members, using the word as only an ex-legionary would do. And Vatinius thought, How odd, that is exactly how Ebenezer and the others regard them.

Then Quintilius said, as a more than usually vicious gust rattled the shutters:

"Travelling South I did not expect such barbarous weather." He gave a little shiver.

"I am at fault," Vatinius said, "I should have ordered a brazier."

He rose to go and shout in the passage; but before he called he listened. The place was not silent; there was the noise, so familiar as to be unnoticeable, of a hundred men busy with their evening routine or relaxation; there were voices, talking and singing, the twang of a stringed instrument, laughter, the rattle of dice, footsteps. All just as usual, and yet . . . Then he knew that it was not his ear that sensed something out of the ordinary, it was his nose. Mingled with the odour of leather, men's sweat, lamp oil and whitewash and cooking there was something else. My scented visitor, Vatinius thought; simply by walking in he tainted the air.

He said, "Bring a brazier," to the man who came running in answer to his call, and unwillingly went back to his room.

When the brazier had been brought and they were alone again, Quintilius said:

"I hope Calirrhoe will do as much for me as it has for Herod. But after all he is seventy or thereabouts; and he is only human. Of his sons which would your ordinary Jew choose to take his place?"

"The younger, Philip," Vatinius said, after some thought. "He's reported to have frugal tastes and is what the Jews call a just man. But the truth is, the Jews don't take very kindly to kings at all. From what I hear, when they had their own, there was always a prophet busy keeping them in order."

"Soothsayers?"

"Not exactly; they use the word differently. Certainly they foretold events, but that was a sideline. Holy men is the nearest word."

He thought how eagerly, in the old days, he would have told Quintilius some of the fascinating stories which in Jewish households were spoken of as sober fact. Elijah, regarding as a miracle, a feast, a few scraps of carrion dropped from the beaks of glutted ravens, for example. It was too late, now; such talk could only be shared with friends.

The dishes were changed again; the slaves brought in small cutlets on a mound of rice, perfectly cooked, each grain separate and fluffy.

Indicating that he had already eaten his fill, Vatinius said, not entirely without malice:

"Small wonder, that you have gout, if you eat like this every day."

"This!" The surprise in Quintilius' voice was genuine. "Why, this is only a makeshift meal, easily carried, quickly cooked. At home eight or nine courses is the rule. After all, Vatinius, eating is one of the *certain* pleasures, and should be made the most of while it is available. Barring the dubious blessing of early death we're all going to end without teeth, or appetite, mumbling slops. A fearsome thought. Do you ever feel time seeping away, like water from a leaky goatskin?"

Vatinius remembered that even as a young man Quintilius had been unusually aware of passing time; the awareness had contributed to his decision. He'd said, I'm twenty and what have I ever had? Half my life or almost, sped, with hard work, hard food, hard beds, and hard words . . .

"I've thought of it; I shouldn't think there's a man who hasn't, at some time or another."

"The thought *haunts* me," Quintilius said; he spoke almost peevishly, and something of his worldliness seemed to drop away. "I look at my boy and see him bald, with a paunch. I take a bath, am well-scraped, freshly clothed, but I *feel* the skeleton there under the flesh and the silk. But I try not to brood. Out of the dark we came, into the dark we go and all we can do about it, all anyone can do, is make the best of the little time we have." He took up his cup and drank deeply.

"There," Vatinius said, "the Jews have the advantage of us. They hold that this life is no more than so much"—he measured a tiny space between finger and thumb—"in a life as vast as the sea."

"Have you ever contemplated turning Jew?"

"Jews are born. I suppose one could adopt their beliefs; but my credulity has limits."

"Mithras promises immortality, too. All these Eastern faiths are much the same."

"I might have taken to Mithras when I was young, but for one thing . . ."

"I remember. Your mother!"

With all that he had seen and been and done and heard, he had remembered, across the years, those conversations on the banks of the Rhone. There was something so disarming, so almost touching about this that Vatinius felt embarrassed. His voice was gruff again as he said, repeating what Quintilius remembered:

"I couldn't have truck with a faith that excluded my mother who was worth any ten men. Let's talk about something cheerful. Your son; nearly thirteen you say. What is his name?"

"His name?" For a second Quintilius looked down at his food, then he lifted his eyes and looked straight at Vatinius.

"Oh, I called him Vatinius, after a friend I once had, in Gaul."

To his complete chagrin Vatinius felt a pulse leap in his throat, and the red blood pour up under his weather-beaten skin. He said in a half-choked voice:

"There was no need for that!"

"No need at all," Quintilius agreed, deliberately misunderstanding, "but boys must have names. And I . . . well write me down as a sentimental fellow."

No sound he had ever heard had been so welcome to Vatinius as the sound of the door opening behind him. He turned in his chair and said, "Oh, Caepio! Enter. What is it?"

Caepio reported, in clipped formal phrases, the arrival of the three trespassers. "There seemed no need to disturb you, sir. I locked them up and intended to report it in the morning. Now one of them is causing a disturbance. He mentions Herod. I thought you should be informed, sir."

"I'll come at once." Deliverance. Just when the situation had become unbearable. Another minute, and they'd have been weeping on one another's shoulders!

"Wait," Quintilius said, quietly, but with authority. "This could be of interest to me. Have them brought here."

Vatinius hesitated. A curious coincidence that in this unvisited place, in one evening, there should arrive Quintilius on some mysterious errand from Caesar, and now three men on Herod's business. It was an axiom that spies were always spied upon.

"What sort of fellow is this? Likely to be violent?"

"Oh no. Very old. Very frail."

"A Jew?" Quintilius asked.

Caepio acknowledged the source of the question by giving Quintilius a glance, but he punctiliously addressed Vatinius as he answered.

"None of them is a Jew, sir."

"Bring him in," Vatinius said.

Melchior, having attained his aim by being noisy, was quiet again. He put his hands in his sleeves and bowed and said in a voice in which politeness, impatience, and petulance mingled:

"Please, who is chief here? I asked, when we were arrested, to be brought to someone in authority."

Vatinius stared, uncomprehending. Quintilius, stirring a little on his cushions, said:

"It is a form of Greek. He asks who is chief here."

I wonder myself, Vatinius thought, angry at having been baulked in his attempt to escape.

"Tell him I am. Caepio, would you fetch Atticus; he's a Greek."

"We came," Melchior said, "to the back of the house, like thieves. I am to blame for that. We are not thieves, we are harmless men on a very important errand, and we are already late. I beg you, let me and the black man proceed. Hold the other as hostage if you must. It is of the utmost importance that I should reach Bethlehem without delay."

"He says," Quintilius said, "that he has an urgent errand in Bethlehem."

"Ask him why he mentioned Herod."

"Simply as a means of gaining attention. It meant nothing. I shouted the most important name I knew."

Melchior was now in a quandary such as he had never imagined. His suspicions of Herod had so worked upon his mind that he felt it would not be safe to divulge his real errand; and yet these men must be persuaded to let him and Balthazar go. And how could that be done?

"What is your errand?" Quintilius asked.

"Harmless. Of no importance to anyone but me. I have to ask for the release of the black man because he speaks for me."

Caepio returned, bringing Atticus.

Glad to exclude Quintilius, Vatinius said, "Now Atticus; ask this old man where he is going, and why, and why he mentioned the name of Herod the King."

Atticus spoke; Melchior answered. Atticus said:

"I'm sorry, sir. I don't understand a word he says."

"I'm not surprised," Quintilius said, "pure Greek is worse than useless. An ear accustomed to attuning itself and a mind capable of making leaps are of more service. Shall I try again?"

"Do," Vatinius said grudgingly. "Ask him how he has made his needs known, speaking a tongue that only you seem able to understand."

"He says," Quintilius said, "that the black man speaks for him."

"All right," said Vatinius. "Atticus, go back to your dice. Caepio, fetch the others. We may as well see them all." He looked at the old man, saw that he was deeply distressed, tremulous and confused, and that part of him which had sympathised with Caleb and Ebenezer, and at secondhand with Josodad, came uppermost.

"Tell him not to worry. Tell him to take the chair and calm himself. Tell him he's in no danger and that I've sent for the friend who speaks for him."

Translated these sentences drove Melchior to the very verge of panic. Balthazar knew that his errand was with the child. He'd blurt it all out, in this place where Herod's name meant so much. It seemed to be a place for soldiers and it was on the very verge of Bethlehem. Oh, what had he done, acting always—except that he had implied to Herod that he would return while determining not to—in a straightforward, honest way. A simpleton, that is what I had proved myself to be, he thought, and I thought I was the wisest man in Korea.

Caepio, thinking, He treats me like an errand boy, but I'll show him that I am at least an efficient errand boy, released the obviously harmless fellow first. To Balthazar, roused from sleep and still dazed, he said, "Walk straight ahead, turn right and wait by the first door." Then he released Gaspar who only two minutes before had regained consciousness, groped for his knife, and was on the point of going crazy again. When the door opened he had been thinking that death by his own hand, by his own knife, would be better than enduring the torture that being shut in this dreadful little cell inflicted upon him. Then the door opened and he thrust the knife, with one of his rapid movements, into the front of his jacket; and his heart rejoiced because, if he were to be locked in again, and thus forced to kill himself, he would kill one or two of his captors first.

Caepio opened the door, and having recognised Gaspar as the dangerous one of the three, would have taken him by the arm; but Gaspar said, "Don't lay your hand on *me!*" with such vehemence that though the words were without meaning, the tone and the look that accompanied them was perfectly clear.

So, let Vatinius, the storekeeper, the fussy housekeeper, the Jew-lover, deal with him, Caepio thought, and he beckoned and pointed, and finally ushered both Balthazar and Gaspar into the room where Vatinius awaited them.

As soon as Melchior saw Balthazar, he said, in a low, sibilant whisper, "No mention of the child. Say anything, but not the truth."

And he was fortunate, for Caepio was, in the same moment saying:

"I think, sir, that this one has a knife."

"You think! Weren't they searched?"

"Yes. This one, I think, concealed his weapon."

Vatinius looked at Gaspar and saw him for what he was, and knew that had he been called, when he *should* have been called, he would have had such an obviously dangerous man stripped to the buff. Caepio, like every other centurion who had ever come here with his century, had made some fumbling, futile attempt to undermine *his* authority. Well, he must learn.

He said, almost casually:

"If you think he has a knife, take it from him."

Testing me, Caepio thought; but alongside that thought ran another. Men returning from their two-months' boring sojourn, all agreed that Vatinius was fussy, strict, a Jew-lover; but they'd add that he never asked anybody to do what he wasn't willing to do himself, that he was brave, a good soldier.

So, with complete confidence that should aid be needed, Vatinius was there to supply it, Caepio went to take away Gaspar's knife—if he had one, if that sudden furtive movement as the door opened had meant what Caepio was almost certain that it did.

But he had reckoned without any knowledge of Gaspar, in whose country one was either quick or dead. There was a brief scuffle; then the centurion, solid and heavy as oak, went reeling back against the wall, pain painting a white band about his mouth and in his mind the certainty that his back was broken. So swift and cunning a throw had never been seen in any arena. Gaspar had not even drawn his knife; but, having thrown Caepio, he leaped upon the table, and stood there, knife in hand, his teeth bared in a wolfish grin, his eyes like a cornered rat's.

Before anyone else could speak or move, Melchior turned, and with a movement swifter even than Gaspar's, brought the edge of his thin old hand down on the desert man's wrist with the gesture of a woman chopping meat for a stew. At the same time he screeched some kind of rebuke or instruction. The knife fell to the floor and Balthazar retrieved it and laid it before Vatinius.

"Get down from there," Melchior said to Gaspar in the tongue that only they shared. "Things are bad enough!" To Quintilius he said, "I beg you, pardon this barbarian; he suffers from claustrophobia, he cannot bear to be shut in. But he is a good man and intends no harm."

"He means no harm," Quintilius translated sardonically.

"No harm," Caepio said, still leaning against the wall, "he's well-nigh broken my back."

Vatinius thought, If you'd made a thorough search in the first place . . . But his voice was kind and concerned when he spoke, reaching for a flask which stood, with others, on the shelf under the maps, "This is good strong liniment. Get somebody to rub you, *hard*, as he would a horse. And tomorrow rest. I will undertake your duties."

Moving like a cripple Caepio departed.

Balthazar had had time to think, to muster his forces, and when Vatinius said to him:

"You speak for this old man, I understand. Tell me, as briefly as possible, where you are bound and on what errand?" he said, smoothly, meekly.

"Sir, my master is an astrologer; he casts horoscopes and he has been asked to go to Bethlehem to predict a favourable day for a wedding."

Melchior, anxious and trembling, had no idea of what story Balthazar was telling, but he saw with great relief that it was received with some amusement.

Astrology had enjoyed a brief and lucrative heyday in Rome, but charlatans had exploited it and gradually it had fallen into disrepute; nowadays only slaves and the most ignorant, credulous people gave it any heed.

"An astrologer?" Vatinius said, looking at the old man. And suddenly he knew that whatever the man claimed to be, he *was*; integrity was written all over him, just as servility was written over Balthazar.

"And who's this hothead?" He nodded towards Gaspar.

"Oh, he rides with us, sir, for protection against robbers."

All three fitted the characters assigned. But Vatinius was nothing if not careful.

"Your master spoke of Herod the King. Why?"

"Because the King received us this afternoon and wishes my master to call upon him as he goes back through Jerusalem." Sheer inspiration visited Balthazar; he knew that he was in a tricky position. Melchior wouldn't be understanding any of this; if the one who could communicate with him asked a question and received an answer that didn't match . . . "It is in order to get back to Jerusalem, to the King, that my master is in such haste."

That sounded reasonable, too. But in Vatinius' mind something jarred a little. Jews, so far as he knew, did not dabble in anything that savoured of necromancy or magic or fortune-telling.

"The family that plans the wedding," he said, "of what nationality are they?"

"Greek, sir," said Balthazar without hesitation. It was a safe thing to say; there were Greeks everywhere. "I speak Greek, too; that is why he needs me."

"And why did you arrive at the rear of this barracks?"

"We were taking a short cut, having been delayed in Jerusalem."

To Vatinius it all sounded satisfactory enough; the old man was what one would imagine a professional astrologer looked like; the black man was somewhat finely clad for a servant, but many people took pride in their servants' appearance, and a servant who spoke Greek and Latin was a valuable one; the third man looked like a guard—and a good one. He was about to say that it was all right, they could go, when Quintilius said softly:

"Very plausible. A little too plausible, don't you think?"

"In what way? What do you suspect?"

"Everything and everybody, except you, Vatinius. May I take a hand here? You"—he addressed Melchior—"take your companions and go and stand by the door. Close to the wall."

Balthazar, understanding, moved without prompting; Melchior spoke to Gaspar who had been standing with his arms folded, hearing the talk as senseless gabble, but ready, at the first sign of danger, to take action. Here, he thought, as he moved without taking his eyes from the two men behind the table, it was exactly as it had been in Jexal, while he watched and waited. It was always the ones clad in silk, the ones with soft hands who gave the orders. And that was not as it should be; that was bad.

Quintilius swung his feet to the floor and patted the place where they had been.

"Sit down; and listen to me." He lowered his voice so that Vatinius had to bring his head very close in order to hear. "It could be a trick. Herod is very wily. Practically every day deputations go to Rome complaining about him, and he may be planning a counterattack. I suppose it never struck you that your nice little sinecure here is a frontier post. What lies between here and Egypt? You take my point? Three men, apparently harmless, come to the rear of a barracks, at night; they tell a garbled tale. If you wave them away by the front door, how does that look? How will it sound? Herod might very well complain that security measures were very slack; and that is something Caesar would take note of."

"How does it sound if I hold them. They say they were with Herod earlier today."

"I've no doubt they were. Cooking up this fairy tale. Truly, Vatinius, the one sensible thing to do, the thing that would vindicate you however it was looked at, would be to send a fast rider to Herod, saying that three mystery men have arrived here and you are holding them until you have word from him as to the validity of their errand."

Vatinius backed away, looking at his one-time friend in horror.

"You want to ruin me? I, a Roman, a soldier, take orders from Herod? Are you in this damned plot, too? The planted, independent, civilian witness?"

"Oh, don't be silly," Quintilius said, a little wearily. "I'm advising you. Send two men if you wish, one to the tribune."

All at once Vatinius felt dizzy. What had seemed to be solid earth under his feet, the daily round of an obscure man in an obscure place, was so swamped with suspicion, trickery, uncertainty that it had turned into a quaking quagmire. It was quite possible, *now*, to imagine Quintilius reporting somewhere to somebody, I arrived, I was received without question, we drank together, and when a decision was called for he obeyed me like an ox. He is not fit to be in charge of a strategic post.

And to be honest, he had never until now regarded his post as being of importance, except as all places where soldiers were stationed were important; place to be manned, kept in a sanitary condition, always alert. Only a very short time ago he had, in a moment of depression, thought that he was nothing but a caretaker; but when Quintilius had asked, What lies between here and Egypt? he had realised that he held and had held, unknowingly for three years, one point of a great Empire's frontier. Not that there was anything to fear from Egypt, that was part of the Empire; but to the South East there was the whole of Arabia. Well might somebody in authority think it worth while to test his alertness, his integrity.

He looked at Melchior and Melchior looked back at him with the urgent, dumb appeal of an animal, endeavouring to convey something, wordlessly. Whom can I trust? Vatinius asked himself; the old man with his look of integrity and other-worldliness; the black man with his facile tongue; my one-time friend?

Well, he thought, if I go down, I go down, making my own decisions; if I'm to be ruined I'll do it myself, by my own calculated error.

He said to Balthazar:

"If your master is an astrologer he should carry the tools of his trade. Where are they?"

"On his camel, sir, if they have not been removed."

"Go and fetch them. The man on duty at the door will show you the way. Bring them here, and be quick."

Balthazar scuttled as all his life he had scuttled in obedience to orders.

Quintilius said in a detached way, "They'll be in perfect order. Herod is no fool."

That thought had not occurred to Vatinius, and hearing it expressed undermined his self-confidence still further, made him feel that he was a simple-minded fool, ill-equipped to deal with a world in which nobody could be trusted.

But he was equipped to maintain an unruffled demeanour in awkward situations, to remaining calm, seemingly confident, however he might feel. He said:

"I am in charge here, Quintilius. I'm ready to take responsibility for what I do."

Balthazar, breathless and sweating, for all the night air was so cold, came hurrying back and laid on the table with the uncleared dishes and Gaspar's knife, the cane chart case, the compasses, the piece of loadstone, the tube with its end of glass, even the bit of sharpened chalk.

Melchior gave a sharp cry, as though someone had stabbed him. He came forward to the table and spread his thin shaking hands over his treasures; they fluttered like distressed parent birds over a threatened nest.

"No! No!" he cried in his native tongue. "They are all I have. All that are left to me. To you they would be useless."

He looked at them, the pitiable remnants of that great fortune, which would have kept any ordinary man in comfort and happiness all his life.

The slow, difficult tears of an old, usually well-controlled man, rose to his eyes and stood there, unspilled, between the scanty lashes.

Nobody, not the best, the most celebrated actor in Rome, however schooled, however bribed, could have put on such an act, Vatinius thought.

He said shortly, "You may go!"

"We may go," Balthazar said to Melchior; Melchior said to Balthazar, "We go." Then he looked from his possessions to Vatinius, and Vatinius answered with a nod. In furious haste Melchior gathered his things, stuffing them into the front of his robe, holding the cane case in his hand, as though it were a wand of office.

For a second the knife lay there. A beautiful knife with a keen, bright blade and a handle of gold shaped to the hand, and with, between blade and hilt, a hand shield, curiously worked. Nobody saw it as a symbol, the knife between the barbarian and the towering might of Rome.

Then Gaspar, thinking that if Melchior could take his gear, he could claim what was his, snatched it up, asking no one's permission.

Balthazar was the only one to take civil leave. Bowing his head, bending his knees, he said in his beautiful Latin:

"Sirs, we thank you."

He was grateful to them because they had been instrumental in restoring some trace of his self-esteem; he couldn't read the stars, he couldn't kill robbers; his dreams seemed to come to nothing; but apparently he could tell, on the spur of the moment, and with no help from anyone, an acceptable tale.

"Come along, come along," Melchior said, now in a frenzy of impatience. "We haven't a moment to lose."

CHAPTER XIV

"This," Melchior said, "is the place." Exhaustion, varied emotions, and that desperate need for haste made his voice shake a little, but he spoke with complete confidence.

The dying star, hanging like a luminous apricot, was now so low that it was possible to pick out from the even huddle of roofs, exactly the one which he had crossed a continent to find. The whole inn yard was awash in mellow light; and looking round he was inclined to hope that, despite all his fears, he might still be in time—but only just.

The end of the long journey appeared to be a shed or a stable; very low, built of clods and roofed with mud and boughs. That a journey planned at the top of a stone and glass tower which had cost a fortune should have ended in this humble place neither surprised nor troubled him. His business was with the child and its parents; the surroundings were quite irrelevant.

He tapped his camel's neck and it knelt willingly. He alighted briskly, defying his weariness; one more effort, the greatest and the last, then he could lie down and sleep; he felt as though he could sleep forever.

Gaspar and Balthazar also alighted, less briskly; they also were spent.

"Now," Melchior said, addressing Gaspar first. "I want no interruptions from you. You will not understand anything that is said, so stand quietly and do not bother us with any foolish questions."

Gaspar grunted. The place where he had hit his head when he fell was beginning to ache and throb, but he ignored the pain, as he had been bred to do and fixed his mind once again on the extremely satisfactory way in which he had thrown that great hulking Roman. He also thought about his plans for the future and began to wonder how best to place his proposals before Melchior and Balthazar, and how long, if they bought fresh camels, it would take them to ride back to Jexal.

Balthazar was now dazed by hunger and fatigue and the speed at which so much had happened, and all so inexplicable; but when Melchior, moving towards the low doorway, said, "Balthazar" his lifetime of slavery, of pushing himself and his thoughts into the background and of concentrating on other people's business, enabled him to say, brightly and attentively, "Yes?"

"Now this is most important. It is unlikely that anyone here will understand me, so you must speak and you must say *exactly* what I say. You must repeat it word for word, and watch their faces. If they look confused, or ask a question, or make a protest, stop me at once. Do you understand? I rely upon you absolutely."

"I will do my best," Balthazar said. Melchior opened the door which moved silently because Joseph had rehung it and oiled its hinges.

It was, as the old man had thought, a stable. A lantern hung on the wall, but compared with the light of the star outside the illumination it gave was poor and dim, and he was obliged to close his eyes for a second or two, screwing them up, to accustom them. Then he looked around and all the vital organs in his body seemed to fall away, leaving him hollow. The disappointment was not to be borne; he would die here of sheer misery, of the knowledge that he had been completely fooled.

For there was no child.

There was a heap of straw and on it two people lay asleep. One was a girl, very young, with what even Melchior's old eye recognised as a virginal look. The other was a man, much older. Father? Brother? He was wrapped in a brown cloak, and he was not sleeping peacefully; he tossed and muttered. There was a long manger, occupied at its farther end by a cow and two donkeys.

No child!

"But this is impossible," Melchior said aloud, in a voice shrill with incredulity.

Then the man awoke and, with a movement as swift as any even Gaspar had ever seen, was on his feet, between them and the woman, alert, defensive; he had a chisel in his hand.

Balthazar said hastily, "We come in peace."

The woman woke then, raised herself and looked anxiously towards the unoccupied end of the manger; Melchior's gaze, following hers found what it sought; there, wrapped like a cocoon, lay a baby, fast asleep.

"Then you are welcome," Joseph said; but he still looked wary.

Melchior acknowledged this with his most formal bow; and Gaspar gave his salute, because he respected a man who could be asleep, awake, armed and ready all in the same breath space. He approved of the brown, sinewy hand. This was a man more like those legendary men-of-the-hills than any he had yet seen; and he must be some sort of outlaw, if this was the best place he could find for his woman to give birth in.

Balthazar bent his head and flexed his knees.

The girl on the straw acknowledged each salutation with a smile and a curiously dignified movement of her head. She looked very pale and very frail, and Melchior regretted that the message he carried would compel her into instant action. Still, it must be done; and there was no time to lose.

"Who are you, and what do you want?" Joseph asked.

"Balthazar, say this: I have come to congratulate you upon the birth of a wonderful child. A child of great destiny. And I have come to warn you." He spoke slowly, and paused to give Balthazar time to put the sentences into Aramaic; but there was no need. As soon as he had begun to speak the man had poised his head as though listening to some distant, just recognisable sound; he frowned in concentration, and at the word "warn" shot Melchior a glance which, though startled, was not surprised. It was almost as though the word confirmed something that he had suspected. And before Balthazar could begin to speak he asked quietly, in bad Greek:

"What is the warning?"

"I can speak to you direct? Good. That will save time. I have come to tell you that this is a very special child."

Joseph said cautiously, "To their parents all children are special." He had just wakened from a terrifying dream; and though these men said they came in peace, and looked harmless—at least two of them looked harmless—he felt it best to be careful.

"But this is different," Melchior said. "I am an astronomer and I read his destiny in the stars, nine months and some days ago, at the time of his conception. I was astounded. You can have no idea of the importance of this child. *If he lives,* he will govern all the world we know, and places as yet unmarked on any map."

He was amazed because the man's face betrayed no astonishment. Surely this was—to put it mildly—an unusual destiny that he was foretelling. Perhaps after all the man did not fully understand.

"Do you understand what I am saying?" he asked.

Joseph nodded. "I travelled a bit when I was younger, and Greek worked anywhere. I know what you're saying."

I will astound you yet! Melchior thought. It was essential to make the man understand the importance of the child before issuing the warning. So he tried again:

"Kings," he said, "will bow down before him. Great armies will march behind his banners—occasionally defeated, but in the end triumphant. He will rule an Empire compared with which that of Alexander was nothing, for his will reach to North and South, to East and West." All innocently, anxious only to inspire belief in a future which present circumstances made almost unbelievable, he moved his thin hand as he named the compass points.

Mary, watching and listening, understanding nothing of what was said, had thought that with his grave dignity, his outlandish garb, his glittering eyes and impressive way of talking, the old man was very much as she had always pictured the prophets to be. When he made his gesture she knew that he was making a prophecy; and he had drawn on the air the sign of the cross. Despite all her faith, all her acceptance, in her heart she cried, Oh no! No! Not that lovely little body, flesh of my flesh, nursed at my breast. But begotten of God, she reminded herself; with every day of his life planned and foreseen, a man of sorrows, and acquainted with grief . . .

She thought again that no other woman had ever been called upon to bear what she must bear. She looked back upon that moment amongst the flowers, when Elisabeth had hailed her as blessed among women, and she had answered that her soul magnified the Lord. A moment of ecstasy, and such came all too rarely. However, God had chosen her, and would give her strength to face what must be faced; but even that thought could not prevent her being sorrowful.

Even the mention of Alexander had not, Melchior observed, moved this father to giving any sign of excitement or surprise. Such words, spoken of a royal baby, lying in a golden cradle in a palace of marble, would have aroused some wonder, surely.

"People who know nothing of him but his name," he said, "will hold it in awe. And his Empire will not split up at his death; if anything his death will *consolidate* it. He will die young —I regret to be obliged to tell you that—thirty-two or -three years will be his lifespan. *If he survives now.* And here I come to my warning. There were very strong counterindications, with influences of the utmost malignancy. Unless precautions are taken he will die by treachery before he is weaned."

Maybe the man's face changed a little then, the anxiety becoming more marked; but still no surprise.

"Until this afternoon," Melchior went on, "I did not, of course, know from what direction danger threatened. Now I am suspicious of a man called Herod, a King in Jerusalem. Most misguidedly I mentioned something of my errand to him, and he knows my destination."

Now he had made an impression. The man's face was that of a man who knows that his worst fears are confirmed; it lost colour and every line in it stood out darkly as though drawn by one of Melchior's sharp chalk sticks.

Melchior said quickly, "But we have a full day. I was not followed, or forestalled, and I think he is depending upon me to go back and tell him where the child is. Tomorrow, when he realises that I have tricked him, he will act, and swiftly. By that time you should be as far away as possible."

There, he had now said it all. His mind presented him with the kind of picture—the whole lifetime in a flash which drowning men were said to see. (But who could *know* that he had asked himself when first he heard that theory, since no drowned man had ever been able to relate his final experience?) He saw himself, as a young man, knowing that astronomy was the only thing he cared about, he saw the long years devoted to the study, the fortune spent upon it, the decision taken on a cold spring night at the top of the tower, and then the journey, probably the longest journey any man had ever yet made. Now it was done; and he was an old, incredibly tired man; and he knew that unless he sat down quickly his legs would give way under him and he would fall.

He looked about and saw the stool.

It was the one which Eunice had allowed Ephorus to borrow from the house in order that Mary might sit on it and the more easily nurse her child. Once, long ago, it had been a fine piece of furniture, with a cover of crimson silk and legs inlaid with mother-of-pearl. Now the cover was shredding and many pieces of the inlay were missing, but Eunice treasured it, and had said, "Even to please you, Ephorus, I wouldn't lend my stool to just anyone. But I know courage when I see it, and that slip of a girl is brave. I could see she was in for a hard time and I told her to yell if she wanted to, there would be nobody to hear her but me. Yet when the time came, and she had good cause for yelling, she remembered that this was an inn and it was night, with people asleep all around. So she stuffed her sleeve into her mouth and bit on it hard. She can have my stool."

So there it was, and Melchior sat on it.

Joseph stood for a moment, thinking about his dream. In it the same angel had come to him again, bringing not comfort this time, but a warning. He was to take the young child and his mother and flee into Egypt because Herod was planning murder. The dream had been so real that Joseph had thought how small his resources were. Fleeing he would not dare to stop, look for work and earn money. He had been on the very point of asking the angel's advice, asking how this was to be done, when these men had arrived and he had wakened.

Now here was this old man, first confirming all the prophecies about the child being the Messiah, and then issuing exactly the same warning as the angel had done; naming the same enemy; setting safety's limit.

Mary, seeing the trouble on his face, said, "What is it, Joseph? What did he tell you?"

He crouched down in the straw beside her and told her, softening everything, trying not to alarm her, yet unable to conceal his mounting anxiety.

Then the three men watching saw her put out her hand and lay it on Joseph's shoulder in what was recognisably a comforting and sustaining gesture.

It reminded Melchior, oddly enough, of old Senya. Not that she had ever touched him; but she had a way of knowing when something in his work, all a mystery to her, had gone wrong; at such times she would put his food bowl before him in a special way, a way that said, Don't worry; you'll manage. This woman's hand on the man's shoulder said just that.

Gaspar noticed the gesture and he stared at the girl who made it with fierce attention. Her hand was small, finely boned, though the skin of the fingers showed that it was the hand of a working woman. The wrist was delicate. So was the girl's neck. She was a pale, frail creature, with great shadowy eyes, in no one way measuring up to his ideal of womanhood. Yet the movement of her hand had not signified weakness or dependence; on the contrary it was strong and heartening, conveying exactly the reassurance which even the most self-sufficient man felt the need of at times. And she had borne a wonderful, strong-looking, beautiful baby, in circumstances as comfortless as any desert woman ever knew.

He thought of Ilya, but in a different fashion from the way in which, at the back of his mind, he had thought of her since the moment when, in the Balcony Room, their eyes had met; not with yearning lust, strictly governed, not with defensive scorn, but with love. The last rational barrier between him and what he wanted went down. Melchior had weakened it, by proving that when necessary a frail body could be indomitable; this girl, with a movement of her hand, had demolished it altogether. It had been his last defence, the thought that a delicate creature must needs be a bad breeder and a clog on a man. It wasn't true; and he knew, with a great uprush of joy, that he would go back to Jexal and stand up in the Sun's eye and mingle his blood with that which in his bigotted folly he had called dregs. And what, he thought, would Lakma say to that? He knew what *he* would say, You great fool, I wanted her for myself, all along. Probably they'd fight again, and Lakma would break another finger for him, and he'd give Lakma another crack over the skull. And it wasn't by any means all sentimental nonsense either; there'd been some truth in what the boy, Malchus, had said; this marriage would unite the old and the new, so that if trouble came Jexal would stand undivided. He could hardly wait for the moment when they would head back for home.

He said to Melchior:

"Have you said all that you came to say?"

"I have said it. And now we must be practical."

Balthazar had also noticed the gesture, but it was rather as though he had seen it through a sheet of glass. Once, long long ago, he had loved his sister; and they'd taken her, kept her in a dark hut, fattened her up and then with flowers and the beating of drums, thrown her into the great river, a living sacrifice to N'Zana. Wasted. And for many years, to him there had been little difference between men and women, and the hand of the woman on the shoulder of the man had stirred nothing even remotely sexual. He had listened to what Melchior had said—the first time that he had heard the whole story—and seemed to have nothing to do with what he had come out to seek, about that he was more confused than ever. In a vague way he felt sorry for this couple, who must now leave this poor shelter and go into the night, into the world that was so hostile to humble people. Also it couldn't be a very pleasant thing to be told, when your child was only a few days old, that he would live so short a time, whatever glory he might achieve in a few years. Considering their plight he studied the animals and hoped that they owned them, though a cow would slow down their flight and the nearest donkey was extremely old, more likely to be a liability than an asset. Balthazar had a shrewd eye for a donkey; the Greek trader had owned many and had been quick to discard a faulty animal.

Melchior addressed Joseph.

"You have told her? She understands? She is fit to travel?"

"She is willing," Joseph said, and the change of word spoke volumes.

"I can see that you are poor. I am poor myself, but I am trying to find a way to help you." He turned to Gaspar and spoke his name. Gaspar came out of his dream and said:

"Yes?"

"If this child is to be saved, he must be removed. They are poor and travel is costly."

"Travel is costly," Gaspar agreed; and he thought, I hope you will remember that, and how much I have spent on you, when I lay my request before you.

"The gold you carry," Melchior said, "which you did not give to Herod—very rightly. Will you give it to these people?"

Just that, the simple request, no reasoning, no pleading; the old man spoke as casually and with as much certainty of getting what he asked for as though, at table, he had suggested that somebody should pass him the salt. A really remarkable old man, old and poor and star crazed, but with the manners of a king.

Gaspar said, "Herod didn't get my gift because I could see that he was useless to me. You, on the other hand, could be very useful. I will give what I carry to these people if you, in return, will do something for me."

And as soon as the words were out he thought, Spoken like a true huckster! Unless I soon get back to my own place and my own people, I shall be thoroughly corrupt.

"And what in the world could *I* do for *you?*" Melchior asked, looking at the man who had financed him, and saved him from the robbers.

"You could come back to Jexal with me and use your skill on

my behalf. A man who can read the stars as you can is not met with every day."

Nor every century, not every millennium, Melchior thought with the supreme satisfaction of a man who has proved himself right. But there was no time for self-congratulation, nor for argument, or even for consideration. These humble custodians of the future Lord of the Earth were like conies, their only safety lay in flight, and the sooner they started the better. When, at the top of his tower, he had visualised himself giving that warning, Melchior had seen armies alerted, guards set, and fortresses manned; now he saw a worried man bundling his wife and the precious baby onto a donkey and making off through the night. Not that it mattered. If the threatened danger could be averted the destiny was quite sure.

"Very well," he said, after what had seemed only a second's thought, "I will do that. But I must ask you to remember that I am no hired Chaldean. I cannot promise to tell you only acceptable things."

"Am I the man to ask that? That is settled then. But there is another thing I must ask you to do for me. I want him, too." He jerked his thumb at Balthazar. "I want him to come and teach tongues to my young men."

"That can wait, surely."

"I want it done now. This is as important to me as your business is to you."

A really remarkable young man, Melchior reflected; ignorant, in many ways uncouth, but issuing orders like a king.

With his own innate courtliness he looked towards the man and the girl and said:

"Excuse us, please. It is your business that we discuss." Then he passed on Gaspar's request, as hastily as was compatible with clarity, to Balthazar, who, faced with this in addition to all that had happened and had not happened, seemed to suffer a lapse from sanity.

"It is not possible," he said. "I have been thinking; I have been wrong. I came out to witness some great thing, and to do that I committed a crime; so I have seen nothing. I am a slave, the property of a Lady living in Edessa. Money was paid for me, so by running away I robbed her. I must go back and make full restitution . . . and take my punishment."

He could hardly believe that he was saying these things, but he was, and in a far more firm and positive voice than he had ever used towards his fellow travellers. Even when he had urged the necessity of entering Jerusalem, the slave wheedle had tainted his voice; now he spoke like a free man.

Irritably now, because of the delay, Melchior translated. And Gaspar turned and looked, for the first time with any real respect at Balthazar, and gave him a cheerful man-to-man blow upon the shoulder, a gesture he reserved for the chosen few of the Five Hundred.

He spoke and Melchior spoke.

"He says you are to reckon your worth, double it, and this woman in Edessa shall have it, in rose jekkals. Also he says that from this moment you are free, because a teacher must have status and authority."

How Balthazar took this astounding piece of news he did not stop to see, for he turned straight back to Gaspar and said:

"Now please, the gold."

"And what," Gaspar said, "about the stinking stuff you carry? You said it had value, equal with gold. Couldn't they have that, and sell it?"

"Oh dear," Melchior said, pushing himself to his feet, angry at the oversight. "Of course, of course." He had tried so hard to be practical. He said to Mary and Joseph:

"We have thought of a way to assist you." But they had asked for nothing; they were decent poor people and had their feelings and their pride; so he added, "They are birth gifts for the baby, and you will honour us by accepting them."

In Balthazar's stunned mind only the word *gifts* made any impact. Of course, to a new baby one brought gifts, and Melchior and Gaspar had come prepared. He had nothing. The child's father, understanding Greek, would know that he was a slave—*had* been a slave, who did not even own himself; but the sweet-faced woman wouldn't know. Judging by his clothes she would think him well-to-do, and mean.

Why he should mind what she thought was as mysterious as the impulse which had prompted his confession; and he had no way of knowing that he was the first of many millions who would wish to please her and shrink from her disapproval. He knew only that he had no gift, and shooting her a humble, apologetic smile, he followed the others into the yard, meaning to stay there and hide his shame, while trying to work out why his venture had been on the one hand so rewarding, making him a free man and a teacher, and on the other, so disappointing.

Neither Melchior nor Gaspar glanced at the star as they used its last light to fumble for what lay hidden at the bottom of their bags of camel fodder. For Melchior its work was done; for Gaspar it had never mattered much; it was not his star.

But Balthazar stared at it, and it was he who saw its end. Just as in his vision, it gathered itself into a great burst of glory, and was gone.

Now the only light in the inn yard was cold and came from a distance, from the ordinary stars and a young, thin crescent moon.

And then, to Balthazar, understanding came in a flash. Melchior's errand and his merged and made sense. It was in the reign of this child, and under his influence, that the old world would end and a new one be born, and the bad things, like slavery, be done away with.

He wished with all his heart that he had a gift to offer this wonderful child; and even as he wished it, he knew that he had. A small gift, but useful. He had the pot of myrrh ointment, stuff of such potency that only two dressings of it had healed his festering sores and the wound the dog had made. And every child had rashes and scratches, fell when it took its first steps and bruised its face, grazed its knees. The old woman had said that the ointment improved with keeping. Remembering her he wished that he had bought an alabaster pot.

So the gifts lay in Mary's lap; the jewelled gold crown that had rolled from the head of a dead king; the frankincense that had been intended for the altar of an unknown god; the pot of myrrh that had eased a slave's sores. She read their meaning plainly; gold for kingship, frankincense for priesthood and myrrh for the anointing of a dead body. Just as it was written. But of what she knew she gave no sign; she thanked each man as he made his gift and smiled with a smile intended for him alone.

"And now," Melchior said to Joseph, "you will leave at once."

"At once. Nothing that I can say can express the thanks I feel. You came from God!"

Gratitude and another unnameable emotion choked him. In the last few days he had lost faith, regained it, lost it again.

Mary had always held that the baby would be born just an ordinary human baby, but privately, in his heart he had hoped for some sign, something out of the ordinary and reassuring, even if it came secretly, to them alone. The birth had been like all others, a painful, bloody business, and Eunice had treated him as the women in charge always treated the man regarded as responsible for such an unpleasant procedure; coming to tell him the news she had said, "You have a fine son; better than you deserve, keeping her on her feet till the last minute, you thoughtless, feckless fool!" And Ephorus had said, "We must drink to the boy." What could have been more ordinary? It had been impossible to shake off the sense of something lacking. Then, when Mary was sleeping, three shepherds had arrived; one of them had seen angels, and heard heavenly voices; one had seen and heard something, the third knew nothing.

But Joseph had taken their coming as a sign, and so had Mary, until Eunice, bringing a bowl of gruel and seeing the shepherds depart, taking with them Joseph's cautious warning not to say anything about this to any but faithful, trustworthy Jews, had said, "Was that Josodad, the shepherd?" Joseph said that he did not know the names of any of them.

"I recognised him," she said. "Poor man, he is demented; he lost his favourite son and has never been the same since. And he drinks. Not here, Ephorus discouraged him; but he drinks."

And the shepherd had talked about seeing his son, dead these five years. So what did one make of that? Drunken men did see strange things; Joseph knew a fellow carpenter who had seen snakes, bright blue ones, in his bed. A man crazed with grief and full of wine, might have had an hallucination and communicated his hysteria to his companions, seen a light, felt the urge to communicate, and then, being a Jew, knowing the prophecies, seeing a newborn child, said all that the shepherd had said.

After that there had been the ordinary days; until tonight when he had had his dream, been about to ask how the journey could be managed and then these men had arrived, bringing the answer. And the old man had spoken with the true prophetic voice.

It seemed to Joseph that he was always falling out of the hand of God, falling, falling, only to be caught again in the hand of God. So, standing there, he uttered a brief prayer, extempore, Lord God of my fathers, I do believe; help me when next I doubt.

But even as he did that he was thinking about Micah's old donkey. Standing idle and well-fed, it had again taken on that deceptive appearance of road-worthiness, and Mary, he knew, would insist upon taking it. And he thought about Anne's jibe that Mary owned two donkeys; it was justified. His faith, like the donkey's gait, flagged, was restored, and then failed again.

Another thought assailed him, had it not been for the broken-down donkey they would not have landed in this place, with the innkeeper so attentive, his wife so competent and both so kind. Nor would they have been here tonight, to be found by this old man who confirmed all the prophecies and who had brought the answer to the question he had been about to ask in his dream, How is this to be managed? It was all—he thought—far beyond the understanding of a plain simple fellow like himself, and the most he could do was to blunder along, doing his best from day to day.

"We will go at once," he assured Melchior and looked at Mary, who, as though she understood, rose up, straight and strong.

"There is no reason," she said, "to rouse the house at this hour. I'll fold the blanket and leave it on the stool, with the coin that Elisabeth and Zacharias gave us. Eunice and Ephorus will understand. But first, I think our friends should see him. I must wake him anyway."

She went to the place where the child lay, lifted him and turned, holding the baby towards them, as though offering them a reward for their journey, for their gifts.

And suddenly they were all smiling. Joseph with his faith restored, Melchior with his errand done, Balthazar who had seen this wonderful thing, and Gaspar who had found his heart. Even Mary, burdened with the weight of knowledge, knowing the end at the beginning, troubled by so much that must be kept locked in her heart, smiled, as any woman does, feeling the weight and warmth of her child, smelling the sweet, clean, milky scent.

So she held him towards them, and the beam from the lantern was caught in the soft fuzz of baby hair, so that to those who watched it seemed for a moment that he wore a halo of light.